Praise for *Highland Jewel*

"A wonderfully refreshing tale filled with fun, adventure, and soul-stirring emotion. I was utterly enthralled from the first page to the last." —Lisa Kleypas

"*Highland Jewel* delivers on every promise. This is truly one of the best Scottish romances I've read in years. Its captivating characters and lyrical prose have earned Terri Lynn Wilhelm a permanent home on my keeper shelf."   —Teresa Medeiros

"A tale as Scottish as tartans and as romantic as violins. A clever romp and an impassioned love story."
—Christina Dodd

Storm Prince

"Hot! . . . Ms. Wilhelm bedazzles with an enchanting tale that makes us smile in utter delight."
—*Romantic Times*

"As enchanting as the mystical sea. . . . Fast-paced, intriguing, believable . . . I was totally mesmerized."
—*Rendezvous*

"A powerful tale. . . . This book is a winner."
—*Old Book Barn Gazette*

"Truly unique. . . . An exciting tale of intrigue [with] one stunning hero."   —*Bell, Book, and Candle*

"Engaging . . . enchanting . . . compelling . . . witty, deeply emotional and sexually romantic. Ms. Wilhelm uses clear, rich, intelligent prose to draw us in to a magical world."

ws

. .

A Hidden Magic

"An absolute delight. Ms. Wilhelm continues to charm readers with her unique sense of humor and inventiveness." —*Romantic Times*

"Very strong. A most enjoyable and entertaining read." —*Rendezvous*

"Unique and fun to read." —*Affaire de Coeur*

"A sensational story. . . . Marvelous and highly enjoyable." —*The Paperback Forum*

"A gothic love story [that] will bring much enjoyment. The resident ghost adds dollops of love, humor, and tenderness to this very satisfying read." —*Gothic Journal*

"Fabulous . . . Wilhelm has penned another beautiful story with well-rounded characters, a sensual setting, and the most memorable ghost I've seen in a novel." —*The Time Machine*

"Hilarious. . . . You're gonna love this." —*Bell, Book, and Candle*

"Wilhelm is growing in popularity with each new book. . . . An especially sexy hero . . . humor, romance, adventure, and surprises as well." —*Old Book Barn Gazette*

"Sweet and memorable . . . Wilhelm can freeze you with the threat of violence or lull you with a soft and melancholy spirit." —Genie Romance and Women's Fiction Exchange

"An enchanting book that beguiles, entertains . . . richly drawn, totally wonderful. . . . Incredible." —Under the Covers Book Reviews

Fool of Hearts

"Filled with poignancy, humor, and a delightful cast of characters. . . . Sit back and enjoy this charming love story and dream of the Highlands and a hero like Calum."
—*Romantic Times*

"A wonderful unique romance that will charm your socks off."
—*Affaire de Coeur*

"An enthralling story. . . . Strong characters, lively dialogue and, of course, romance make this story a winner."
—*Rendezvous*

"A great story with a wonderful cast of characters. Readers everywhere will be anxiously awaiting her future books."
—*The Paperback Forum*

"Her characters, drawn with the lush richness of the tapestries that hang in the great halls of medieval castles, easily win the heart. Mystery, betrayal, and passion ensnare the reader."
—Under the Covers Book Reviews

Shadow Prince

"Terri Lynn Wilhelm weaves a rich and spellbinding story."
—*Romantic Times*

"A taut relationship drama that will emotionally fulfill readers with its uplifting message." —*Affaire de Coeur*

"An excellent blend of mystery and romance . . . Wilhelm has created a world peopled by larger-than-life characters who pull the reader into the story with them and who don't let go of your heart, even when you reach the last page."
—*Rendezvous*

"Wonderful, sensual, vivid. . . . Will leave you, the reader, breathless. . . . Pure romance magic."
—*Gothic Journal*

"A sensual delight."
—*The Time Machine*

THE
MOON LORD

Terri Lynn Wilhelm

A SIGNET BOOK

SIGNET
Published by New American Library, a division of
Penguin Putnam Inc., 375 Hudson Street,
New York, New York 10014, U.S.A.
Penguin Books Ltd, 27 Wrights Lane,
London W8 5TZ, England
Penguin Books Australia Ltd, Ringwood,
Victoria, Australia
Penguin Books Canada Ltd, 10 Alcorn Avenue,
Toronto, Ontario, Canada M4V 3B2
Penguin Books (N.Z.) Ltd, 182–190 Wairau Road,
Auckland 10, New Zealand

Penguin Books Ltd, Registered Offices:
Harmondsworth, Middlesex, England

First published by Signet, an imprint of New American Library,
a division of Penguin Putnam Inc.

First Printing, October 1999
10 9 8 7 6 5 4 3 2 1

 REGISTERED TRADEMARK—MARCA REGISTRADA

Printed in the United States of America

To Gregory,
who slays dragons every day.

When he shall die,
Take him and cut him out in little stars,
And he will make the face of heaven so fine
That all the world will be in love with night,
And pay no worship to the garish sun.

Romeo and Juliet, Act III, Scene II
—WILLIAM SHAKESPEARE

PROLOGUE

1192, *The Holy Land*

Tancred de Vierzon raced across the bailey toward the guarded gates of the Saracen fortress Bâb Al-Muhunnad as flames leapt into the night sky. The air rang with the clang of swords, with the shouts and cries of men, and the screams of horses in the stables close to the burning barracks.

The pounding of Tancred's scarred bare feet against the hot, hard-packed earth was lost in the chaos as English, French, and Swedish crusaders lashed back at their cruel Musselmen captors. Hatred, humiliation, and desperation fueled their pale, starved bodies as they struggled to beat back the armored, better-fed enemy long enough to open the fort to the army of King Richard Lion Heart.

Tancred prayed that the king had received the messages smuggled out of the well-defended stronghold, at no little sacrifice to the senders. That he did not believe it all a trap. And, above all, that he was waiting outside the walls.

It was a terrible risk. Tancred had known that from the beginning. His years of fighting to free the Holy Land from the yoke of unbelievers had stripped away what little idealism remained in him. Bickering sovereigns, disease, and arrogance had all but delivered victory to the Saracens. Only values and standards learned from his patient foster father, Eudes de Epernay, had kept Tancred from growing thoroughly discouraged . . . or corrupted.

Let it please God to take pity on his servants now! If it did not . . . well, He would very shortly be minus many of them.

Tancred saw the Saracen's sword arc downward in time to jump back, but he failed to completely escape its range. Pain seared down his bare arm. Before the Saracen could lift the weapon again, Tancred slammed his heel into his enemy's groin.

With a pained moan, the Saracen doubled over. Tancred seized the sword from the other's hands, then swung down the blade. His enemy's head dropped to the ground.

Clad in only a ragged clout and armed with an alien blade he used again and again, Tancred de Vierzon doggedly made his way through the battle to the towering gate. In the turmoil, he did not immediately notice that no arrows came from the direction of the guardhouses that flanked the top of the gate. Only when he arrived almost directly beneath the guardhouses could he glimpse the limp, arrow-punctured arm dangling over the threshold of one gatehouse door. Quickly he turned his gaze to follow the top of the fortress wall. No one manned the battlements! No one, that is, but a few arrow-riddled bodies.

For the first time in three months, Tancred laughed. The message had made it into Richard's hands! The Lion Heart had brought archers of his own to eliminate at least some of the Saracen's ability to stop the prisoners.

Tancred set his naked shoulder to the great beam that bolted shut the gates. Carved from the massive trunk of a Cedar of Lebanon, it moved only fractionally. Months of deprivation and torture had robbed Tancred of much of his strength, but it would ever take more than a solitary man to bolt or unbolt these gates.

Wildly he looked around him for aid, squinting against the sting of thick, acrid smoke. He spied another prisoner, distinctive in his bearded near nakedness, the filthy clout pale in the flame-shot dark.

"Ho, D'Arganton!" he shouted. "To me, D'Arganton, to me!"

The other crusader lopped off the sword hand of his opponent, then drove his own captured weapon down between the Saracen's shoulder and neck. The foe toppled. Hastily retrieving the fallen enemy's sword, D'Arganton leaped over the bloody corpse as he ran toward Tancred. His teeth gleamed in his wild, dark beard.

Together, they set their shoulders to the enormous beam. Together they strained to move it beyond its stout iron brackets. Another crusader, a Swede, fought his way clear to join in their effort, his lash-striped shoulder pushing against the rough wood with theirs.

With a shout, a Musselman charged the Swede, who stumbled as he struggled to avoid the enemy's sword. Before the wet blade could reach him, Tancred shifted his position and lashed out with his own sword, deflecting the blow. D'Arganton drove his blade through the armored Saracen's eye and into the brain.

Again Tancred and his brother crusaders shouldered the timber. The massive shaft slid free of one iron bracket . . . then the other. The three men scrambled to pull open the towering gates.

Into the citadel thundered the army of Richard Lion Heart, King of England.

Hours later, Tancred followed the king's squire to the large tent, trying not to sway on his feet. There had been no time to do more than have his wound attended, thus starvation still gnawed in his hollow belly, his hair remained wild and matted and his body unwashed, clad only in his ragged clout.

It was like Richard to have no care for another man's dignity, he thought. It was also like Richard to summon him to come alone into the royal presence . . . alone before the inevitable flock of powerful lords and Tancred's knightly peers who always filled the king's quarters after an important battle.

The squire paused at the closed flaps of the tent. Calling up the resolve that had kept him alive through months of hell, Tancred painfully straightened, rolling back his emaciated shoulders. He would go before his king as a *man*.

Drawing aside one large flap, the boy stepped into the opening and announced in a high, youthful voice, "The chevalier, Tancred de Vierzon!" With a respectful bow, he motioned Tancred inside.

The masculine boom and murmur of voices abruptly died. The heavy smell of sweat mingled with the sweetish odor that issued from the hanging oil lamps and the tang of drying blood. These knights and lords had come directly from the battle. Mail chimed softly and shuffling feet whispered against jewel-colored carpets as the men present opened a path for Tancred.

Often when a Christian knight was taken prisoner by the Saracens, he was held for ransom, sometimes even treated as a guest during the wait for payment. Often, but not always. There had been no such fiction of hospitality at Al Muhunnad. And Tancred knew that, more than once, the mutilated body of a prisoner had been dumped into a crusader encampment by night. The commander of the notorious fortress was half mad with his burning hatred of Christians.

How long had Christendom thrown her valiant sons at those high stone walls gleaming under the harsh sun that seared this alien land, only to come limping away, defeated? Months? Years? Tonight it had finally fallen into Richard's grasp.

As Tancred passed them, lords and knights alike silently raised their cups to him in salute.

He stopped in front of Richard, who remained seated, still attired in his hauberk and chausses, his rich surcoat torn and stained. Slowly, Tancred went down to one knee before his sovereign, bowing his head.

"So, Tancred," Richard Lion Heart said, "it seems our paths are never to separate for long." He snapped his fingers, and the squire hurried forward with a stool. "Sit, sit. I will keep you but a short time before I send you to sup and sleep."

"You are kind, Majesty." Tancred carefully hauled himself onto the stool.

Sharp blue eyes examined him. "Nonsense. It is a small liberty to grant a favorite of one's sire."

Tancred went very still inside. Richard had lost no love on his father, the late King Henry II. "Had I been a favorite, my liege, he would have kept me beside him. Instead, he chose to give me into the care of three bachelor knights among the royal host." Two of them had died within three years, leaving a ten-year-old boy to be raised by one, unmarried fighting man.

The king's mouth moved in a smile that lacked any real warmth. "I remember. The Holy Trinity, many called them, so high were their standards of conduct. Most excellent knights."

"Yea, my lord. Most excellent." Eudes de Epernay had begun by doing his best to train a coltish, unwanted boy, and in the end, he had become more of a loving father than Tancred's true sire had ever been.

"He let you live," Richard said, his words so low that only Tancred was close enough to hear. His tone suggested that, had the decision been Richard's, things would have gone differently.

Though weary and weak with long hunger, Tancred carefully chose his words to one of Christendom's most temperamental and powerful men, reminding himself that Richard was the son of the king who had spared him. "Why slaughter the perfectly fit pup of a prize hunting hound gone mad?" he asked, his words equally as low-pitched.

Richard's gaze bore into Tancred's. "Because he had vowed he would."

Tancred felt the tension crackle throughout the pavilion. The two of them had been down this path several times before. Tancred wearied of it, but their strange relationship had given him some idea of how Richard's humor worked. So he lifted an eyebrow and smiled. "Had he fulfilled his vow, Al Muhannad would yet stand against you, my king."

Richard blinked at Tancred's audacity—then barked a hearty laugh. "Name of God, but you've a nerve about you!"

"Do I lie, Dread Majesty?" Tancred inquired politely.

Sobering, Richard shook his head. "No. I have never known you to tell anything but the truth. As you do now."

"I am gratified," Tancred murmured.

"I much doubt that." Dragging in a long, loud breath, Richard abruptly huffed it out. In a louder voice, one calculated for all to hear, he proclaimed, "What you have done goes beyond mere bravery. You deserve to be rewarded. I have certainly rewarded men for less." He gestured impatiently to his squire. "The list, I would have the list I made."

The boy hurried over with a sheet of parchment. Richard snatched it from his hands and shoved it into Tancred's.

"Choose one of these estates," he said. "The usual obligations go along with such a gift, you understand."

"Of course, Majesty." In the shadow-shifting light of oil lamps and torchieres, Tancred's gaze glided over the list of properties. A few of the names he recognized and knew to be respectable holdings. But he knew the one he craved would not be on this list.

"You may give me your answer tomorrow, Chevalier Tancred," Richard said, generously allowing time for consideration.

Tancred was sensible of this sign of favor. After all, this was an important choice—one most knights never had a chance to make. Every knight dreamed of acquiring an estate. Land provided stability, a permanent home, and a source of income less fickle than an employer's whims. Land elevated a mere fighting man to the far greater position of a lord. Land meant wealth. Wealth meant power.

To a landless knight such as Tancred, the promise of a holding was like the offering of a torch in the land of eternal dark. How he hungered for a place of his own!

But there was something that Tancred must first do. Something that might jeopardize gaining this grant from Richard.

The rage that had clawed at Tancred's vitals had burned to white-cold fury during his months in Al Muhunnad. Tancred had a debt to settle with Arnaud Bourton.

He raised his gaze from the parchment he held. "I would have Wynnsef," he said quietly.

Richard's red-gold eyebrows drew together in question. "Wynnsef? I do not recollect that name."

"It is the fief of Arnaud Bourton, Your Majesty."

"Ah."

Tancred struggled to compose himself as he sat, filthy, near naked, and starving, on that stool no man of his height should ever be required to fold down upon. His heart thudded heavily in his chest. He could lose all that he might have gained this night and with it the hope of justice.

The Lion Heart frowned faintly and launched himself from his chair. The gathering quickly made way when he began to pace. "I have heard from the others about your accusation against Bourton. I know that you believe you saw Arnaud Bourton conferring with Our enemy just before your garrison was set upon by Saracen troops," he said. "But you are the sole witness. Am I correct? The sole witness. And this charge you make is grave indeed."

"Only a grave charge may accompany a black deed."

Richard nodded slowly. "Yea, that is so."

The Earl of Quorley spoke up. "Bourton had a leman, Your Majesty. She was Saracen."

The king's lips curled with distaste, but he made no reply.

"There was one other witness, sire," Tancred said.

"Eh? But why has he not come forth? It is his duty!"

Tancred strove to suppress his bitterness. "He died in a dungeon at Al Muhunnad."

Richard stood still for a long moment. No one else in the pavilion stirred as the king stroked his short beard, his gaze focused off into the distance. Finally, he spoke.

"You have ever been a gallant knight, Tancred de Vierzon," he said. "No one can doubt your fidelity or your courage."

Tancred clenched his jaws on angry words. He had seen what he had seen! Bourton had delivered the garrison into the hands of the enemy. He struggled to swallow his anger. "There is more to it than my belief, Your Majesty."

"My liege, the Saracens could not easily have learned the code word for that watch," a powerful baron pointed out. "It was closely guarded. Only three of our own men knew it. Bourton was one of them."

The king nodded thoughtfully. "While the evidence points toward Chevalier Arnaud, still it is not quite enough to damn him as a traitor. This is a serious offense. The penalty is death in a most hideous manner and the confiscation of all that he owns." He turned to face Tancred. "You may have Wynnsef, chevalier . . . if you can take it from its present master. I will allow God to decide if Bourton is guilty or not." He smiled coolly. "God and the good right arm of Tancred de Vierzon."

ONE

1194, England

Flames crackled in the vast fireplace of Wynnsef's great hall, casting their warmth over the slumbering wolfhounds sprawled on the rushes in front of the hearth. The hall's lime-washed stone walls were colorfully painted and hung with jewel-toned tapestries from the East to keep out the cold. Small panes of polished horn in the high, narrow windows allowed through the thin morning light, but not the gusting wind of early spring.

Seated on her brother's thronelike carved chair upon the dais, Rosamund of Wynnsef poured over the accounts with Brother Felix, who sat next to her at the trestle table, his goose quill scratching across parchment as he scribed the notes she dictated.

Suddenly, the outside wooden stairs thundered with hurried footsteps. The heavy oak door banged open, and John Willsson, the stocky captain of the castle guard, strode swiftly across the hall to the dais.

"My lady," John said. "I beg pardon for this interruption, but I knew you would wish to be told at once."

"Does my brother return?" Rosamund asked, but before hope could lift in her breast, the expression on her captain's ruddy, lined face crushed it.

"I would that it were so, my lady," he said grimly, "for Godfrey Fitz Clare is on the march."

Rosamund rose to her feet. "So. 'Tis no surprise to us, eh, John?" She hoped that her voice sounded more calm than she truly felt. She had feared Fitz Clare would move against them at the first opportunity, and so she had pleaded with her brother, Arnaud, to give up his plan of laying siege to a lordless castle in the north. The spy she had earlier set to watch Fitz Clare's demesne of Heddon had sent word of activity there, a gathering of forces. Arnaud had scorned her concerns, telling her that Lord Fitz Clare would never be foolish enough to assault the fief of a king's man. It was true that Wynnsef was held directly from the crown, but it was also true that King Richard was presently embroiled in the machinations of keeping his kingship independent of his former captor, German Emperor Henry VI. What was the worth of one vassal compared to that of an empire? Her brother had left her with no knights and barely a handful of foot soldiers to defend the only home she had ever known. The home that Arnaud took too much for granted for Rosamund's liking.

"When will Fitz Clare arrive at our gates, do you know?"

"Soon. They are visible from the wall walk. That is how we discovered them."

Sweet Mary! "Why were we not warned sooner by our informer?" she asked now, her mind racing down a mental list of all that must be done. So little time. Too few men.

"He came himself to warn us, but his horse broke its leg in a badger hole on the way," John explained. "He just arrived."

Quickly, Rosamund turned to the monk. "See to the chapel and its supplies, if you will, Brother Felix. And we must needs use its space for sleepers this night."

The old monk nodded his tonsured head as he capped his inkhorn. "Yea, my lady." He hastened up the inner spiral stairway that led to the floors above the great hall.

Fourteen-year-old Helvise of Cheyham, her pretty face pale and her brown eyes wide with anxiety, came running with Rosamund's fox-lined mantle. With a smile of thanks for her fosterling, Rosamund absently donned the luxurious garment, fastening it at her throat with an opal-studded brooch.

"Go and pack your belongings, sweeting," she told Helvise. "I would not have you here when Lord Truf- flenose arrives."

Despite her worry, Helvise giggled at the name they shared for the arrogant, porcine Godfrey Fitz Clare. In the next instant, her amusement fled. Her rosebud mouth trembled. "Have a care for yourself, my lady."

Embracing the girl, Rosamund kissed her on each cheek. "And you, my little daisy."

Rosamund gathered her skirts in both hands, then headed swiftly for the door, fresh rushes rustling at her every step, John Willsson at her heel. Sweeping down the outer stairs, she saw by the gathering crowd that the news of Fitz Clare's advance had spread. As she crossed the inner bailey to the watch tower, she rattled off instructions. A messenger must be sent to Arnaud. The villagers and villeins had to be warned and brought within the castle walls, and accommoda- tions for them made. Helvise needed an armed escort, but it would have to be much smaller than Rosa- mund liked.

Inside the tower, she climbed the stone steps that clung to the convex inner wall. Finally, she strode onto the roof, where the cold wind tore at her wimple and veil, tugged at the heavy drapery of her mantle, while John's heavier leather mantle scarce moved in the stream of wind.

Her gaze followed the direction in which he pointed. She looked out over the gleaming lime-washed castle and its inner curtain, over the moat beyond the east- ern outer curtain, and the forest.

Past the forest, her search abruptly ended. Fitz
Clare, who held nothing more than a generous manor,
had hired mercenaries . . . but not enough. He did not
present such an overwhelming display of might that
throwing open the gates of Wynnsef was the only
sane response.

"This man is a thorn in my side," she said, glaring
at a band of approximately two-dozen armed men.
Oxen plodded before a wagon bearing a mangonel.
"And it appears that his spy is better than my spy."

"It would, my lady," John agreed. Beneath his
helm, his weathered face wore a bleak expression.
"But then, all that would take is one man sitting by
the side of the road, counting the number of knights
and foot soldiers Lord Wynnsef took with him. He
made no effort to keep his departure secret."

Rosamund sighed. "No. He did not." And now they
were faced with the slow starvation and sickness that
came of long sieges. At the advanced age of nineteen,
she had seen and heard and survived enough to know
what lay before them. "We will have to destroy anything Fitz Clare and his mercenaries might be able
to use."

"The grain bins and cottages, my lady?"

"Yea, John," she said dully. "And the crops." She
hoped her brother found his sally into the north worth
the price.

At any other time, this showing by Fitz Clare's
would have been laughable. With the garrison de-
pleted by Arnaud's mad quest, it posed a serious
threat.

"Do you know if my lord brother called on all who
owed him knights' fees for his enterprise?" she asked
John, never swerving her gaze from the enemy who
marched toward Wynnsef.

"By my count, he did, my lady."

She exhaled heavily. "So I thought." Arnaud had
no staunch allies close by to whom she could appeal.
Indeed, if other barons heard Wynnsef was so weak,

there would be more than Fitz Clare with which to contend.

Returning to the great hall, she wrote the letter to be delivered to Arnaud. After that, she set about organizing the incoming peasantry and craftsmen. Imperious geese, burdened donkeys and oxen, bleating sheep, wailing, frightened children accompanied eighty-seven worried folk who did not normally dwell within the castle walls. The beasts were set to graze in the outer bailey, while places within the inner bailey were found for the people. There was scarcely room to put one's foot, so crowded were the old keep, the hall, and all the other buildings of the castle proper.

Rosamund dispatched the messenger carrying her letter, watching him spur his horse through the small postern gate, heading north. Helvise and her single armed escort headed out only minutes later, galloping southwest, toward her father's manor. Behind them, the heavy oak-and-iron door was shut and barred.

Rosamund wanted nothing so much as to rush to her private walled garden for a moment of respite from the commotion and the anxiety, but that was out of the question. There would be time, too much time, for such things after the drawbridge was raised and the portcullis lowered.

"My lady!" One of John's men came running, the iron bosses on his leather gambeson winking dully in the thin sunlight. "My lady, another force approaches from the south."

"Who?" she demanded. It could not possibly be Arnaud. Only a miracle could have brought him here so soon.

"I do not know, my lady. The sentry at the south tower saw 'em. Says they're not ours. He's never seen the pennon before. All black, it is, with a silver moon and stars."

Who? Rosamund hurried toward the stables. Finally, she gathered her skirts and broke into a run. She found her horse already waiting. Immediately she

rode to the south tower, where John awaited her with
the sentry. Filled with dread, her gaze followed the
beaten track that was a well-traveled road. There, having passed beyond the concealment of a bend in that
road behind a swath of forest, came an array of
knights, armed and mailed and ready for battle. As
the guardsman had said, the pennon was strange, and
not a little odd. Yet somehow familiar.

Then she saw it: a second pennon streaming in the
breeze. A red cross mounted on a white field. Her
heart lifted. "Crusaders!" she cried. Holy warriors.
Praise be!

Were they come to save Wynnsef? Had her prayers
and those of the others crammed within these ashlar
walls moved God to aid them? Half fearing to hope,
she crossed herself and sent up a silent prayer of
thanks.

"John, perhaps we are saved," she said.

"Do not rely upon it, my lady."

"There are fewer of them than Lord Trufflenose
commands, but most of them are knights—and the
favored of God." Why did the device on that pennon
strike her as familiar? She had not seen it before, but
she was certain she had heard of it. A silver moon . . .
"We shall hope this man comes as our savior."

John glanced at her, his salt-and-pepper brows
drawn down in concern.

"We have prepared for a siege," she pointed out.
"We will do what we can. Is the drawbridge raised?"

"It is. The mangonels stand on their tower and the
rocks are being winched up. The oil is heating. My
men are ready." He did not mention that the few men
Arnaud had left him could not possibly cover the wall
walks effectively. "Allow me to arm some of the
craftsmen and more reliable villeins, my lady."

This was no light matter, but there was no choice.
She nodded. "At worst it will look as if we are not
so grossly undermanned, at best they will prove somewhat effective."

John surveyed the crowd below, many of whom struggled to settle in cramped, temporary quarters, knowing the strong possibility that all they had labored for in this world might soon perish. "They will fight for their lives," he said.

Rosamund thought of Wynnsef. Here, smiling nurses had once held her hands as she learned to walk. She remembered her father's love for this land, and of her own joy in making green things grow here. Her fingers clenched into a fist. "So shall we all."

Shortly after None, the crusaders sent a herald to Fitz Clare. When the herald returned to them, they rode toward Fitz Clare's marching force, bypassing the village and castle as if they were invisible. On the wall walk, Rosamund felt her heart sink as her last hope vanished. The crusaders had thrown their lot in with Lord Godfrey.

But they left the road before they came into the view of Fitz Clare, heading off in a northwesterly direction, keeping a thick peninsula of woods between themselves and the force marching toward Wynnsef. As she watched the last crusader vanish on the far side of the woods, Rosamund remembered why that odd pennon had been familiar.

"Tancred de Vierzon," she muttered.

John looked at her. "Eh?"

"The strange pennon the crusaders flew. I just placed it. The black, the silver, the moon. It is that of Tancred de Vierzon."

The captain looked startled. "The knight the troubadours sing of? I was not certain he was real . . . or living."

"As that strange pennon is famous for being his, it seems he is both real and very much alive."

" 'Tis well, then, that he and his men kept riding."

"One less problem," she agreed. For she was not *really* foolish enough to hope that Chevalier Tancred de Vierzon would risk his life and those of his men to help Wynnsef.

Champions rushing to aid damsels in distress were song fodder. Such lays were entertaining on a bleak winter's eve, but only silly children believed them, not old maids of nineteen. And certainly not wellborn old maids who planned to enter a convent.

Fitz Clare and his men moved steadily toward Wynnsef. A messenger brought the expected ultimatum: Surrender or pay the consequences. Rosamund sent her terse response.

The baron and his men arrived. The mangonel was moved into place across the moat from the castle.

Within the castle walls fell a strained hush.

A deep rumble issued from behind Fitz Clare's line of soldiers, causing them all to turn.

Suddenly, out of the forest thundered massive war horses bearing men with white crosses on their streaming mantles. One of their number raised an eerie, ululating battle cry that sent a shiver through Rosamund.

She and the others on the battlements watched in amazement as the skill and ferocity of the crusaders gradually hammered back Fitz Clare's greater numbers. The onlookers exclaimed when the first arrow was fired by a mounted archer. Working with astounding ease and accuracy from the rocking backs of their horses, white-crossed archers armed with oddly shaped bows rapidly took their toll against the foot soldiers and bowmen of Fitz Clare.

Finally, the surviving mercenaries forsook their employer. That started a panic among the foot soldiers, who apparently had little faith in their leader. Soon, all were fleeing in the direction from which they'd come. Behind them, the bodies of their dead and wounded lay strewn about the field between the abandoned siege machine and wagons.

Rosamund wanted to shout with relief. They had been saved! No wonder Arnaud had not been concerned over leaving so few of the garrison at Wynnsef.

Doubtless these crusaders were friends he'd made in the Holy Land. It all made sense now. Arnaud had known they were coming here.

How like him not to tell *her*.

Resentment pricked Rosamund. Then, as she'd done uncounted times since her father's funeral, she thrust it resolutely away. What good to brood on the slight? Arnaud would have his way until she could persuade him to release her to enter Hembley Abbey.

The knight, attired all in black save for a large, silver crescent moon and tiny stars broidered on his long surcoat and blazoned on his shield, broke away from the crusaders, who were moving into four long lines. His great black war horse cantered across the littered meadow to the edge of the moat. From there he called out to those standing on the allure over the main gate.

"I am Tancred de Vierzon. Who speaks for Wynnsef?"

"I speak for Wynnsef," she answered, studying him with interest.

So he claimed to be the fabulous Moon Lord, who, in all the *chansons de geste*, was the fairest to look upon, the bravest and most skilled warrior, a man of unsurpassed cunning when it came to outwitting the Saracen. He was King Richard's man. From the battlements she looked down upon him, her gaze moving over his solitary figure donned in black mail, surcoat, and great helm. She suppressed a shiver. How ominous and unknowable he appeared.

She doubted the man in black armor on the far side of the moat was the Moon Lord at all. Likely he was only a knight, though admittedly an impressive one. If a woman were silly enough to take the gilded words of jongleurs and troubadours as truth, she would believe every brave knight to be a Galahad with the powers of an archangel and the cunning of a fox.

Silence stretched between them, yet she sensed that he watched her.

"I claim this castle as mine," the self-proclaimed

Tancred de Vierzon declared. "Do you open your gates to your new master now, and I will enter in peace. Deny me at your peril."

Rosamund's fingers gripped the edge of the stone merlon. This man was no friend to her brother! So, when the gravy was reduced to pudding, even the great Tancred de Vierzon, or at least his impostor, was naught but a landless soldier on a horse, hungry for land. She should have known.

She cast a glance at John, who frowned as he studied the meadow and its occupants. "The man must be a fool," she said in a low, cutting voice.

"What trickery have you up your sleeve, de Vierzon?" he muttered.

"You do not have sufficient men to lower a siege on this castle," she exclaimed to the dark knight, who waited patiently for her answer.

To her embarrassed surprise, the four columns of men behind him burst into laughter.

The black great helm turned toward the men, and she saw his shoulders shake. The varlet was laughing at her! Before she could form a retort, he turned in his saddle to face her again.

"These men are sufficient to any task," he said. "Surrender or stand against me and surrender later. I will have your answer now."

"My answer is *no*." Her defiant words rang through the ashlar walls of Wynnsef. She tried to shut out her awareness of those in the bailey below her, their anxious faces raised to her, of the tense men-at-arms, who would be the first to die should she be mistaken.

De Vierzon wheeled his great stallion and galloped back toward the other knights. Their columns parted before him, as the Red Sea before Moses. As grain before the knife.

He rode into the shadowed forest, followed by his men.

*   *   *

Hours passed with no sign of the Moon Lord or his men. Tension in Wynnsef mounted, exacerbated by crowded conditions. Nightfall stretched nerves tighter still.

Rosamund restlessly prowled the wall walk, pausing to speak with each sentry, hoping to encourage them on their long watch. The same questions haunted them all. Was Tancred de Vierzon part of a larger force soon to come? Or had he rescued Wynnsef at Arnaud's behest, only to jest cruelly with those he had saved? Had he gone for good, or would he return?

Again and again, she told herself that so small a force as they had seen could never hope to successfully lay siege to any castle, much less one the size of Wynnsef. No, it seemed more likely that he might harass the villeins and freemen and any commerce traveling to and from the castle. When Arnaud arrived, he would put an end to that.

The moon had begun its descent by the time John quietly stepped beside her. She knew he had worked ceaselessly, making what improvements to security he could with the limited resources available.

"You should be abed, my lady," he said. Moonlight gleamed dully on his conical helm.

"As should you. You cannot hope to stand every shift with no rest."

In his salt-and-pepper beard, his mouth almost smiled. "In times like this, a soldier learns to snatch a few winks of sleep whenever he may. But you have not. And you, my lady, are the one to whom everyone looks. You are their torch in a fearful storm, and so you must not burn yourself out. Please, go sleep awhile. I'll send to you should anything unusual pass."

Rosamund sighed wearily. "A torch, am I? I feel more like an ash."

Now he did smile. "Mayhap there is some small resemblance."

Despite herself, she chuckled. "Oh, where is this talk of torches, now, Silver Tongue?"

He did not speak for a moment, instead looking out over the meadow where, earlier, the mercenaries had been allowed to haul away their injured, and the dead that had been left behind. The charred remnants of the mangonel stood where it had been abandoned, a victim of an incendiary quarrel shot by a castle crossbowman. Not far from it lay the ash heap that had been the wagon-load of bundled rushes.

"If you don't mind my saying so, my lady," John said, "your father would have been proud of you."

The captain had been in service to her father well before Rosamund had been born. The two men had come through countless battles together.

"Thank you, John."

"Castles have been held for days by fewer men than we have," he pointed out.

What he didn't mention was that someone had come to their aid in time. Arnaud's ability to offend his peers had resulted in a distinct dearth of allies for situations such as this.

Rosamund went to the chapel, where she lighted a candle and said a prayer for Helvise's safe journey home and for the messenger carrying the letter to Arnaud. Then she hurried downstairs to the great hall.

As she left the new keep and crossed the courtyard to enter the old tower keep which housed her small bedchamber, it pleased her to think of her father's approval. Even if Tancred de Vierzon did bring back more men, Arnaud would receive the letter she'd sent within several days. If they could hold the castle for a fortnight . . .

It could be done, she thought as she washed her face with the icy water from the ewer. It must be done.

Quickly, she undressed and slipped between the frigid linens, where she lay shivering until the heat of her body was captured and held by the wool blankets and the finely dressed bearskin. With a sigh, she snuggled deeper into the thick nest of covers.

A prickling of awareness lifted the delicate hairs on

her nape. Before she could move, a large hand descended over her mouth, firmly pinning her head to her pillow.

"Now," said a deep masculine voice near her ear, "I will accept your surrender."

Two

She tried to bite his hand, but his black leather glove and his snug grip defeated her.

"Ah," he murmured, his breath stirring a wisp of hair at her cheek. "The lady is in truth a vixen."

In the flickering bronze glow cast by delicate flames dancing in the brazier, Rosamund tried to glimpse the face of the speaker, but he remained out of her line of vision. She scowled to cover the thundering of her heart.

Three oddly spaced knocks sounded at her chamber door, and she struggled to free herself to shout for help. To her surprise, her captor released her.

Rosamund flew to the door, but when she jerked it open, she found the stairway empty. She screamed for help.

No one came running in answer. She bolted from the chamber. No sooner had her bare foot landed on the third cold step than iron-strong arms hauled her back into her chamber.

Frantically she fought to win free, hammering and clawing at any part of his body she could reach.

He flung her on the bed. The ropes supporting the mattress creaked sharply as she landed. Slightly dazed, she lay panting, glaring at his back as he shut the door. Then he turned to face her, and for the first time Rosamund actually saw her captor.

He was tall and clothed entirely in supple black

leather that seemed to absorb the light like velvet.
His garments were like none she'd ever seen, with an
indecently short tunic sashed at the waist and odd,
long braes that were cross-gartered. His soft boots
reached midcalf.

What little of his skin that had been left uncovered
had been darkened by soot, and in the low illumination she could determine little about his features. A
black cloth, knotted at his nape, concealed his hair,
and a mask of the same fabric covered the bottom
half of his face, from the bridge of his nose to below
his chin. Only his eyes were not dark, but from where
she lay she could not determine their color. She could,
however, detect their movement.

His gaze moved slowly over her body. In the wake
of that leisurely trail, her skin throbbed with awakened sensitivity. With a jolt, Rosamund recalled that
she sprawled naked before him. Hastily, she snatched
up the embroidered bed curtain and clutched it to her.

He tugged off his mask, exposing more sooty skin.
"When I told you that I would accept your surrender,"
he said, amusement lurking in his rich baritone, "I
had no notion you would make that surrender
so . . . complete."

She tossed her head in defiance, and her heavy hair
shifted against her shoulders and breasts. "I'll die
first."

He bared startlingly white teeth in a slow smile.
"Wynnsef's is the only gate I wish to breach this night,
lady, and that I have already done."

He had breached Wynnsef's gate? Impossible! She
swallowed hard. Impossible . . . unless he did not
work alone.

The door opened and on the threshold stood a man
clad identically in black and almost as tall as her captor. "All have reported back," he said, his words
strangely accented. "We will await you in the great
hall as you have instructed." He glanced at Rosa-

mund. "Would that I had drawn such an onerous task."

"Yea, Kadar, I should have assigned this to you. By now you would have charmed her into eager compliance."

Kadar laughed as he withdrew, closing the door behind him. The sound of his mirth echoed back through the tower's stairwell.

"Who—" The word stuck in Rosamund's arid throat. "Who *are* you? What do you want here?"

"Why, I would have thought that apparent, Lady Rosamund. I want Wynnsef."

He strode to the ivory-inlaid casket she kept on the table by her bed. Flipping open the carved lid, he reached inside and took the precious ring of keys that was not only essential to the security of the castle and its store of foodstuffs, but the symbol of Rosamund's importance to Wynnsef.

She scrambled across the bed to make a grab for the keys. "No!"

He evaded her lunge with ease. " 'Tis done. Denying it will not undo the fact. As to my identity, I think you know that."

"Many men desire Wynnsef," she said stiffly. A woman should have so many suitors! "Which one are you?" Who was this son of the night, this brother to shadows?

"I am Tancred de Vierzon, damoiselle, and I have done what I said I would do."

As she stared at him, astonishment warred with a sense of betrayal. Crusaders were God's warriors, men of faith who had trod the same streets Christ once walked. They did not slip through the dark hours like assassins.

"You lie," she snapped. "Tancred de Vierzon is a crusader. He is," she said, her cheeks hot with anger, "King Richard's man. My brother, also, is a king's man and a crusader, perhaps even an acquaintance of Chevalier Tancred. While you, sirrah, are no better than a thief. Whoever that man out on the meadow was today, whoever you are, I do not believe it is Tancred de Vierzon. Now I ask you again, *who are you*?"

The tall stranger regarded her with hooded eyes. "I, lady, am the new master of Wynnsef." He went to the door, the keys dangling from his fingers. "You'll do well to remember that. I'll send for you at cock's crow."

Before she made it halfway across the room, he had smoothly exited the door, closing it firmly behind him. She heard the jingle of keys. Ha! He couldn't know which of the keys fit this lock. Planting her bare feet on the plank floor, Rosamund pulled on the door handle. It opened a little, but quickly jerked shut. She tried harder. The fourth key he tried was a match, and she heard it turn in the lock.

She was more a prisoner of Wynnsef than ever.

As pink dawn tinted the silvering sky, Rosamund followed the guard sent to escort her to the great hall.

Every story she had ever heard of the rapine that followed the conquering of a castle had kept her company through the endless dark hours. Thus, when the time had come for her to prepare herself to meet the conqueror, she had taken care in her appearance, using it as a warrior used his armor. Without a puissant male to protect her, a woman's only defense was the world's perception of her. Rosamund had done what she could to make that perception one of power. To that end, a wimple of white silk swathed her chin and throat, and a fillet of stiffened azure linen embroidered with gold thread held her white silk veil in place. Over her good yellow kirtle she had donned the azure tunic, then her girdle of gold links set with amber.

She was Rosamund Bourton of Wynnsef, daughter of a powerful baron. During the four long years since her father's death, despite her older brother's lavish spending, she had managed to keep Wynnsef profitable. All, that is, but the year the crops had failed.

Rosamund rubbed her thumb over the small scar near her bottom lip, as she had a thousand times before. Catching herself, she dropped her hand and straightened her shoulders.

As she and her guard entered the hall, she was struck by the quiet. No raucous masculine laughter, no feminine cries of anguish assaulted her as she had expected. Indeed, there was no sign of any females, which was alarming in itself. Instead, there was the occasional snap from logs burning in the fireplace. Three men unfamiliar to her, dressed in good woolen tunics and hose, sat by the hearth, scraping the blades of their swords with wet stones, which they periodically dunked in the bucket set on the floor between them. Two others, not far from them, sat over a game of chess, her brother's ivory-and-ebony board and pieces on the small table between them. Within easy reach of every man was a cup, so Rosamund guessed the servants were up and working, but making themselves scarce.

Her attention was captured by the man on the dais before her.

Tall and dark, he sat on the thronelike lord's chair as if it had been made for him. Unlike the previous men who had occupied that chair, he was not dwarfed by its size—an observation Rosamund found disturbing.

He was clean-shaven, and his raven hair was cut in the short style favored by knights. The fitted sleeves of his black tunic came to his wrists. Over them, the sleeves of his black surcoat were wider and ended just below his elbows with a frieze of silver embroidery. A black kid belt fastened with a buckle that formed a silver disk. The hem of his ankle-length surcoat was expertly dagged and skillfully worked with more silver thread. He wore boots of soft black leather. As Rosamund came closer, she saw a wide cuff of silver set with four polished moonstones on each of his wrists. Draped over the arm of the chair was the invader's sword belt, keeping within easy reach his black, leather-worked scabbard and the long, heavy sword within.

Her escort stopped at the foot of the dais. Quietly, he withdrew, leaving her in the middle of the hall, alone with the conqueror of Wynnsef.

Deliberately continuing to examine the sword, Rosamund did not look up to meet her captor's gaze. Willing herself not to react to the heavy silence, or the magnetic pull of his attention, she noted that the quillons of the weapon were masterfully wrought to resemble a falcon's wings. Set into the round pommel was an orb of flawlessly clear rock crystal.

With a sinking feeling, she realized this was no ordinary weapon. She had heard it described several times, each in a different *chanson de geste.* No longer could she deny that this man was indeed Tancred de Vierzon.

A large hand dropped into her view. It grasped the haft, then swept the sword from its scabbard with a metallic hiss. Startled, she looked up, directly into the face of the Moon Lord.

Black slashes slanted over eyes of such pale, brilliant gray that one could only comprehend them as silver. One high, prominent cheekbone bore a brand. The size of a seal made by a large signet ring, a circle containing two stars scarred the smooth skin in strange perfection. His nose was straight. Below it, his mouth formed a strong bow that invited a second glance, but it took Rosamund a moment to discover why: the superbly sculpted top lip was slightly fuller than the bottom.

"The damoiselle is interested in my sword," he said. To her chagrin, it was not spoken as a question. She recognized the deep, masculine voice from last night.

He held the weapon out for her inspection, the flat

of the deadly blade resting on one palm. Clearly he did not fear that she might wrest it from him.

"It is a sword," she said coolly, resisting the urge to touch the gleaming thing. "I have seen many of them."

Without comment, he slid it back into its scabbard, but she suspected she had not fooled him. The unique sword was almost as famous as the man. Doubtless he had fools gaping at it all the time. How annoying that she could now be counted among them.

"Wynnsef is mine," he said bluntly. "I have already released those who came here for safety; they are in no danger. Fitz Clare will be a while in recovering."

"My brother is a baron," she said tightly. "Do you truly believe the king will not come to his aid?"

"Your brother can expect no help from Richard."

A prickle of alarm went down her back. But then she thought, What else would such a clever fellow say? Would he admit he was a rogue knight? Not likely. "Oh?" she said, not bothering to conceal the skeptical note that leaked into her tone. "Pray, tell me why a baron cannot expect his liege lord's aid?"

"The king did tell me that, were I to take Wynnsef, it would be mine." He spread his arms, indicating his men comfortably in residence about the hall. "As you can see, I have taken Wynnsef."

The prickle of alarm returned. Had Arnaud done something to displease King Richard? "I don't believe you."

Tancred shrugged.

"Why would King Richard say such a thing to a mere knight?" she demanded. " 'Take this barony from my loyal man and it shall be yours'? I cannot credit such a thing."

"Believe what you will."

"My brother will be back," she declared.

His lips curved slowly upward. "Lady, I am counting on it."

The man was insane. Absolutely, irrefutably insane.

Rosamund had heard the stories brought back by crusaders. The heat of the Holy Land could cook a man's brain. Obviously it had seared Tancred de Vierzon's to a crisp.

"When my lord brother returns, he will take Wynnsef from you," she said stoutly. "He will give you cause to wish you'd never been born." She hoped.

"That he has already done."

What had Arnaud done? What could he do that would be terrible enough to make a man such as this wish he had not been born?

Ha, said a clear voice at the back of her anxious mind, *but of course this man would say something to cause you doubt, anything to make you less loyal to Arnaud.*

Rosamund regarded him down her nose—no mean feat considering his height advantage. "You speak in riddles. If you have something to say, sirrah, do so now. Soon Arnaud will be upon you, and you'll find it difficult to speak after he mounts your head on a pike."

He settled back comfortably in the chair. "My head on a pike? Sounds painful."

The wretch was amused! "When he does retake Wynnsef, he won't have to sneak around like a snake to do it."

His amusement vanished, and in its place she glimpsed something else, something he quickly shuttered from her. "Lady Rosamund, your brother's cunning imitation of a snake astonished many in Outremer."

His reaction confused her. She frowned. "What—"

"I will attend to your brother when he arrives," he said flatly. "Until then, you will see to it that those who live on the demesne, the fees, and in the village go about their work and cause me no trouble."

"Must I remain here? Am I to be your captive?" she asked indignantly, outraged, but not naive enough to believe women were never held against their will.

One black eyebrow lifted. "Captive? That is too

harsh a word. Rather, let us say that you cannot bear to leave Wynnsef when things are in such a state of uncertainty."

Furious blood beat in her cheeks. "You think me a traitor to my brother? Well, I will *not* aid you, Chevalier Tancred. I will not make smooth the way for you as you try to take over my home!"

He leaned forward in the chair, his hands resting on the carved-oak griffins that formed the arms. Alarmed by the potency that radiated from him, Rosamund took a step back before she caught herself.

"Would you rather I settle unwanted distractions with a whip?" he asked softly, his voice the more menacing for its control.

She shook her head.

His compelling starlight eyes held her gaze in thrall. He leaned nearer. "Believe me, lady, when I tell you I have little time for treachery or petty disputes. Normally I am a patient man, *but not now*."

Rosamund stared at him for several heartbeats more before she remembered to breathe in. She wanted nothing more than to wipe her damp palms on her kirtle, but refused to give him the satisfaction of letting him know how well he intimidated her. "I . . . I will do as you ask, up—upon one condition."

He straightened, both eyebrows lifting this time. "You issue terms?"

"One." She cleared her arid throat. "For now."

Absently, a forefinger smoothed back and forth over the rock crystal in the pommel of his sword. "I would hear this condition of yours."

By now they had the attention of every man who had been sitting in the great hall when she had arrived and several more who had come in after.

"Leave the females of Wynnsef alone," she said.

In the silence that swallowed the great hall, Rosamund's words seemed to boom. The murmur of masculine voices that abruptly rose carried an indignant edge. Tancred held up a hand, and silence returned to the chamber.

"You insult us, damoiselle," he said softly. "The conduct of my knights is of the highest standard."

"Women ever suffer for the ambitions of men, Chevalier Tancred," she said, again denying him the title of "lord." "Therefore, if I have misjudged you and your knights, I beg pardon. Are you then all chaste?" she asked sweetly. Improbable, unless they have been made eunuchs during their captivity by the Mussulman. But that was too much for which to hope.

He frowned. "We are not monks, Lady Rosamund, but neither are we beasts. No man of mine will force a maid. However, if she bats her eyes at him in flirtation, I much doubt she will be disappointed."

Male laughter filled the hall, accompanied by nods of approval and a bit of back-slapping.

"We know the difference between invitation and rape," he finished bluntly.

"Will your knights know the difference when they have drunk deeply?"

"You may ask that of any man."

"But you are new to this place. Neither you nor your men are familiar with our ways. How easy it would be to misread intentions when not only the woman, but her customs, are unknown to you."

His thumb continued to stroke the jewel. "Perhaps."

"You say you hold yourself to the highest standards." She shrugged. "I have seen no sign of it."

"We have not sacked this castle," one knight pointed out loudly enough to be heard by all. The hall rumbled with tenor and baritone voices muttering agreement.

Rosamund heard, but when she spoke, it was to Tancred. "All that proves is that you are not the lowest of barbarians . . . and not completely stupid. Only a fool destroys his gain."

Tancred's lips curved faintly. "True enough."

"You entered Wynnsef in the manner of thieves,

not knights," she continued, still rankling over what she considered a low action.

A growl of dissent vibrated off the stone walls from the growing numbers of knights.

He regarded her with hooded eyes. "I gave you fair warning, damoiselle. You refused to comply. Would you have been better satisfied if I had spent the lives of your men and mine in battle?"

She seethed over how easily he had made her appear not only bloodthirsty and heartless, but in the wrong. "You would have lost."

"Spoken like the defeated."

Rosamund swallowed a hot retort. The deed was done; she feared Wynnsef had fallen into the hands of a knight whose heart might well be as black as his surcoat. Now she must extract from him what concessions she could as she waited for her brother and his force to arrive. Pray God the messenger rode like the wind to get to Arnaud.

"Yea, Chevalier—"

"I am your lord now," he said, his voice velvet-gloved iron.

She nearly choked on her resentment. "Yea, my lord," she managed. "You have defeated my attempt to hold this castle for my brother. Thus, I have only the hope that the songs about you are true."

"They are *songs*," he drawled. "Diversions for idle moments."

"Then . . . you were not fostered by three valiant knights chosen for their virtue?"

"Yea," he growled. "That part is true."

"Did they not teach you their virtuous ways?"

He did not reply immediately. "They did."

"Are you not the *beau chevalier* known far and wide for *his* virtue and noble conduct?"

Tancred scowled. "I am no saint."

"Yet you expect your men to rise above their base urges, my lord?" Those last two words nearly stuck in her throat.

"Come to your point," he demanded curtly.

"It is said that you are no ordinary knight, but what you have just said reflects a very ordinary outlook. Too often, women's bodies are considered booty by a conqueror and his men, chattel to be used like a bench, a quintain, or a . . . a—"

"A scabbard!" someone in the crowd shouted.

The laughter choked off at a quelling glance from Tancred.

"Are you truly so stark?" she flared. "Can you not understand how terrifying it is for women when their home is conquered?"

"You conceal your terror well, Lady Rosamund," he observed dryly.

She drew a deep breath and eased it out, wishing her heart would stop hammering. "I must. Many depend upon me."

These large strangers surrounding her were the victors, but the fact that they were not already forcing their attention on the women of Wynnsef suggested she might have a chance.

"They must learn to depend upon their new lord," Tancred said.

Rosamund saw the opening and pounced. "Then perhaps my request will serve us both. If you honor my request they will be less frightened of you."

Those in the great hall fell silent, expectation hanging in the air like a morning mist.

"One month is what I ask. Lord Tancred," she added.

He made no comment.

"In that month neither you nor your men will take a woman until she expressly asks it. Not with the swaying of hips or the fluttering of eyelashes. Not with sighs. With words and words alone." Rosamund was certain only the boldest strumpet or the oldest wife could bring herself to ask that of a man. "Then there can be no mistaking intention."

Tancred remained still for a moment, his expression

unreadable. From the corner of her eye, she glimpsed
outrage in the faces of his knights.

"Lady, do you toy with me?" he asked quietly.

Her nerves jangled under her skin. "I am not foolish, my lord." *Only desperate.* "But look around you.
See you any servants here? In truth, I thought to ease
the fear of you among the people of Wynnsef. For
two generations, they and theirs have known only the
rule of my family. Such a dictate would go far to win
their unreserved loyalty. And it is my experience, sire,
that such loyalty among your people is like having
additional eyes and ears against a very harsh world."

Tancred made an indeterminate sound in his throat.
"Lady, these people do not know how harsh the world
can be."

"But you do. Would you bring that harshness here?"

He didn't reply, but she drew her answer from his
thoughtful silence.

"Why a month?" he finally asked.

"A fortnight is too little time for the high blood of
conquest to cool, and a quarter perhaps too long. I'm
not trying to be unreasonable. Unless you think there
is not sufficient willpower among your host to last a
month?" She slanted him a querying look.

"Do not think to manipulate me, damoiselle."

"I would not dream of it," she assured him with a
meekness she did not feel.

"Hmph." The Moon Lord regarded her over stee-
pled fingers. "I think you may have misjudged how
charming these knights can be."

"My lord, no woman objects to *true* charm. But base
lies are an offense before God."

He nodded slowly. "So they are. Very well. You
shall have your month." A slow, wolfish smile curved
his lips. "And I shall have your cooperation."

After hearing Mass, Tancred and his men returned
to the great hall for a quick meal of ale, bread, and
cheese before going to their duties. The other castle

folk joined them there to break their fast, as had apparently always been the custom. Tension weighed on those gathered like the heavy heat in Outremer.

Lady Rosamund saw fit to absent herself.

"It seems the beautiful dove is missing," said an exotically accented voice as Kadar came to stand at Tancred's shoulder. "Think you that she's flown?"

Tancred quaffed the last of his ale and thrust his great, carved-oak chair back from the trestle table on the dais. He stood, then turned to look at the lean, swarthy man whose family, for centuries, had been lords in that far, sun-baked land. Enemies, the Holy See named them. Unbelievers. Saracens. But then, the Pope had not witnessed the conduct of those he had sent on a holy quest. Tancred could only believe Jesus wept over what had been done in His name.

"I would know if she had." Tancred headed for the door.

Kadar fell into step beside him, his choice of attire as brilliant as Tancred's was somber. "Ah. Such a comfort, omniscience."

Tancred cut him a sidelong glance, but did not immediately reply. When he finally spoke, it was not to address his methods for keeping track of Rosamund. That was no secret. "She believes that she has only to wait, and her brother will return to save her."

Kadar shook his head. "She is brave, that one. I would not underestimate her."

"Mayhap. Still, she is only a woman."

"A very beautiful one, my friend. Another man, in your place, would have already taken her to his bed."

"Ha! As if I would lie with Arnaud Bourton's sister! I do not kennel with vipers, Kadar."

"You do not kennel with anyone," Kadar observed mildly.

"Not that you know of, you meddlesome Mussulman. I do not cover every woman willing to spread herself for me."

Kadar's smile was unruffled. "Women are meant for

pleasure, my friend. Who am I to deny the delightful creatures that which I am capable of giving them?" His smile grew. "They are marvels of Creation. Their dulcet voices. Their wondrous fragrance. The taste of their lips, of their skin, of their—"

"I see this month will go harder on you than I thought," Tancred said with a lift of an eyebrow.

Kadar shrugged. "Sometimes fasting is good for the soul. It heightens a man's . . . appreciation."

Tancred laughed. "Your appreciation sounds high enough." His gaze traveled over the interior of the inner bailey. "Have you ever seen anything like this?" he murmured, half to himself.

The amount of greenery he saw astonished him. Oh, there were the usual physic and kitchen gardens, though these, which he had earlier seen by the rising sun, were extraordinarily lush.

No, it was all the other growing things that surprised him. They were everywhere he looked. Barrels cut in half and packed with soil yielded flowering peas, yarrow, and cowslips. Earth-filled troughs burst with lush greenery and blossoms alien to him. Plant beds in unexpected places cheered the eye with budding daffodils, irises, and foxglove and insured good eating with the likes of hart's-tongue and parsley and a host of other plants. On the roofs of the less strategic towers he'd discovered bee skeps, those domes of twisted straw where bees made their homes and their honey.

While his life among fighting men had provided limited contact with creatures other than war horses, hounds, falcons, and men, he knew enough to guess that within the confines of Wynnsef Castle alone these bees would find plenty of nectar. And likely there were a myriad more skeps out in the blossoming orchards he saw from the western wall walk.

Moveable gardens draped a rainbow of flowers down well-maintained limestone walls. Tancred thought this must be how the hanging gardens of Babylon had looked.

"I have never seen a fortress like it," Kadar admitted. "There is a touch of Paradise here."

They talked a bit longer about this unusual place, then parted ways, each to attend to his respective tasks in consolidating the control of Wynnsef into the hands of its new master. This was not the first citadel they had secured in such a manner. The difference lay in that the others had been captured in the king's name.

Tancred had already taken the measure of the captain of the guards, one John Willsson. Although John had spoken no word against Arnaud, Tancred had learned to read men well enough to sense disapproval. Arnaud was not a master John could respect. John, on the other hand, was respected by his men as a soldier and as a fair and evenhanded commander. That much had been apparent as Tancred had moved among the handful of exhausted guards Arnaud left to defend Wynnsef.

It did not hurt matters that crusaders were held in high regard, or that Tancred's methods of taking the castle had been new to them, almost magical. If the castle folk regarded him and his men with a touch of awe or fear, so much the better. That would work to his advantage when Arnaud finally discovered someone else held his honor and came to retake it.

Freemen and villeins went about their work as usual, though subdued and uncertain for their futures. As Tancred walked the busy inner bailey, he saw no one who did not appear at least adequately fed. As a stranger in a closed community, he drew stares and stirred low-voiced comment.

Tancred strode toward the stable. Never had he wanted anything more fiercely than he'd wanted Wynnsef. And now it was his.

After a lifetime of garrisons and camps, he finally had a home. By the Grace of God, he would keep it, to the fury and great hurt of the traitor. But the loss of his estate was not the gravest of the punishments

Tancred had planned for that faithless cur, the one that would bring the most satisfaction.

Arnaud of Wynnsef would pay for his betrayal . . . with his life.

THREE

At noon, a page found Rosamund in the laundry, listening to the complaints of the head laundress regarding the condition of the aging tubs and troughs.

"I crave your pardon, Lady Rosamund," the boy said, clearly unhappy over having to interrupt her in the course of her duties. "But Lord Tancred bade me deliver this message to you."

The mere mention of Tancred's name was sufficient to cause Rosamund to tense.

For the small page's sake, she smiled. "What message is that, Piers?"

The child scowled down at the toes of his dusty shoes as he concentrated on getting the words right. "He said, my lady, that you should present yourself at the great hall, prepared to ride."

"When?"

"Oh. At once."

Rosamund stiffened, her eyes blazing. *The arrogance of the man!* He wanted the castle to continue to run smoothly, but she must drop what she was doing to attend him, as if she were a villein.

Safer than any other woman in the world—Indeed!

The laundress, a sturdy woman at least a score of years older than Rosamund cleared her throat. "My lady, you know I mean no disrespect . . . "

"Speak, Mattie," Rosamund said. "I will listen."

"The man holds your life—all our lives—in his sword hand." Her broad, usually ruddy face was pale.

Rosamund recalled the choice he had given her: the whip for those who might distract him, or her cooperation in keeping things running smoothly. Without her there to intercede and interpret, would he truly unleash that promised whip upon the people of Wynnsef?

She remembered the strong gloved hand on her mouth. The deep, deadly voice in her ear. Tancred de Vierzon, lounging upon the carved-oak high seat like a black-jeweled dragon. Powerful. Dangerous.

Rosamund took a deep breath and huffed it out. "We'll finish this task later, Mattie."

With a look of relief, Mattie nodded.

"Thank you, Piers." Rosamund started in the direction of the great hall, but stopped when she saw the boy's face.

His small blond eyebrows wrinkled with distress. "I think 'immediately' may have come and gone, my lady. I . . . I couldn't find you. I did look. I looked everywhere!"

She patted Piers's thin shoulder. "I'm certain Lord Tancred will understand." She wasn't certain of any such thing, so she hurried toward the great hall.

Before she was halfway there, three knights in helmets and mail guided their warhorses into the courtyard and stopped in her path.

Her stomach clenched. Forced to look up, Rosamund shielded her eyes against the bright spring sun.

From beneath the edge of a conical helmet, separated by the helmet's metal nasal, two silver eyes stared down at her. The ventail of the mail coif that fastened to the helmet concealed the rest of his face. It did not matter. Rosamund would have recognized those eyes anywhere.

"I have waited on you, damoiselle," said the voice that was as deep and dark as a bottomless tarn.

"I was unavoidably detained, my lord."

"I mislike waiting."

Piers came flying up from behind Rosamund. He threw himself in front of her, making of his small body a shield, though there was terror in his wide blue eyes. "My fault, my lord!" he cried.

Afraid that he might alarm that black giant of a horse and be struck by one of those hooves that were as large as his head, Rosamund pulled Piers back. The horse never moved.

"My fault," Piers repeated, with only the faintest quaver in his childish voice. Through the practical wool of her work-a-day kirtle Rosamund felt his clutching fingers tremble. "My Lord Tancred, she did but j—j—just receive your message!"

The startlingly light eyes turned toward the boy. "Did you dawdle, Master Piers?"

Vehemently, Piers shook his head. "No, sire. I didn't know where to find her."

Rosamund held him protectively against her legs. "He is a good lad, Lord Tancred."

Tancred's gaze moved from the boy to Rosamund. "I can see that. Very well, Piers, you have brought the lady as I asked."

Rosamund's fingers could not resist smoothing the tousled locks. "Thank you, Piers. Now go join the other young gentlemen in their lessons. You would not wish to offend our Brother Felix, would you?"

Again he shook his head, sending his blond hair back into motion. "Oh, no, my lady." He cast an uncertain glance toward the tall, dark knight, who gave a slight nod.

In a small flurry of wool and leather, Piers sprinted toward the great hall, where the good monk was today giving his lessons.

Rosamund's sleek gray barb was brought around, and once she was mounted Tancred led the way toward the main gate of the castle. The two knights Tancred introduced as Bernard of Glathe and Osbert of Lede accompanied them.

Rosamund held her peace as the wooden draw-bridge thundered under the mighty war horses and her elegant barb. When they reached the narrow track that led away from Wynnsef, she could no longer restrain her curiosity.

"To where do we go, my lord?" she asked.

Tancred did not bother to look at her. "I desire that you show me Wynnsef."

Surrounded by knights on heavy destriers that dwarfed her and her daintier mare, Rosamund turned La Songe westward, in the opposite direction of the village, her fingers tense on the mare's reins. "For certes, you will want to enjoy this honor while you can," she said sweetly.

Tancred's eyes crinkled with amusement. "Believe what you will for now, damoiselle. You will see soon enough that Wynnsef is mine, and so it shall remain. My son will rule it after me, and his son after him."

Osbert, the oldest of the three men, laughed. "First you must take a wife, Tancred,"

Tancred shrugged one broad shoulder. Mail rattled. "There are women enough to serve my purpose when I am ready."

Rosamund bristled. Did this man's arrogance know no bounds? "Pray, inform the ladies now of their good fortune," she muttered under her breath. "Doubtless they will wish to line up to await your esteemed attentions."

"Doubtless," he said quietly, without turning his head to look at her.

Annoyed with the heat that rose in her cheeks, Rosamund made no reply. Instead, she welcomed the questions the knights asked her regarding Wynnsef. She answered the ones which would give them little or no useful facts to use against Arnaud and his force.

For the first time in her life, being a woman proved an advantage. She could say "I know not" to queries for even elementary information, and they believed her!

Considering how short their stay would be at Wynnsef, she decided Tancred de Vierzon truly didn't *need* to know how many acres were under cultivation for wheat, the number of capable adult male villeins belonging to the fief, or how many head of cattle were owned by Arnaud. So she assumed what she hoped was a "simple" or "innocent" look. After all, was she not a member of that gender that was reputedly incompetent *and* the source of sin? Privately, Rosamund considered such drivel a convenient fabrication by males, who did not hesitate to heap responsibility upon the much narrower shoulders of their wives or sisters.

With a properly demure smile, Rosamund did actually confirm the obvious: that wheat was grown on Wynnsef, that there were, indeed, adult male villeins, and that Arnaud owned cattle.

"We have forest," she said proudly. Her father had planted it when he'd first come into possession of Wynnsef. It had reduced the income for the honor, but had, in the long run, made it more valuable. "There is good hunting there." Let him eat out his heart when he controlled Wynnsef no more.

"Are there birds in the mews?" Tancred asked.

Her first impulse was to deny the existence of the Wynnsef mews, but she knew he probably would not believe that. "Yea, lord."

"What sorts of hawks are there?"

Arnaud had, of course, taken with him his new favorite, a white gyrfalcon from Greenland. But there was still her own lovely Matilda, a merlin, a lady's hawk. "A peregrine, two sparrow hawks, two lanners, and two sakers." Arnaud had brought the peregrine home with him when he had returned from the crusades. Despite his efforts to win it over, the magnificent falcon had never taken to him.

"Sounds well-stocked," Osbert said in his gravelly voice. "My father always kept an excellent mews, and he had a falconer that was the envy of the shire. My brother inherited, and now he spends more on his falcons than on his wife."

"Your brother's falcons are sweeter-tempered than his wife," Bernard teased.

The men laughed.

Bernard turned to Rosamund. "Your brother, lady—he has never wed?"

She tensed, uneasy. "No."

"How came that to be?" Osbert asked, appearing to be genuinely interested. "The firstborn male, your father's heir. I would have thought him betrothed while in the cradle to secure an alliance with another strong family."

Like the swift advance of a changing tide, old bitterness she'd struggled to banish swept through Rosamund. Had Arnaud wed as he should have, she, his sister, would have been free to go her own way. "He was."

"Did the maid die before they could wed?" Bernard inquired solicitously.

She sliced Tancred a fulminating glance and found his even gaze unreadable above the edge of his dark mail. "No. My father did."

They all turned their gazes on her, waiting. If she did not tell them, they might inquire of someone else.

"My brother delayed the marriage that normally would have taken place upon his fourteenth natal day until he was eighteen, and his prospective bride twelve. My parents indulged him. Then, first my mother died, then my father. Arnaud called off the betrothal. He has not found a suitable prospect since." Not that he had troubled to look.

"Did he not like your father's choice of mate for him?" Osbert asked, clearly curious.

Rosamund worried the inside of her bottom lip and considered ignoring the question. She weighed the consequences with what she might gain or lose, and decided that the way Tancred was regarding her, the

odds were she would stand to lose what little control
she had retained.

"No," she said at length. "She had a limp from a
childhood accident."

"She speaks of Lady Margaret of Cranthorp," Tancred said.

Bernard's eye widened. "Holy Face! He gave up
such a lovely lady?"

"Such a *rich* lady," Osbert added.

"We've had the privilege of making Margaret of
Cranthorp's acquaintance," Bernard explained to Rosamund. "A more pleasing lady one could not hope
to meet. Yea, there was a tiny limp, but it was of no
consequence. Her charm outshone it."

Arnaud had raved on about the girl's "ungainly,
lumbering" walk. Rosamund had thought the limp
slight.

"Her husband seems pleased with her," Tancred
said.

Osbert nodded. "And she with him."

"Then all is well," Rosamund said stiffly. "I am
happy for her."

Nothing more was said as the sun inched to its ze-
nith. The only sounds were the dull, syncopated thump
of hooves, the swish of grass against the horses' legs,
the occasional creak of leather, and the energetic
courting songs of birds. Invaders or no, Dame Spring
would not cease her rituals of rebirth.

"We cannot ride the entire manor in one day," she
said. "If we do not turn back soon, we'll not make
the castle by nightfall."

On the edge of the forest, they stopped to let the
horses rest and munch tender spring grass while they
attended nature's call and stretched their legs. In their
turn, Osbert and Bernard walked into the heavy shade
of the forest, leaving Rosamund and Tancred to watch
the horses.

Restless with him so near, she strolled over to the
clear, chuckling stream. Primroses grew along its

mossy banks, like cheerful droplets of sunshine clustered amid leaves of quilted emerald. As she idly watched the water, a fingerling struggled against the current.

Suddenly, Rosamund sensed someone behind her. She whirled, her hand instinctively going to that place on her girdle where she had always worn her knife in its vermeil sheath set with agates. Her fingers encountered only a plain girdle; the guard had taken the blade from her that morning before escorting her to the great hall.

She found herself facing Tancred completely alone and unarmed.

He had loosed the ventail of his mail coif from its fastening at the edge of his helmet, leaving his lower face exposed. "I did not mean to startle you."

"Then you should not have sneaked up behind me." She sidled a little farther away, uneasy around such a potent presence.

He watched her, but made no move to close the distance she'd put between them. "I did not sneak. 'Tis only that I am quiet when I move."

"So I've noticed. Altogether too quiet. 'Tis unnatural," she informed him. "A man in mail should . . . should *clink* when he walks. It allows one time to get out of his way."

"That is one of the reasons I've learned how not to clink. Another is that it allows me to observe people."

She sat down on a rock several feet away, but kept a wary eye on him. "No reason to watch me. I assure you, I was doing nothing at all interesting."

"In that you are mistaken."

Rosamund frowned. "Very well. Tell me what I was doing that was worth observing." She noticed that he had removed his mail mitten gauntlets. Now one large hand rested easily on the pommel of his sword, the other hand propped on one lean hip.

A corner of his mouth lifted. "You were avoiding me."

She laughed bitterly. "One hardly needs stealth to discover that. You have stolen my home, Lord Tancred. You hold me prisoner. You have made it clear you would gladly do my brother harm. If you are expecting me to seek out your company, then you are doomed to disappointment." Rosamund rose to her feet. "In plain terms have you declared your enmity on me and mine. Do not expect me to love you for it." She strode away, new meadow grass tugging at the hem of her kirtle.

He did not try to stop her, nor did he follow her, and for that Rosamund was thankful. Weariness sawed at her bones. There had been no sleep for her since the night before last, and her nerves were strung taut from uncertainty and dread.

She went to La Songe, needing to touch something living, breathing, and familiar. As she ran her palm over the sleek gray neck, the mare lifted her head to study Rosamund with large brown eyes. La Songe huffed a breath out her nostrils that sounded much like a sigh, as if she sympathized with her mistress. Then, as if accepting what Fortune had dealt them with a philosophical shrug, she went back to snatching at tender green blades with strong, no-nonsense teeth.

Soon after, the three knights mounted their destriers and took up their formation around Rosamund. They headed north, toward the castle.

"Has there been trouble with brigands?" Tancred asked, his gaze surveying the distance ahead of them.

"There is always trouble with brigands," she said. "Arnaud has done better than most at keeping them at bay."

"When he is not away indulging in brigandage on his own."

Rosamund's jaw tightened. If only she could deny the truth of that comment. She had tried—how she'd tried!—to dissuade Arnaud from his addlepated expedition.

"Many of the brigands are knights returned from

the Holy Land and who have been left lordless. They are the worst, for they are skilled and equipped," she continued, refusing to acknowledge his thrust. "They savage the farms and the village. 'Tis as if they learned naught of Our Lord while they served in the land of His birth," she ended indignantly.

"I wager they learned much in Outremer," he said tonelessly.

Rosamund looked at him, curious. She had always believed that a knight who had taken the cross and fought the blessed war to retake the Holy Land from the heathen must surely earn an inner peace that could not fail him, just as the Holy Father in Rome promised every crusader an honored place in Heaven. Tancred de Vierzon was renowned for his many feats of bravery in that hot and distant place, yet, if ever there was a man bereft of tranquility, it was he.

His branded face revealed no hint of what lay in his mind. She was careful not to stare, but stole furtive glances at him, trying to learn something, anything. As she studied him, it was clear to see why troubadours sang of his manly beauty. His straight nose beneath the nasal of his helmet, those intriguing lips and that firm chin combined to form a profile that would easily win maidens to his side. But any who were not stout-hearted might shrink from the fierce light in his eyes.

Pulling her attention from the inscrutable man riding beside her, Rosamund lifted her face to the azure sky, enjoying the feel of the sun on her cheeks after a long, cold winter. A playful zephyr ruffled the edges of her veil. She breathed in the heady green fragrance of burgeoning leaves and hoof-trampled grass, the friendly smell of sun-warmed horse, and the fainter, musky odor of man.

In the distance, she could see Wynnsef Castle, its towering limestone walls gleaming pale and bright above the verdant plane that spread out around it. To her surprise, Tancred guided them away.

"Where do we go?" she asked, her brows drawn together in consternation.

"The village," he replied shortly.

Her spirits plummeted. She'd thought she had managed to detour him from that place for at least a day or so. Now it seemed there was no escape for those who lived in the cluster of thatched-roofed, wattle-and-daub hovels that surrounded the small stone church.

Families labored in their fields, sowing newly turned earth with barley and oats, peas and vetches. On the common green, a small girl herded a flock of geese, driving them toward the mill pond, where, at the far end, the mill's waterwheel churned. The women gathered at the town's well chattered as they drew water to fill their buckets.

As Rosamund and the three knights approached, a couple of mongrels barked at them. The geese flapped their wings and honked noisily at the intruders. A coltish lad sprinted from a nearby field, in the direction of the village headman's cottage.

The laughter at the well died to cautious whispers. As the destriers and the barb picked their way through the muddy street, men walked out of byres and barns. Women left their tasks, some carrying babes in their arms, others with toddlers riding their hips. The brawny miller ducked under the lintel of his door and joined the growing crowd. The village priest came out to stand on the steps of the church, where Tancred drew his horse to a halt.

"Good morrow, Father," Tancred said with a slight inclination of his head. "I thought to call upon you to advise you of a recent change."

Father Ivo, a wiry man in his thirties, his tonsured hair a dark fringe, bowed in return, his arms remaining folded in front of him, hands tucked into the wide sleeves of his roughly woven brown robe. "I give you welcome, Lord Tancred. I've been told that you are now lord of Wynnsef and therefore, of Attewell."

"You have been told aright."

"These are good and loyal people," Father Ivo said, spreading his arms to indicate the village, the surrounding fields, and all who lived and worked within. "I entreat you to deal with them fairly."

Silver-gray eyes took the priest's measure. "I intend to."

Father Ivo turned to Rosamund. "The mysteries of our Lord passeth all understanding, do they not, my lady? 'Twould seem that at last He has made to grant your dearest wish."

Rosamund's stomach tightened. Father Ivo was too innocent. Now was not the time for him to bring this up. She must stay. She must hold Wynnsef for her brother. What if Tancred decided that sending her away would be more convenient than putting up with the bargain she'd struck with him?

Rosamund forced a smile.

At that moment, Uehtred, the stocky, flaxen-haired village headman, arrived, trailed by the members of the village council and one barking dog. A village woman silenced the disturbance by shooing the cur away, then Rosamund performed introductions. It was clear to her that the villagers gathered here were familiar with the *chansons* about Tancred de Vierzon's feats of valor. They seemed much more impressed with him than they were her brother. But then, no one had composed poems or songs about Arnaud's knightly excellence.

The dog that had been chased away took up his barking again, this time from the safer distance of the common green. The combination of clamorous cur and strangers invading the village proved too much for the aggressive temperament of the geese. Hissing and honking, they charged away from their small warden, straight toward the horses.

"*O-o-nk! O-o-nk!*" The fowl thrust their heads forward and arched their wings. Calling to them, the goose girl ran after them. She waved her willow wand at them, which only served to enrage them further.

Even as Rosamund worried over the notoriously high-strung temperament of destriers, La Songe edged nervously to one side. Bernard's heavy horse pranced restlessly. Tancred's mount stood rock solid in its place.

Osbert's destrier snorted and sidled. Just then Rosamund saw the frantic child dart after her charges between the legs of the horses.

"The child—!" She got no further. A white-feathered head shot toward La Songe's fetlock. With a shrill cry, the barb reared. Rosamund managed to keep to her saddle. She worked to calm La Songe, to prevent her from trampling the girl, who shrieked a heart-tearing child's cry of terror. Restively, Osbert's mount snorted and sidled.

Another fowl struck, and Bernard's heavy horse lunged upward, iron-shod forehooves churning the air like a murderous windmill. That set off Osbert's destrier, who reared, stamped and snorted and reared again.

Swiftly, Tancred guided his great beast forward, into the deadly melee. A few hundred pounds of iron mail and man leaned down out of the saddle. In a single, fluid motion, he scooped the screaming child into his arm. Then, as if they were two well-meshed parts of the same machine, man and horse deftly eluded the enraged destriers' hooves to canter a safe distance away. As they moved by her, Rosamund heard Tancred murmuring softly to the terrified girl, who clung to him.

He delivered the child into the arms of a frantic woman. She hugged the little one close and burst into tears.

The villagers cheered. It started as a ripple and gradually rose to a roar. Gazing at their faces, Rosamund supposed that yet another feat of bravery would

soon be immortalized in *chansons de geste* about the
Moon Lord.

By the time they left Attewell, the sun skimmed the
red-gold horizon. As the rhythmic swaying of La
Songe lulled Rosamund into a near-somnolent state,
she remembered something that had surprised her
when it had happened earlier that morning.

Tancred had known the page's name. He had called
Piers by name. Even her brother had never managed
to get that right, and he had known Piers most of the
boy's life.

Beside her, she heard the now familiar, yet still almost mystical, baritone, the softly spoken words little
more than a rich vibration of the golden twilight air.

"Tell me, lady, of what did the priest speak? What
wish is it that God has seen fit to grant you?"

FOUR

Rosamund looked into the eyes of the conqueror. "My wish," she said, "to become a nun."

The slanting, black-slash eyebrows rose in surprise. "A *nun*? You?"

She bristled at his incredulous tone. "Pray, what do you find extraordinary about that?"

"I cannot envision you as a meek, obedient sister robed in black." He eyed her red kirtle.

Annoyed, she tossed her head. "Little you know."

The corners of his mouth lifted, and she found herself staring. Holy Rood, but he was marvelous to look upon. As beautiful as an archangel, as secret as a walled garden.

He made no reply, but the flush that crawled up his neck suggested that he had caught her staring, and that it embarrassed him.

Turning her face away to hide her own warm hue, she caught a glimpse of his mail-covered thigh where it parted the side slit of his black surcoat. Such long legs. Long, well-muscled legs.

Her blush deepened, and she chided herself for even noticing his body. A true nun, she told herself firmly, did not see men as men. They were . . . uh . . . Why, they were merely one of God's creatures, though more noisy and overbearing than most.

That last thought made her feel a bit less harried, and the heat gradually ebbed from her cheeks. With a relieved breath, she glanced at him from beneath her lashes. *Just a creature*, she quickly reminded herself.

No more was said between them as the small party rode over the drawbridge into the outer bailey. Looking up at the wall walk, Rosamund saw that her few men-at-arms had now been joined by many of Tancred's. The invaders were not as small a force as she had thought. The realization left her feeling sick.

"What has captured your attention so completely, Lady Rosamund?" Tancred asked as he swung out of the saddle. He handed the reins of his destrier to a stable lad.

She dismounted, then cast him a chilly look. He knew, curse him.

He smiled coolly. "My men make a much-needed addition to the paltry number with which you thought to hold this castle. They are seasoned warriors, skilled in many forms of combat. A few such forms will be unknown to Arnaud."

"I much doubt that," she snapped, but she remembered waking to his whisper in the dead of night; waking to find that she was the prisoner of this brother to shadows, and that the castle was his.

Perhaps Arnaud had learned these strange ways of fighting, but had kept them concealed to gain the element of surprise against his enemies. "Mayhap you are right," she said, hoping to confuse Tancred. Alas, he appeared not one bit confused.

He struck off toward the great hall, then stopped and turned back to her. "You did not grace us with your presence when we broke our fast this morn."

"I was . . . busy."

"In future you will not be so busy that you cannot take your meals with the rest of us."

Although Rosamund had purposely avoided breaking bread with this usurper, she had been busy. He'd told her he'd wanted no distractions. That meant everything must run as smoothly as usual, which required long hours of hard work and vigilance from her, as it always had. More so now, with an invader in their midst. "This morning you said—"

"I know well what I said this morning. *Now* I am adding this: You will take your meals with the rest of us. You are a princess no longer."

She stared at him. *Princess?*

He strode away, flanked by Osbert and Bernard.

"Insufferable simpkin," she muttered, glaring over her shoulder at Tancred's retreating form as she turned to go back to the laundry.

She collided with a solid chest clothed in gorgeous colors.

Instantly, hands came up to steady her. "My pardon, lady, for choosing an inconvenient place in which to stand." The smiling masculine voice was exotically accented, like none she'd heard before, until she'd heard it in her chamber the night of the Moon Lord's invasion.

Her head snapped up, and she saw she was standing in the loose embrace of a swarthy man with laughing dark eyes. On his head he wore a dark blue turban. The brass spike that projected from the top center gave the simple affair a distinctly military look.

Startled, she backed out of his grasp. All the nightmare stories she'd heard of the enemy's evil flooded back to her. "Saracen!" she hissed in alarm.

With courtly grace, he touched the fingertips of his right hand to his forehead, then to his chest, as he bowed. "It pleases your people to call us by that name, O Flower of Wynnsef. I am known as Kadar."

She eyed him suspiciously. "Th—that is a pagan name?"

He straightened. "No, Lady Rosamund, for I am not a pagan. Our God is the same, yours and mine, known only by differing names. For there is but one God, is this not so?"

"I—Why, yea. Of course." Her eyebrows knotted in confusion. "Then why—"

He waved a hand in an elegant gesture of negation.

"It is a political matter, as much as a religious puzzle, best left to distract those who possess far too much power. You need not fear me unless you harm Tancred de Vierzon."

Rosamund pressed her lips closed, a hairline crack *pinging* in her patience.

"He has annoyed you." Kadar sighed sympathetically. "This was inevitable."

Nagged by distrust, she regarded him through narrowed eyes, but curiosity finally got the better of her. "Why?"

"Why?" Kadar echoed incredulously. "Because he is a stubborn gentleman, and you, O Beauteous One, are a stubborn gentlewoman. Your power has fallen, while his has ascended. But fear not; his standards are foolishly high. I doubt he will take you against your will."

"It is the only way he could take me!" she blurted. Embarrassed, she snapped her jaw shut against any other undignified statements.

Kadar laughed. "Ah, but you perceive, do you not, that any other man in his place would have already claimed you as his rightful spoils. His men would have shared the other women amongst them."

She stiffened. "I'm the daughter of a baron. King Richard would never stand for it." But Rosamund knew that he would. She was no great heiress to bring her guardian the rich fees that would come with managing estates.

Kadar shrugged. "Your king told my lord Tancred that he could keep Wynnsef should he take it. No restrictions were laid upon what was found here."

"My thanks," Rosamund said tartly, "for pointing out to what humble depths my station has fallen."

"The lady mistakes me," he said. "I sought only to reassure."

"But of course." *And oxen can dance*, she thought, heading toward the laundry once again. She reminded herself that patience was a virtue.

"Wait," Kadar called. "You go in the wrong direction."

"The laundry is this way," she said.

"But you would not presume to bathe Lord Tancred *there*, would you?" he asked.

Exasperated, Rosamund stalked back to Kadar. "What I am going to do now is check the laundry troughs, to make certain his high puissance and his oh-so-honorable minions will find clean garments when next they need them. We wouldn't wish those good knights to be forced to wear soiled clothing whilst they grind their victims under their heels, would we?" Fie on patience! She would work on it tomorrow. "What I am *not* going to do is bathe your lord!"

Rosamund scowled at the great wooden tub as Aefre dumped the last bucket of steaming water into it.

" 'Tis not right, m'lady," the sturdily built fifteen-year-old girl said hotly. "Not with you wantin' to be a holy sister."

"*Wanting* to enter a convent and actually doing so are clearly very separate things in the minds of men." Rosamund sighed. "Well, 'tis not as if I've never attended to a man's bath before. I've been doing it since Mama died."

"Yea, m'lady, for nigh unto four years now. But those men were *guests*. M'Lord Tancred is no guest."

"No, he is not," Rosamund agreed. *Oh, hurry, Arnaud!*

Aefre's pretty face lighted. "Are you going to cast a spell over him with your green magic?"

Rosamund shook her head. She'd all but given up trying to make her people understand that her gift with growing plants and with using them in everything from cooking to healing had naught to do with sorcery. "I'll not risk his wrath when we have only to wait for my lord brother to return and take back Wynnsef." She smiled, trying to reassure the girl. "Orva will

have your supper ready with the others now, Aefre."
The servants ate their meals before being called upon
to serve the lord and his crowd their victuals.

When the door had closed behind the servant, Rosamund opened the small pouch she had brought with
her from her herbarium. She crumbled the dried
leaves between her fingers and sprinkled them over
the hot water. The air in the underground chamber
grew redolent with the scent of rosemary and mint.

Arnaud had claimed this room from a storage chamber when he had returned from the Holy Land. Nothing
would do but that a special fireplace be constructed
to heat the place and the water that was drawn from
the deep well on this level. The tub had been built
here, for it was too large for the doors to accommodate. A tent enclosed the tub to keep the water hot
longer. Outside of the tent, however, everything
echoed against the stone walls and high, vaulted ceil-
ing. The only illumination came from the fire in the
large fireplace and the candles on their tall stands.
Rosamund preferred to take her baths in the much
smaller tub brought to her tower chamber. This vast
cavern was far too isolated for her ease.

She heard the outside door beyond this chamber
open, then close. Footfalls of someone descending the
stone steps echoed hollowly. Minutes later Tancred
entered the low light that hugged the lower portion
of the room. He had on the padded gambeson and
arming hose that were worn under mail hauberks
and chausses.

"Lady, why do you choose to set the bath here, in
a gloomy cave?" he asked, his voice cascading off the
arched walls and ceilings. "This is the sort of place
where murder is done." His gaze seemed to miss nothing as he advanced toward her.

"You refused to have a tub placed in your room,
Lord Tancred, and so I bethought you desirous of
using the large tub, here in the bathing chamber."

He looked skeptical. "This? A bathing chamber?"

"Yea, my lord," she said, still curious why he would not wish to bathe in his own quarters, the most spacious private chamber in the castle. "The temperature of these underground vaults stays ever more constant than the buildings above. In the winter, they are warmer than the upper structures; in the summer, cooler."

"As are the catacombs of Rome," he replied dryly, but he strolled over to the bench by the fireplace.

Piece-by-piece his clothing came off, until he wore only lightweight linen braies and chausses. Then even these were stripped off. Careful not to look at him, she folded each garment and placed them neatly on the bench.

Rosamund had seen naked men before, yea even naked knights, for it had been her duty as chatelaine to offer hospitality. Always she had averted her gaze from the more personal parts of their bodies, concentrating on soothing, relaxing, scrubbing their backs where they could not reach. The ritual was not meant to be intimate, though she had heard of instances, at other holds, where the experiences had become very intimate indeed.

Never, before now, had she been so nervous. Mayhap it was because this man held her life and those of her people in his fist. Or because he was so much taller than other men, his shoulders so much broader. It might be his fierce, masculine beauty that unsettled her, though she made a point of not looking at it now. Whatever the cause, a heated tension thrummed beneath the surface of her skin.

Determined to finish this ordeal as quickly as possible, she went to the tent, where she threw open the flap. Steam wafted out into the cooler air like a playful wraith. Humidity moistened her skin.

From the corner of her eye, she glimpsed Tancred's approach. Quickly, she turned away as he passed her. She heard his low chuckle as he ducked into the tent. As he passed close to her, her heart beat faster.

"Many women catch sight of a man's body without losing their souls to Satan, Lady Rosamund," he said.

Her back turned to him, she worried her bottom lip between her teeth. *They have never seen* you, *Tancred de Vierzon.* Aloud, she informed him primly, "It is my intention to become a nun, not some knight's *mie.*"

The water splashed softly as he entered it. His contented sigh reached her ears. She stepped out of the tent and closed the flap, giving him his privacy, with her own sigh of relief.

"Damoiselle," he said, "I require your assistance."

She exhaled sharply through her nostrils. Then she counted to ten . . . slowly.

"Damoiselle," he said again, his voice low and patient.

She counted to twenty.

Snatching open a flap, she marched back into the pavilion. "What?" she snapped. "One would think you could at least wash by yourself."

He raised an innocent gaze to her. "I could if I had soap."

A swift glance around revealed none. She spun on her heels. In seconds she returned with a ball of her own herbal soap. This she plunked down beside the goblet of wine on the small table at his elbow.

"I desire your company," he said before she made it to the door of the tent. "Won't you sit and speak with me awhile? Then, when I am ready, you may lave my back for me."

She glared at his bare back, until, in the low light provided by a few candles, she saw the scars there. They covered his back in long, silvery white stripes. This man had been whipped, cruelly whipped. The shocking sight reminded her of the brutality of his life. Grudgingly, she admitted to herself that Tancred made no unreasonable request . . . under normal circumstances. But then, these were not normal circumstances.

He drew in a long breath. "What is this smell?"

He sniffed again. " 'Tis something in the water." He scooped up bathwater in one cupped hand to inspect the specks of dried leaf.

"Rosemary and mint," she informed him warily.

Tancred leaned back against the wall of the tub and rested his arms along its rim. He tilted his head so that he could see her. "Why?"

"Why what?"

"Why have you put something good in the bathwater of your enemy?"

There in the humid heat of the pavilion, she studied his face for a moment. Surely not even the fallen angel, Lucifer, could be so beautiful. Steam swirled around them as her gaze moved over his thick, raven hair, his intelligent brow, the black slashes of his eyebrows, his oblique eyes, and straight, imperious nose. Those high, slanting cheekbones. That mouth . . . Against her will, she found herself staring, watching it move with each word he spoke. Those provocative lips, the top one slightly fuller . . . edged by the shadow of dark new beard at the end of the day, which only served to draw attention to their splendid shape . . . their inviting texture . . .

His sensual lips moved. They formed her name. *Rosamund*. Never before had she noticed how lips moved to form that word.

"Lady Rosamund, are you well?"

She blinked. "Uh—" Blood rushed to her face, and her chest tightened with her humiliation. "I beg your par—" Her voice cracked.

His eyebrows drew together. "Lady?" The word dropped from his lips as he rose from the water without warning. He grasped her arms with his warm, wet hands.

Only thoughts of tortured saints allowed Rosamund to tear her gaze from the full magnificence of Tancred's naked body. Holy Face, what temptation!

He gently guided her to the stool beside the tub, where she sat down with a limp-kneed thump. When he made to step out of the tub, she hastily waved him back in.

"For certes 'tis the heat," she said, fanning her face after he had settled back into the water, his manly essentials, and much of the rest of him, neatly blocked from view by the wall of the tub.

Tancred looked skeptical. "The only thing truly hot in here is the water."

How uncourtly of him to debate the point with her. "Very well," she replied crisply, "the *moist* heat."

He studied her for a long moment, driving her to the verge of squirming beneath that intense silvery gaze.

"You appear sounder than that," he said.

"Oh!" Was this the way he behaved in King Richard's courts? If the troubadours could hear him now Rosamund doubted they'd be likely to compose yet another song in praise of him. "I assure you, sir, I am quite sound of wind and strong of limb. Do you wish to check my teeth, as well?"

He scowled down at the water, but he didn't appear to be looking at anything. "You put words in my mouth," he muttered.

Careful not to glance into the tub, Rosamund went to the small table where she had set the customary flagon of wine and a cup. She thrust the goblet of wine at him. "Drink," she snapped.

He accepted the cup. "Who could refuse such a gracious offer?" With only a slight hesitation, he drank. He grunted his approval of the flavor.

It annoyed her that he should take all her refinements of hospitality—things that had always set her apart as a superior chatelaine—for granted . . . if indeed he noticed them at all.

This barbarian had invaded her castle. He had accosted her within her own chamber. Now, like her brother, he held her captive and used her talents and abilities for his convenience.

Rosamund seized one of two filled ewers from the

table. Without warning, she doused his head, wetting his hair for washing.

The water had been hot when she'd filled the ewers, but it had since turned cool. She realized her mistake too late.

With a roar, Tancred surged to his feet. Startled, she backed away, but not fast enough. He swept her up in his arms, and she shrieked with alarm.

Unexpectedly their gazes collided. Her protest died into silence, its echo fading among the stone vaults. He went still. Rosamund felt as if she were being drawn into the gleaming silver and black of his eyes. Her breath caught in her throat. His gaze lowered to her lips, which she vaguely realized had parted. He stared for the length of several rapids heartbeats. Abruptly his jaw tightened.

Then he dumped her into the tub.

She shrieked with outrage, splashing and floundering about in the water, becoming ever more entangled with her long sleeves and skirts. "Knave!" she sputtered.

"Shrew," he snarled.

Someone pounded on the stout door at the top of the stairs. "My lady!" came Aefre's worried voice. "My lord, please! Open the door!"

Rosamund tore her sodden, drooping wimple away from her throat and threw it on the floor. "Aefre, enter!" she called. "It is not locked."

"Yea, it is," Tancred rumbled.

She glared at him. "Is it not enough that you have ruined my kirtle?" she demanded angrily. "Do you seek also to ruin my good name?"

"Your good name," he sneered. "Who would dare malign the honor of the sweet-tempered little nun-to-be? I refused to have my hour of luxury disturbed by some gawping maid or stripling."

Using the wall of the tub as a support, she raised herself to her feet, weighed by ells of sopping cloth. With the back of one hand, she pushed a dripping mantle of hair out of her face. "You flatter yourself overmuch, my lord," she jeered.

Standing across the tub from her, his eyes widened. "Oh, do I, damoiselle?"

"Yea, you do," she retorted with a haughty lift of her chin. "What female in her right mind would give a puffed-up toad like you so much as a second glance?"

With an impatient jerk of his hand, he sluiced the water off his face. "Then you, madam, are quite insane, for you've ogled me like the worst camp follower."

Rosamund launched herself at him with a cry of furious humiliation. They went down in a churning tangle of arms and legs, sending a wall of water over the wooden side of the tub.

Tancred wrestled to the top and spat water. "God's Teeth, woman, you've surveyed me like a harlot on payday. Nun, my ar—"

She reared up and shoved his head under the water. "Swine!"

He snatched her under.

All her frustration, embarrassment, and anger burned through her limbs as she struggled with Tancred under the water, wanting badly to throttle him. He had sneaked into the castle and taken it from her control. He had opened her to her brother's certain ridicule and wrath. He had upset her carefully laid plans to finally obtain Arnaud's permission to enter a convent, where she could live in peace. Tancred was commanding and arrogant, and she detested him!

Just when Rosamund thought her lungs would burst, Tancred thrust her up out of the water, pushing her back against the planks of the tub's side, where she lay gasping for air. Before she could escape, he rolled on top of her, pinning her neatly in place without crushing her. As he panted, his deep, solid chest pressed rhythmically against her breasts. His face was so close that even in the dim light she saw his nostrils flare with each breath.

She looked up and found his gaze trained on her from beneath thick, raven lashes bejeweled with water droplets.

Abruptly he framed her face between his hands and claimed her lips in a carnal, openmouthed kiss. His flesh burned against hers. His thighs, which rode the outside of hers, tensed. Against the tender cradle at the apex of her legs, through the drenched layers of clothing, she felt him grow hard and thick and searing hot.

Although what was happening was beyond the realm of her experience, she responded to him. Her fingers gripped his wet hair, her tongue clumsily returned his strokes and thrusts. Her blood pounded in her ears with every wild beat of her heart.

Some dark, unfamiliar power surged through her, sending her arching up to make the contact between their bodies more complete. Tancred groaned deep in his throat, a sound that fueled her blind excitement, She nipped his bottom lip and tasted the tang of blood.

He growled and thrust his hips against her. A low moan of pleasure escaped her throat, into his mouth. He moved his head and fastened his mouth to the side of her neck and sucked. She had never felt its like before. He thrust his hips again. Some primal instinct sent her hand questing, reaching for him.

The door at the top of the stairs slammed open, and the bang of oak against stone echoed through the vaulted chambers.

Startled, Rosamund and Tancred stared at each other, the searing spell that bound them shattered. They sprang apart. He swiftly stood, then stepped out of the tub. In seconds he'd procured a linen drying cloth and wrapped it around his hips.

Encumbered by heavy, clinging skirts and sleeves, Rosamund made a slower, less graceful exit from the tub. When he started to assist her, she sent him a glare.

· "Touch me not," she hissed, thoroughly shamed that she should have wallowed with the enemy.

Ignoring her, he lifted her, streaming, out of the water and plunked her upright onto the ground. He tossed a drying cloth at her, then strode from the tent.

"Ah, John," she heard him say. "I regret we could not answer the door. There was an accident, you see. Lady Rosamund stumbled and fell into the tub."

Aefre burst into the tent. She stopped in her tracks when she caught sight of Rosamund. "Oh!" Snatching up a drying cloth, she rushed forward to protectively embrace Rosamund and then feverishly try to dry her. "*He* did this," she whispered angrily as she blotted. "You are too distressed for it to have been otherwise."

The men remained outside the pavilion.

"It is not customary to lock the door when my lady is alone with a man—any man—Lord Tancred," John Willsson said stiffly. "My good lady was performing a courtesy in attending you at your bath, and it is not just that you should invite gossip by locking the door."

"I desired privacy," Tancred said, his voice losing some of its amiability.

"Then you should have chosen your page to assist you, not an unwed lady."

Tancred's baritone issued low and hard as iron. "You go too far, Captain."

Giving up on making any creditable repairs to her appearance, Rosamund hurried out of the tent, unwilling to have John take Tancred's wrath upon his head for defending her. Aefre followed on her heels, still wringing and dabbing.

John took one look at Rosamund and fixed Tancred with a cold, narrow-eyed stare. As he opened his mouth to speak, Rosamund rushed to divert a possible calamity.

"It is as he said, John. I—I stumbled. 'Twas clumsy of me. Pray, do not distress yourself on my account."

A heavy silence settled over the chamber for a long

moment. The only sounds were the faint hissing and popping of the logs in the fire and the intermittent *plop* of water dripping off Tancred and Rosamund onto the stone floor.

Gently, with one hand, John raised Rosamund's face slightly upward, into the torch's light. He touched the raw place on her chin Tancred's nascent beard had abraded, and she winced.

"And did you also scrape your face, my lady?" he asked, his outrage more disturbing for the softness of his tone. "When you fell?"

She grasped his hand and met his simmering gaze with pleading in her eyes. He was as an uncle to her. He had bounced her on his knee in the great hall when she had been little more than a babe in swaddling, and he had taught her how to ride a horse after she had taken her first steps. Her heart could not stand the loss of him.

"Yea," she lied. "As you say, I scraped it when I fell." *Please*, she beseeched him silently. *Do not be rash in my cause.*

"It will not happen again," Tancred said quietly, meeting John's gaze squarely. No one could mistake his meaning.

John searched her face, then accorded Tancred a curt nod. He unfastened his leather mantle and draped it over Rosamund's shoulders. Without waiting to be dismissed by his new overlord, he escorted the women up the stairs of the keep.

As Rosamund swept up the stone stairs, she did not need to glance back to know that Tancred watched her. And she didn't need to see his face to know it would have a closed, unreadable expression as he stood there alone in the gloom.

FIVE

Upon fleeing from the keep, Rosamund made straight for her tower chamber. Inside, with the door bolted, she peeled off her sopping clothes and flung them away in a rare fit of temper. She silently submitted to Aefre, who clucked and shook her head, but who was wise enough not to ask questions while her mistress was so agitated. As the younger woman went about buffing Rosamund dry, she surreptitiously checked her mistress's body, but she wasn't subtle enough.

"What are you doing?" Rosamund asked impatiently.

"Looking for bruises, my lady," Aefre replied, unruffled at being discovered. "Never have I seen you so disturbed over the mere bathing of a man. And Lord Tancred *did* bolt the door."

The memory of those moments spent pressed against Tancred in the bathing tub flooded back to Rosamund. His large, hard, indisputably male body . . . the arousing hunger of his mouth . . . Nothing had ever stirred her like that before. She had never imagined—

Her face flamed with confusion and shame. "There are no bruises, Aefre. Lord Tancred did me no harm."

But she felt certain what they had done was wrong. It had to be. Anything that made her feel as if sweet, heated honey were being poured over her body, *through* her body, must be forbidden.

Aefre offered no other comment until she had

helped Rosamund into a fresh kirtle and cotte, and Rosamund had sat down at her dressing table. A hundred times Aefre pulled the boar's bristles brush through the wet blond mass, but it was hardly drier when she finished than when she had begun. It was decided that plaiting the hair, dressing it like a crown, might leave less of a wet mark on the veil.

Rosamund worried her bottom lip. How was it possible that such an annoying man—and an enemy at that—could have affected her in such a manner? She thought she ought to go directly to Brother Felix to confess her stolen pleasure with the Moon Lord, but it was too embarrassing. Perhaps it would be better to wait to confess to Abbess Matilda when she arrived. Rosamund hoped the abbess, who usually took a personal interest in overseeing the caravan of supplies ordered for Wynnsef, did not simply turn the caravan of supply wagons around and return to Hembley Abbey when she heard the castle had been captured. But that seemed unlikely. By no means was the abbess faint of heart.

Rosamund noticed that Aefre was being unusually quiet, which instantly drew her attention from her own thoughts. "What is it, Aefre?"

The girl pressed her lips together tightly and shook her head, but her gaze avoided Rosamund's.

"Come," Rosamund encouraged softly, remembering the loyalty this young farmer's daughter had always shown her. "What's amiss?"

Aefre's eyebrows drew down as she continued braiding. "Lady, he marked you."

"Marked me?"

"Yea, on your neck. A—a . . . love bite."

"*What?*" Rosamund snatched up the hand mirror of polished brass from the dressing table. To her horror, it reflected a purple bruise the size of a finger nail on the side of her neck. "That . . . that *swine!*"

"Did you not feel it, then? When he, uh . . . when he bit you?" Aefre inquired hesitantly.

"I—" Had she? Slowly she shook her head. No. She had been in thrall to luscious sensation. "We struggled in the water."

Aefre's eyes widened. "He sought to force you?"

"No, no," Rosamund denied hastily. As much as she resented him, she would not falsely accuse even Tancred de Vierzon of such a vile deed. "I dumped water on him, and—and he took exception to my manner. 'Twas temper that drove him to dump me into the water, not lust."

Aefre made no immediate comment as her fingers continued to work Rosamund's damp hair. Her gaze remained fixed on her task with more interest than she normally displayed in weaving hair into simple braids. "My ma does say as how sometimes anger is but a cover for love."

Love? Ha! "Your mother is a wise woman, Aefre, and you know I have harkened to her advice more than once—"

"Yea, my lady, but—"

"But I harbor no love for Lord Tancred, and he certainly has none for me. There is only enmity between us. Deep, burning, mutual enmity. Did he but know that I await the sound of my brother's trumpets so that I might throw open the back gates to him, Tancred would have cast me out of Wynnsef ere I had time to pack. No, he holds me in low esteem. He is certain I am naught but a pampered princess"—she forestalled Aefre's surprised objection with a wave of her hand—"and I would that he continue to think me so. The less he learns about the workings of Wynnsef the better. There will be less damage to repair after Arnaud has driven that upstart knight away. Then all that will remain for me to do before entering Hembley Abbey will be to finish Helvise's training in the running of Wynnsef and convincing my brother that Helvise will be a perfect bride for him."

"He will never think that."

"He will. I must simply persuade him."

Aefre draped a veil over Rosamund's head and scowled as the damp plaits stained the silk with moisture. "Her breasts are too small."

"She has the perfect figure for a lady," Rosamund insisted. "Besides, she will, by then, know how to manage Wynnsef as efficiently as I."

"Not as efficiently as you, ever. Lady Helvise has not your green magic."

Rosamund sighed. "I have no magic."

Aefre arranged Rosamund's wimple, careful to fully conceal the love bite. "Your hair is damp. You should allow it time to fully dry before you leave your chamber. Even in plaits, it soaks your veil, and you cannot wear a wimple without a veil."

Abruptly, Rosamund rose to her feet. "Staying here until my hair dries is not an option. *He* has decreed that I am to attend meals in the hall."

Her temper simmering, she stalked to the great hall, where all had taken their places. The vast stone chamber hummed with myriad hushed conversations, punctuated by an occasional burst of laughter. The food was just being brought into the great hall from the kitchens.

Hoping to go unnoticed, Rosamund slipped onto the bench at the table her brother had assigned her for when he was in residence. No sooner had she nodded congenially to her surprised new trencher mate, one of the Moon Lord's senior knights, than Piers appeared at her shoulder.

"Lady Rosamund," he said, "my Lord Tancred desires that you take the place befitting your station."

A stone plunked into Rosamund's stomach. Was she now to be forced to take an even more lowly place? One below the salt cellar? That would explain Tancred's insistence that she attend the communal meal.

"As my lord desires," she replied tonelessly.

To her astonishment, Piers led her to the high table, and it occurred to her that the new lord might wish to humiliate her in person.

Tancred rose from his chair, tall, dark, and attired in somber gray. "Welcome, lady," he said, drawing back the other chair at the high table—one only slightly less grand than the one he claimed, the one that had belonged to her mother for many years. "I would deem it an honor if you sat with me," he said blandly, but beneath the surface smoothness of his words cut an edge of steel.

She eyed the chair warily, then lifted her gaze. It clashed with his.

Sensing the tension between them, Piers turned a worried face to Rosamund. Conversation in the hall ceased.

Uncertain of what Tancred might be capable, she reluctantly sat in the proffered chair. "You are too kind, sir," she murmured.

With a reassuring nod, Tancred sent Piers to join his fellows at their suppers, then signaled the cup bearer to fill the beaten silver goblet set at her place. Once that had been accomplished, and the cup bearer had departed, he turned to her. "Your hair is still wet, lady. It has soaked your veil."

Tense over this new, unwanted seating arrangement, nervous at being so close to him after their encounter in the tub, she looked down at the roast fish on her trencher. "You ordered me to attend the meals in the great hall." With her knife and spoon, she procured a small slice of fish.

"Had you sent word to me, a plate could have been taken to your chamber. You will find I am not an unreasonable man . . . when left unprovoked."

She rankled at that last. "I am your hostage, dread lord, and do quake at the thought of incurring your anger," she replied with false meekness.

His bark of startled laughter drew the attention of those around them. Ignoring the blatant curiosity of the other diners, he grinned. "In truth?" he said, his deep, night-velvet voice soft and for her ears alone.

"So cunningly do you conceal your quaking, I might have mistaken it for defiance."

"I would not dare, my lord." *Unless I see the chance.*

"If that is so, lady, then remove your veil, that your hair may dry as we eat our meal. I would not have you sicken on my account."

"Indeed, sir," she said sweetly, unable to force another syllable of submission to her lips. " 'Twould be on your account that I would most likely sicken."

One black-slash eyebrow lifted in warning, and she went still, fearful that this time she'd gone too far. Her heart pounded so hard it threatened to leap up her throat.

"Did I not have it otherwise from your own lips," he drawled, "I might mistake your words for sarcasm. But then, we both know quaking hostages are fortunate if they can summon spit, much less derision. Is that not so, Lady Rosamund?"

"Yea, my lord." *Curse him.* Was that amusement lurking in those silver eyes?

He broke off a bit of manchet loaf. "See that your trembling does not jar your bones sufficiently to distract me. I hear there is a troubadour to entertain us this evening, and I would not have him drowned out by the clattering."

She lowered her eyes, torn between seething and amazement. "I will bear that in mind."

A server stopped to offer them more sauce. When Tancred saw that Rosamund wanted none, he sent the servant on.

"Do not stint yourself on my account," she said. "Though you will soon discover the larders of Wynnsef are finite."

He studied her for a moment, the sweep of his thick, lashes concealing his eyes from her. "I am a fighting man, damoiselle, and have been all my life. I am used to simple fare."

"What of all those dishes you have enjoyed at the king's board?"

She had taken the trouble to learn as much of him as she could, mostly from John, who had, with her father, served the old King Henry on several occasions. He had been there when a rebellious baron's only son, a black-haired boy the age of Piers, had been given to Henry as hostage against that baron's good behavior.

The baron had broken the truce, knowing his son would be hanged. But at the last minute, as the child stood on the gallows with the noose around his neck, Henry's heart had proved too soft to kill the boy he had come to like. The king's heart had not been too soft to have the father drawn and quartered as a traitor after he'd finally been captured.

That Henry had provided for Tancred's training as a knight was all else that she knew of this man beside her until his exploits in the Holy Land had set the bards to such feverish activity.

"Many of the dishes at the king's court," Tancred replied, "were as wondrous to behold as they were rare. Still, I'd not want to eat them every day. Or even often, in some cases. Nor have I any wish to exhaust my own castle's storerooms," he added with blunt finality.

Rosamund simmered over his proprietary reference to Wynnsef's supplies, supplies that *she* had worked to collect.

"Tell me of the troubadour who will entertain us," Tancred said. "Is he a nightingale?"

Will was more like an awkward nightingale fledgling. One who worked very hard at growing into a glorious songbird. He was still young; he would improve as he grew older.

"He is a local lad, and he has remarkable . . . potential. Ever ready with his lute and a song, is our Will. He knows the *chansons* that are much requested amongst the manors and castles, and he also composes." That part needed more work. Much more work.

"Ah."

That single syllable was far too articulate for Rosamund's comfort. "He is most earnest in his efforts," she said. " 'Tis only that he's . . . well . . . "

"Not very good?" Tancred suggested helpfully.

"Yea. No!" She sighed. "He will improve. He's still a youth, and it takes years of practice and dedication to make a good troubadour, just as it does to make a good knight." A bit of inspiration, that.

"With one essential difference, perhaps."

She smothered a sigh.

"When a troubadour makes an error, he seldom dies for it."

"Would that not depend on his patron?" she asked.

A corner of Tancred's mouth curled upward, and Rosamund noticed for the first time how young he was. He had attained such fame that she had expected him to be at least near the end of his thirtieth year, but now she saw he probably wasn't more than five-and-twenty. The force of his virility—especially powerful at this close proximity—and his confidence distracted one's attention from his youth.

When someone two benches down hailed him, Tancred turned his attention toward the man, one of his knights. Rosamund took the opportunity to conduct a stealthy survey of the Moon Lord, this time close-up, without the water and the steam.

In the dancing light of the wall torches, his thick, cropped hair shone as glossy and blue-black as a raven's wing. High, broad cheekbones bespoke a Northman's ancestry, but she knew not what heritage accounted for the slanting eyebrows, the compelling silver-gray eyes or that wide, marvelous mouth.

Distractedly, she pushed her food around on her trencher, lacking appetite for the fish. It did not seem just that an enemy should possess such a comely appearance. Or the power to attract one's glance. To charm one's most secret thoughts. To bend one's righteous anger into flame-hot desire . . .

A blush pulsed in her cheeks as she remembered her abandon in his arms. She stared down at the white linen covering the table as he conversed with his knight. He seemed so untouched by an experience that had shaken her profoundly. Her passion, the searing intimacy with which he had touched her, things she had shared with no other man, clearly meant nothing to Tancred. Yet they haunted her.

Against her will, Rosamund's gaze stole back to the scar that rode the crest of his cheekbone. A brand, burned into smooth skin. Two stars within a circle, of the size made by a signet ring. Who had done this thing to him?

Like everyone else in England, she had heard how he'd delivered the impregnable Saracen fortress of Bâb Al-Muhunnad into Christian hands. Why, he'd accomplished what King Richard and his army could not. And Tancred had done it while being held prisoner. Was this brand then the work of a cruel Saracen?

Instinctively, her eyes sought out handsome Kadar. His faith and his accent marked him as a foreigner and therefore, an outsider. Even his name was strange. Yet, judging from her conversation with him, he seemed determined to protect Tancred. Rosamund doubted he had been the one who had applied the searing metal.

Tancred shifted his weight, settling back into his carved chair. Her nerves twanged.

To distract herself, Rosamund captured another bit of fish with the tip of her spoon. As she set it to her lips, her gaze moved over the occupants of the great hall. If he could forget their kisses in the bathing tub, so could she.

They were of no import. None at all. Indeed, they had already fled her mind.

Forcing herself to focus on the room before her, she saw men and women taking their last meal of the day together. It was more of a feast, actually, and served rather later than usual. Rosamund supposed Tancred had ordered a celebration of his ascendency.

A cool, moist nose nudged her elbow. Ordinarily, such ill manners in her favorite wolfhound would have invited a reprimand, but this evening Rosamund absently slipped Fleet a tidbit of perch.

As sneaky as it had seemed to her, at least Tancred's silent invasion had brought with it neither death nor rape. Not even destruction. Although she noticed resentful looks cast by some of the Wynnsef people at the knights, she did not miss the smiles, the small bursts of laughter, or the good-natured flirtation here and there between members of the two factions.

A servant passed behind them, creating a draft that swept across the damp patches of Rosamund's veil. A strong chill passed through her, and she shivered.

Tancred noticed at once. "Wet hair cannot be healthful for you. Would you feel better if you retired to your chamber? A servant could bring you some hot mulled wine."

His offer was tempting, but not since her father had died had Rosamund sat at the high table by right. Though it was her due as a wifeless lord's sister and as chatelaine of Wynnsef, Arnaud never permitted her to sit at the high table in his presence. Only when her brother was gone did she ascend the steps of the dais. And now, at the Usurper's invitation she sat here in full view of everyone. It was almost a heady experience.

Suddenly an unwelcome thought occurred to her. Would she be perceived as a traitor to Wynnsef and Arnaud? Seen to be in collusion with the enemy? Perhaps even suspected of having thrown open the gate for this brother to shadows?

Her stomach tightened at the thought. Only Tancred's men had been present in the great hall when she had struck her bargain. Only John and Aefre knew that Rosamund but worked to keep the peace until her brother arrived.

Then a new and terrible thought dawned on her: What would Arnaud conclude? Would he think she had aided Tancred?

Her stomach clenched into a knot. He might believe the worst of her in this matter. He had in so many others.

"Lady Rosamund?"

At the sound of Tancred's voice, she looked up to find him regarding her, his eyes veiled by black lashes.

"Er," she managed. Such finesse. Still, she did not like the idea of turning tail, of scuttling off to hide. She was *not* a traitor. "I, uh . . . I'll stay here for a while, thank you."

Besides as much as she might want to leave, this place gave her a clear view of the way his knights behaved with at least those females of Wynnsef gathered here. Who could tell what might happen after Tancred's men downed several cups of ale?

And once alone, in the dark, your fears will multiply and grow more fearsome, the knowing voice of her conscience whispered.

Tancred inclined his head. "As you wish."

That moment brought another draft across her damp scalp. She shuddered, her jaw clenched against chattering teeth.

"If you insist on staying here," he said, impatience touching his voice, "at least remove your veil so your hair may dry. Why are you so stubborn over the removal of a mere veil?"

Her eyes widened in surprise, but her flash of temper came from a roiling stew of indignation and frayed nerves. "I am not a woman of easy virtue that runs about with her crowing glory revealed to one and all," she retorted. "I like to believe I am a lady, thank you. And ladies wear their veils in public." Even villeins covered their hair.

Tancred's expression grew shuttered.

Where was that tightening of his jaw now? That flash in his eyes that, even in the short span of their acquaintance, warned he would tolerate no more? His reaction perplexed her.

Then a thought occurred to her, and the steam in her ire leaked away. "Didn't you know that?"

He ignored her question. "Your pardon, Lady Rosamund. No insult was intended."

"I rejoice in hearing that," she said tartly. His abrupt withdrawal made her feel as if he'd slammed a door in her face. She didn't know why that should bother her, but it did. Which annoyed her.

Tancred regarded the other tables in the hall as he took a swallow of wine. "Your food is getting cold. I would not keep you from it."

A careful survey of the great hall revealed no serious fraternization between Tancred's knights and Wynnsef's women. If, later, someone should break the truce, she would hear of it. Staying here now, with the chill moving ever more thoroughly into her flesh, was not strictly necessary. And heaven knew, the scintillating company of this man—her worst enemy—certainly offered no inducement to remain.

"I shall retire now," she informed him coolly. "I find I have grown quite weary."

Only the slightest narrowing of his eyes told her that she'd scored her point. "As you wish, damoiselle. I would not keep you."

She rose, and then, without another glance in his direction, descended the dais steps. With stately dignity, she swept out of the hall and down the stairs into the courtyard. The brisk spring evening wafted cold against her wet scalp. She started toward the keep.

Inspiration struck. She changed direction.

She made her way to the corner of the castle that housed a thatched-roofed, one-room cottage surrounded by the large herb garden she used for medicaments, scents, and cooking. Here she tried new combinations and mixed old ones. As she stepped inside, the green fragrances of herbs, the heavier notes of spices, the dusty scent of scrupulously swept earth closed around her.

So familiar with this place was she that, in the dark, she moved unerringly about the single large room with its work benches and cupboards. By touch, she located the pottery jar she sought. Carefully, she withdrew the objects she needed for her plan.

Dodging the notice of the guards Tancred had set at various points about the baileys proved a challenge, but one she met with success. By descending to the offices on the first floor of the new keep, she came up into the hall well behind the dais, out of sight in the passages that connected the kitchens and pantry, little used by this time of evening. Will, the troubadour, had just begun his first song and still held the attention of most of those in the hall.

Swiftly, Rosamund climbed the spiral stairs up to the solar, which had once been her parents' chamber, then her brother's, and now Tancred's. Nothing had yet been changed from her brother's arrangement, which served her purpose. In the dark room, she needed no lighted candle to guide her to the large bed.

With a wicked smile, she eased back the blankets. Carefully, she placed first one spiny thistle, then the other. Then she smoothed the covers back into place.

Tancred's yowl would be heard throughout the castle, when he rolled naked into bed, for if he was lucky enough to miss one thistle, he would certainly find the other.

She grinned all the way to the old keep.

Her tower chamber there possessed no fireplace, so now she fed the three braziers on their tall, brass tripods. With more energy than was warranted, she removed her veil and wimple. She took down her braids, then proceeded to unplait them, at last shaking out the rippling, thigh-length fall of her hair. Her damp hair.

Seizing her brush, she set dragging it through her tresses in long, violent strokes, as if each were a strike at her captor. "Fie—on—him. Fie—on—him!"

But it was herself with whom she was angriest. No matter how dangerous, how unreadable, how *infuriating* Tancred was nor how badly Arnaud's arrogance had served Wynnsef, she had been in charge of the honor when it had been lost, and she had behaved as a wanton with the very man who had taken it.

A man who must feel the lowest contempt for her. A contempt she justly deserved.

Each merciless stroke of the brush tugged at her scalp.

His indifference to their moment of conflagration in the dark vault beneath this keep had left her confused, torn between relief at his making no reference to their shared insanity, embarrassment that she seemed to have been the only one shaken by the experience, and self-disgust for her weakness in having permitted his bold embrace, much less in thrilling to it.

Well, it would not happen again. She was determined on Hembley Abbey and the life of a nun. Proper nuns had no interest in men's hands, in their solid chests, and most assuredly *not* in their warm lips. Nuns' lives were serene. Peaceful. As a nun she would slip away from having to make all the decisions, from shouldering all the responsibilites. She could become just another slat in the waterwheel.

Tancred would never learn that his kisses had shaken her, and she certainly had no intention that he should see the mark his mouth had made on her neck.

But tonight she would enjoy the music of his howls when he landed on her small revenge.

SIX

In the wavering light from the fireplace, Tancred stripped off his clothing, preparing for bed. Out of habit learned in snake- and scorpion-infested Outremer, he carefully pulled back the bedcovers.

No startled snake struck at him. He discovered not even one prancing scorpion arching its tail. What he found were thistles. Two dried thistles.

Tancred stared down at the thorny brown things lying on the linen sheet. He supposed it was possible they had hitched a ride while the cloth had been hanging out to dry beside the laundry hut.

Possible, but improbable.

It was also improbable that two large thistles would have gone unnoticed by the laundresses. A more likely mode of travel for the sharp things was two feet. Two feet clad in soft kid shoes. Dark blue kid, to be precise.

The Green Witch, they called her. Her people appeared to take pride in the title, which seemed odd to him. The subject of witches seldom evoked pride in villeins or villagers. Usually it stirred fear among them.

Not in these people. At least not the subject of this particular alleged witch. They came to her for healing, for advice. From his conversations with the local folk, he had learned that even farmers consulted her regarding the best way or time to sow. Everyone swore she wielded magic, and a man needed only to look around the castle, much less the lush fields surrounding it, to believe they might be right.

There was, however one place in the castle where a man could not look. That place was enclosed by high, solid walls, and a sturdy door. A large iron lock secured that door, the key to which, he had been told, only Lady Rosamund held.

It was not on the ring of keys he had taken from her; he had tried them all. He'd gathered from the scraps of what he'd heard that only Rosamund was allowed to enter that place. Arnaud, as any simpleton could see, was restrictive when it came to his sister, but even Arnaud did not go there.

From the wall walk Tancred had seen the tips of leaves, which confirmed what he had been told—a garden lay beyond those walls. And what was one more garden when there were already so many?

He shook his head in puzzlement. Were the peasants right after all? Did she indeed invoke magic from green things?

His vision turned inward, to the image conjured by memory. Tancred had been here only one full day, and already one pilgrim returning from Lourdes and one knight on his way home from crusade had stopped at Wynnsef, asking to see the Lady Rosamund. Each had treated her with profound respect. Each had brought her a different plant from a different far land, carefully kept alive, its ball of soil and roots wrapped in linen and frequently moistened.

She had welcomed each traveler with that smile of hers, the one that made a man feel as if he were witnessing a glorious, and somehow miraculous, sunrise. She'd greeted them like boon companions feared lost, though Tancred suspected she had met them only once before, on their journey out. For an instant, he had envied them. That smile would never turn toward him.

His gaze returned to the twin thistles nestled in his

bed, and one corner of his mouth lifted partially in a crooked smile. No, for him there were thorns.

'Twas better that way.

"I would look at the accounting rolls for Wynnsef," Tancred announced the next morning as the castle residents broke their fast.

Rosamund nearly choked on the bite of manchet loaf she'd taken. The accounting rolls had been clasped together as a book, and that book was the last thing she wanted him to see.

"Also summon the seneschal," he added.

"He's not here," she said quickly. "He's gone to visit . . . um . . . a far property. Yea, a far property. It's inspection time, you see. When he returns, I'll direct him to you immediately."

Tancred idly glanced into the cup of ale he held. "What far property?"

Her brain spun frantically. "Oh, 'tis very far."

"What is the name of this property?"

Eh? "I cannot recall all the lands that came to my brother. Such things have been of no concern to me."

"I have a list of those lands your brother inherited," he said amiably. "As well as the dower lands that are to come to you. Or go to the abbey when you finally take your vows. Perhaps I should have it fetched. I could read it to you and you could indicate whither the seneschal has gone. Unless, of course, you read. Then you can read the list yourself."

Fie on the man! Rosamund thought, struggling to appear unconcerned. Other than Wynnsef's accounts journal—and she knew he hadn't obtained it from *there*—there was only one other source for that information.

The king.

She almost slumped in her chair. Then it occurred to her that a deftly placed bribe to a royal clerk might also obtain such a list. Until she could speak with her brother, she had to believe that. Surely, if Arnaud had displeased the king, she would have learned of it. She could spot anxiety in Arnaud from across the bailey, so poorly did he conceal worry or guilt.

She turned what she hoped was a vacuous smile on Tancred, and thought about crossing her eyes. She wanted to look like every knight's dream female—docile and ignorant—but she wasn't willing to look completely stupid. "I read . . . a little." A compromise.

"Could you pick out the name of where the seneschal has gone?"

Rosamund pretended to think about it a minute, then nodded.

He gave her a peculiar look. "Last eve did you not make every attempt to dry your hair?"

She stared at him. Why was he talking about her hair? Had it something to do with the thistles? Did he suspect who had left them?

Rosamund had listened for some time last night, but, to her vast disappointment, she had never heard the expected howl from within the solar above the great hall.

"Yea, my lord," she said. "Why do you ask?"

" 'Tis of no great import, I suppose," he said blandly. "I feared you might have taken a cold in your head. Or a fever in your brain."

"No. My hair dried, and I have suffered no ill effects."

He nodded as he sliced a bit of cheese from the wedge they shared, then popped it into his mouth. "You are in fine fettle, you say?"

"Y-e-a," she answered, suspicious of his intent. "I am well."

His black lashes swept down, veiling his eyes. "I pray you forgive me, Lady Rosamund, if I have confused you. I am unused to working with women, you see, and so forget that their minds require greater . . . *care*."

She straightened in her chair. "And, pray, what does *that* mean?"

"Only that women's brains were never intended to plan, to comprehend, to—"

"To *think*?" she offered acidly.

His eyes were still concealed from her. "Well . . . "

Rosamund's lips pressed together in annoyance. She had wanted him to think her empty-headed, but she hadn't expected to find success so irritating.

He made a strangled noise in his throat, and she thought she saw his shoulder shake.

Her eyes narrowed as she detected a twitch at the corners of his mouth. She inhaled sharply through her nose as she drew herself up in majestic indignation.

When Tancred glanced at her from the corner of one eye, he could no longer hold back his laughter. It rumbled up out of his chest, deep and rich. And it continued, curse him.

"Stop it," she snapped, her voice low, as she realized that they had become the center of attention of everyone in the great hall. "I fail to see what you find so amusing."

"You," he choked. "Oh, you, most assuredly."

"How very gratifying to find I can be mistaken for a court fool." She kicked him under the table. "Stop it!"

He leaned back in his thronelike chair and regarded her with those lightning eyes. Slowly his smile faded. "Never strike me again."

What possessed her when it came to this upstart knight? Not since girlhood had she struck anyone. She had learned the stern self-discipline that ruled her life. What was it about Tancred that sent her temper soaring so easily? It was not just that he had succeeded in taking Wynnsef where other men, men with armies, had failed. She had lived through a siege here, endured the anxiety, fear, and hardship that came with it. Would she have preferred another such ordeal? her conscience demanded. To that question, she had a ready answer: No!

Although she sensed danger behind Tancred's calm manner and his soft, controlled voice, her pride refused to allow her to submit. She had been in the wrong. She knew it.

Still, she found herself lifting her chin and meeting his gaze squarely. At that elemental contact, a tremor vibrated through her. "You provoked me."

One slanting raven eyebrow lifted. "And now you have provoked me."

Rosamund found it more difficult to breathe. She moistened lips suddenly gone dry with the tip of her tongue. "What . . . What are you going to do?"

His gaze fell to her mouth. "I will think on it."

A peculiar tension spread through her chest, making her conscious of each breath she drew.

Tancred scowled and looked away, reaching for his ale cup. "For now, I want the account rolls."

"I told you—"

"I *know* what you told me, damoiselle. It is what *I* told *you* that matters."

"You are arrogant."

A shadow of a smile touched his lips. "If you say so, Lady Rosamund."

"I do," she insisted, knowing even as the words escaped her lips that she should have remained silent. What possessed her? "Arrogant and—and—"

"Lord of Wynnsef."

She clamped her jaws shut.

"And the Lord of Wynnsef," he continued, "desires to see the rolls for his honor."

"I said I would attempt to find them."

He nodded agreeably, and uneasiness rippled through her. With long, tapered fingers, he popped another bit of bread into his mouth. He gazed out over the great hall, where a cacophony of conversation and the clatter of eating utensils and cups provided a curtain of privacy for any discussions taking place at the high table.

"I sense a certain reluctance on your part," he said, still surveying the activities taking place in the hall.

Rosamund made no reply. It was a sin to lie.

"Therefore," he continued pleasantly, "until the

rolls are in my possession, you will attend me at my bath."

She stared at him, openmouthed with shock. "After what happened— After your last— You must be mad!"

Slowly he shook his head. The dim light of the early morning sun through the polished horn panes of the high windows gleamed on his blue-black hair, glinted in his silvery eyes. "Annoyed, perhaps, but not mad. I'll not bar the door, and you'll not throw cold water on me."

"I did not throw cold water on you. It was tepid. And you deserved it."

His only answer was a cocked eyebrow.

"If the door is not barred, what is to keep someone from coming to my aid if you assault me again?" she returned with a trace of smugness. If her people could open the door, he would not wish to be caught behaving in a dishonorable manner. After all, she thought snidely, he was the vaunted Moon Lord, baron of goodness and light.

"My guard outside the door."

Her eyes widened. "Do you seek to ruin my reputation?"

He gave her a guileless look. "Lady Rosamund, the guard is for my protection against your deplorable violence."

"You are loathsome," she hissed.

He shrugged one broad shoulder. "The rolls, damoiselle. That is all I ask."

"I don't know where they are!"

"Unfortunate." He pushed back the heavy lord's chair with a negligible movement of his legs, then rose to his feet. "Alas, a lord's lot is a dirty one," he said blandly as he turned to leave. "I shall require a bath every night."

Rosamund glared at him as he paused to exchange with Kadar a few words and a companionable slap on the shoulder. He moved on to rouse Osbert and Bernard from a good-natured debate. Then, accompanied by the three men, Tancred strode out of the great hall.

Sweet Mary, what was she to do? Rosamund thought frantically. If she gave him the book, he'd know everything about Wynnsef. The accurate dimensions of the castle and its moat. The locations, capacities, and inventories of all the armories, granaries, cellars, wells, barns, and brewing house were listed in meticulous detail on those pages. Also recorded in that great, heavy book were the exact number of cows, horses, sheep, and other livestock. The pages revealed what the fish ponds had produced each season. Listed there was the number of men and women who owed Wynnsef service, as well as the acres under tillage.

In short, Tancred would learn that he could hold Wynnsef almost indefinitely against Arnaud. And as much as she wanted to believe King Richard would come to Arnaud's aid, she was unwilling to blind herself to the possibility that Arnaud had incurred his overlord's displeasure. The fact that her brother had no allies among the other lords was, to her at least, a telling reality. Even if Arnaud was in good standing with Richard, the king was occupied trying to preserve his sovereignty. Reality might be harsh, but it was still reality.

If Arnaud was to swiftly reclaim Wynnsef, Tancred must not learn how well-provisioned the castle stood. There was no preventing the Moon Lord from ascertaining its defensibility; that he could, and would, do without her help. The best way in which she could assist her brother was to prevent Tancred from claiming possession of that book.

Rosamund found Brother Felix in what passed for his office just off the upstairs chapel. He sat at his writing desk on a high stool, the rasp of his goose-quill pen on the thick, lambskin parchment the only sound in the chilly room. On one wall hung a large rosewood crucifix and against another wall stood a rudimentary case of shelves, stuffed with parchment rolls and letters, a few precious, dog-eared books, and some of the paraphernalia of his office as chaplain to Wynnsef.

As if sensing her presence in the doorway behind him, the good monk peered over his shoulder. When he caught sight of her, he slid off his stool and came forward to greet her.

"Lady Rosamund, I was just composing a report to my abbot, and you have saved me from having to ask Lord Tancred for a messenger. At least for a while." He came fairly close to her before he could determine her expression, for Brother Felix was somewhat myopic. Then his eyes widened slightly. "Oh, my dear lady. It doesn't take the omniscience of our Lord to see that you are fretting over something." He blinked. "Well, of course you would be worried, wouldn't you? You've just lost your home."

Rosamund closed the chamber door against possible unseen eavesdroppers. "Brother, we must hide the journal."

He looked startled. "Eh?"

"Wynnsef's accounts journal. We must conceal it from Lord Tancred."

His shaggy eyebrows drew together in consternation. "Do you think that wise, my lady?"

She struggled to be patient, anxious over the loss of time. "Not only wise, but necessary. Arnaud will soon be here to retake Wynnsef. If Tancred gets those books, he will learn that, with our present supplies, he could hold out for a year against my brother and his men."

"Will not the king come to your brother's aid?"

"The king is busy. His brother, John, has conspired against him with the King of France and, of course, there is that problem with Emperor Henry."

"Oh." Brother Felix thought a minute. "Is it true that Lord Tancred has said the king gave him Wynnsef if he could take it?"

"That is what he says. But does that sound like anything Richard would say?"

Brother Felix folded his arms, slipping his hands into the full sleeves, his expression troubled. "Who can tell? The ways of kings are—"

"Sly and unreliable."

"I—"

"Please, Brother," she entreated. "You are the only one to whom I can turn in this dark time. Please help me."

He sighed. "As you wish, my child. Our Savior only knows how valiant you have been through of all this. The least I can do is to help you hide one book."

First Rosamund went to the tanner, where she procured a generous square of supple oiled leather and several lengths of narrow leather cord. As soon as she was out of sight of anyone, she rolled up the sheet of leather, and tied it to her thigh, under her skirts.

Next, she and Brother Felix collected the large tome from its usual hiding place at the back of a linen cupboard. Concealing it under folded sheets and altar cloths, one at a time, they left the great hall and made their way to the dark, vaulted storerooms beneath the old keep.

Rosamund led the way, holding aloft a torch of resinous pine with one hand, balancing the journal on her head while holding it in place with her free hand. The roll of leather bound to her leg made walking awkward, but not impossible. She couldn't help but glance in the direction of the bathing room.

"Where are we going, my lady?" Brother Felix asked in a low voice, struggling to keep up with her younger, longer legs. His words echoed against the high stone walls like susurrous brook.

She leaned close to his ear. "The vault in the well."

Abruptly he halted. In the torchlight his eyes grew wide. "Lady, you cannot mean it. Why, 'tis impossible! I am old and, er, stout. 'Twill be most dangerous. I'll not be able to *breathe*!"

"Calm yourself, Brother Felix. I know your fear of close places. Besides, I have not the strength to handle the pulley for such weight. For a man full-grown," she added hastily, unwilling to hurt Brother Felix's feelings. "I will carry the book down. It is my responsibility."

He shook his head, the fringe of his hair flying out. "No. Certainly not. The risk is far too great. Why, what would your father have said?"

"He'd have said, 'There's my good girl. I knew I could count on you.' "

Brother Felix fretted. "I don't think he would have said that at all. Not at all." Distractedly, he looked around. "There are other places to hide it. Who would think to look for the journal anywhere down here?"

"Servants come here because of the storerooms and to heat water for the bathing tub. No, the only place it will be safe is in the well vault. Only you, Arnaud, and I know of its existence."

Brother Felix opened his mouth to continue his protest, and she cut him off.

"Come," she said. "We must have done with this before Thurkill and the others arrive to draw and heat the water for Tancred's cursed bath."

Nearly an hour later, Rosamund was feverishly praying. With every creaking, uneven turn of the windlass, she jerked deeper into the stone-lined stygian pit. A thick rope was knotted around her waist for caution's sake, but it was the large loop through which she'd fitted her feet that bore the brunt of her weight. The journal was bound to her by her knotted tunic so that she carried it like a peasant carried her infant with her to the fields—slung against her chest.

Rosamund could not recall ever being this nervous. The single taper she held with trembling fingers gave off a pitiful glow that skimmed damp stones fit precisely together and velvet clumps of moss growing here and there.

"Do you see it yet?" Brother Felix whispered loudly enough for anyone beneath the keep to hear.

Rosamund squinted into the dank, eerie gloom. "Just a little farther down." No wonder the license to crenelate and other important papers stored in the vault had remained safe for so long. Only a lunatic would attempt to reach them. Not that anyone would ever think to look here. This was probably the safest place in all of England . . . if you were a license. Or a journal.

"Stop," Rosamund called softly. There, just within the aureole of weak light, she saw the triangular stone about which her father had told her so long ago. And it appeared just large enough to accommodate the book if it was quite deep. "A little lower, please."

A full, squeaking revolution of the windlass brought her lurching to exactly the right place. Well, it would have been exactly right if the sides of the well had been closer than the knuckles of her outstretched hand.

"Brother, can you move the rope a bit to your right?" Her voice echoed hollowly in the vertical stone tunnel.

Slowly, Brother Felix lowered her one more turn. Then . . . nothing, save for a soft grunt.

She peered up. "Brother?" From above the coping, his brown-sleeved arm made a swipe at the rope, which hung close to the center of the well. He missed.

"Patience, child," he wheezed. "My arms are not quite so long as yours." He leaned farther over the coping and tried again, his short, stubby fingers outspread. This time he came closer to the target.

Rosamund's fingers gripped the rope. "Brother, careful you don't fall in. Perhaps if you can find a long stick, or a hook, that would help."

"Excellent suggestion. I'll be back directly." He vanished.

Never had Rosamund felt more isolated. She cast

the candle she held a worried glance. It was burning lower.

Time sluggishly oozed out, its dark unknown filling the space around her. There was only Rosamund clinging to the rope, the weight of the book in its makeshift sling dragging at her shoulders, the faintly foul stink of the tallow mingling with the dank wet-stone smell of the well. She began to worry that something had befallen Brother Felix.

Finally, she could stand it no longer. "Brother?" she whispered loudly. The tunnel caught the sound and bounced it back, elongated, distorted.

When she received no answer from Brother Felix, she tried again, this time a little louder. Her voice caught in her parched throat.

Suddenly, his head popped into sight above her, his candle sending flickering shadows over the dear, round cheeks and short, turned-up nose. "Here I am, my lady." He sounded out of breath, as if he had been running. Bless him.

"Hold on," he told her. He raised his taper to see her better, but apparently that failed. "Are you holding on?"

"Yea, Brother." As tightly as she could.

He snagged the rope with a rake and slowly pulled it toward him until he could reach it with his hands. "Is that better?" he asked when he grasped her lifeline in both hands. He maneuvered the rope until her shoulder brushed the wall.

"Perfect," Rosamund called softly. From her shoe she pulled the knife she'd earlier filched from the kitchen. She went to work prying out the triangular stone.

After what seemed an eternity of scraping and gouging, she managed to pry the stone from its snug fit. Although the thing was heavy, it wasn't as weighty as she had feared. It was just thick enough to stopper the hole and keep the contents from exposure.

It was at that moment that she perceived a problem,

one she silently berated herself for not realizing before. "Brother, do you have it in you to pull me up to place this stone safely on the floor, then to lower me and raise me twice more?"

He hesitated. "I fear not, my lady." Dejection saturated his voice.

Rosamund sighed. She had not really expected that he could. She knew she was no air-light butterfly.

"I am sorry," he said humbly.

"The fault is not yours," she assured him. "Miles the Blacksmith would be strained to accomplish it."

"Shall I pull you up now?"

"No. I shall somehow manage." While she sounded confident, she did not quite accomplish the belief. Still, she had no choice. She must try.

Balancing the stone plug with one hand, she struggled to extract the large book from its sling.

Rosamund lightly braced her body against the wall, enabling her to ease the book into the black vault hole. She clamped her lip between her teeth as she forced herself to shove the journal back the full length of her arm, plunging her valued appendage into the unknown. To jerk her arm out as quickly as she wanted would have unbalanced her, so she endured the excruciating process of slowly withdrawing it.

Saint Martha only knew what condition the license and other valuable papers must now be in. Rosamund refused to worry about that now. When her brother regained control of Wynnsef, he could attend the matter. The important thing was to keep the book out of the hands of Tancred de Vierzon.

Who would soon be here for his bath.

The thought of the tall Moon Lord as he had been at his bath last evening slipped into her mind like the serpent into Eden.

Tall, broad-shouldered, flat-bellied—

Rosamund shied from that path. She had important matters to think about, which did *not* include silver eyes that flashed in the candlelight . . . or steam-dampened, sun-burnished bare skin . . . or marvelous, warm lips . . .

She jerked from that all-too-clear recollection. The triangular stone slipped from her fingers. Instinctively she lunged, grabbing for it. Her fingers closed around the stone as one foot slid from the rope loop and the other tangled in it.

With a strangled squawk, Rosamund toppled.

The rope knot around her waist held, saving her from plunging into the water far below. Instead, she dangled upside down, the skirts of her kirtle and tunic settling down around what normally constituted her upper body, leaving the rest of her bare.

She clutched the stone, her heart racing wildly, her thoughts scattered. Her legs and bottom quickly grew chilled.

"My lady, what has happened?" Brother Felix called, his echoing voice filled with anxiety. "Lady Rosamund?"

As her fear eased, the first thing she realized was that, from her waist down—or rather up—she was completely exposed, except for her shoes, and the short length of stocking on each of the legs waving in the air. Her nether regions were now quite naked.

"Don't look!" she cried, her words muffled by her skirts. "*Do—Not—Look.*"

"But—"

"Brother, please. If you value my feelings, don't look at me."

"Very well. I will not look at you. But what can I do to assist you?"

The blood was rushing to her head. "Er . . . Pull me up just a turn. Slowly. Yea, like that." She had yet to fit this miserable stone back into its place. "Stop." Her naked legs wrapped around the taut rope above her, her head throbbing, she fumbled the triangle back into the vault entrance. "Now pull me up. Pull for all you are worth. Just do not look into the well."

The outside door of the keep opened, then closed. Footsteps sounded on the stairs.

Holy Sepulcher!

Rosamund's heart beat faster. Oh, God, oh, God, please let that be Aefre! Or John. Or even Abbess Matilda. Please, please, please, don't let it be—

"Brother Felix, what are you doing here?" Tancred asked.

Rosamund wilted against the ropes.

"Er . . . " Brother Felix managed deftly.

"Has the other well gone dry?" Tancred inquired, his voice indicating he was coming this way. "I heard nothing of that."

"No, no. The other well has not gone dry."

The light of a torch slanted down across the inside of the well. "Why, Brother, you're most red in the face. And you are sweating." The tone of Tancred's voice changed from friendly to concerned. "Surely drawing a bucket of water would not be such a strain on you. Are you ill?"

The torchlight grew brighter. Rosamund felt more helpless than ever as she dangled at the end of the rope.

"No! Do not look down, my lord!" Brother Felix must have loosened his hold on the hand of the windlass in his effort to keep Tancred from seeing inside the well.

Rosamund plunged downward, shrieking.

She jerked to a halt, swinging slowly back and forth.

"Who is down there?" Tancred demanded. The glow of the torch did not penetrate the gloom far enough to illuminate Rosamund.

Her head pounded. The rope gnawed at her waist, ground against her bottom ribs. Her naked buttocks and legs ached with chill. And she was about to be discovered by the enemy—if she did not first drown.

"I ask you again," Tancred said, his patience clearly wearing thin. "Brother Felix, who—"

"My lord, I had thought to spare the poor child's

dignity, but I think now, we must just pull her up and discuss it when she is safe."

"*What* poor child?" Tancred growled.

"Lady Rosamund. Pull her up. Please, Lord Tancred, pull her up now. But don't look down. Oh, this is dreadful. Dreadful!"

Tancred swore softly, but the well amplified his vivid oath.

Compared to her excruciatingly slow descent, Rosamund fairly flew up the well. Tancred was reeling her up so swiftly, Rosamund feared she would slam into the windlass beam.

"Don't look!" she wailed as she burst up into the torch's light. "My Lord Tancred, *please*. Do not look at me. I'm tangled in the rope. Ups—side down. 'Tis most unseemly!"

"Avert your eyes, Lord Tancred," Brother Felix implored.

"I am, I am," Tancred snapped. "Sacred Blood, it does complicate things, trying to hold the handle in place and find the little witch by feel alone."

His groping hand came down smack in the center of one cold, bared cheek. He squeezed gently. Rosamund squeaked in surprise.

Tancred laughed. "Yea, my lady, you are indeed in a most unseemly position." He slipped his palm down—or rather up—the back of her leg. Gritting her teeth, she forced herself to submit.

"Wait—I have her ankle," Tancred announced. "Tell me this is an ankle, damoiselle, and that I have not—"

"It is my ankle," she grated.

"Praise be," Brother Felix exclaimed with obvious relief.

From beneath the edge of her lopsided veil, Rosamund saw that both men had indeed averted their faces. Guided by his grip on her ankle, Tancred dragged her over to the edge, where he righted her. Then pulled her over the coping and into his arms.

Rosamund clutched at him, shuddering in his arms with the force of a few dry sobs. Never had she felt such a welcoming embrace, one so unyielding, so protective . . . so safe.

After a few minutes, her breathing eased. Gradually, she realized that she was pressed against his body. It grew clear that she was, perhaps, not quite so safe as she'd thought. She thrust herself away from him. He made no attempt to stay her.

"Now," Tancred said with a sharp glance at Brother Felix before he turned his compelling silver gaze on Rosamund, "you will tell me how you came to be hanging upside down in the old keep's well."

Her mind raced, trying to fabricate a believable lie. She failed.

"She fell," Brother Felix blurted. God bless him!

"I fell," she echoed promptly, nodding emphatically.

"Ah." Tancred looked not in the least convinced. "You fell."

Faced with Tancred's disbelief, both Rosamund and Brother Felix nodded.

Pointedly, Tancred looked at the well. "I see no broken masonry. How is it that you fell in this sturdy, walled well?"

Rosamund thought she now knew how a rat trapped by a cat must feel. "Er. Well. I was, uh, coming to check the supply of . . . of beeswax. I had no more reached the bottom of the stairs when my candle flame went out."

"Doubtless from one of the many gusts of wind that come up so suddenly down here," Tancred said dryly.

Rosamund ignored him. "I became lost in the dark."

"And that is when you fell into the well?" Tancred inquired with honeyed politeness.

"Yea, Lord Tancred."

He strolled away several paces, his hands folded behind him. "I find it somewhat interesting that you fell into this well—this vast well—and yet you are not wet."

"I grabbed the rope," Rosamund replied. "As I fell. I grabbed it. The rope."

Tancred's eyebrows lifted. "Indeed? You are most resourceful, damoiselle." He eyed the knotted and looped rope. "And far stronger than you appear."

Brother Felix chimed in instantly. "I heard her shouts for help and came immediately. She . . . she told me not to look. She was as you found her."

Tancred paced slowly around Rosamund and Brother Felix. "You fell into the well."

Rosamund felt as if her nerves might unravel. "I fell into the well, and was scarcely able to save myself," she said sharply. "It was just shy of a miracle, but you act as if I should have considerately fallen to my doom. Shall I apologize for managing to grab hold of the rope?" She glared at him. "I grant that it was not the most graceful thing I have ever done, but you will understand if I was not greatly concerned with grace at that moment." What did it take to convince this man? But she already knew the answer to that.

The truth.

"Hmm. A miracle indeed," Tancred finally replied.

She disliked the edgy feeling that ate at her, and she hated this continuous lying. Rosamund focused her simmering temper on Tancred. "And what brings *you* down here at such a convenient moment?"

"Simple," he replied. "I was passing the door outside and heard you wailing."

Feeling like a simpkin, Rosamund jerked her tunic straight. "Oh."

Abruptly, Tancred turned to face her. He accorded her an abbreviated bow. "I rejoice in your rescue, damoiselle." He bowed briskly to Brother Felix. "Brother." Making a show of lighting the monk's candle with the torch, he then set the torch in a wall bracket. Candle in hand, he swiftly took the stairs up to exit the old keep.

Rosamund and Brother Felix waited a few minutes, then flew up the narrow stone steps, to the outer door and the long-shadowed sunlight of late afternoon.

The book was safe.

The sun was nearing the horizon when Tancred relented and called an end to the exercise. For hours he had loosed his pent-up impatience in the violence of sword practice, there in the outer bailey. He had driven himself hard, and his men had known better than to slacken their own efforts.

Now squires lugged buckets of cool well water among the sweating knights, who drank their fill, then ladled the refreshing liquid over their already damp heads.

"You are as a fiery *Jinn*, Tancred," Kadar said as he wiped his neck with a drying cloth offered by his squire. "What demon gnaws at you?"

Tancred relished the invigorating rush of water as he emptied a ladle over the top of his head. He shook his head and raked his hair back from his face. "No demon." He set a foot on a bench and laid the flat of his sword across his leather-clad thigh. In the mellow light of the near twilight, he examined the blade's edges for nicks.

Kadar grinned. "No demon—a witch. She whom they call the Green Witch. She is a mystery, that one. She appears a lush willow, one who sways with the wind. Yet she possesses a deep strength of will." His expression grew solemn, but glee lit his dark eyes. "She will bear you strong sons."

Tancred snorted. "The only thing I'll get from Lady Rosamund is a pain in the arse."

"Ah, but you want her. Who cannot see your blood rise when you are near her?"

"You mistake apoplexy for lust."

Kadar turned his own blade this way and that, studying its edge. He clucked his tongue in mild admonishment. "You are not the same with her as you are with the other women."

"She is a lady, not a camp follower," Tancred replied. Why was Kadar so persistent in this?

"Even ladies need love, my friend."

Tancred straightened abruptly. He thrust his sword back into its scabbard. It slid home with a metallic hiss. "Enough. That lady wants to be a *nun*, Kadar. A bride of Christ. Mayhap He can love her; I cannot. Her blood is poisoned. She is Arnaud's sister."

Sloe eyes studied Tancred. "And you are Stephan de Vierzon's son."

Tancred's gut knotted. He shot Kadar a warning look.

The Saracen shrugged. "It seems a waste for that one with lips like a *houri* to lock herself away in such a manner."

"Her choice. It concerns me not. My interest lies in holding Wynnsef."

Before Kadar could reply, a bright-eyed youth hesitantly approached them.

"My—my Lord Tancred," he stammered nervously. "I cannot tell you how exciting it is to have the Moon Lord here, in the very castle where I live." He flushed a deep crimson. "*The* Moon Lord. N—never was a humble troubadour so fortunate." At Tancred's blank look, he added in a faint voice, "I am Will, sire. Will of . . . of . . . well, of Wynnsef. I performed for you in the great hall last eve."

With crashing clarity, Tancred recalled that freckled face now. God's toenails, the lad's voice had cracked mercilessly and often.

"Yea, Will," Tancred said. "I have cause to remember your performance." His ears still hurt.

Conscience nudged him. As Rosamund had pointed out, the lad was young yet. The voice problem would pass in a year or so. His skill with the lute was another matter. That would require much practice.

Tancred noticed from the lad's speech that he was

no peasant. Why, then, was he not in training to be a knight?

The youth's face lighted. "You liked my music?"

Looking into Will's narrow, freckled face, Tancred could not bring himself to hurt the boy's pride. " 'Twas something I'll never forget."

"Nor I," Kadar agreed.

"You are too kind, my lords," Will said with flushed dignity. "Lord Tancred, would you would allow me to observe you as you go about your weighty business? I want to learn all about you, my Lord Tancred, the better to immortalize you with my music."

"No," Tancred replied with more force than he'd intended. Jesu, there were too many of those cursed songs already.

Will's smile deflated. His open face failed to conceal his confusion, his embarrassment and disappointment. Tancred felt as if he'd kicked an unweaned pup.

"Y—y—your pardon, my lord," the lad stammered, staring down at the dust on the toes of his shoes. "I will not bother you more." He turned away and walked back toward the inner bailey.

It was then that Tancred noticed the boy's awkward gait. A glance gave the reason: a club foot. No wonder, then, Will did not train to be a knight.

A man made of his life what he could.

With a muttered oath, Tancred threw down the drying cloth he still held. He raised his voice. "Will."

The young troubadour halted. With obvious reluctance, he looked back to Tancred. "Yea, my lord?"

"I grant you your request."

Will stared at him a moment, as if unable to believe what he heard. Then he smiled as brightly as if Tancred had offered him the world on a platter of silver. "Oh, thank you! Thank you, beau sire. I'll not get in your way, I promise."

"See that you do not," Tancred said gruffly.

"You won't even know that I'm there."

"On the morrow, then."

"Yea, my lord." Will was beaming happily as he hobbled away.

From within the inner bailey, the horn sounded, signaling that it was time to wash before the final meal of the day. The sound underscored the fact that Rosamund had not come forth with the account rolls. Tancred smiled grimly.

Bath time.

SEVEN

Rosamund's footsteps echoed in the cavernous bathing chamber as she moved about, testing the temperature of the water, arranging the towels in a convenient location, placing the vermeil wine flagon and goblet on the small table beside the tub. Although her first inclination had been to bring the odorous soft laundry soap made from rendered hog fat for Tancred to use, she'd thought better of it and had chosen a ball of rosemary soap from the Mediterranean, which possessed a luxurious olive oil base. No doubt she was casting pearls before swine, she thought tartly, but why make a bad situation even worse? He would be gone before long. Then he would have to find his own soap . . . and another hostage to scrub his back.

Grudgingly, she admitted to herself that he would likely never suffer from a dearth of women willing to help him with his bath. Oddly, the thought of him lounging in a tub, surrounded by a bevy of comely, fawning women, annoyed her.

She heard the outside door at the top of the stairs open, then Tancred's voice.

"Mind you do not leave your post at this door, Ranulf," he said, his words echoing hollowly through the labyrinth of vaulted storage chambers. "If you hear me scream, come running. My virtue may be at stake."

Rosamund heard men's laughter, then the sound of

the door closing. Footfalls—from *large* feet, she thought spitefully—reached her ears.

He carried his helm under one arm and still wore his mail. Over his hauberk, he wore a long black surcote edged with minute silver stars and crescent moons. A wide black sword belt, its buckle fashioned in the shape of a silver disk, was slung around his hips. From it hung his legendary weapon.

Her nostrils twitched at the strong musk of his scent, and she eyed him from head to black-booted toes. "You are sweaty and dirty."

He grinned, his hard, even teeth startlingly bright in his sun-browned face. "Yea, lady, I am. I am a warrior. Battle is a sweaty and dirty business."

"Your squire should have removed your mail," she pointed out acidly.

"I had other work for him. You are strong. You may assist me in his stead."

Rosamund clamped down on her indignation. For whatever reason, he seemed certain she had the book. It was evident that he would make her pay for her refusal to turn it over to him. She only hoped that he did not lose patience with her before Arnaud arrived.

"And how, pray, do you know I'm strong?" she asked. In the gloom of the chamber illuminated only by a fire on the hearth and a handful of candles, she clearly saw his slanting eyebrow lift.

"Why, damoiselle, I have felt you." He ignored her gasp of outrage. "Two nights ago I held you against my body as you struggled. Your firm muscles rippled beneath your smooth skin. Then, last eve, you did attack me. So ferocious were you in your assault of my person, it was all I could do to keep you from hurting yourself."

"You are a villain, sirrah."

"No, Lady Rosamund, I am a hero, a champion, a—what was it one troubadour called me?—a dark Apollo." He sat on a bench. "Now assist me. If I must do it myself, you will again find yourself with wet hair come time to sup."

Reluctantly, she moved close to him. Tancred was right; she was strong. As strong as many squires. Well, the young ones, anyway. She had helped her father and brother and countless guests remove their hauberks. So why was she uneasy about being close to him? He had not offered her harm. It must be her anger that made her feel this way around him. Yea, her anger, for no one called it forth in her like Tancred de Vierzon.

She took a firm hold of the weighty chain garment and lifted. That is, she tried to lift.

The hauberk scarcely moved.

She tried again, grunting with effort. Holy Rood, the thing must be made of lead. Of course, she thought defensively, Tancred was much taller than either her father or brother, both sizeable men. Indeed, he was much *larger*.

Tancred lifted his hands to grasp the hauberk at his shoulders. "Now try," he said.

With his help, she managed to haul off the garment of iron chain, which he set on the bench beside him.

Groaning with relief, he rolled his broad shoulders. "For certes, I've worn this thing so long I'd forgotten how good it feels to have it off."

Standing behind him, Rosamund could not help but smile at the memories his words invoked. As a child she had heard those very words from her father when he had been relieved of his hauberk. How it had amazed her to learn that her beloved baron-father-god was actually quite human.

She removed Tancred's quilted gambeson, then peeled off his damp linen shirt, leaving his upper body bare. The golden firelight glistened along the smooth curve of shoulder and long-muscled arm to cast into shadow the valley between arm and ribs and the taut, ridged plane of his belly. A V-shaped, midnight mat of curly hair narrowed down the length of his deep chest to a trail that disappeared beneath the buckled waistband of his dark mail chausses.

Rosamund turned away to unfold and refold linen drying cloths as Tancred divested himself of his remaining mail and clothing. So silently did he move that she did not hear him walk into the tent. When she heard the sound of him entering the water, and his drawn-out sigh of pleasure, she entered the tent bearing more towels than he would need.

Wordlessly, she handed him the goblet of Burgundy wine. Then she sat down on a stool she had placed behind him, a safe distance away.

He took a long swallow of wine, then eased back against the wood-planked wall of the tub, his tanned, outspread arms resting along the rim. Several minutes passed in which the only sound came from the wood crackling in the great fireplace beyond the pavilion walls.

"Have you taken a vow of silence, little nun?" he asked softly without turning to look at her.

"No, my lord."

"Ah. How meek we have become of a sudden."

"Yea, my lord." She would give him no cause to touch her again.

He took another drink of wine, nodding slowly as he lingered over it. He swallowed, but offered no comment.

She eased out a breath of relief.

"To whom should I give my thanks for subduing you, damoiselle?"

Her eyes narrowed at the back of his head. Was that a smile she heard in his voice? "God," she answered tartly.

"Well, all know He moves in mysterious ways. Did not Father Ivo say that very thing?"

She regarded Tancred with suspicion. "He did."

He took another swallow of wine, then set the cup on the table. Taking up the ball of soap, he sniffed at it. "Hmm. Do I smell thistle?"

Rosamund jerked upright on the stool. "There are many kinds of thistle," she said cautiously.

"This would be the spiny variety. Dried. Sharp."

He was only guessing, she thought. He could not be certain. "Do they have a fragrance, my lord?" she asked, all innocence.

"Yea, lady, and I can smell them out even from their hiding places."

"How odd that thistles should hide."

"Just so. How odd." She heard it there in his rich, deep voice, a warning, an implicit promise: Next time he would take action.

He handed the soap to her over his shoulder. "Wash my hair and my back. Then you may go."

Staring at the soap, at the large, long-fingered hand that held it, Rosamund struggled with her affronted pride. Her first inclination was to grab the hard ball and bounce it off his head.

"Damoiselle, I am waiting."

"Yea, my lord." She forced the words through tight lips. With a restraint that Rosamund was certain even Abbess Matilda would approve, she took the soap from his High Puissance of Toads, careful her fingers did not graze his.

After briskly pushing up the long sleeves of her kirtle and tying back the pendulous sleeves of her tunic, she dipped the soap into the herb-scented water—far from Tancred's body. Then she tested the water in one of the ewers to make certain it was pleasantly warm. Satisfied of its temperature, she slowly poured it over his thick cap of hair.

In the moist heat of the tent, she returned to the stool behind him. With brisk efficiency, she lathered up the soap until she was satisfied she had enough. Washing a man's hair was an ordinary chore, one she had performed uncounted times before.

The instant she touched Tancred's head, things changed.

All at once this routine task took on an unnerving

intimacy. The warmth of his scalp heated her. The raven silk of his hair swathed her fingers, mingling with the creamy foam on her palms.

She felt him tense at her touch. A moment later, she realized that neither of them had moved. In the candlelight, she saw his muscles had grown as hard as granite.

Discovering that she had not breathed, Rosamund inhaled deeply. With the steamy air came the rich fragrance of rosemary and mint, the smell of burning candles, and the scent of warm, wet male.

Hesitantly, she began working the pale foam through his dark locks, her fingers uncustomarily stiff.

Still, he did not move.

His quiet and the misty heat in the pavilion combined to cast an increasingly heavy net of languor over her. The motion of her fingers slowed as she massaged his scalp. They swirled through the creamed-silk texture, moving over the crown of his head to his nape, where she saw that his dark hair grew down to a perfect point. She paused over it, fascinated. His nape was otherwise smooth, paler than the sun-browned skin lower down, a hidden tender area on the strong, masculine neck. Indeed, it might be the only tender place on his large warrior's body. And here it was, naked to her gaze. Without thinking, she stroked it slowly with her thumb.

"Cease caressing me, damoiselle," he said hoarsely, "unless you desire to become wet again."

His harsh voice broke the spell of her reverie. She snatched her hands away.

" 'Twas no caress," she said haughtily. "I merely tried to remove a bit of dirt." She supposed she would have to confess the lie to Brother Felix.

Tancred's only response was a grunt, but somehow he managed to imbue it with suspicious doubt.

Or maybe it was just her guilt nibbling at her.

She decided his hair was sufficiently clean. Conscientiously, she rinsed it thoroughly. When she went to pour on the diluted verjuice, he stopped her.

"What have you here?" he demanded. "You have rinsed my hair once already." He sniffed at the ewer, abruptly drawing back and wrinkling his nose against the sharp odor of the fermented grape juice.

"Diluted verjuice will remove any cloud on your hair the soap has left."

He regarded her with a narrowed gaze. "You do this for me?"

What arrogance to suppose she did something special for him! "I do this for everyone I bathe." She lifted her chin. "Guest or tyrant."

"Very well." He turned back around.

She frowned. "Very well what, *my lord*?" The last two words fell from her lips like chips of ice.

He ignored her pique. "Attend me."

The effrontery of the man! She was no body servant, though he chose to treat her as one. Temper lifted the ewer to fling the diluted verjuice at the back of his head. Good sense lowered it again. Though she gripped the handle of the ewer so tightly her knuckles grew white, Rosamund gently poured the liquid over his hair, thinking of all the other things she could have added to that final rinse to make it smell even worse.

A knocking at the outside door to the keep echoed through the vaults.

Tancred sighed. He flung one long, well-muscled arm out in a gesture for her to leave. "Go. Reassure your watchdog that I have not dishonored you. When he has satisfied himself that you are safe, return to me."

She walked to the tent flap, where she paused to turn back to him. "How do you know it is John?"

" 'Twould be what I'd do were I in his place."

Just as Tancred had predicted, she encountered John stalking down the stairs.

In the light of her thick candle, she saw his relief.

"I am well, John," she assured him, her heart warming at his concern for her.

He gave her a curt nod, but she saw much of the tension leave his weathered face. "I am pleased to find you so."

She reached out and rubbed her hand up and down the side of his mail-clad arm in a restrained show of affection. Beneath her palm she felt a myriad of tiny metal links, and beneath that the solid bone and muscle of a man who had spent his life fighting, first at her father's side, and, more lately, at hers. Words could never express to him her affection and trust, and she suspected that they would embarrass him. So she curled her fingers around his large arm and gave him a silent, warm squeeze.

He patted her awkwardly on her shoulder.

From the corner of her eye, she glimpsed a motion in the doorway at the top of the stairs. She turned to find Aefre peering around the doorway.

"You are well, my lady?" she called.

"Yea, Aefre. Look, my hair is even dry."

Aefre laughed.

"As it should be," John said wryly.

After her two champions left to return to their duties, Rosamund went to the fireplace and removed the hefty kettle of water she'd earlier left heating. She lugged it into the pavilion.

"God's eyes, woman, do you seek to do yourself an injury?" Tancred demanded when he saw her with the kettle. "Put it down at once."

She continued toward the tub with it. "There is no one else to deliver to the tub more hot water."

Tancred rose up out of the water. *"Put the cursed kettle down!"* He left the tub.

Rosamund dropped the kettle. It thumped against the stone floor.

Speechless, she watched him pick up the kettle, then return to the pavilion. The image of a stallion flitted through her mind.

"There are servants to do this work," he said as she entered the tent to find him pouring the hot water into the tub. He lifted an eyebrow when he saw her standing stock still just inside the entrance. He rested his hands on his bare hips. "So, this is how ladies behave," he drawled. "Were a harlot to size me up so brazenly, damoiselle, the next step would be for me to inquire her price."

Blushing hotly, Rosamund averted her face. "I do beg your pardon, my lord."

What more could she say? Her conduct was inexcusable. She could not say for certain why she behaved so improperly when she came into the company of this man. She felt as if she were slipping out of control, and she did not like the feeling at all.

He strolled closer to her.

She squeezed her eyes shut against the temptation to look at him, to view the details of his magnificent body more fully. She felt foolish and ashamed. Even so, she could feel the heat of him as he drew near to her. Very near.

"I will not touch you," he murmured, his voice as deep and beckoning as sin. "But you may touch me."

His breath sent a thrill through her, and she shivered even as her body flushed. She caught her bottom lip firmly between her teeth.

His silky hair brushed her cheek. "You know you want to."

"No," she denied, her eyes still shut, her face still turned away from him. But even to her own ears her refusal sounded breathy and weak.

"Come," he invited softly. "Unclench you hand and place it—"

Her fingers opened slowly.

She caught herself. Her near-capitulation frightened her. "No!" She whirled away from him, then met his gaze, her eyes blazing. "Are you always so cruel? Do you torment all your prisoners in such a manner?"

His sensual lips curved into a smile. "No."

She backed away a few more steps. "Why do you torture me so?"

"Damoiselle, you have no idea what torture is."

"The songs tell of your own captivity, of the terrible tortures you endured."

"They are only songs, lady. They were composed for the entertainment of bored lords and ladies."

She straightened. "Have you grown bored with your many *chansons*, lord knight? Is that why you now seek to draw your entertainment from me?"

The candles behind him threw most of his face into shadow. Only one dark-pooled eye and the upper ledge of one high cheekbone glowed in the amber light.

"I never asked for those accursed songs. Never wanted them. As for you, you have only to give me the account rolls for Wynnsef to be free of the onerous chore of coming here each eve."

"I have told you already: I do not have them. The seneschal—"

"Would not take all the rolls with him. He might not even take one, but press his tallies and notes into wax or mark them on a tally stick until he returned and could safely scribe his findings on parchment."

Rosamund swallowed. "He . . . he has ever taken the rolls with him. To consult, should need arise. He prefers to write directly on the rolls."

Tancred reentered the tub. "Indeed?" He resumed his seat, lounging back against the wall of the linen-lined tub.

Like some all-powerful potentate, she thought resentfully. A great dark wolf certain of his supremacy. His return to the tub signaled the continuation of his bath, in spite of what must be tepid water.

He took a leisurely drink of wine, then began to lave his arms with the soap. "So," he said casually, "your brother's seneschal prefers to take valuable documents with him when he travels around the honor."

She didn't move from where she stood, but regarded

him suspiciously. "Yea. And an excellent seneschal he is."

"Does this fellow's insistence on risking the very memory of Wynnsef's economy not concern your brother?" The lather streaked and foamed pale against his muscular, sun-browned arms.

"My lord brother has every confidence in his seneschal," she lied. "Naturally Arnaud sends an adequate escort of knights and men-at-arms."

Tancred stroked the lather over his impressive chest, where it mingled with whorls of crisp black hair. "I find it strange that this person—What is his name? You have not mentioned it."

"Er, his name is . . . Nigel. Nigel of—" Her mind raced. It seized on the first distant place that came to her. "London. Yea. Nigel of London."

Tancred paused in his bath and cocked an eyebrow up at her. "Nigel of *London*. I trow he might as well have taken the name 'Nigel Everyman.' "

"A most excellent seneschal."

"So you've said." He washed his broad shoulders. One bore a large pale scar.

She had seen such an injury, freshly done. During a melee, an opponent's lance had penetrated deeply into the knight's shoulder. The wound had proved mortal.

Apparently, Tancred de Vierzon was made of sterner stuff.

"I find it strange," he continued, "that this Nigel of London would leave Wynnsef at such a time." He held the soap out to her.

She glared at it.

"My back," Tancred said.

Rosamund stalked over to him and snatched the slippery ball from his palm. She thumped down on her stool and began to roughly scour his back.

His hand struck like lightning, seizing her wrist in a firm grip. "Damoiselle," he said, his voice like midnight velvet, "do you wish to join me in this tub?"

She attempted to pull from his grasp. It was like trying to win free of iron manacles. "You will do with me as you wish anyway," she told him through clenched teeth.

"There is but one way to find out."

She remembered the madness of need that had swept through her blood like a May fever.

She remembered the thrilling, carnal kiss.

She remembered John.

Abruptly Rosamund ceased tugging against Tancred's hold.

"Ah. Much better." With his free hand, he retrieved the soap from the bottom of the tub. He offered it to her. "Now gently, little nun. You wouldn't want to injure me."

Seething, Rosamund washed his back. She wished what she held in her hand was a knife, not a ball of fragrant soap. When she finished, she returned the soap to him, and he completed his ablutions.

With his back still to her, he rose to his feet, water cascading off him. His body gleamed wetly in the candlelight.

Tearing her gaze away from the sight, she tested the water in the large ewer on the floor. " 'Tis but tepid," she announced sullenly.

"It will do."

Standing on the stool, she poured the water—gently—over his shoulders, rinsing away the soap.

"As I was saying," he went on as he stepped out of the tub and then wrapped a large linen drying cloth about his hips, "I find it strange that Nigel of London would leave Wynnsef just as his master was sallying out the gate, on his way north. With his employer absent from the baronial estates, his first duty was to remain here. And if your brother could not spare sufficient men to guard his castle, I much doubt he would part with them to protect a hireling. Excellent," he added, "though he might be." Tancred strolled out of the tent.

Rosamund reluctantly followed him as she tried to whip up righteous indignation. "Are you naming me a liar?"

"Yea, Lady Rosamund. I am." He began drying his torso with a fresh cloth.

She hadn't wanted to lie, but she was certain God would forgive her, given the circumstances. Or at least Abbess Matilda would. But Rosamund had never expected to be baldly confronted with her deception.

"Hmph," was the best that she could do, and even it nearly caught in her throat. What would he do to her now?

Tancred pulled on his tunic. "Go, now, and ready yourself for the meal," he said, not bothering to look up as he lifted a fresh surcote from the bench.

It was all she could do not to run for the door.

"Oh, and one more thing," he added in a soft voice that halted her in her tracks.

She turned to look at him, waiting, her heart pounding.

He regarded her with hooded eyes. "Be on time to dinner."

EIGHT

"God on the Cross, we must find those accounting rolls," Tancred said in a low, heated voice.

Rosamund had sat next to him, chill and distant, for less than an hour before she had excused herself to retire to her chamber. Kadar had wandered over to drop into the chair she had vacated.

Kadar's eyebrows lifted in surprise. "You know our search is diligent. Men are scouring the castle. I myself have become too well acquainted with the old keep's cellars. With that well and such vast stores of food, we will not starve when Arnaud returns to raise a siege against us."

"Yea. I have seen them, as I have seen Bernard's tally of Wynnsef's herd of cattle, of its goats and sheep and fowl. And all the other tallies I have set the men to collect. But the information they can obtain cannot begin to tell me what the rolls can. I need to know who are my villeins and who are freemen, who owes me labor and how many hours. Who does owe me rent and how much. Who hold their fees from me, owe me their loyalty. And more, much more." Tancred stared across the great hall at the door through which Rosamund had left. *"I want those rolls."*

Kadar studied Tancred thoughtfully. "There is more here than records, I think."

Tancred clenched the metal stem of his goblet, and the moonstone on his wrist winked in the torchlight.

"I mislike the punishment I decreed for Lady Rosamund."

Somber of expression, Kadar said, "If she does not please you, O Seeker of Tallies, have her whipped. She is the sister of your enemy."

Tancred cut a sharp glance to Kadar and noticed at once the amusement lurking in the depths of those dark eyes. "You know better than that."

"Yea, I do. Who knows better than I?"

Tancred made no answer, instead taking a long swallow of wine.

"The fair Rosamund, she is not a proper chatelaine?" Kadar finally asked, breaking the silence.

"A more proper chatelaine would be difficult to find. I know she loathes the very air I breathe, yet she makes certain the water is the perfect temperature, and that it is sweet-smelling with herbs. The soap she uses is not the common stuff made here, but the rich soap they make in Italy, with the oil of olives." He gazed moodily into his cup without noticing its contents. "Jesú, she even sets wine on a table near the tub so that I may drink when I desire."

"Ah. But the wine is not what you truly desire, is it, my friend?"

Tancred's jaw tightened. "Wine is all I will take."

Kadar grinned. "She draws you to her, that one. Whether she wills it or no."

Tancred laughed, but he felt little amusement. "Rosamund of Wynnsef does not will it, of that I am certain. Nor do I. When I need a woman, I would find a lusty widow and make her my leman." He shook his head. "An innocent with the face of an angel and the body of Venus is a combination likely to drive the wits from any man. Best she hide in some abbey, where only God may appreciate her beauty."

"Wed her," Kadar said.

Tancred stared at him. "What mad thought is this?"

"You are a man of substance now," Kadar persisted. "You need a wife. Who better to take than a woman born to this place? A woman, who, even under difficult circumstances, conducts herself with grace and honor?"

"I want an heiress, Kadar," Tancred said flatly. What he *didn't* want was a female who had the ability to provoke his temper even as she sent his body into a flaming state of arousal. God on the Cross, he felt like an uncontrolled green stripling when he was around her. He didn't understand what power she held over him, but he did not like it. Perhaps there was witchery here, as the peasants said.

He shook his head. Foolish imaginings. Next he'd be looking for a salamander.

Kadar popped a bit of honeyed pear into his mouth. "How do you know Lady Rosamund is not an heiress?"

"Because a creature such as Arnaud would have married her off as soon as he could in order to obtain whatever advantage her new husband might bring. Look for yourself. She is long in the tooth for never having been a bride of any kind, either of Christ or man."

"You know well she is a flower of womanhood."

Tancred sighed heavily. "You are determined to be contrary in this matter."

Kadar smiled, but there was a faint wistful element to his expression. "I would have *you*, at least, with a tender wife and babes in the cradle."

Concerned, Tancred leaned closer so that he might not be overheard. He gripped his friend's arm. "I told you that you would never be happy in England."

"What is happiness to my family's honor?"

"I never questioned either your family's honor or your personal honor."

"It was for that very reason that it became important. But we have said these things too many times already. I am doing what is right."

"Mistake me not, Kadar. You are as close to a brother as I have ever known, and it would grieve me to lose you from my side, but I do not believe you will be content until you return to your people."

Kadar placed a deceptively elegant hand over his heart and bowed in his chair. "You, O Right Hand of Wisdom, are my people. As I am yours." He straightened. "Also, I have become too corrupted by your English ways," he added, his expression solemn, but his dark eyes gleaming. "I would not sully the paradise of my father's house with my tainted person."

Tancred knew that Kadar sought to divert the path of their conversation and decided to let the matter rest for the time being. He was selfish enough to want Kadar to remain, yet he knew how lonely his friend must often feel, and it troubled him. But now he eased back against the high, carved back of his chair and smiled.

"Then perhaps what you need is a bath in my excellent tub, Kadar, with a ball of Italian soap and the assistance of a pretty woman."

Kadar's eyebrows lifted. "The Rose of Wynnsef?"

As swift as lightning, as sharp as a sword, an unexpected emotion tore through Tancred, leaving him surprised, unsettled.

"I jest," Kadar said. "I would not subject a Christian woman to such duty. It would be unjust. I will bathe myself, as ever." He released an exaggerated sigh.

From experience, Tancred knew that, soon enough, women would step up to assist the handsome Saracen with his ablutions. In no time they would vie for the privilege.

Tancred grinned. "Brave fellow. You are a shining example to all men."

From the center of the U formed by the trestle tables came the strummed chord of a lute. Tancred looked up to find that Will had taken his seat, ready to begin the evening's entertainment.

The first song was a standard, one that was a favorite in every court in England that Tancred had visited.

He had heard the many verses countless times, performed by various troubadours. The *chanson de geste* concerned a knight who sacrificed his life defending the honor of his faithless lord . . . and so on and so on. This time, Tancred found himself paying closer attention than usual.

As he listened, he realized that Will's voice would be a vibrant tenor when he finishing shedding the higher octaves of his boyhood. The lad was competent on the lute, but competent wasn't good enough if he wished to maintain his position as Wynnsef's court bard.

The consideration of what to do with Will could not hold Tancred's attention for long. Not while a question still burned in his mind.

Where were those cursed rolls?

The moon had begun its descent as Tancred silently slipped out of his room and down the stairs, into the great hall where servants and some of the junior-ranking men-at-arms slept on straw pallets on the benches—now pushed against the wall—or on the floor. From a dark corner came the strangled squeaks and moans of a man and woman tupping. Snores loud enough to frighten horses sawed back and forth within the chamber.

A young archer wrapped in a felted wool blanket raised up on one elbow.

"Is aught amiss, my lord?" the lad whispered.

"All is well, Ranulf. Go back to sleep."

The lad lay back down, and Tancred passed on. The heavy, iron-studded oak door closed quietly behind him.

Attired in the black garments he had worn the night he'd taken Wynnsef, Tancred kept to the night shadows of buildings to escape the attention of sentries, wanting only a time of privacy, of peace. And to meet a challenge that had been thrown in his teeth.

Finally he came to his target. For a long moment

he studied the stone walls of the locked garden, which rose stark black and silver in the light of the gibbous moon. From the wall walk, he had already observed that the limestone walls were approximately one foot thick—nothing at all like the twelve-foot thickness of the two curtains and the massive walls of the old and the new keeps. On his first day as master of Wynnsef, he had examined the heavy, ironbound door that led inside. When he had tried it, the thing had remained solidly in place. And Lady Rosamund professed to have lost the key. Oh, he remembered well how the light in her summer-sky eyes had danced as she had uttered that bald lie.

No, if the key had indeed been lost, that door would have been swiftly removed. In the light of day, he had managed enough time alone to examine the hinges and had concluded that they'd been oiled and cared for. It was a good, strong door, and Tancred had decided to leave it in place.

From his belt, he removed the coiled rope with the grappling hook on one end. With the ease that came of experience, he sent the hook hurling over the top of the high wall, directly over the door, allowing enough rope for the hook to hit the ground on the other side, and thus avoid the noise of steel striking stone, which was sure to attract the attention of the wall walk sentries.

Slowly, he drew in the line until he felt the tug of resistance. If he was correct, the grappling hook was caught in the embrasure of the door on the other side of the wall. He pulled on the rope. It held. Within seconds, he secured his end of the rope to the sturdy wheel of a nearby wagon. Swiftly, silently, Tancred scaled the wall, slithering over the top, where he was most visible, and down into the forbidden interior.

It was not a large garden; it couldn't be. Within the inner bailey of a castle, space was too precious to be spared for nonessentials. The fact that it was this big suggested an indulgent master. Arnaud? Tancred doubted that. During his acquaintance with Arnaud of Wynnsef, before that raid by Faris Sabih Ibn Qasim's forces, the man had displayed a distinct preference for the company of women, one Turkish woman in particular. And a distinct lust for wealth.

He had lacked the gold to pay the scutage, which would have released him from physical service to his overlord. So instead of paying the coin that would have allowed King Richard to pay for mercenaries to take his vassal's place, Arnaud and the knights who owed him service had been forced to accompany the king to the Holy Land. 'Twas a tale that any and all heard whenever the sniveling cur had downed a cup or two of wine. Others had doubtless been in the same situation, but they'd possessed the grace to keep it to themselves.

Tancred thrust back thoughts of Arnaud, and the rage that always came with them. That whore's son had nothing to do with this magical place. It would be evident in an instant to anyone who knew him.

Daisy-flushed grass covered the ground and two turf benches. Across one end of the garden grew a row of fruit trees, frothing with delicate blossoms. From an elegant fount in the center of the garden, water channels radiated out to beds of plants lush with tight buds. Across the garden from the trees stood a tunnel arbor, some thirty feet in length. Rosebushes and honeysuckle formed its walls, and grapevines, their leaves not yet fully opened, formed the rounded roof. As the days grew longer and the sun brighter, grape leaves would unfurl to take on a dappled translucence that provided cheerful shade.

Now moonlight touched everything with strokes of silver, turning the fragrant garden into a faerie realm. He listened to the tranquil music of trickling water from the fount and felt, for the first time in many years, at peace. The walls that rose on each side of this secret place held the world at bay. In here there was no concern over Fitz Clare joining forces with

Arnaud to attack the castle before Tancred could put
his plan into effect, no thoughts regarding Tancred's
own inexperience in managing a baronial estate, or his
need for the essential information the rolls held.

Here, in this secret, forbidden place, green life
flourished with mysterious opulence and timeless di-
versity. Soothing calm enfolded Tancred like the balm
of Paradise. A paradise tended and protected by Rosamund Bourton.

Rosamund.

She was half angel, half elf in the form of Venus.
Her face took form within his mind's eye. Hair of
spun sunbeams, eyes the color of the summer sky, a
smile that could melt any heart—every heart. Rosamund tended and protected those who needed her. As
she had stood a prisoner before him that first morn
after his conquest of Wynnsef, surrounded by her enemies, she had championed the helpless. He had heard
the faint tremor in her breath. She had been afraid,
yet she had fought, using the only weapon she'd possessed: her wit. Such courage was far too rare, even
among men. Perhaps especially among men.

He remembered how she had pulled little Piers
against her, away from the perceived danger of Van-
del's hooves. She had faced the lord of the castle,
prepared to do battle in defense of a fatherless boy.

Rosamund—*Lady* Rosamund—was like no woman
Tancred had ever met.

And she was quite forbidden to him. Still, he could
enter her secret garden, which sighed her presence
with each opening bud, each drift of heady fragrance.
He would stroke the delicate petals and enjoy the perfume that gathered here. Then he would allow the
peace that lay within these walls to assuage the cares
of the day.

Tancred chuckled as he absently followed a slender
water channel, a darker line in the dark night, to its
source at the base of the fount.

Not for one moment had he believed that ridiculous

story about Rosamund accidentally falling down the
well, but the strange experience of hauling her out of
the dank pit—as she dangled upside down—had made
him suspicious. Now he believed he knew were the
rolls were hidden.

Most of the castles he had taken for Richard had
possessed gardens, and he had walked in them all.
Many had even managed to avoid the ravages of the
desperate warfare undergone before Tancred and his
men had been sent to slip inside the fortresses to quietly seize control.

Richard had always preferred the messy way of taking
power. It was wasteful and vainglorious to Tancred's
way of thinking. It squandered life and resources need-
lessly. Still, Richard was king and would have his way.
He made snide remarks about the lack of honor in
Tancred's methods, but without those methods far
fewer castles would have fallen into Richard's grasp.
Even Richard had—only privately, of course—admitted that.

Tancred dabbled the fingertips of one hand in the
cold water of the font's wellhead, his thoughts drifting
in the rare peace. A man might wish to remain here
forever. In the tranquility, he again recalled an incident out of his past, as he had when he had helped
Rosamund out of the well.

After Tancred and his men had taken an adulterine
fortification by stealth, then opened the gates, Richard
and his army had charged inside, triumphant. The king
had demanded certain letters from his disgraced vassal, letters that would have proven the treachery of
one of Richard's inner circle. The baron, however, had
already concealed the damning correspondence, keeping them as a future bargaining chip. He denied
knowledge of them.

Seeing which way the wind blew, his leman had betrayed him. She had taken the king's men directly to
the spot where the letters had been concealed.

Rosamund had shown such courage, he had been

inclined to let her have some time to savor her momentary triumph. But her time was up. It was not wise for him to delay longer. Tancred smiled.

After one last look around the garden, he strode to the rope then scaled the moonlit wall.

By the Grace of God, Rosamund of Wynnsef would not be assisting him with another bath.

After Mass, Rosamund went to the kitchens to confer with the cook over certain supplies, which were running lower than she liked. The cinnamon was almost gone, the cloves not far behind. Both were among the purchases she had commissioned Hembley Abbey to make on her behalf. She fretted that the wagons had turned back when it was learned Wynnsef had been taken by the Moon Lord.

That was still on her mind when she entered the great hall to break her fast with the others, as his Puissant Majesty of Toads had commanded. She swept across the floor, rushes rustling under her feet and the trailing hem of her kirtle, her thoughts occupied. It wasn't until she mounted the steps of the dais that she perceived the strange silence that filled the hall. She glanced around.

Everyone was watching her.

Quickly she glanced down to see if she had gotten something on her garments while in the kitchens. No, her clothing was as it should be. Filled with uneasiness, she took her chair beside Tancred, who was practically the only one in the chamber not looking at her.

"A pleasant day to you, Lady Rosamund," he said politely.

In the presence of others, he always treated her with courtesy. 'Twas a consideration she appreciated, having often suffered the lack of it from Arnaud.

"And to you, Lord Tancred," she replied as she tried to detect what was causing the odd behavior of the others.

He lifted his cup to drink of his ale, and she saw
what lay on the table on the other side of him.

The shock of seeing Wynnsef's large journal at his
elbow snatched the air from her lungs. Her heartbeat
hammered in her ears.

The reason behind the stares of the others now
came clear.

"Eat your cheese and bread, damoiselle," Tancred
said softly. "I would not have you swoon."

"How . . . how did you find it?" she asked
tonelessly.

"You are not the first to keep your valuables in the
wall of a well."

Rosamund met his gaze. She wanted to hate him.
She *should* hate him.

Her sense of fairness made it difficult. He was keeping his promise regarding his men and Wynnsef's
women. He had not shunned Will, despite the lad's
club foot and inexperience as a troubadour. He had
risked his life to save a peasant's child.

Still, he was a dangerous man who had taken something she did not want him to keep: her home.

Also, her brother's honor. Part of that honor, the
pretty manor of Belleborne, originally part of her
mother's dower, was to have been hers. Arnaud had
kept it from her, promising again and again to turn it
over to her soon, always soon. Although her father
may have wanted to leave it to Rosamund directly,
conveying grants of land by will were illegal. Strictly
speaking, all land belonged to the Crown. In practice,
however, a hefty fee—a heriot—to the overlord of the
deceased would usually gain his consent for the heir
to be invested as new master—or in a daughter's case,
mistress—of the land in question.

Without Belleborne, Rosamund must needs enter
the abbey as a pauper, and that she was not yet ready
to do. She was also not ready to appeal to the crown
for justice. A decision could go either way, as women
had no true legal right to the courts, but either way

it went, she would lose the only family she had left. Arnaud would never forgive her.

"What now, Lord Tancred?" she asked, trying not to think of the possible consequences of her defiance of him in concealing the journal.

"Pray, eat your food, lady, and I will tell you."

She looked down at the cheese and manchet loaf. Her appetite had deserted her, but she cut a slice of cheese and ate it. Doubtless she would need strength for whatever came now.

"I have looked through this book," he said, laying one hand on the heavy leather cover. "It tells many tales."

One of them was that he could read and figure, she thought as she chewed her bread. But then, what would one expect from the Moon Lord, that wonder of knighthood, that marvel in mail?

"There is no seneschal for Wynnsef, is there?" It was more statement than question.

Rosamund choked on her bread.

Swiftly, Tancred began patting her on her back.

"Stop," she rasped. "Please, no more." He was close. Too close. Instead of helping, he only unsettled her more. As she gasped for air, she distractedly waved him back into his seat. Was this to be her end, then? Murdered by a crumb of bread?

Gradually the choking and coughing passed.

"Your pardon, lady," he said when she was breathing more easily. "I did seek only to aid you."

When she had finally filled her lungs with air and eased out a soft sigh, she nodded. "Yea, I believe you." She dabbed at her eyes with the napkin, then managed a ghost of a smile. "If you desired my death, I should suppose you would use a more direct method."

"If I desired your death, you would be dead," he said bluntly, clearly not amused.

Her smile grew frigid. "Oh, but I am so convenient, am I not? Better than a villein, for I know more that is useful to you. Indeed, you have only to play at your sword games while Wynnsef manages itself."

"You confuse me with your brother, damoiselle."

"You would like to think it, but in this matter the two of you have much in common."

Tancred scowled. "I am *nothing* like Arnaud of Wynnsef."

His statement was so adamant Rosamund was forced to wonder again what grudge he held against Arnaud. But she would not give Tancred the satisfaction of her asking. To do so might seem as though her loyalty to her brother could be doubted.

She knew her brother possessed certain imperfections of temperament. But she also knew what most others did not: Arnaud had suffered for years—because of her.

"If you are so flawless a seigneur," she said, "I pray you explain the difference between what you expect of me, and that which my brother expects of me."

"The difference may lie less in our expectations, damoiselle, than in the point that I am a conqueror, a stranger to you, but he is your brother."

His words stabbed deeply into her, burning like a poisoned blade as it laid open a truth she could not bear to face.

In that moment, Rosamund felt more alone than she had since the night of her father's death. In a world filled with war and wolves, there were none she could call on for their strength. She stood alone, her arms outspread to shield those who loved her, for their stations in life were even more precarious than hers.

With a gaze that she hoped would conceal the hollowness she was feeling, Rosamund said, "Yea, he *is* my brother."

"A fact I do not intend to forget."

Purposefully, she sliced another piece of cheese and nibbled at it. "Which brings us back to my question. What do you intend to do now?"

Just by chance she caught the flicker of his eyes as

his gaze dropped to the sliver of cheese . . . and then to her mouth. It lingered, then lifted again.

Was he remembering their kiss? she wondered. Did the memory hover at the back of his mind, as it did hers?

She caught herself. Tancred thinking of her? Such a ludicrous idea. This man, after all, was the Moon Lord. Likely many an elegant lady in many a sumptuous court had been kissed by his warm, skillful lips. And had eagerly kissed him back. By comparison, Rosamund must seem like a silly rustic mouse.

She glanced at him through her lowered lashes. Was he privately laughing at her? The thought that he might believe her silly—or, worse, ridiculous—disturbed her.

Since her fosterage had been cut short by her mother's death, Rosamund had not left Wynnsef. First, because her father had been heartbroken over the loss of his dear lady and believed no place he had ever seen was as agreeable to him as his own demesne, and then, after his death, because Arnaud feared she might fly away and leave him to care for his own estates. Consequently, she was accustomed to being an important fish in her remote little pond. Tancred, however, was a shark accustomed to the sea.

He frowned down at the table. "I have been fighting all of my life. My time and strength and whatever small gifts I may possess have gone to learning how to stay alive, then learning how best to do my liege's will, which is, and always shall be, to win. I know how to read, write, and figure. But . . . "

For the first time, she observed hesitation in him. Surprised, she waited for him to finish.

"I must learn to live with peace," he finally said.

Peace? "And so you took my brother's lands," she observed sourly.

His beautiful dark-angel face grew shuttered. "There are matters yet to settle. Still I would learn what must be done in such times."

"Why are you telling me this?"

With one hand, he carefully opened the intricately wrought leather cover of the heavy journal. His fingertips slipped over the first page of thick parchment in a movement akin to a caress. Rosamund watched, powerless to look away.

"Because," he said softly. "You are going to teach me."

NINE

Just past Sext, a sentry at the inner bailey gate called out. In minutes the news had spread that the Abbess of Hembley waited without, accompanied by one novice, an escort of eight knights, a dozen mounted men-at-arms, and a line of loaded wagons driven by nuns. Large, burley nuns.

Rosamund stood in the courtyard issuing orders to a handful of hang-dog villeins faced with the task of cleaning out the castle's numerous cesspits. When she heard the sentry's shout, she quickly set the workmen about their tasks, then gathered her skirts and dashed up to the wall walk beside the gatehouse.

Never had there been a more welcome sight than the slim, regal figure of Abbess Matilda, sitting astride a gray palfrey whose trappings bore the symbol of the industrious abbey.

Delighted and relieved, Rosamund hailed them and waved. The women smiled and waved back.

Tancred strode up to stand beside her, gazing down at the well-armed group.

"Tell the abbess's captain," he said to the sentry, "that the abbess, the sisters, and the wagons are welcome. He and the rest of her escort will be allowed in only on the condition that they render their weapons to our armorer."

"He won't agree to that," Rosamund protested. "Would you, in his place?"

Tancred's lips moved in a faint smile. "No."

"I know the abbess. It is to Hembley Abbey that I wish to go. And we need what is in those wagons."

He studied the column of wagons and the armed men below. "We do?"

His casual question, so naturally spoken, jarred against Rosamund's sensibilities, releasing a tangle of resentment and longing. If only there were a man she might consider a partner. Quickly she squashed that mad thread. There was no "we" here. There was only the Moon Lord and his hostage.

"Yea, Lord Tancred," she replied. "We do. Hembley Abbey serves as my agent. They purchase the goods I cannot—" She broke off, refusing to admit to this man that, though Wynnsef was her home, her brother had made her a virtual prisoner here. She must act the steward for Wynnsef, yet she could not leave to inspect the other lands that belonged to the honor, or travel as necessary to keep the estates supplied with iron, salt, dried fish, wool, hides, and other things that either could not be produced here or produced in sufficient quantity. "They bring those things I have ordered for Wynnsef. Turn them away, and you'll have no salt, no spices, no . . . well, you will do without many things."

He turned his head to look at her, lifting a black eyebrow, but he made no comment on her change in reference.

"I cannot allow that many armed men into my inner bailey. While this lady is a daughter of the church, I know her not." He considered a moment, then spoke to the sentry. "I will speak with the lady abbess myself."

The wind caught his long mantle as he strode down the stone steps from the wall walk, and it billowed out behind him like a dark flag. The door in the greater gate was opened for him, and he walked out to stand beside the palfrey.

Rosamund watched as he conversed with Abbess

Matilda for a few minutes. Then he walked back into the castle. Minutes later, she heard the gates creak open and the heavy chains rattle as the winch turned, raising the portcullis. The nuns clucked to the teams of horses, and the supply caravan entered, hooves thudding against earth, wagon wheels creaking.

On the seat of the first wagon, sat Edeva, the abbey's perpetual novice. The petite brunette had been given to the abbey by her large family when she was a child, but it had soon become apparent that Edeva was not suited for the life of a religious, being too inquisitive. By that time, the abbess and sisters of Hembley Abbey were much more her family than mere, uninterested blood-kin.

Raw-boned Sister Dameta sat next to Edeva, holding the reins.

Swiftly descending the stairs, Rosamund saw the abbess's men-at-arms render their weapons to the castle armorer. The knights of the escort were permitted to keep their swords, but delivered up their shields, axes, lances, and maces.

Tancred himself stepped forward to assist Abbess Matilda down from her palfrey, but she impatiently waved him away.

"I am not so long in years that I cannot dismount from my own horse," she told him in her brisk, no-nonsense manner.

"I did not imply you were, madam."

Rosamund went directly into the embrace of the abbess, who gave her an affectionate squeeze and a kiss on each cheek.

"Would you assist this one to dismount?" Abbess Matilda demanded of Tancred, indicating Rosamund with a sweep of her hand.

Tancred's gaze moved over Rosamund then centered on the abbess's elegant, ageless face. "I know her to be hale and sound of limb, but if she wished it, I would help her down. You, my lady abbess, are unknown to me. If those ells of brown wool you wear concealed an afflicted leg or knee or foot, would you still insist I let you be?"

Abbess Matilda regarded him for a moment. "I detest being put in my place, boy."

Tancred's mild expression did not change. "And I detest being called 'boy.' "

Just as Rosamund worried that this meeting would culminate in disaster, the abbess nodded slightly. "I had heard from a dear friend how that meeting between you and the king's grace went after the fall of Bâb Al-Muhunnad. I am more inclined to credit his account of it now."

Tancred briefly glanced at Rosamund, but spoke to Abbess Matilda. "Then you know our king told me that if I took Wynnsef, it was mine."

"So I was told. But you have not yet fully taken it, have you? That will be decided when Lord Arnaud returns. Oh, news—*some* news—travels quickly. I know that he was north somewhere when you arrived. And that you drove away a much greater force than your own before you quietly took this castle. Do not count on such ease with the lady Rosamund's brother. He is sullen and lazy, but not entirely stupid."

Rosamund stared at her in surprise.

Abbess Matilda laid a manicured fingertip under Rosamund's chin and gently lifted. "Close your mouth, sweeting, there are flies about."

Tancred gestured toward the new keep. "Come. Allow me to offer you and the good sisters refreshment."

With an imperial dip of her head, the abbess agreed, and they walked toward the great hall. By tacit agreement, her knights accompanied them, along with several of Tancred's own knights.

"I am familiar with Arnaud's tactics," Tancred said as they walked, continuing their conversation, "and with the strength of the force he commands." The corners of his mouth lifted in a minute curve. "I have my plans."

They mounted the outside steps to the first-level great hall.

Tancred guided them to the dais while pages showed the abbey knights to tables that had not been in place less than a quarter of an hour ago. Servants hastened to draw out the heavy chairs on the dais.

"You will, of course, desire that I take Lady Rosamund back with me for her safety," Abbess Matilda said, thereby winning Rosamund's gratitude.

"I think not." Tancred turned a cool smile on the abbess. "She is safer here." He handed the prelate into her chair.

He attended the courtesy of assisting Rosamund into her carved seat before taking his own. She noted that he did not yield the high seat to Abbess Matilda. As a baron and lord of Wynnsef, his station would be much higher than hers, for the lands and estates of the honor encompassed much more of England than did those belonging to Hembley Abbey. And much of those vast properties were within view of the highest place in the castle, the watch tower. Belleborne was one of those estates beyond such sight. Rosamund had not laid eyes upon it in years.

"How can you say she is safer here?" Abbess Matilda asked as she dipped her hands into the silver, rose-water-filled basin offered by a servant.

" 'Tis simple." Tancred submerged his hands in the basin offered by another man. "I say it because it is so."

"You know Lord Arnaud will lay siege to Wynnsef to get it back."

Tancred wore a bland expression. "I know no such thing, my lady abbess. Nor do you."

Before more could be said, the nuns were escorted in by Tancred's knights, pointing up the lack of courtesy in Hembley's men. Immediately Rosamund's gaze sought out Edeva. She found her walking beside Kadar, sneaking glances up at him. As usual, the Saracen was attired in gorgeous raiment. Today he wore

a brief turban bearing a large ruby above the center
of his forehead.

If Kadar owned a ruby the size of a falcon's egg,
why did he remain with Tancred, as one of his men?
Indeed, why had he made the long journey to England
at all? A Christian kingdom would not be a pleasant
place for him to live.

"Do you not agree, Lady Rosamund?"

At Abbess Matilda's question, Rosamund realized
she had missed something in the conversation.

"I fear I did not hear what was said, Abbess
Matilda."

"I said that we should leave the decision to you as
to whether you would feel safer here or at Hembley
Abbey."

There was no question in Rosamund's mind where
she would be safer—from a siege and from the will of
Tancred de Vierzon. As she parted her lips to reply,
he caught her eye with his level silver gaze. Its intensity stopped the words in her throat.

Their first meeting came back to her.

I will do as you ask, upon one condition.

Very well. You shall have your month.

How would everyone else at Wynnsef fare if she
now took this escape? The quiet grimness in Tancred's
words rang again in her memory.

*Would you rather I settled unwanted distractions with
a whip?*

The people of this barony were unused to such
harshness. She had always tried to govern with compassion and justice. What harm might they stumble
into with this man?

When Arnaud returned to take back Wynnsef and
found her gone, would he be so furious he would refuse to give over Belleborne? Would she be faced with
seeking the king's justice or living the rest of her life
as a prisoner? Arnaud could be rude and petulant and
even petty, but he could also be charming and make
her laugh, when he chose. And he was her brother.

Rosamund met Tancred's compelling gaze. "Mayhap I would feel safer at Hembley," she said quietly, "but my duty lies here at Wynnsef."

Abbess Matilda looked surprised for an instant, then assumed an expression of calm acceptance. "I disagree, my child, but I understand your loyalty to your lord brother."

Not for an instant did Rosamund believe Abbess Matilda, the woman who had managed to obtain every supply—including seed of the jessamine plant—from Rosamund's every list over the past two years, had given up so easily. Rosamund would later need to explain her reasons for staying so her mentor would truly accept the wisdom of her decision.

A simple meal was served the guests, the hour being too early for supper to be ready and much too late for the Spartan repast of the morning. Rosamund left Tancred to face the sword-sharp intellect of the abbess while she went to arrange accommodations for the extra people. Some would sleep upon straw pallets on the floor of the great hall, but the nuns and Abbess Matilda should be housed in proper chambers.

Rosamund decided to try to find a chamber close to her own for Edeva. She had grown quite fond of the perpetual novice. Of an age with Rosamund, Edeva was curious about everything and yearned for adventure. The two young women had spent many hours with their heads together, whispering secrets, giggling over outlandish fancies.

The ladies from Hembley Abbey would have to share quarters in order for there to be sufficient chambers enough for all of them. Edeva would fare best with Sister Octavia, Rosamund decided. Sister Octavia was not as severe as Sister Philomena, as timid as Sister Dameta, as bossy as Sister Mary, or as easily shocked as Sister Clemence.

No, Sister Clemence would especially be a poor choice to share a room with Edeva, who was full of questions regarding her faith. Some of them had even shocked Rosamund. But every now and again Edeva's questions would return to niggle at the back of the mind: How could one know all that there was to know about God—or at least as much as was purported to be known? God was omniscient, omnipresent, omnipotent. Man was not. Did that mean man only *looked* like God? And if God possessed the same shape as a man, didn't that limit Him? It certainly limited men.

Putting those unsettling thoughts aside, Rosamund turned her attention to what must be done. Some of Hembley's knights would sleep in the great hall, the others, along with the abbey's men-at-arms, would have pallets in the garrison with Wynnsef's men-at-arms. Abbess Matilda would take the chamber reserved for guests of state, two floors above the great hall on the end opposite from Tancred's quarters. It had not been used often since her father's death, but she had seen to it that the chamber was kept scrupulously maintained. One would not wish to offer a bishop or the King of England—and by *no* means the Abbess of Hembley—a musty room or a mildewed mattress shredded by rats.

After a careful inspection that took in the freshness of mattresses and sheets, the quality of the newly spread rushes on the wooden floors, and, in the abbess's room, the shine of the polished horn panes in the largest window of the castle, the Abbess Matilda's trunks and the more meager possessions of the nuns and Edeva, were transferred from the wagons to their chambers.

While the nuns and Edeva freshened and rested after their long, arduous journey from Hembley Abby, Rosamund and Brother Felix, equipped with ink horn, quill, and parchment, returned to the courtyard to check the goods against her list and have them taken to their proper places. Already assembled were her people, who knew what to do when one of the abbey's caravans arrived.

No surprise to Rosamund, Abbess Matilda was

there also, ready to make certain everything was as it should be. In one slim hand she grasped a parchment scroll which doubtless detailed the wagons' contents.

"My lady abbess, would you not prefer to rest?" Rosamund said, concerned that Matilda at the venerable age of five-and-forty might be jeopardizing her health. "Brother Felix and I can easily see to this." Only a slight exaggeration. Accounting for and supervising the placement of these many commodities was no small task, but Rosamund was responsible for most of it anyway.

Abbess Matilda waved away the suggestion. "I realize, my dear, that I saw the springtide of my life long ago, but I am not yet so ancient that I cannot fulfill my responsibilities."

"You know well I did not imply you were incapable. 'Tis your comfort I consider."

Eyes twinkled in the austere elegance of Matilda's face. "I will be considerably more comfortable after I know what you ordered, and the exact quantities in which you ordered them, has been delivered to you in good condition. Then I may breathe more easily."

Rosamund's eyebrows drew slightly downward. "Do you fret so with every commission you fulfill? If so, you must be ever worried."

"Were it not for your commissions, Rosamund, there would not have been others. You made it possible for Hembley Abbey to prosper. Who else would have thought to request our abbey act as an agent in making purchases? Now we have sufficient commissions that we are able to purchase many items at once, in such quantities that we may save our patrons many marks. That, in turn, has brought more patrons."

A deep, familiar voice spoke behind Rosamund. "It sounds as if Hembley Abbey is indebted to Wynnsef."

Abbess Matilda arched a silver eyebrow. "It is indebted to Lady Rosamund of Wynnsef, Lord Tancred."

"I perceive a fine distinction."

"There is. Now, the sooner we undertake our task at hand, the sooner we shall all be finished." With that, she unrolled her scroll and strode to a wagon farther down the line. Clearly uncertain if he should go with the abbess to get started or stay with Rosamund, Brother Felix cast the latter a questioning look. Rosamund inclined her head in the direction of Abbess Matilda. He walked after that lady.

Rosamund turned. Tancred stood close behind her, his thick cap of raven hair gleaming in the sunlight. Today he wore a black tunic, and over that a gray surcoat.

"Is there something you wish, my lord?" she asked politely, easing a step away so that she didn't have to crane her neck to see his face.

His gaze following the abbess and Brother Felix, he said, "Yea, Lady Rosamund, there is."

She waited, wary of what he might want this time.

He looked at her. "I want you to teach me what to do when supplies that have been ordered arrive at Wynnsef."

"You are responsible for many men, Lord Tancred. Have you never kept records of the supplies they would need? Of food or—or"—she searched her brain for something such a collection of knights and mounted men-at-arms would need—"feed for their horses?"

He lifted an open hand in a gesture indicating the many loaded wagons. "Nothing equal to this. For the most part, the men tended their own equipment and clothing. My cook ordered what he needed for food. I paid out the coin, so I know what certain foodstuffs in that quantity cost. Hay is cheap and can be purchased from farmers as it is needed. In summer the horses grazed." He shrugged. "Now I would know the things a castle requires, the quantity and where they are stored."

Rosamund watched Abbess Matilda stride briskly

from wagon to wagon. There certainly had been no love displayed between the abbess and Tancred.

She slanted him a shrewd glance. "Shall I presume you would prefer your lessons not to be . . . obvious?"

He smiled, and his eyes warmed with humor. "You shall."

She found herself smiling back at him. "Very well. Quickly, now, for we must attend my lady abbess before she grows impatient. The quantities of everything are going to be counted. She will check the list from which she purchased—the list I sent her—and I shall consult my copy. The number of goods counted should correspond with them."

"And if they don't?"

"If the goods come up short, the difference comes out of the fee I pay Hembley Abbey. But that has never happened."

"There has been no pilferage?" he asked, clearly surprised.

"No one who knows the abbess would dare." Rosamund noticed that Abbess Matilda had stopped. "Come. She greatly dislikes to be kept waiting."

"That matters to you?"

As they walked toward the end of the wagons, Rosamund shot him a sharp glance, but she could detect no derision or criticism in his tone, only genuine interest.

"Abbess Matilda has been kind to me," she said.

"And you have been good to her, or so it sounded when I arrived."

"I suppose. If Hembley has derived some benefit from me, I am happy for it. But she was kind to me ere I ever asked if she might fill a commission for me."

They caught up with the abbess and Brother Felix and then began the long process. As an item was counted and found to comply with the lists, Rosamund's people removed it from the wagon—whether it be hides, ingots, bags of wool, loaves of sugar, or the like—then hauled it away to an assigned place within the castle.

Tancred walked beside Rosamund, watching, listening, once in a while lowering his head to hers to ask a quiet question. In short, he did nothing to cause her nerves to vibrate as they did. She told herself she was still disturbed over him finding the journal, despite the simple prayer Brother Felix had suggested she might find calming. The prayer consisted of only four words, yet it managed to reflect a universe of philosophy.

Thy Will be done.

Initially, she had found it soothing. Why wasn't the prayer—which she repeated faster and faster in her mind—working now? When had it ceased to calm? She frowned slightly, trying to remember. Then it came to her, and she wished she hadn't attempted to recall, because the instant bloomed in her mind, as clear as if she were reliving it.

It had ceased to soothe the moment Tancred had smiled and asked her to help him.

She glanced up at him through her lashes. *Had* he cast a spell on her? Was he *trying* to unsettle her?

Almost as quickly as that occurred to her, Rosamund cast the suspicion aside, making a small noise of self-disgust in her throat. She was getting to be as superstitious as a villein. Holy Rood, he was a *knight*, not a sorcerer. Very well, she admitted, a courageous knight. Also a stealthy one. But that hardly made him the boon companion of Beelzebub.

"Did you say something, Lady Rosamund?" Tancred asked as he lifted the cover of a small box and peered inside.

"No."

"What is this?" he inquired, studying the brown, wrinkled-looking pieces of root.

"Galingale."

He looked at her over his shoulder. "The spice?"

She nodded. The dishes prepared at Wynnsef made full use of spices and herbs.

"Do you receive a list with the prices of each type of goods you have purchased?"

Thy Will be done, Thy Will be done, Thy Will be done. "Yea, Lord Tancred. There is a full accounting given me."

"And this is recorded in the journal?"

"It is copied into the journal," she agreed.

And so the afternoon proceeded until the last wagon had been emptied, and the numbers tallied and compared. As they always had before, the lists matched. Looking pale with weariness, Abbess Matilda excused herself to go luxuriate in a steaming bath. Brother Felix departed to his own duties, taking the rolls with him.

"I thank you, damoiselle, for your patience," Tancred said. "I have learned much."

He left her then, heading in the direction of the stables, and Rosamund stood there, watching his tall, broad-shouldered figure stride away. He had done nothing to interfere with the process of transferring the goods Abbess Matilda had delivered. Even the abbess could not have found fault with his conduct.

Grudgingly, Rosamund admitted to herself that he learned quickly.

Too quickly for her peace of mind.

TEN

It was midafternoon when Tancred found Kadar in a deserted area of the outer bailey. The sun was smothered by clouds that presaged rain before nightfall. Faridah, Kadar's favorite horse, grazed on new grass, flicking her long, well-groomed tail. The Arab mare was still saddled and wore a damp sheen on her coat.

Facing southeast, Kadar knelt on the rectangle of tapestry he had carried with him from his homeland. He bore his weight on the base of his heels, his hands extended along his thighs in the *julūs* position of his *Salāh*, his ritual prayer. His handsome, hawkish face wore an expression of serenity Tancred envied.

Silently, Tancred waited a few minutes to see if Kadar was nearly finished. He was nearing the end of the sequence, but might choose to begin another. If so, Tancred would speak with his friend another time.

Kadar looked over his right shoulder, then his left, intoning the *taslīm*. He went quiet, gazing into the distance, still facing southeast. Then, with a barely perceptible sigh, he rose to his feet. Stepping back, he picked up the tapestry, shook it once, then began rolling it.

Tancred cleared his throat.

Kadar turned. He smiled when he saw Tancred. His hands continued to brush grass and bits of earth from the bottom of the tapestry as he rolled it into a tube, which he placed inside a leather bag designed for the purpose.

"I have been exercising Faridah," he said with a nod toward the elegant bay. "I have neglected her shamefully while I have worked with Zahir."

Zahir was Kadar's destrier, a handsome young stallion he had purchased in Flanders as he, Tancred, and the men who now made up the core of Tancred's force, made their way to England. European cavalry tactics differed markedly from those used by Kadar's people, thus he had decided it wise to obtain a "lumbering" European war horse.

But he had educated the stallion as he had all his horses, and, while Zahir would never be able to swerve or stop as sharply as the lighter, more nimble Faridah, he had put the destriers of Tancred and the rest of the men to shame. Now, everyone in Tancred's host—including Tancred—employed training techniques Kadar and his family had learned from the Seljuk Turks, who were famed for their equestrian feats. Tancred had also incorporated some Saracen techniques in his stratagems, which often confused the enemy enough to give Tancred an advantage.

"I hope I did not disturb your prayers," Tancred said.

"No, you were as silent as a fox. I did not hear you."

Tancred looked back over his shoulder.

"Are you pursued?" Kadar asked, casually reaching for his sword and belt, which he had set aside. He moved with an ease that, to someone who did not know him, might have fully concealed his tension.

"No. Well, yea, I am pursued, but by none who carry a weapon. At least, not a weapon merciful enough to offer instant death. Haste! Think of something to divert him at least for a while. Mercy, I beg of thee, brother."

Kadar grinned as he caught sight of Will, hobbling in swift pursuit of Tancred. "Ah. Your admirer, the aspiring troubadour. You *did* tell him you would spend a day with him. Would you crush his joy for lack of patience?"

Tancred scowled at Kadar. " 'Tis only that I need a respite. A moment without *questions*. I am not as marvelous as he believes."

Kadar arched his eyebrows. "Shall I aid you in dispelling his ideals?"

Suddenly, Tancred did not like the thought of being made smaller in Will's eyes. "No. Time will see to that."

Panting, Will arrived. "Your . . . pardon . . . my lord. I . . . was not attentive. I did not . . . see you . . . leave."

Feeling small and unworthy of this boy's admiration, Tancred gave him a curt nod. "The fault is mine, Will." The boy had doggedly kept up with him all day, asking question after question in his subdued voice, all the while excitement danced in his gray eyes. "Come, we'll watch Kadar work with his Arab."

"Alas," Kadar said smoothly, with no sign of regret, "I have already worked with Faridah. Why don't *you* work with her awhile, dread lord? I will tell Will of your many glorious feats of bravery."

"I would not have you bore the lad, Kadar." Tancred narrowed his eyes threateningly at his friend over Will's head. "Besides, Faridah is unused to me."

"Faridah adores you. She takes apples from your hand. For none other will she do this, save me. And Will wishes to see you put her through her paces, do you not?" Kadar looked to the lad for an answer.

"Oh, yes, sir!" Will exclaimed. "All know the Moon Lord excels at all he undertakes."

"Yea, my fearless lord," Kadar agreed, a smile lurking at the corners of his mouth. He gestured toward the grazing Faridah. "Go. Bedazzle us with your skill and grace."

There was no way to win this contest without being boorish, Tancred decided, and he'd already done a fine job of that once today. So he performed a lavish bow and waved away their applause and cheers.

He strode to Faridah. He spoke softly to her, stroking her nose, her sleek neck. She nuzzled his hand, looking for an apple, but took her disappointment at finding none with good spirits.

Tancred mounted her, then nudged her into a slow canter back to where Kadar and Will sat. He bowed from the waist. Murmuring the proper command to Faridah, he watched as she lowered her exquisite head in a distinct bow of her own. Will laughed with delight, and Kadar, who had taught the mare that maneuver, smiled.

One by one, Tancred took the Arab through the exercises he had practiced with his destrier, Vandal, and his own Arab. He charged across the field, and reined for a sudden stop. Faridah executed the halt so precisely Will was impressed. Tancred found he enjoyed the lad's delight. Next came the abrupt swerve and from there a few other exercises.

Then Tancred drew the mare to a stop. He got down and unsaddled her. When he mounted her again, he felt the warmth of her against his buttocks and legs. He nudged her into a walk, then a canter. With Faridah going at a full gallop, Tancred leaned far to one side, the muscles in his thighs and calves tightening, their strength the only thing preventing him from falling beneath iron-shod hooves. Reaching out, he plucked a yellow dandelion from the sweet young grass. Muscles toned by years spent riding, walking, and sprinting while wearing a hundred pounds of mail, pulled him into place on the horse's back.

Smiling at Will's unrestrained enthusiasm and Kadar's good-natured heckling, Tancred noticed the approach of Sister Edeva. Wearing the white of one who has not yet been initiated into the order, her hair respectably concealed by veil and wimple, the little novice carried an earthenware jug and a willow basket.

He smiled. "Good day to you, Sister," he said, sliding off Faridah.

"Good day, Lord Tancred," she answered.

Kadar swiftly rose to his feet, turning to face her. Will followed suit. Tancred started toward her to relieve her of her burdens, but before he took two steps, Kadar stood before her.

"Allow me," the Saracen murmured, carefully holding out his hands in an unmistakable gesture offering to take the basket and jug, moving as he would with a skittish mare. He had learned the hard way that some English women found the strangeness of his garb and his swarthy coloring alarming on first sight.

Clearly not Sister Edeva, Tancred thought as he saw her give her burden into Kadar's hands with a shy smile.

Kadar's expression remained grave.

"Your cook thought you might wish these, my lord, since you were absent from the noon meal," she said. "I told her I would find you and deliver this." She slipped a quick, curious sidelong glance at Kadar, who had not moved, as if he'd been turned to a pillar of salt.

Tancred almost laughed aloud at the sight of his friend, usually suave and courtly with women, now stone-faced, cradling a common jug in one arm and a basket in the other as if they were swaddled babes. Well, Kadar customarily accorded nuns the deepest respect, tending to be more grave in their presence than usual. Perhaps it was just that this pretty young woman was soon to be a nun that had him so quiet.

"I thank you, Sister Edeva," Tancred said. "Will you join us in this bounty?"

"You do me honor, sir, but I have promised Lady Rosamund I would help her with the spinning."

"Spinning? Lady Rosamund spins? Wool?"

Sister Edeva laughed. It was a gay, musical sound. "But of course. Wool. Flax. Whatever is needful."

This came as a surprise. Rosamund acted as sene-

schal to Wynnsef *and* spun? While he did not know
how to run an estate, he did know that it took most
of one's waking hours. He had met a seneschal or two
while in the king's host.

"Do you know the lady Rosamund well?" he asked,
careful to sound casual.

A guarded look came into her dark eyes. "We are
friends." Her tone, while still pleasant, now carried
with it a distant quality that did not invite questions.

"I suppose the two of you are of an age." Though
well past the age when most girls were wedded and
bedded, Rosamund was still young. Still thoroughly
desirable. For a traitor's sister.

"Yea, my lord."

Though he wished to ask more about Rosamund,
Tancred decided it was unwise to ask it of her friend,
a female friend at that. If he asked more than what
seemed like an idle question or two, Sister Edeva
would likely go straight to Rosamund and inform her
of his curiosity.

"Thank you for bringing these to us," he said, indicating the jug and the basket. "If you have a promise
to keep, I will not stay you further."

With a small bow of her head, she left.

Kadar watched her, his expression still somber.

Tancred gently removed the burden from Kadar's
arms. Kadar didn't move. His gaze followed Sister
Edeva until she left their sight.

"Let us enjoy this unexpected bounty," Tancred
said to Will. "He will join us when he finishes with
his staring."

Will grinned.

"I do not stare," Kadar informed Tancred with lofty
dignity as he followed. "I wished only to make certain
she entered the inner bailey safely."

"Excellent thinking, Kadar," Tancred said as he sat
cross-legged on the grass. "All here know this outer
bailey is fraught with peril."

Will and Kadar joined him on the grass.

"Sister Edeva is very pretty," Will said innocently.

Tancred flicked a knowing glance at Kadar, who pointedly ignored him. "Yea, she is pretty indeed. And well spoken. No simple farmer's daughter, I would venture."

Will's gaze fastened to the roast rabbit Tancred removed from the basket. "No, sire. Her father was a lord in Shropshire, who held his fee from—" He frowned slightly, trying to recall. Finally he shrugged. "I misremember now. No baron, though."

"Did you hear, Kadar?" Tancred inquired mildly. "Her father was a lord."

Kadar accepted the hunk of rabbit Tancred offered. "I heard." His inflection was one of indifference.

Will scarcely restrained his enthusiasm when he was offered a portion, too, and Tancred remembered Rosamund's defense of the lad, how she had put his lack of polish as a troubadour down to youth. And Tancred was forced to admit he was rather young. Not more than twelve or thirteen. It was, perhaps, Will's height that led one to believe him older than he was.

Tancred, too, had always been tall for his age. It brought advantages, but it carried disadvantages as well. More was always expected of you, required of you. The carefree years of ignorant youth were vastly shorter for a tall lad than for his shorter peers.

For one who intended to be a knight, that, in time, would prove an advantage.

For a lad who had been born with a club foot, it would place him more apart from everyone. It would be yet another disadvantage.

He studied Will's narrow, snub-nosed face. If Will could learn to play a lute well, when his voice changed, he would have something people would want.

"Can you read and write, Will?" Tancred asked.

"Yea, my lord. Lady Rosamund bade Brother Felix teach me when he gave her lord brother's squires and pages their lessons."

Tancred chewed a bit of rabbit as he considered what a happy mixture that must have been for Will. "Did that prove difficult for you?"

Will swallowed a mouthful of meat. "The lessons? No, my seigneur. And I was glad for them."

A breeze ruffled Tancred's hair "Not the lessons."

Will flushed. He looked down and plucked a few blades of grass. " 'Twas no different."

Tancred had thought as much.

The other boys were bound for lives of hard physical activity and there was the very real possibility that many of them would be disfigured, dismembered, or slain before they reached the prime of their lives. Like most of the very young, they had no tolerance for someone who could not do the things they could, someone whom they perceived as being unable to keep up . . . to measure up.

Tancred remembered what Rosamund had said about Arnaud breaking his betrothal to Lady Margaret of Cranthorp. Apparently, some never outgrew their intolerance.

"Do you sing in the great hall every night?" he asked, striving to make the question sound offhand and unimportant. He sensed Will's tension immediately.

"No," Will said softly.

So. Arnaud would not have the boy around him.

"Lady Rosamund speaks fondly of you," Tancred said.

Will brightened immediately. "She does?"

"Did you not know?"

"Yea, sire. That is, I have hoped that she was pleased with me. I am trying very hard," Will said earnestly. "She is very kind to me. I would never willingly disappoint her." His dun eyebrows drew downward. "It would be easier if my voice would quit cracking," he muttered.

Kadar smiled. "That will come with time, young Will. It is something all men go through."

Will sighed. "Yea, that is what my Lady Rosamund says."

Tancred could see the busy hand of that very same lady behind Will's struggle to become a troubadour. "How does your father feel about your desire to, uh, sing?" And play the lute, presumably better than he played it now.

"He tells me to listen to Lady Rosamund, my lord. 'Listen to our lady Rosamund.' " Will grinned. "Says it like she walks on water. 'She knows what she is about.' 'Course he would like her. 'Twould be wrong if he did not."

Tancred offered Will another piece of rabbit, along with a hunk of the loaf he discovered in the basket. The lad had devoured his first piece of meat. Kadar helped himself.

"Your father, he admires the lady Rosamund?" the Saracen asked.

"Indeed he does, sir. He was an archer, but he lost his arm. In battle, you understand," Will added quickly, lest there be any question as to his father's courage, apparently. "His lord cast him out. Said he was no good to him anymore. We would have starved were it not for Lady Rosamund. She found a place for him."

Tancred savored the flavor of the bread. The cook and his helpers were very good. "Does your father work here at Wynnsef?"

When Will didn't answer immediately, Tancred looked up. The lad wore an expression of worry.

"Do you think me less beneficent than Lady Rosamund?" Tancred inquired, careful to lay no blame.

"He carves. My father carves. My older brothers build chairs and trunks and cupboards and the like, and Papa makes them . . . grand."

Tancred took a swig of milk from the jug. "Did he make the high seat?" He passed the jug to Will.

"Oh, no, sire. We were not here when that was made. It was created for Lady Rosamund's grandfather, so she told me. Sent all the way from Normandy when her grandfather was made a baron of King Henry."

Kadar nodded. "Lady Rosamund, she comes from a line of nobles, it seems." His mouth curved in a faint smile. "Like you, dread lord."

Tancred stroked the rock crystal jewel set in the pommel of his sword, which lay beside him. His ancestors had been high lords with great lands on this isle ere William of Normandy had been a twinkle in the eye of his low-born mother. Others of them had been—and still were—landed lords in Burgundy. Tancred's father had sundered that long legacy of privilege and power with his treachery. He had willingly consigned his only son to death.

Good King Henry's generosity had stayed the hangman's hand and let the traitor's son live, had even given him into the care of three goodly knights. By God's Grace, one of them had become the loving father Tancred had yearned for.

Eudes de Epernay, Tancred's teacher, companion, and father in all but blood had been slaughtered through the cowardly treachery of another traitor— Arnaud Bourton of Wynnsef. That same treachery had led to Tancred's capture and torture. He had witnessed comrades die in pain, debased by the enemy.

This traitor would pay for more than his disloyalty to the king.

This time, Tancred would have his revenge.

Rosamund sat on a turf seat in the castle's small pleasure garden, the one open to all who dwelled here. The weather was too lovely for anyone to want to stay inside if they could help it. She had spread a cloth on the daisy-dotted lawn to protect the washed and carded wool she spun on a lightweight spindle.

Four knights sat under a nearby apple tree, their masculine voices courteously pitched save for an occasional burst of laughter. Not far from them, two workmen basked in the sunshine, sharing half a loaf of coarse bread, a chunk of cheese, and a skin of ale as they took a respite from their labors.

Her fingers dexterously twisted the wool as she fed it to the whirling drop spindle. Where was Edeva? It was unlike her to make an engagement and not keep it. Abbess Matilda had commandeered Brother Felix and was attending to her correspondence. This would be Rosamund and Edeva's first chance to chat since the arrival of the supplies.

The temptation to meet Edeva in the walled garden had been strong, but only she and her father—oh, and the servant, Bened, who sometimes helped her—had ever been inside. A plaisance, her father had laughingly called it on the day he had unveiled his plans to her. He had intended it as his gift to her on her twelfth birthday but had been so delighted with the idea he had been unable to wait.

A garden, a private place, instead of a husband, he had later told her sadly. With his dear wife gone to God, he could not bear to also lose his beloved daughter. Could Rosamund understand and forgive him? he had asked in that quiet voice that had become his after her mother's death.

So he had commissioned the walls to be built, the iron-studded door, complete with lock, to be hung, and together they had designed and planted most of the garden. They had always shared a love of the land, the joy that came from green things, from planting and tending, then being rewarded with new leaves and, ultimately, with flowers or fruit.

So Rosamund had left the door locked and suggested Edeva meet her in the castle's communal pleasure garden.

A slight figure in white appeared in the arch that marked the opening of the garden. Quickly Edeva surveyed the area. Her face lighted when she saw Rosamund, and Rosamund's heart lifted at that silent, sincere greeting.

As straight as the flight of a bee to nectar, Edeva made a path directly to Rosamund, who swiftly set aside her work and rose to embrace her friend with genuine gladness.

"You look as lovely as ever," Rosamund said as they both sat down on the turf bench. Smiling, she took up her distaff and spindle again. "White must become you."

Edeva laughed, which drew the admiring attention of the men in the garden. Rosamund doubted her friend even noticed.

"I am glad to hear it," Edeva said, "for it will likely be the only color I wear for the rest of my days."

Rosamund once again set the spindle to whirling. "So nothing has changed?"

Edeva helped herself to the spare spindle and a wool-wound distaff from the basket beside Rosamund. "No. I have prayed and waited, and prayed more, but nothing has happened. No inspiration. No revelation. Not even confidence that taking vows as a nun is what I am supposed to do."

It had been convenient for her family to place her in Hembley Abbey, and had accrued points in favor of their entrance into Heaven. Rosamund already knew that not one of Edeva's relations had ever gone to visit her at the Abbey. That seemed wrong to her, even if they had disapproved of Edeva's mother.

"So you still feel that you were not meant to become a nun?" Rosamund asked.

Edeva set her spindle in motion. "I don't want to be a nun. Yet the nuns at the abbey are dear to me. They are my true family."

"Do they desire that you leave the abbey?"

"No. Nor do they try to push me into taking my vows." Edeva smiled. " 'Tis as if they have accepted that I'll never become a nun. But what of you? Will Lord Tancred free you to enter Hembley?"

Rosamund slowly shook her head. "Not yet. He wishes me to keep Wynnsef as ordered as it has always been. He also wishes me to teach him how to keep it that way."

Edeva's sloe eyes widened with surprise. "Indeed?"

"But he will have little time to learn," Rosamund said more optimistically than she felt at that moment. "Arnaud will not give him time."

"Oh? Have you been in communication with your lord brother?"

"No." Rosamund worried her bottom lip.

"I saw no sign of him on our journey here, but then we came from the south, and he would be coming down from the north."

"The messenger I sent would have ridden straight to Arnaud. If he rides hard, he will reach him tomorrow or the next day. Arnaud will push his men as hard as King Henry ever pushed his. My brother will take the Usurper by surprise."

For a long moment, Edeva made no reply. She frowned down at the spindle, yet she appeared not to see it.

"What is wrong, Edeva?" Rosamund asked, her fingers unerringly working the wool into fine thread.

Edeva looked up at her with apology plain on her face. "I dislike telling you this, but I believe you should know. At every inn at which we stopped on our way here, people spoke of how the king told the Moon Lord that if he could take Wynnsef, it would be his."

Rosamund's fingers jerked to a halt. There it was again. It was what she feared most: that Tancred de Vierzon told the truth.

"No," she whispered. "It cannot be." She said it as much to allay her anxiety as to champion Arnaud, but she found no comfort in her words. Staring down at a trampled daisy, she dragged in a long breath and then evenly forced it out.

"Did you, perchance, hear the reason why?" she asked, her gaze still riveted to the crushed flower.

"No one seemed certain, but rumor had it that there was treachery involved."

Rosamund hesitated. "Tancred's?"

Edeva looked down at her hands, now still in her lap. "Arnaud's."

" 'Tis a lie!" Rosamund snapped. "This is Tancred's work. Arnaud has no treachery in him!" He lacked the subtlety required.

"Would you not say that what he has done to you is treachery of a sort?" Edeva said in a low voice. "I do not believe your father intended you to lead the life you do now."

"That is different. Arnaud . . . He has suffered. I have been the cause of much of it. But he would never truly hurt me." She noticed Edeva pointedly looking at the small scar near her mouth and flushed. "A mistake. He was greatly wroth with me. He felt I had failed him."

"Perhaps he felt the king, too, had failed him."

Rosamund looked sharply at her. "Do you truly think that?"

Edeva sighed. "I do not know your lord brother that well."

"Well enough. Do you believe him capable of treachery so foul the king would be moved to award his properties to another?"

"Well . . . perhaps not."

"Nor do I. Mark my words, Tancred is behind this. Somehow he has even managed to win the Earl of Quorley to his side. Now, with the king so occupied, it would be a simple matter to spread lies to back his present actions. You know how people love to gossip, especially when it involves the blackening of a lord's character."

"Yea, that is so."

Yet no matter how badly Rosamund wished to believe in the innocence of her brother, she could not entirely convince herself of Tancred's villainy. Why that was so, she was not sure. After all, the man had slithered into the castle like an adder the night he had taken it. If he had captured Wynnsef as an honest knight would, he would have raised a siege.

He would have used battering rams to destroy the outer curtain gate, mangonels to hurl large stones into the inner bailey, where it would have destroyed buildings and stonework. Men, women, and children would have died. He would have set sappers to undermine the corners of the walls as, above ground, he loaded a trebuchet with the decaying carcass of a cow or horse and then launched it into the inner bailey, where it would have rotted and caused sickness. Flaming arrows would have set the place afire. In the end, the deaths on both sides would have been numerous, and the castle would have been badly damaged. If he had tried to take Wynnsef like an honest knight.

As her brother had gone north to do to a lordless castle.

Instead, Tancred had harmed no one here. He had even given John Willsson and the handful of other men-at-arms who had been left behind by her brother the choice of serving him or leaving unmolested. To a man, they had chosen to serve him.

Of course, she thought spitefully, in these difficult times, serving the Moon Lord was better than serving no master at all . . . and starving.

Rosamund's innate honesty and sense of fairness rushed up to expunge her spite. In truth, John's defection had not surprised her. He was a fighting man born, and she had always sensed his disapproval of Arnaud, who had insisted on paying scutage rather than fighting for his liege lord. Unfortunately, when King Richard had taken the cross, poor crops had left Wynnsef without enough gold to pay the scutage, and Arnaud had, for the first time, been forced to physically fulfill his obligation to his overlord.

Arnaud had never noticed John's reservation toward him, and for that Rosamund was thankful. She had never questioned John's loyalty when it came to preserving her personal safety and the continuity of Wynnsef. Indeed, she did not question his loyalty now. Her brother had shown poor judgment in leaving a jewel such as Wynnsef undermanned. He had, she supposed John believed, deserted the castle and all who depended upon it for their livelihoods and safety.

While the *chansons* might glorify men who died defending the honor of indifferent overlords, John had always been too practical to believe any but a want-wit would surrender his life so pointlessly. Like Abbess Matilda and Rosamund's father, John did not suffer fools gladly.

Rosamund set the spindle back into its whirling motion. Well, she had never heard anyone accuse Tancred of being a fool.

Her greater concern now was how to avoid becoming one herself.

ELEVEN

The great hall was crowded with petitioners and accused, spectators and those come to lend moral support from the castle and its two villages. Many of the castle folk had also come here, unwilling to miss anything out of the ordinary.

The guttural utterances and hammered inflections of English predominated, with the more fluid-sounding words and singsong intonation of Norman French heard here and there throughout the hall, becoming concentrated near the dais. So many voices at once produced a hollow roar in the colorful, towering chamber, occasionally pierced by the high-pitched shriek of a cranky child.

Fleet, Rosamund's favorite wolfhound, sat at her feet, watchful of the crowd. John stood beside her carved seat, which, in turn, was arranged beside the massive chair occupied by Tancred. On his other side stood Kadar, who, perversely Rosamund suspected, wore his spiked turban and the most Saracen-like clothing he could have chosen. His handsome face was impassive as he surveyed the crowd.

He leaned slightly to speak with Tancred, and his words reached Rosamund.

"I like it not, Tancred," he said. "This should have waited until the matter of this castle is settled between you and the Fair One's brother. What if he and his men have come here in disguise?"

"All have been checked for weapons, Kadar. Even the man carrying the disgruntled goose."

Kadar lifted a single elegant eyebrow. "I see my concern amuses you."

"Not at all," Tancred replied. "But I cannot continue to put off the business of Wynnsef. These matters have gone too long unattended."

Two sennights had passed since that night Rosamund had awoken to a gloved hand on her mouth. In that time, she had been kept busy doing the things she had always done in the course of administering Wynnsef.

She tried to avoid Tancred when they were not sharing the high table at meals, but something about him drew her gaze whenever they happened to be within sight of each other. More than once she had turned to find him looking at her, his expression unfathomable. At those times, she felt as if a warm gale had blown through her, crashing against her finely drawn nerves. He would accord her a slight nod, then turn back to his business at hand, leaving her unsettled.

Abbess Matilda had decided to stay at Wynnsef Castle, announcing that it was improper to leave Rosamund in the clutches of an invader, with no female companion of her own rank. Rosamund smiled faintly. A chaperon, she had meant, more for the protection of Rosamund's good name than aught else, since, lately, no man had done more than glance at her. Besides, she had John and Aefre, Fleet, and her own good sense to protect her. Still Abbess Matilda would not be dissuaded. Not that Rosamund had tried very hard. She enjoyed the company of the abbess, the nuns, and, especially, Edeva. All of them now sat on benches that ranged out from each side of the dais. Brother Felix sat at a small table beside Abbess Matilda, armed with quills, pots of ink, and sheets of parchment. On the other side of the abbess sat Father Ivo, who served as priest for both the villages of Attewell and Cloptune, both now represented by plaintiffs and defendants.

Because Rosamund had always served as seneschal *and* judge, Dunton, the butler, had always attended to keeping order among those coming before the judge.

"Give Dunton a nod, so he knows that you are ready to begin the proceedings, my lord," she told Tancred in a voice meant for his ears only.

Tall, lanky Dunton, who was watching for the signal from Rosamund, almost missed it when Tancred gave a slight inclination of his head. Strutting to his place in the vacant area directly in front of the seated nuns, he pounded the stone floor with the elaborate staff Will's father had created just for the purpose. Gradually, the crowd fell quiet.

Dunton unrolled his list. "If it please Your Honor," he declared loudly enough to be heard out in the stables "Lord Tancred, baron of Richard, by the Grace of God king of . . ." He continued on for some time. Then he repeated his speech in the harsher-sounding English.

Rosamund restrained an impulse to roll her eyes over Dunton's absurd pretentiousness. She supposed the man might be forgiven. After all, no lord had presided over the manorial court for the past three years, one of which Rosamund's father had been too ill to attend.

Tancred moved slightly so that his lips were close to her ear. Despite his close morning shave, a faint bluish shadow touched his upper lip, his chin, and angular jaw, a promise of new beard before Vespers. "Does he do this every time?" he murmured.

She tried not to smile, aware that those who saw it might take that as belittling to this important occasion. Turning her head slightly, she met his gaze. The impact of that meeting caused her to draw her breath more sharply. "No." She heard his faint sigh of relief.

Finally, Dunton arrived at the end of his flourishes and went on to state, in French, that Anfeald of Cloptune did claim Gimm the Younger of Cloptune had traded him a goose that did not lay. Again he repeated the information in English.

Clutching the annoyed goose that periodically struggled within his grasp, Anfeald glared at his neighbor, Gimm, who glared back at him.

Tancred regarded the men thoughtfully in the heavy silence of the hall. Someone at the back of the crowd coughed. Gradually, the rustling of shuffling feet grew audible.

"Gimm the Younger," Tancred said in English. "When you traded the goose to Anfeald, were you aware that the goose did not lay eggs?"

Stunned by his fluent use of English, Rosamund stared at Tancred. Most knights she'd met had never bothered to learn the language of the lower orders, and so she had been prepared to translate for him. A lord who knew their language, and deigned to use it, could forge a powerful tie with his people. But most lords still left English to their seneschals. When had Tancred learned it? And why? His ease with it suggested much use.

Gimm tugged on his forelock. "My lord, Gerty is a fine goose. She laid eggs just like the rest o' my geese."

Anfeald's face grew mottled red with indignation.

Tancred looked at Anfeald. "Has the goose laid any eggs since you brought her home?"

"Nay, Lord Tancred, she has not!" Belatedly, he jerked on his forelock. "Not one egg has this creature laid."

"What did you receive in exchange for Gerty?" Tancred inquired of Gimm.

Ah, Rosamund thought. He asked an astute question—one she doubted Lord Trufflenose would have asked—if he ever bothered to attend his manorial court.

"A piglet, my lord."

A fair exchange.

"And are you unwilling to return the piglet to An-feald and receive back your goose?"

Very good.

The Moon Lord's first lesson in the tedious side of lordship, Rosamund thought. He would now discover how dull this life would be compared to the one he was used to. She could just imagine Arnaud sitting here, listening to peasants squabble over a goose. On second thought, she could not. He had attended pre-cisely one manorial court, but he had stalked out of the hall before the first dispute had been settled. Tan-cred displayed amazing patience with these folk to whom a goose and a piglet were vastly important. He seemed willing to listen to and to learn of their mod-est affairs.

"My lord, I had a goose to spare. What I needed was a pig to fatten for my brother's wedding come the autumn."

Tancred's gaze flicked to Rosamund, who barely in-clined her head, signaling that Gimm's brother was indeed intending to wed in the autumn. It did not cease to astonish her that this arrogant warrior not only sought her aid, he actually took it.

"Anfeald, do you keep the goose with others?"

His query puzzled her. Where was he leading?

"I have only the one goose and her mate, my lord. 'Twas my intent to start a small flock of my own from them."

"Ah. Could someone be taking the eggs from your new goose?"

"There are no eggs for anyone to take, my lord. I check the nest every day."

"Are there any who might wish to inflame ill will between you and Gimm?"

An excellent thought!

At this, Gimm and Anfeald looked at each other in question. They shook their heads.

"Very well," Tancred said. "Anfeald, you claim the

goose does not lay eggs. Gimm, you claim that it does. The goose shall remain here for a period of—"

He turned to Rosamund and asked in a low voice, "How long does it take for a goose to lay an egg?"

Rosamund smothered her smile. "Geese and ganders are very particular as to their mates. Unlike most creatures, they will not mate on first acquaintance. They require time to become accustomed to each other. And you may wish to ask Anfeald if his goose is older than his gander. Sometimes they will not mate if that is so."

"Foolish couple," he muttered as he cast her a twinkling glance.

Unbidden, the image of Tancred rising from the bathing tub flooded her mind. The hunger and yearning that had gripped her as they had shared that shameless kiss flashed through her now.

Rosamund blushed.

Tancred raised his voice. "Anfeald, have you ever raised geese?"

She struggled to compose herself.

"Nay, my lord," Anfeald answered.

"Has your good wife?"

"Nay, my lord. We do have chickens and cocks, though."

"Is your gander younger than the goose you got from Gimm?"

His questioned pleased Rosamund. He had taken her advice. Arnaud would never have done that.

"Oh, aye, my lord. Wanted a randy young gander to serve the females," he replied earnestly. There was a spattering of titters throughout the hall.

"I ask that you remember the sensibilities of the ladies present, Anfeald," Tancred said mildly. "Many are unfamiliar with the ways of livestock, and we would not wish to embarrass them, would we?"

"Nay, Lord Tancred. Never."

Rosamund noticed the pink cheeks of the nuns.

"Are you aware," Tancred continued, "that sometimes a goose will not mate if the gander is younger than she?"

Anfeald looked startled. "Eh?"

Gimm turned his head to look at him. "You did not know that?" He snorted in obvious disgust. "You've not the sense God gave a flea. Geese and chickens are different. A body would think you would ask someone about such things before you traded away one o' your pigs."

Anfeald bristled. "They both lay eggs, do they not? At least *most* geese lay eggs."

"Aye, they do!" Gimm returned hotly. "When they are given a proper partner. Not some gosling expected to do a gander's work."

"He's a proper gander!"

Dunton sharply rapped his staff on the floor. "Silence in the court! Do you forget where you are?"

Apparently they had, for the two men promptly ceased arguing and looked chastened.

"Anfeald, you will leave the goose here," Tancred decreed.

Rosamund stiffened. Was he, like so many lords, going to enrich himself by penalizing those who came to him for help?

A Wynnsef man-at-arms promptly stepped forward and took the struggling goose from Anfeald's arms.

"She will be placed in the company of older ganders. If, in the fullness of time, she lays eggs, we shall know what caused the problem."

Still tense, Rosamund waited.

Anfeald appeared a bit paler than he had minutes before. "And if she does not?"

"Then Gimm will take her back, and return the pig to you. In the same condition he received it, is that clear, Gimm? Also, Gimm will give you six fertile goose eggs, to be placed under a sitting hen until they hatch."

Rosamund could have laughed with relief. Tancred

was *not* like so many of the others. He was better, so much better. There was justice in him.

"Aye, my lord," Gimm replied. "But what will happen when Gerty lays? I've lost a day's work because Anfeald here cannot tell the difference between chickens and geese."

The great hall echoed with laughter at that, and Rosamund felt certain that, if the goose laid eggs, Anfeald would hear about this in his village for the rest of his days.

"If Gerty lays eggs," Tancred replied, "then you get the eggs, you keep the pig, and Anfeald will stand on the village green and ask your pardon."

Gimm the Younger grinned. "Aye, lord, that is fitting justice."

The jury agreed, and both men left, apparently satisfied with the arrangement. Rosamund quietly made certain that Anfeald was given a receipt for the goose.

Rosamund regarded Tancred through a veil of lashes. There was certainly more to this man than *chansons de geste* and the favor of the king. "May I inquire where you learned about fertile eggs and laying hens, Lord Tancred?"

He smiled, and something fluttered within her breast.

"Surprised you, did I?" he asked. "My mother's people were Saxon landholders before ever William of Normandy turned his eyes to this isle. They hold some land still, and it was with them that I lived before"—he seemed to reconsider what he had been about to say—"before my sixth summer."

She guessed he had been about say "before my father gave me to the king to hold hostage." Rosamund knew it was the way of the world, but she had always abhorred the taking of a child as a hostage. In Tancred's instance, a child of six years had been held to account for his father's treasonous actions. The boy had known as he'd been given over to the king's custody that he would hang if his rebel father again went against his sovereign. Every soul in England was familiar with the story. Tancred de Vierzon, son of a traitor, had received King Henry's mercy and been given to three bachelor knights of great virtue to foster. The Crown had been rewarded tenfold for that single act of clemency. King Richard, however, was no Henry.

"That would explain where you learned English," she said, "not your knowledge of poultry."

"Ah, but if you had known my grandfather, you would not say that. He believed no sensible man remained ignorant of the ways of his assets."

She chuckled softly. "My father believed that, also." Her father had been an estimable lord, and his people and his lands had prospered. Her smile slowly faded. Tancred and her wise, fair-minded father might have more in common than she cared to believe.

Dunton stalked forward to pound the floor with his staff, and Tancred turned to direct his attention to the next dispute. From the corner of her eye, she studied him. She had never questioned her parents' affection for her. It had always been there, showing itself in a myriad ways. Would Tancred have been the same man he was today if his father had loved him?

Several other cases were presented after that. Tancred listened with patience to the complaints and the defenses—some of which sounded decidedly flimsy to Rosamund. He did not hesitate to consult with her when he needed information. It was amazing how often their minds seemed to run alike. His suggestions were astonishingly just and in the case of the thief, even merciful. The young man would be whipped. By submitting to a public whipping, he was allowed to remain in Attewell to support himself and his elderly grandmother by farming her croft. Usually, punishments doled to repeating thieves were more severe, and included hanging, facial branding, severing a hand, or banishment—the latter being almost always a certain death sentence.

Rosamund could see that the jury—made up of men

from the two villages—were also impressed. It was to them that the final decision fell, and they used as their measurement the "custom of the manor."

For the first time, Rosamund wondered if Wynnsef might fare better under the Moon Lord than it did under the rule of Arnaud.

Immediately, she felt a traitor. Yet, as the day wore on, and Tancred patiently listened to the complaints of peasants and merchants and craftsmen, weighing the evidence presented in each case, she was reminded more of her father's caring supervision than of her brother's indifference. More than once she met John's gaze, and found she was not the only one reminded of better days.

The court adjourned before vespers, its business completed. Some of those who had walked from the villages would stay the night before undertaking the journey home. That meant more to seat and feed. Edeva accompanied Rosamund as she arranged for the changes. Afterward, they took their spinning to a chamber two floors above the great hall where the looms and already dyed yarns were kept. Many a pleasant afternoon had been spent here as women spun and wove. Today they had the room to themselves, this not being the usual time of day for such work. They set their spindles twirling.

"What thought you of Lord Tancred?" Edeva asked. She grinned. "I found him the best seigneur I had ever looked upon."

Rosamund's lips curved in a faint smile. "Yea, he is a comely man."

"He is indeed. Yet so somber. He made a most excellent official."

Rosamund merely nodded, unwilling to speak of the thoughts that plagued her like the tempting promises of the devil.

"Both he and his heathen friend are quiet sorts, are they not? They must be dull fellows indeed."

"No, not dull," Rosamund said, feeling her cheeks

heat. "Besides, how can you think Kadar is dull? He dresses like a foreign prince and has courtly ways."

"Yet he is manly, do you not think so?" Edeva asked. "Good to gaze upon, too. But much too solemn."

"Kadar?" Rosamund asked. "Too solemn? Do we speak of the same man?"

"The heathen is Kadar, is he not?"

"Yea. He is . . ." She tried to recall the trail of names he had given when he had introduced himself to her. "He is Azim Kadar Ben Haroun Marzuq Tamir. I think. And he is not a heathen. He insisted he was not. He said that we believe in the same God." She frowned slightly as her fingers encountered a tiny bit of twig that should have been carded out. "I'm certain, though, it's not as simple as he would have it sound. Otherwise there would be no need for crusades."

Edeva seemed to study her spinning spindle as she fed it with a twisted strand of wool. "A few of the crusaders, who have stopped the night at the abbey's guest house on the way home from the Holy Land, have talked about all the . . . all the blood that has been shed. Christian blood. Spilled by other Christians. Our knights."

Rosamund's eyes grew large. "*Christian* blood? Our knights have killed other Christians? No. They must have been mistaken."

Edeva shook her head. "I don't believe they were. Rosamund, these men were deeply affected by the slaughter they witnessed. Unarmed men, women, and children. Nuns ravished." She shook her head again. " 'Tis too horrible to envision."

"But . . . why? Why was this thing done?" Rosamund asked, unable to believe it could be true.

"They were Christians guided by that patriarch left over from Byzantium. The patriarch is to them what the pope is to us. Some in the West call them heretic Christians, but how is anyone to truly know? We have only the words of men to go by. Perhaps inspired men, but men for all that. And men, I have learned, even sheltered in the abbey as I have been, have their own interests at heart more often than not."

Rosamund was forced to agree. Although she had been shut away in Wynnsef, it seemed their—hers and Edeva's—news of the world, of what was right and wrong, holy and unholy, came from the same source: men. A man in Rome claimed the Christians in the East who looked to the patriarch for guidance were *wrong*. That the patriarch was wrong. Both the patriarch and the Pope claimed to be acting in the interests of God, but Rosamund much doubted God had ever declared it was fitting to murder men, women, and children who honored him and who devoutly tried to observe what they believed were his wishes.

"I keep thinking," Edeva said. "What if knights from *there* came on crusade *here*. Would they claim we at Hembley Abbey were heretics? Would they dishonor us, murder us, as those poor sisters were in the Holy Land? As if we had not lived our lives to serve God? Surely, it is the same God we all pray to."

"That will never happen, Edeva." But then, had those unfortunates in the Holy Land expected to be slaughtered by Christian knights from Austria, France, England, or Denmark? Had those people in that far-off land even heard of those kingdoms?

"Why?" Edeva asked. "Because God is with *our* knights only?"

So Rome would have them all believe, Rosamund thought, uncomfortable with the doubts this conversation inspired. Life was easier to face when one thought one knew the rules, and, that if one followed them, one would be safe. But there were too many examples that conflicted with such a simple belief. Not even the powerful were safe.

"I do not truly know why. Mayhap because they already have the Holy Land. Or they are not so brave. So well equipped. Or so arrogant."

"Or because we do not have something they want," Edeva said wryly.

"Yea. Always that."

They spun in silence for a while, each sunk in her own thoughts.

Lady, these people do not know how harsh the world can be.

Whatever Tancred had experienced during his time in the Holy Land, it had been terrible. It had scarred his flesh and his soul.

Perhaps she was being naive, Rosamund thought, but, as maddening as that man could be—and often was—she could not imagine him committing the foul deeds of which the knights who had stayed at the abbey's guest house had spoken.

But then, what did she really know about Tancred?

The lofty, isolated moon shone like ancient silver in the dark sky as Rosamund inserted her key into the well-oiled lock. On noiseless hinges, the door swung open at her touch. She exhaled before she stepped across the threshold, into another world. Quietly she closed the door of the walled garden behind her and locked it. Then she inhaled deeply, drawing in air fertile with the smell of moist earth, with the sharp, green scent of burgeoning, rain-washed plants.

With one hand she held the lighted candle, with the other she pulled off her shoes and stockings. She closed her eyes as she curled her toes into grass affluent with tiny daisies, wetting her feet, luxuriating in the fresh tickle. Of their own accord, her lips curved upward in contentment.

She cocked her head, listening. Here there was only the sweet, pure sound of trickling water from the fount. Somehow, that soft music kept out the distant, occasional sound of male voices from the gatehouse or wall walk that she had heard on the way from her bedchamber, leaving this place untouched by the outer world.

This garden was her place. Hers alone. Here, no demands were placed on her, no criticisms voiced against her. Here she found only welcome. Serenity. Peace.

Of late, she had been given little opportunity to come to her garden. No time at all during the day, when she might enjoy the color of each growing thing. Still, the night lent a mystical, faerie-realm quality to this private place.

Slowly, she walked along the wall, lighting the torches set in blackened iron brackets with her taper, waiting and watching at each until flame took hold on resinous wood. After that was done, she went to the fount, where she set her candle in one of the stone notches that ringed the top, just below the carved stone rosebud from which the water flowed.

Golden light and charcoal shadows filled the garden, bringing it to life as the flames danced. Rosamund laughed softly, feeling young and unfettered for the first time in a very long time. Abandoning the dignity expected of a lady of her considerable years, she began to sway with the shifting shadows, imagining a tribe of carefree faeries frolicking among the Madonna Lilies and up in the blossom-laden fruit trees.

Laughter bubbled up from her throat as she flung out her arms and began to twirl. Round and round she went, her bare feet skimming over the lawn, delighting in the cool air streaming against her bare forearms. Sweet Mary, it felt good to forget her worries, her responsibilities, and simply enjoy the peace and quiet of this place. Here no one could ask her what was to be done next, or what *she* intended to do. Here the sickening twist in her stomach over when Arnaud would come, and what he would do when he arrived, eased. Within these walls she could escape the unsettling presence of the Moon Lord. Escape from the way her body warmed and hummed when he came close. From the way her breath came more rapidly under his compelling silver gaze.

Rosamund stopped twirling, dizzy, gasping for air. She would *not* think of Tancred. She would not allow him to disturb her peace of mind, as short-lived as it might be.

She walked to the entrance of the tunnel arbor. Moonlight spangled the stygian interior, forming glowing shafts through the gaps in the grapevines where tender leaves had not yet fully opened. For a moment she hesitated, then turned aside, unwilling to sit by herself in the gloom. It was enough that she lay alone, awake long into the night, every night, since Tancred had slipped into her bed chamber to clasp his hand over her mouth and whisper in her ear his demand for her surrender.

Lifting the skirts of her kirtle and tunic to her knees, she felt the chill of a spring evening on her bare flesh. With long-legged strides, she returned to the fountain, where she scooped up glistening handfuls of liquid crystal, droplets trembling on her wrists, turned magically into jewels by the candle's light. She splashed her face with the icy water, gasping and laughing at her own foolishness, reveling in sensation and the freedom to enjoy it. The water flowed sweetly across her tongue.

Something glinted in one of the fount's upper stone catches, which remained perpetually filled with trickling water, creating a small waterfall into a lower, slightly larger basin. Licking the water from her lips, Rosamund leaned closer, curious to find what sparkled under the shallow water.

It lay at the bottom of the little basin. Frowning, she dipped her fingers into the catch to fish out the object. Lifting it from the water, she held it to the light.

There on her palm lay a silver disk.

In its center gleamed a single, cabochon moonstone.

Tancred stood alone on the dark wall walk, listening to her delighted, throaty laughter. He ached to hold her in his arms, to press his mouth to her creamy throat, to her slender shoulder, to feel her stir against his body as her passion awakened.

Jesú, to be wanted by this innocent, spirited woman would be as much as a man could ever crave.

But she was not for him. She was destined to pass into the stone embrace of a convent, living a life of prayer and devotion. Unsullied. Pure.

No, she was not for him, not for one who was . . . unclean.

Yet he would not part with her. Not until she had taught him what he must know to rule Wynnsef with a wise hand. And until he killed her whoreson brother.

He watched as the light inside the garden diminished, as if torches were being swiftly snuffed. He flinched inwardly as he heard the door slam.

Still he kept the bobbing candle flame in sight until it had safely passed into the old keep. Then Tancred turned and gazed northward. He set clenched fists on the stone merlon.

Please God, let Arnaud come soon.

TWELVE

As Abbess Matilda, the nuns, and Edeva filed into the chapel to hear Mass early the following morning, they seemed to scoop Rosamund up with them, so that she stood with them during the service, separated from Tancred and his men by a row of knights and a row of shorter, muscular nuns. Not that she would have seen him, anyway, since he was behind her.

The silver disk set with the glowing moonstone lay in her locked casket by her bed. More than once, last night, she had opened the lid of the vine-and-leaf-scrolled box Arnaud had brought her from the Holy Land to look at it. Her temper had roiled, making sleep impossible until the moon hovered over the horizon. Now she struggled to stay awake as Brother Felix droned on in Latin. Her knowledge of that language didn't prevent her from drowsing when his voice took on that singsong quality that had the power to lull one's senses when one was shy so many hours of sleep.

Edeva nudged her in the ribs once, and directed a significant glance in the direction of the abbess. After that, Rosamund managed to keep her eyes open.

Afterward, as they all broke their fast in the great hall, she took her place at the high table with Tancred and the abbess, giving Tancred only the chilliest of courtesies, which he seemed not to notice, much to her annoyance. He appeared to be wrapped up in his own thoughts.

Likely planning another invasion of her garden, she thought darkly. It was too much to hope for that he might be planning the invasion of someone else's castle.

A man-at-arms strode into the great hall and presented himself before Tancred. "My lord, the Swede has arrived."

"The Swede has a name, Henry."

Henry grinned. "Yea, Lord Tancred, but he laughed and said to tell you that 'the Swede is here.' "

Tancred smiled for what seemed the first time that day. "He will never allow me to forget that I could not remember his name when I most needed to. Tell Sigurd Lukasson that I will be there directly. Notify the marshal those extra horses have arrived."

Henry bowed to his lord, then spun on his heel and made for the door, wasting no time to carry out his orders. With a quirk of his finger, Tancred summoned Piers. The small page hurried across the chamber, skipping a few steps until he remembered his dignity and that of the lord he served.

Tancred bent in his chair to keep the child from having to crane his neck to see Tancred's face. The man spoke softly, quickly, and the boy nodded.

"Yea, my lord!" he finally said, then flew out of the great hall, in the direction of the kitchens.

Rosamund watched it all with growing alarm. Who was Sigurd Lukasson? What were the horses for? But Tancred made not attempt to satisfy her curiosity. She cast a glance at Abbess Matilda, who lifted her eyebrows to indicate that it was also a mystery to her.

After politely excusing himself to the abbess and Rosamund, in a tone that gave them no choice, he left the hall. Worried over anything that even faintly resembled reinforcements, Rosamund cast aside decorum and hurried after him.

"Who is this Swedish person?" she asked when she caught up to Tancred outside the new keep.

"A fellow prisoner at Bâb Al-Muhunnad," he replied absently, his gaze focused on the main gate, still securely closed. His long legs ate the distance so quickly, she had difficulty keeping up with him.

"What horses?" she demanded.

"Return to the abbess, where you belong, damoiselle. I have matters to attend that are no concern of yours."

"They *are* my affair," she insisted. "This castle is—"

"Mine." Tancred halted abruptly, and she nearly ran into him. His silver gray eyes blazed. "This castle is mine now, lady. Not yours. Not your precious brother's. *Mine.* You fear that I am bringing in reinforcements. Then worry all you wish, for they are here, and there are more on the way."

She felt the blood drain from her face.

"Go back and finish your meal," he said gently.

"These—these reinforcements of yours had better hurry, because my brother is on his way here," she told him. Bravado, sheer bravado, but she knew not what else to say, and she wanted badly to shake that infuriating self-contained stillness about him that seemed to spit in the eye of all the doubts that haunted her.

"Your brother does not even know I am here."

"He does by now!" Surely the messenger would have reached him by now.

The soft morning breeze lifted a raven lock of his hair. "No, lady. He does not."

Rosamund felt as if she had fallen into a world where everything moved abnormally slow, including her thoughts. "But you said—"

"I said Lady Helvise of Cheyham had made it to her home safely. And she did. Her father offered her to me for my bride when he learned I had taken Wynnsef."

How vastly practical was Helvise's father, Rosa-

mund thought dully as she remembered her fosterling
had ridden in a different direction than the messenger.

"What did you do to him?" she asked.

"Why, I turned him down, of course. She would
have to be a greater heiress than she is for me to take
to wife a timid child." His lashes lowered, concealing
his eyes. "Fit meat for your brother, apparently."

"Not the Lord of Cheyham. My messenger. What
did you do with my messenger?"

As if to allow privacy, Tancred looked away. "I fear
he is dead, Lady Rosamund. He refused to stop when
my men hailed him. He was your loyal man to the
end."

For a moment, the world spun around her and
began to fade into white. She gasped for air, afraid
she might faint, desperate not to show such weakness
before the Moon Lord and his men. She felt his warm
grasp on her elbow.

"Unhand me," she ordered, but her voice wavered.

His hand remained where it was. "You did what
you had to do, lady. The castle was about to be
attacked."

"I've never . . ." Her throat clogged with remorse.
"I've never sent anyone to his death before." She
began to shake. "Dear God . . ."

Tancred gently enfolded her in his embrace, an embrace that offered warmth and comfort and an understanding solace. "He had a choice, *ma églatine*. He
chose to try to get through. A good man, loyal to you.
Likely he believed my men were with Fitz Clare and
sought to trick him. But perhaps it did not matter to
him who my men were with if they were not with you
or your brother. He died swiftly, and he died honor-
ably. That is as much as any man can ask."

Her throat tightened, clogged with tears. "He . . .
he could have died in bed. An old man. Surrounded
by m—many grandchildren." She swallowed hard,
then drew a ragged breath.

"Ah, *ma églatine*," Tancred said softly, "he was

dressed as a man-at-arms. If he had planned to die of old age, he would have been a merchant." His strong, broad palm smoothed up and down her back, consoling, soothing.

He was trying to cheer her. But she knew, as he did, that few had the luxury of choosing what they would be. For most that was settled by dire necessity. For others by family. And some few, such as Tancred de Vierzon, by destiny.

She pressed her palms against his chest, and he promptly released her. He studied her for an instant, his expression one of concern. Then the shutters closed, leaving his dark-angel's face unreadable.

Tancred signaled a young man-at-arms, who came trotting across the courtyard to them. "Ranulf, see the lady Rosamund to her chamber. She is feeling unwell. Inform Abbess Matilda."

"Yea, my lord."

"No, wait," she objected, "I am well."

But Tancred was already gone, on his way to welcome his reinforcements.

"Come, Lady Rosamund," the young man said, coaxingly. "Please allow me to see you to your chamber."

She didn't want to go to her chamber. She wanted to see how many made up this first group of reinforcements and to try to determine how well they were equipped. Rosamund managed to take precisely two steps before the young man-at-arms barred her way.

"My Lord Tancred gave me an order, Lady Rosamund. I have no choice but to obey."

She drew herself up and gathered her most imperious air about her. "How old are you, boy?"

He laughed. "Nineteen years, lady, and I'll wager I'm older than you."

"Oh, very well," she said with a decided show of ill grace. "Escort me to my chamber if you must."

As she stalked toward the old keep with the man-at-arms at her heels, she heard masculine shouts and laughter. Chains rattled as the portcullis was raised.

Tancred finally found Kadar in the bathing chamber. Feminine giggles from within the pavilion warned him that Kadar was not alone.

"Is this a bad time for you to receive visitors, Kadar?" he called.

He heard Kadar's low voice and then bursts of more giggling, from two separate sources.

"Come in, Tancred, come in. I am enjoying the hospitality of your new home."

Tancred ducked his head as he entered the tent. Steam engulfed him.

Kadar lounged in the bathing tub, attended by two pretty, young servants, who crowded slightly closer to him as Tancred approached.

On the tunic of one, directly on the curve of a full breast, was a wet mark in the shape of a large hand. Both of the girls possessed lips that were rosy and slightly swollen from kissing.

Kadar followed Tancred's glance and then smiled.

"Do your husbands know that you are here?" Tancred asked the girls.

Three pairs of eyes widened.

"You did not mention husbands, my sweet little strawberries," Kadar told his companions in mild reproach.

"We have no husbands, my lord," one strawberry replied.

"Not till we prove we can breed," said the other. "And our men have been trying and trying, but so far . . . nothing."

Kadar looked up at them in surprise. "Was I to be put to stud?"

The girls blushed and giggled.

"It seems you have your answer." Tancred smothered a smile. "I would remind you of the promise I made to Lady Rosamund. You have not lured . . .

uh . . ." He lifted his eyebrows, silently requesting their names.

"Daisy," one said promptly.

"Cwen," offered the other.

Kadar sighed. "I could have told you that, O Assassin of Delight. And I have not made false promises. Indeed, I have made no promises at all."

"Please, my lord," Daisy said to Tancred, "do not blame him. Cwen and me lured Lord Kadar here. Promised to bathe him right good, we did. Well, ye see we had to do something to get him alone, when we couldn't get him tipsylike. Even brewed him our special ale."

Cwen nodded her agreement. "But he wouldn't drink it. His Allah won't let 'im."

Kadar rolled his eyes at the mangled interpretation.

Tancred almost laughed. Clearly, Cwen and Daisy weren't interested in Kadar's religious abstinence from alcohol other than it had required a change in their plans.

"So we planned to ply him with fresh mare's milk and . . . well . . ." Daisy had the grace to blush.

"Ply him with us, also," Cwen finished in an embarrassed rush. "He's so sweet-natured, is Lord Kadar. And real good to look at."

Sweet-natured? Kadar? Tancred smothered a grin.

Daisy traced a half-circle on the stone floor with one bare toe. "We thought he might . . . oblige us."

"Give us babes as pretty as he is," Cwen said with a shy glance at Kadar.

Tancred thought it wise not to point out to the two blondes that their pretty babes might possess swarthy coloring. At this rate, likely more than two babes born on his estates in the coming years would possess such complexions. Kadar always honored his bed partners and took responsibility for the support of his progeny. Fortunately, he possessed great wealth.

"Kadar, I see you are otherwise occupied," he said

with a short, crisp bow each to Daisy and Cwen. "Ladies."

He hadn't taken two steps toward the tent flap before Kadar spoke up. "If you took the trouble to find me, Lord Tancred, your business with me must be *extremely* urgent. I would be remiss in seeking my own pleasure before . . . er . . . before—"

Smoothly, Tancred picked up on Kadar's veiled plea for help. "Yea, I do have urgent business to discuss, but I was bedazzled by your beauteous companions."

Looking apologetic, Kadar turned in the tub. He took the hand of each of girls. "Vital affairs demand I part from you now, my little strawberries, but your confidence in my, uh . . . in my charms, it has given me great joy." He kissed their hands.

Trying not to look disappointed, Daisy and Cwen left.

Waiting to hear the outer door open, then close behind them, Tancred sauntered over to the small table that, for him, had always contained a flagon of wine and a goblet. Now there was a pottery jug and a drinking horn filled with milk. Kadar waved his hand, offering Tancred the filled cup. Tancred murmured his polite refusal.

The outer door closed.

"I do not understand, Kadar. Few men are fortunate enough to be wooed by two nubile females with tupping on their minds. Why did you send them away?"

Kadar drank down the horn of milk. "I am a fool. A *fool*." He replaced the cup on the table with a thump, then stood.

Tancred handed him a drying cloth. "Some might say so."

Kadar wrapped the cloth around his hips. "Ordinarily, I would have welcomed two such bright-eyed little partridges." He stepped out of the large tub and headed to the benches where his clothing lay, in front of the stoked fire.

"Then why?"

"Ayee*ah*!" Kadar raked his fingers through his dripping hair in evident frustration. "It is maddening, this this *indifference* I feel. It must surely be a terrible sickness."

"Surely," Tancred agreed gravely, trying not to smile.

"They came to me, Tancred, I would not dishonor your pledge to the Flower of Wynnsef."

"I have their own testimony on it."

Kadar stared into the fire for a long moment, running the fingertips of one hand over his short, neatly trimmed beard.

Tancred sobered. "Have you been thinking of that little novice, Edeva?"

"Yea." Kadar's voice was barely audible. "Yea, she haunts my thoughts. I find I am always . . . wondering about her. She has such quiet ways, yet she is filled with such life." He shook his head. When he spoke, his voice was nonchalant. "It will pass, this interest in her. I am only curious, that is all."

"Certainly."

"Still," Kadar pronounced, whirling to face Tancred, "she is different from those other, hulking females, you must admit that is so."

Tancred nodded sagely. "It is so."

"And she is lovely, fragile—"

"Dark, sloe-eyed—"

"Yea! Her eyes, they are like the soft eyes of a doe. And her lips"—he seemed to recall he was discussing a prospective nun—"are quite adequate." Quickly, he proceeded to don his clothes. "With them, she will doubtless say her prayers often."

Tancred studied Kadar, who was his brother in all but blood. Together, in countless battles, they had fought back-to-back, their trust in each other a third shield in their defense. Aside from Kadar's own people, Tancred's foes had been accepted by Kadar as his own foes, by choice. By honor.

Had it not been for that same stiff-necked honor, Kadar would have remained in his own land, a lord of importance, eventually surrounded by sloe-eyed, adoring wives and many handsome, spoiled children. Instead, he had come out of his sun-drenched land with Tancred. He had lived amongst Tancred's men as one of them, accepted by them, yet apart. Separated by a faith that he observed alone and with an unspoken determination made elegant by its very purity, he had not tried to bridge the distance, accepting it as the price of living among barbarians. Often likeable, earnest, and honest, but barbarians all the same.

And now Kadar had become infatuated with a Christian novice.

At least, Tancred devoutly hoped what Kadar felt was only infatuation. That it would soon fade from his mind . . . and leave his heart untouched.

"But you did not come into this great dark cavern to hear about nuns," Kadar said as he pulled on his soft leather boots. He stood, the cloth he would have used for his turban in one hand, his black hair still wet. "So. I await to gather the pearls of wisdom as they fall from your lips." He grinned. "Has young Will driven you into hiding again with his adulation?"

Tancred turned and led them toward the stairs. "No, but he is one of the things I would speak of."

"Indeed?"

"Yea, Kadar. I know you have noticed he is somewhat lacking in his skill with the lute—"

Kadar halted abruptly. "No."

Tancred had expected some resistance. "I would not ask you to help him, save you are the only one I know who is exceptionally skilled on the lute."

" 'Tis a woman's instrument. I should never have learned to play the cursed thing. No."

"It is not considered a woman's instrument *here*," Tancred reasoned. "It is considered a sign of accomplishment for a knight to also be able to compose and play the lute. Why, the finest *chansons de geste* have been written by men."

Kadar folded his arms across his chest. "Should that comfort me? *Here*, few men bathe regularly."

Tancred rested his hand on Kadar's shoulder. "He is but a lad, Kadar, one Fate has cheated. You know as I do that he has not the choices other boys have. Likely, he would have preferred to be a knight, but what he *can* be is a troubadour. And with your help and the fullness of time, he can be an exceptional troubadour, sought after, one who will bring distinction to any hall he enters."

Kadar glowered down at Tancred's hand. Tancred, knowing his friend well, did not move it.

"You are evil, Tancred de Vierzon," Kadar finally grumbled, and Tancred knew that he had won a fine instructor for Will.

"Perhaps," he said with a smile. "But Will is not. Admit it: You like him, too."

"Well enough." Kadar fixed Tancred with a narrowed look. "But if those hyenas, Bernard or Osbert, so much as chuckle over this, you will have to replace the lute I break over their hard heads."

"You would damage your lute?" The lute was of Persian make, given him by his favorite uncle upon parting. Knowing how Kadar prized the instrument, the threat surprised Tancred.

"Never," Kadar said. "I would use that clumsy box of Will's."

They walked up the narrow stairs toward the outside door.

"Never let Will hear you say that. His father made that lute for him."

They emerged into the sunlight of afternoon. The air was filled with the clanging of metal being worked on an anvil in the blacksmith's shop, of wood being sawed, of mens' voices as stones for the mangonels were unloaded from a wagon. Somewhere, a child laughed. The smells of goats and horses, of sawdust and churned earth, of dung and sweat struck Tancred's nostrils. But through it all, like a quiet song in a hall of revelers, the sweet fragrance of flowers reached him. Curious, he looked around and found a trough filled with pea plants loaded with blossoms. As he savored that scent, an image bloomed in his mind, an image with hair the color of gold and eyes the exact shade of a summer sky. An image with the face of an angel and the spirit of a falcon.

"What is it, O Patron of Music?" Kadar asked.

"Hmm?" Tancred shook his head to clear it. "What did you say?"

Kadar shrewdly eyed Tancred, then the trough of flowering peas. "Your thoughts were on the Fair One again."

Tancred scowled. "What do you mean 'again'? I smelled the sweetness of those flowers, that is all."

"And thought of her."

Tancred struck off toward the stables. "She is the only one who would stick plants all over a castle. What foolishness in a military garrison. All those troughs and barrels—they get in the way."

Kadar easily kept apace. "Then have them removed."

Tancred's scowl grew fiercer. "I have not the time."

"Then I will give the order for you."

Black lashes lowered slightly. "No." The sound was softly explosive, dangerously quiet.

Laughing, Kadar threw up his hands as if in surrender. "They are safe from me, those plants so much in the way."

Warmth crept up Tancred's neck. He stalked into the stables thinking he should have chosen an estate from Richard's list when he'd had the chance. None of them would have brought him the trouble that came along with Wynnsef and its green witch.

But he'd wanted to inflict as much pain on the traitor as he could think of, and what better way to do it than to take all that he owned? His home, his wealth and, finally, his worthless life.

What Tancred hadn't anticipated was his sister. It ought to have been easy to despise her as much as her brother. Two treacherous snakes from the same nest. It had been inconvenient to learn, even before his return to England, that the sire and dam of that nest were good and loyal souls. Now it appeared that Arnaud must be a changeling, for even his sister—a *female*, by the Cross—was made of worthier stuff.

As Tancred went to Vandal's box, where the stallion lifted his head in greeting, something inside him went still and sick as he thought of Rosamund's unflagging loyalty to the only family she had left. She either did not know, or did not believe, her brother's treachery had been responsible for the deaths of forty-seven of his fellow crusaders, and the imprisonment, and subsequent torture, of another thirty-one. Either way, she would soon be deprived of the last of her family.

Tancred set his jaw. It would give her another soul to pray for when she entombed herself in Hembley Abbey with the rest of the nuns.

As he fished a dried crab apple from the soft leather pouch that hung from his belt, Kadar came to stand beside him.

"Tell her," he said softly. "Tell her how you feel about her."

Tancred remembered the sound of the garden door slamming closed. "Her future is settled, Kadar. So is mine. There is naught to discuss."

"Perhaps she would not wish to become a nun if she knew—"

"Kadar." The word was a growl of warning.

Kadar's dark eyes flicked a glance at him, then returned to Vandal. "Fool," he said gently.

As he offered his war horse the apple on the flat of his palm, Tancred thought his friend might be wise, but he, Tancred, was right in refusing to turn the thoughts of a woman set on dedicating her life to God. "Besides," he murmured, "she would not want me after I killed her brother."

"Her brother treats her like a slave," Kadar replied indignantly.

Tancred looked at him. "He is her only family. You do not know what it is to have no family."

Kadar's expression softened. "Yea, Allah has blessed me indeed."

They stood in silence for a while, their gazes on Vandal, their thoughts elsewhere.

Finally, Tancred dragged in a long breath and exhaled it sharply. "Another reason I sought you out was to tell you that word arrived from one of my informers. Arnaud has learned that I've taken Wynnsef. He and his men have stopped their siege of that northern castle. They are on their way here."

THIRTEEN

As the magical glow of early twilight brushed Wynnsef with gold, Rosamund sat on the edge of her
bed and stared at the silver disk she cradled in her
hands. As if drawn by a spell, her thumb smoothed
over the polished moonstone set in the precise middle
of the disk. The stone was perfect, though smaller than
those set in Tancred's wide silver cuffs.

She had meant to cast it with contempt onto his
trencher this morn. Or better yet, throw it at him—
though she knew she would not dare. Oh, the words
she had practiced last night had been scathing. How
dare he invade her private garden!

Gradually, her shock and wrath had burned down,
allowing room for reality. Wynnsef was Tancred's
now . . . until her brother arrived to take it from
him. Therefore, the garden was no longer *her* private
garden—it was Tancred's. Yet he had not removed
the door as she had feared he might after she'd told
him that the key was lost. Indeed, but for this disk,
she would not have known anyone else had entered
her garden.

He must have gone over the wall. Once inside, he
had left this, his badge, to tell her that he had been
there. That she could not keep him out.

Yet he had not barred her from the garden and the
delight it brought her.

She did not doubt that Tancred could have the key

from her if he desired. He had found the journal, had he not? The corners of her mouth lifted and fell. What was a key to a man who conquered castles without a siege?

Rosamund regarded the smooth silver disk in her hand. It warmed to her touch. Its austere beauty made it a pleasure to gaze upon.

She had said nothing of the garden.

Rosamund stroked the moonstone. Then, she placed it back in her casket. locking it away.

The next day, Tancred's second group of knights—like the first, comrades from the Holy Land, various Continental battles and tourneys and those who wished to enter the service of the legendary Moon Lord—arrived. On foot, behind them, marched men-at-arms. There were many rough embraces, much shoulder-slapping and masculine laughter. The horses that were led off to the stables seemed to form a dark and dappled river from where Rosamund, Edeva, and Abbess Matilda watched at the spinning room window. That vantage point gave them a clear view of all that went on in this corner of the inner bailey.

"I should call you away from this window," the abbess grumbled. She moved up onto her tiptoes for a better view. "This gaping out of windows in full sight of so many men is most unseemly."

"So very many," Edeva mused, but Rosamund noticed that her gaze followed only one man—the dark and brilliantly clad Kadar.

"How do they compare to your lord brother's host?" Abbess Matilda asked Rosamund.

Swiftly Rosamund estimated how many fighting men now garrisoned Wynnsef. "There are not so many here as left with Arnaud, but he may have lost some men if he laid siege to that castle."

"Lord Arnaud is a fool," Abbess Matilda said, curtly frowning down at the courtyard filled with armed men.

Edeva patted Rosamund's hand, out of sight of the abbess. "Perhaps Lord Arnaud did not expect he would be the target of someone's dislike."

"From what the Earl of Quorley told me," the abbess said, "he should have."

A stone sank in the pit of Rosamund's stomach. The Earl of Quorley was known far and wide for his honesty. In spite of that, she said with quiet firmness, "I will ask you to remember that it is my brother of whom you speak, my lady."

While the abbess did not apologize, she said no more about Arnaud as the three of them watched the activities in the inner bailey. A shout from the gate sentry caught their attention.

"What did he say?" Abbess Matilda asked impatiently. "Really, one would think it would be necessary to learn to shout clearly if one were a sentry."

"Something about 'approaches,'" Edeva murmured.

Rosamund leaned farther forward, every muscle in her body tense. Who? *Who* approached? Had Arnaud somehow gotten word of what had passed at Wynnsef?

She watched as the tall, somberly attired figure of Tancred separated from the sea of men clustered in the courtyard and jogged up the stone steps to the wall walk. He strode toward the gate, but she could not see where he stopped; the upper gate house stood in her way.

"I cannot stand not knowing," she said. "I am going to find out." She edged her way from between Edeva and the Abbess Matilda before they had time to move aside.

"Do not go out there!" Abbess Matilda ordered. "Not without me." She hurried after Rosamund

Edeva hastened to catch up with them. "Wait for me!"

As they hurried down the spiral stairs into the great hall, they were met by a breathless Piers.

"My lady," he gasped, "my lord Tancred says that

Lord Godfrey waits outside the gates. My lord thought perhaps you might wish to join him anon in the great hall." The boy dimpled. "He said to look your best and to bring my lady abbess with you. He asks that you join him on the dais when you are ready. My lady," he added in a rush, "he intends that you enjoy your triumph over Lord Trufflenose!" Piers dimpled. "Lord Tancred laughed when I told him what you and Lady Helvise did call Lord Godfrey."

"Piers, please tell Lord Tancred I"—she glanced at the abbess, who nodded—"that is, the lady abbess and I will be pleased to join him on the dais."

"Yea, my lady." Piers dashed away to deliver her answer to his adored master.

"I must change my garments, see to my hair," Rosamund said, feeling suddenly flustered, determined to look as triumphant as she could, considering her present situation.

"I'll find Aefre," Edeva volunteered.

Rosamund flew through the passageways that led outside to the kitchens, Abbess Matilda as hot on her heels as she might and yet maintain her dignity. Staying out of sight of the main courtyard, they darted into the old keep and straight up the stairs. They had been in her chamber only minutes when Edeva and Aefre arrived.

"So," Aefre said, whipping off Rosamund's embroidered linen fillet. "You will have the satisfaction of staring old Trufflenose in the eye and smiling at his loss. I doubt he'll try his tricks with Lord Tancred in charge." The veil and wimple quickly followed the way of the fillet.

"He didn't try them when Arnaud was here, either," Rosamund told her testily as Aefre quickly brushed out the hip-long drapery of golden blond hair.

"Such lovely hair," Abbess Matilda said. "So very gold."

"Is it not?" Aefre said, ignoring the silent place of a serving maid. "Never been cut."

Off came Rosamund's everyday tunic and kirtle, on went a fresh damask tunic of mulberry, a sendal kirtle of pale blue, and a white silk wimple and veil, and a circlet of gold links studded with amethysts. With a hug to Aefre, Rosamund strode out the door, accompanied by Abbess Matilda and Edeva.

The great hall was filled with Tancred's knights in mail, with their shields and swords, his men-at-arms in their leather gambesons bossed with metal disks, also wearing swords at their hips. Osbert, Bernard, and Kadar had positioned themselves next to the dais beside Tancred, and next to the good sisters, who had apparently insisted on being present.

With imperial dignity, the three women walked up the center of the great hall. Edeva went to stand beside Kadar, who glanced down at her without a change in his impassive expression. Rosamund followed Abbess Matilda onto the dais, where Tancred rose from his carved seat. The abbess sat to his right and Rosamund to his left.

Tall, broad-shouldered with a supple grace and a blatantly virile presence, Tancred was the essence of a powerful lord. His raven hair gleamed in the sunlight filtering through the horn panes in the high windows. His silver eyes seemed to miss nothing that passed within the hall. Attired in a tunic of dark blue, a black surcoat edged with ermine, and his soft black boots, he settled back into his great chair. His arms rested on the carved griffins that formed the rests. Each of his strong wrists bore its customary silver cuff set with four polished moonstones.

Suddenly the murmurous din in the hall escalated, then fell away to silence. Lord Godfrey, flanked by two of his knights, strode into the great hall, and then down the aisle in the center cleared by the crowd.

Short and stocky, with a thick layer of fat accrued through years and prosperity, Godfrey Fitz Clare, with his unfortunate porcine nose, resembled nothing so

much as an ill-tempered boar dressed in a green tunic
and a scarlet surcoat. A sword hung at his hip.

He stopped at the foot of the dais, apparently surprised to see that there was no vacant seat ready to
receive him. He tried to make the best of his cool
reception by smiling broadly.

"I give you greetings, Lord Tancred."

Tancred's eyelids half lowered in an air of idleness
that would have fooled anyone unfamiliar with him.
"To what do we owe the . . . pleasure . . . of this
visit?"

Fitz Clare's gaze raked hungrily over Rosamund,
which made her want to plunge into a tub of hot water
and scrub her skin with soap. Instead, she lifted her
chin slightly and regarded him down her nose. Finding
no welcome from her, he nodded respectfully to the
abbess, then looked at Tancred.

"I heard one of King Richard's champions had
gained Wynnsef and thought to make a neighborly
visit," he replied.

"Indeed?" Tancred drawled. "I could not help but
notice that you brought a somewhat smaller escort for
this neighborly visit than for the one you intended to
pay Lady Rosamund last time you passed this way."

Fitz Clare smiled. "Bourton does not appreciate
what he holds." His gaze moved around the richly
appointed great hall, sliding over Rosamund with an
avidity that set her stomach rolling before returning
to Tancred. "I would."

Tancred smiled back at him, and only a lunatic
would not have perceived the deadly danger there.
"Perhaps Bourton did not sufficiently appreciate his
possessions. But those possessions are mine now." His
smile deepened fractionally, growing even more lethal.
"And I do."

Staring at Tancred, like a mouse fascinated by a
viper, Fitz Clare lost some of his color. Nervously, he
licked his full, red lips. "W—well of course you do.
Fair, green Wynnsef would be a trophy for any man."

Tancred made no reply.

"What . . . " Fitz Clare cleared his throat. "What of Lady Rosamund?"

"What of her?"

"Is she"—his right hand came to rest on the pommel of his sword—"is she one of those possessions?"

It took great effort for Rosamund not to react to the offensive question, nor to send a questioning look in Tancred's direction. Truth must be faced. She was a woman. More than that, she was—or rightly should be—a woman of property. That meant she was almost certainly *someone's* chattel. A father's. A husband's. The king's. What was hers, essentially, was his, or at least in his control. Her body and undervalued mind came with the property. A nuisance, that, she thought wryly, knowing her person would always come secondary to the incomes from her estate.

"Lady Rosamund," Tancred said softly, "wishes to enter Hembley Abbey. And I would remove my hand from my sword, were I you, Lord Godfrey. My bowmen are ever eager to show off the astonishing accuracy of their aim."

Startled, Fitz Clare quickly lifted his hand from the handle of his sword. He looked around the hall, then spied the armed archers standing on the landing above the great hall.

"Is this how you receive your neighbors?" he demanded angrily.

"No. But when my first experience with a neighbor has involved his mercenaries and his siege machine, trust comes somewhat slowly. You see, I have never considered bloodshed to be a requirement of neighborly love." Tancred shrugged. "It seems you believe differently."

Crimson inched up Fitz Clare's neck. "I did not know *you* would be Wynnsef's new lord." His voice rose fractionally up the scale.

"But Lady Rosamund is fair game?"

"Yea, Lord Tancred, as you well know." Crimson suffused Fitz Clare's face.

Tancred's lashes lowered a little more. "What do you imply, sir?" he asked quietly.

The hall went deathly silent. If someone's stocking had fallen, it would have been audible in that moment.

"Uh . . . " Abruptly, Fitz Clare appeared to realize he had gravely erred. "Only that it was also an opportune time for you to take Wynnsef. I meant no disrespect to the lady or to your intentions."

In point of fact, Rosamund thought, Tancred *had* found her brother's absence quite convenient. But he had offered her no harm, nor did he seem inclined to force her into marriage. A shudder ran through her as she considered what her fate might have been had Fitz Clare succeeded in taking Wynnsef.

Tancred made a motion, and servants brought a chair for Fitz Clare. "As I have said, Lady Rosamund wishes to enter Hembley Abbey. Is that not so, Lady Rosamund?" he asked her, looked at her for the first time since Fitz Clare's entrance.

"Yea, Lord Tancred, it is indeed so," she answered.

"Lord Godfrey," Tancred continued, "I presume you have already met the Abbess of Hembley Abbey?"

"No," Fitz Clare said faintly. "I have not that honor."

Tancred turned toward Abbess Matilda. Rosamund didn't miss the light of approval in the abbess's eyes as she looked at Tancred, who made the introduction. "Do you wish to receive Lady Rosamund into your flock?"

"For certes, my lord. Until then, I remain here to protect her good name from those who would foully slander it." She cast a gimlet eye on Fitz Clare—and a less severe version of it on Tancred, who did not acknowledge the unspoken warning.

"So you see, Lord Godfrey," Tancred said, his expression bland, "all is well here."

Rosamund began to suspect that the only reason Fitz Clare had been allowed inside was to witness that life went on as usual within the castle walls here—and to allow him to see that Wynnsef was no longer undermanned.

"I would not have assumed otherwise," Fitz Clare professed smoothly.

A lie if ever Rosamund had heard one. *He has come here sniffing for discontent, for weakness.* He had also come to meet the Moon Lord, to judge for himself the man behind the legends, of that she felt certain.

At some invisible signal from Tancred, a servant stepped forward to offer Fitz Clare a goblet of wine and his choice from a plate of savory wafers. He accepted them graciously with murmured thanks to Tancred. Rosamund hoped he choked.

"Tell me, Lord Tancred," he said, all oily innocence, "what will pass when Arnaud Bourton and his many men return?"

Tancred met Fitz Clare's audacity with a look impossible to read. "I have my plans for Arnaud Bourton."

Fitz Clare stayed only a little longer when it became clear that he would get no more information from the new lord of Wynnsef. He made his excuses for needing to return home. Tancred did not attempt to dissuade him. Finally, Lord Trufflnose and his armed escort departed for his own manor.

"Perhaps the disagreeable man has finally accepted that Lady Rosamund is out of his reach," Abbess Matilda said with a sniff of disdain.

"Some men will go to any lengths for land," Rosamund said.

A minute flare of Tancred's nostrils suggested a stronger reaction than he otherwise revealed. "Fitz Clare may covet your land, Lady Rosamund, but make no mistake, it is you he wants."

She made a moue of distaste. "The thought of that creature—It is enough to give me night terrors."

Tancred smiled, and, for the first time, Rosamund noticed the shadows of fatigue beneath his eyes.

The abbess must have noticed at the same time. "You look weary," she said bluntly to Tancred.

He shrugged one shoulder, but offered no comment.

" 'Tis no wonder," Abbess Matilda persisted. "You could not possibly have gotten much sleep last night. That shouting was enough to wake the dead."

He smiled faintly. "If it disturbed you, I ask your pardon."

"Who shouted?" Rosamund asked.

"One of the men. He has ill dreams."

"Ill, indeed," Abbess Matilda agreed, "to cause him such distress."

"If you wish it, I can have him removed to other quarters while you remain."

The abbess waved a slim hand in regal denial. "Not necessary. I will take a potion before I retire. Should have been taking one, anyway. It will help me rest better."

"Perhaps I should make something for the fellow," Rosamund volunteered. "I—"

"No." Tancred's quick, sharp answer verged on discourtesy.

Rosamund covered her surprise at his response with a facade of acceptance that she hoped concealed her dismay at such curt rejection. They were his men, she told herself. He knew them best. Mayhap they believed what they heard about her witchery. That might be enough to worry a man.

What matter to her? She had duties enough without tending to the health of the Usurper's men.

She left the great hall, heading toward the old keep to change back into her everyday garments before she returned to her many duties. As she walked, Rosamund wondered if her appearance on the dais with Tancred might be used against her when Arnaud returned.

*   *   *

Rosamund paced the floor of her chamber, restless, unable to sleep. She wanted—no, *needed*—the peace that her garden offered, but since the discovery of the moonstone disk three days ago, she had not returned.

During those days, she had passed the door of the garden countless times, and each time she had checked the door she had found it secured. Twice she had even slipped her key into the lock to see if it still worked. It had.

She went to her open window, feeling the pull of that walled sanctuary.

Outside, moonlight gilded the night scape of dark stone structures and smaller, wattle-and-daub buildings with dabs of silver and plains of matte onyx. Barely visible were the white tops of the garden's lime-washed ashlar walls.

Why was she staying away? Rosamund suddenly wondered. *He* was not keeping her out, as she had tried to do with him. She had never even seen him go near the garden.

She gazed longingly at the tops of those walls and imagined she stood on the daisy-flushed grass, curling her bare toes through it. Oh, those heady green smells. That soothing white music from the fount's trickling water. Had the leaves of the arbor's grapevines opened yet?

Whirling away from the window, she hurried to the chest at the foot of her bed, from which she grabbed a plain, woolen kirtle and pulled it on over her linen chemise. She stuffed her bare feet into shoes, snatched up a lighted candle, then dashed from the chamber.

Swiftly, she made her way down the winding stone steps and out of the old keep. Cupping her hand to protect the candle's flame from the breeze created by her speed, she made her way through the castle to her walled garden. Outside its door, she paused, listening. She heard only the soft chuckle of trickling water and the distant cry of a night bird.

As she applied her key, she dropped the taper. Its fragile flame winked out, casting her into the dark.

For a moment, she stood there, her eyes closed. The moon, she knew, was not full, but it was bright enough to move by if one was familiar with her surroundings. Rosamund had never viewed the garden without the light of the sun or a taper or torch. Now she would see things through the eyes of brownies and faeries. She smiled, taken with her whimsy.

She stepped into the garden, then eased the door closed, unwilling to disturb the tranquility of this place with the sound of clanging metal. Her hands still on the latch, her back to the garden, she closed her eyes again. The sound of gently falling water poured over her, refreshing her spirit. She breathed in the crisp, clean scents of growing things. Soon, she thought, there would also be the sweet fragrance of flowers. Woodbine. Roses. Lavender.

Smiling, her eyes still shut, she turned slowly, trying to locate the direction of the fountain by sound alone. When she felt certain that she faced that way, she opened her eyes.

And froze.

There, beyond the fountain, on the other side of the garden, knelt a man.

FOURTEEN

Tall, broad-shouldered, attired all in black, with a tunic but no surcoat, he knelt with his back to her, facing the far flower bed.

Even with only the moon for illumination, Rosamund knew it was Tancred. She also knew him to have acute hearing, and she thought it odd that he appeared unaware that anyone had entered the garden. Then it occurred to her: She had been careful to move as silently as possible, and the fount that chuckled between them would have obscured any little sound she had made.

Remaining where she'd stopped, her muscles tense, she watched Tancred. His body blocked her from seeing what he was doing. His head never moved. It remained facing straight forward. Then he moved, only about a foot to his side, still facing the flower bed.

Gradually, curiosity overrode her resentment. Moving quietly, careful to keep the fount between them, Rosamund moved over to give herself a better angle from which to view his activity. When she achieved her first glimpse, she abruptly stopped.

He knelt in front of a patch of alehoof, which stood only about ten inches high. Few of the plants in the beds stood taller. In the daytime, it was easy to admire the flowers and the ragged, kidney-shaped leaves. Now their pale violet blossoms and their bright green leaves were varied tones of black and gray.

Tancred did not see those somber shades.

His eyes were closed.

He nimbly learned the shape of the plant with his hands, as if he were blind. With his palms and fingers, he measured the height and width. Then his fingertips traced a few of the leaves. From there, he edged a fragile bloom with a delicate touch. Lowering his face to the plant, he slowly inhaled.

She knew he smelled its strong aroma. It was not a strictly ornamental plant. Indeed, it was most useful in the brewing of ale, in making tisanes, and its tender shoots and leaves went into salads and soups. Still, she thought alehoof a pretty plant, and so she always grew it here as well as in the physic garden. But why would it claim such attention from a knight?

His eyes still closed, Tancred moved to the group of plants beside the alehoof: wodebroun.

These could be found in almost any moist woodland mead, but the rich, deep blue flowers that grew on spikes were so lush and colorful that Rosamund would not consider the garden complete without them. But, again, Tancred would not know that. Only through the devoted touch of his fingers, through a long, softly indrawn breath, did he acquaint himself with the wild-flower. Yet it seemed to Rosamund that he grew to be on more intimate terms with these plants than she who had brought them here and tended them.

She moved closer, unwilling to miss anything he did.

Instantly he sprang to his feet, his hand swooping for the long-knife at his side.

Rosamund gasped and lunged backward, almost stepping in a bed of young foxglove.

Tancred stayed his hand. "You." The word was an accusation. He rammed the weapon back into its sheath. "Has no one ever told you *not* to sneak up on an armed man?"

She started to bristle, then realized that he was likely more irritated over the fact that she'd caught him in the act of touching flowers than over her catching him unawares. Rosamund smiled.

"Of course," she said.

"You should have listened."

She decided not to comment on the subject of advice. It always sounded so much wiser years afterward than at the moment given. Instead, she thought how uplifting it felt to know something about the magnificent Moon Lord that he did not want her to know. Why, it could make a woman positively glow with the delight.

"You're standing in my garden," she informed him with cheerful cheek.

He was standing too far from her for Rosamund to discern his expression. His face was a stark mask of moonlight and shadow. So she walked closer to him.

He towered over her, all masculine grace, bone-deep power and breath-stopping virility. She thought about easing back a step or two, but pride stopped her. Looking up, she saw that, from this closer distance, the moonlight softened the fierce beauty of his face. It was the pools and planes of ebony shadow that lent it severity. Slanting slashes lifted in silent question, but she held her tongue. If he wanted answers, then he must ask. She refused to guess at questions.

"I did not think you would return," he said softly.

The world seemed to tilt off balance in that still, moon-spun moment, and his simple statement took on more depth and new meaning. Why that was, Rosamund could not fathom. Yet something was different. *He* was different. Perhaps even . . . she was different.

"I could not stay away," she answered.

She would not mention the silver disk. No word of the crimson silk pouch she had foolishly made for it would pass her lips. Both lay locked securely in her casket.

He nodded slowly. "There is a strange peace to this place."

She smiled. "Magic. That's what my father called it." And because it seemed to twinkle in the night air all around them, she whispered to herself, "Magic."

Tancred paced to the fount. From the stiff tilt of his shoulders, and his measured steps, Rosamund gathered the impression he might be uneasy with the subject of magic. He had taken the cross and followed his liege lord to fight in the Holy Land. Perhaps it was only natural that the mention of magic did not sit well with him. It was an old power, a pagan power, and the Church preached it was wicked. But had not God overseen the world before the birth of Jesus? Everything bespoke His power. Even magic. Perhaps, especially magic. Rosamund smiled to herself. Brother Felix would be shocked to hear this of her. Mayhap she had been listening too much to Edeva's many questions.

She did not move from where she stood. "I have heard it said that a garden is God's special place."

"Yea, I can believe that it is."

Water sprang from the top of the fount through the center of a carved stone rose. In the glistening flow, his long, lean fingers traced the folds of the petals. Watching his hand, a warm shiver passed through Rosamund's body.

"What were you doing?" she finally asked in a quiet voice.

He made no answer.

"When I came in," she persisted, "what is it that you were doing?"

Tancred turned his head slightly, as if he would avoid her gaze. At first she thought he would refuse to answer her, and had already decided to leave be when he finally spoke.

"When I was fighting with King Richard in Outremer," he said, his voice as soft and deep as midnight smoke, "I and many others of my garrison were taken captive by Sabih Ibn Qasim's men. We were driven like cattle to Bâb Al-Muhunnad."

Rosamund recognized that last foreign name. It was the mighty fortress that Tancred had delivered to King Richard. Its commander had hated Christians with a passion approaching insanity. The only Christians to ever have escaped alive had been those who followed Tancred in his uprising.

"There, I was thrown into a dark cellar," he said. "No light penetrated that hole. My hand placed before my face was not visible to me."

Rosamund shivered at the prospect of being in such a terrible place. The thought of it seemed to draw the air from her lungs.

"They kept me there for weeks. I lived like an animal. A blind animal. My cage held a few others. A few who were dead and had begun to rot. One who was dying. A crusader who had gone mad within a week. And me."

Without thinking, she moved to the fount, too. Facing him across the wellhead, she began to reach out to him, but abruptly realized what she was doing. Not wishing to drive him away, she dropped her hand to her side. "How terrible for you," she said. Although heartfelt, the words seemed too lame to signify her true feelings. What could one say to fully express one's horror, one's sympathy over something so terrible? Words seemed so inadequate as to sound false.

"Now," he continued, "when I am in the presence of great beauty, I try to remind myself how fortunate I am. And . . . I try to draw on all of my senses. Those leaves"—he indicated the alehoof—"I can see their shape, the scalloped edges, but to try to discover that with only the fingers makes them more immediate. More . . . intimate. Your mind learns a shape, but your hands, your body, also learn. You *know* the smell, the texture, the sound it makes as you brush your fingertips across it."

His words ignited a flame in Rosamund. " 'Tis as if you become more a part of the garden?"

Tancred turned his head and looked at her. "Yea.

That is it, precisely. The presence of these growing things becomes more *tangible*. And . . . " He frowned down at the unfolding rose of stone beneath his hand.

"Yea, Tancred de Vierzon?" she coaxed softly.

"There was a time when I did not believe I would ever see such loveliness again. It seemed certain I would die in the dark. That my flesh and my bones would turn to dust and no one save my enemy would know." He cupped a tiny pool of crystalline water in his palm. "There was no one left to care."

She stared at him as he studied the water in his hand. How could this be so? How could the death of such a man go unmourned? "No mother?" she asked.

"She died long ago. After my father gave me as hostage to King Henry."

"No sisters or brothers?"

He slowly shook his head, as if preoccupied with the water.

"No—" She broke off, her face going hot.

Tancred's lashes lifted as he turned his gaze on her.

All too aware of that gaze, she forced the words out. "No lovers?"

He remained silent, his shadowed face betraying nothing of his thoughts.

"I ask pardon, it is none of my concern," she muttered, feeling maladroit and flustered. She might want to know, but it certainly was none of her—

"None." Moonlight caught and glimmered in the endless depths of his eyes.

No lovers. Why that answer should lift her spirits, Rosamund could not guess. Still, that was years ago. He had risen up and delivered that fortress and many others both in the East, on the Continent, and in England to their king. By the time Tancred had arrived here, songs of his brave deeds were already being sung throughout the kingdom.

She thought about what he had said earlier. Learning through touch, memorizing with not only the mind, but with the body.

She leaned toward him, pressing her hands against the pouting stone petals of the rose. "Teach me."

He regarded her from the corners of his eyes. "Teach you what?"

Her steps hurried back to the flower beds. "Teach me how to learn with my body as well as with my mind. Teach me to be closer to my garden."

"*Your* garden?"

Rosamund swallowed, finding it difficult to smile at the hint of humor she heard in his voice. "Yea, my lord. Help me to become closer to it, that I may take a bit of this place with me when I part from Wynnsef."

He made no move to join her. "And when would that be, my lady?"

"Soon perhaps," she said, her throat constricting with sorrow. All that was known to her, all that was dear, would be left behind when she entered Hembley Abbey. For a reason she had no wish to examine, she now felt a breath of uncertainty over committing herself to a life of obedience and chastity.

By the time Arnaud returned with his men thundering around him, he might have already fixed Rosamund in his mind as a traitor. Evidence was there for one who wished to believe. Tancred had taken the castle without a siege. Rosamund had not been sent into a convent, she now sat at Tancred's side during meals, during the manorial court, and even when guests came to call. Doubtless, were it not for Abbess Matilda's presence, Rosamund would already be known as the Moon Lord's harlot.

Tancred left the fount and came to stand in front of her. In the moonlight, their gazes met. Slowly, he reached out to touch her cheek.

She shivered beneath the warmth of his fingers. No man had ever touched her with such tenderness. And, oh, there had been times when she'd thought she would die of longing for just such a touch.

As she stood with Tancred in the secret garden, all her years of loneliness moaned through Rosamund like the wind through an empty tower. She turned her face more fully into his callused palm. Her lips accidentally brushed his skin

Startled by the glide of warmth against her sensitive flesh, frightened by her lack of restraint, she pulled back.

He dropped his hand to his side. "I would never harm you, Rosamund."

"I—We—I am going to become a nun," she blurted.

Her heart was still racing as Tancred quietly left the garden, closing behind him the door that she had forgotten to lock.

The next morning after Mass, where as usual the incense set her to sneezing, Rosamund found an excuse not to go directly to break her fast in the great hall. It was cowardice, pure and simple, but she wasn't ready to face Tancred again. Not after she had all but kissed his palm and then behaved like a frightened child. She could only imagine what he thought of her erratic behavior. If it was worse than she thought of it, Rosamund was certain to be seared by his contempt.

She was halfway to her physic garden and the cottage that served as her herbarium, when she turned around and started back to the great hall. Arriving late would only draw everyone's attention to her. If she slipped in with everyone else, she would not further insult Tancred and no one would suspect there might be something amiss.

As Rosamund slid into her chair behind the trestle table, the sight of Tancred's empty massive high seat sent a ripple of distress through her. She hadn't wanted to face him after last night, and yet, at the same time, she had anticipated seeing him again all night, waiting with an excited dread that had made sleep impossible.

Apparently, Tancred experienced no such anticipation over her.

The lump in her throat made it difficult to swallow.

Well, who could blame him? she thought. Not only
had she nuzzled his hand, she had then turned around
and, with a complete lack of grace, rejected his gentle touch.

"Where is Lord Tancred this fine morn?" Abbess
Matilda asked as she took her place.

In no mood for conversation, particularly one regarding Tancred, Rosamund muttered something
about his likely having business to attend.

Abbess Matilda shrugged off his absence. "When
you make my sleeping draught for tonight," she said,
"would you please see to it that 'tis strong enough to
see me through a night of noise? That man-at-arms
must have had the most terrible night terrors last
night. Fortunately, it lasts but briefly. Doubtless until
he wakes himself, poor fellow. I think Lord Tancred
is most unreasonable in not allowing you to dose the
man."

"I am certain my reputation for witchery makes
Lord Tancred and his men uneasy," Rosamund said,
distractedly wadding a bit of manchet loaf between
her fingers before eating it.

The abbess waved an elegant hand, her signet ring
winking in the light of the new day pouring through
the window. "Nothing to that. Anyone with a crumb
of sense knows you have a God-given gift with
plants." She smiled. "I plan to make good use of your
talent when you come to us at Hembley Abbey. *We*
will welcome such a gift."

"Too kind," Rosamund murmured, feeling like a
traitor. For a long moment, she felt Abbess Matilda's
gaze on her. Then that lady turned her attention to
the light repast before her.

Restless, Rosamund surveyed those present in the
hall as she ate. Kadar was absent and so were several
other knights. As soon as she politely could, Rosamund excused herself with Abbess Matilda, then went
to her herbarium, stopping along the way to send a
page to have her horse saddled.

Inside the cottage, the air was redolent with the rich smells of basil, comfrey, blackthorn, and a host of other herbs. Rosamund threw open the shutters to let in the cheerful spring sunshine, then went about packing her usual two willow baskets with earthenware bottles of lotions and newly brewed tinctures, salves in crockery pots, muslin packets of freshly picked leaves and of dried mixtures to be used in the making of medicinal teas and poultices. Into one of the baskets also went clean linen rags that had been torn into strips and squares.

Father Ivo and Attewell's headman, Uehtred, had both contributed to her list of names needing her aid in that village. She would make her trip to Cloptune later in the sennight. Tancred's arrival had interrupted her visits, and those who usually came to her—those who could walk—had been fearful of entering the castle.

A knock at the cottage's door announced a smiling Edeva. "Fair morn to you, Rosamund," she said. "I thought you might welcome some aid."

Rosamund tucked the last packet into her basket. "I would, indeed. And I know the good people I will call on would welcome the sight of a sister from Hembley Abbey."

"You know I am no nun, nor even, in truth, a novice."

"Yea, Edeva, I do know it. But the folk of Attewell see you as one, and, today, that is what matters."

Before Edeva could further protest, Rosamund laughingly thrust a basket into her hands and then shooed her out the door. As they walked the path through the garden that would take them to the stables, they encountered Sister Dameta.

"Lady Rosamund, I thought you might have some task for me. At the abbey I have often worked in the garden. Mayhap I can be of some assistance to you?"

For Sister Dameta, that was a long, forthright speech. The strapping nun was usually quite timid.

Edeva looped her arm through Sister Dameta's and said, "You are ready to go mad with boredom, are you not, Sister?"

Sister Dameta pinkened. " 'Tis only that I am used to working. Your marshal would not allow me to help in the stables. I—I am rather good with horses."

Rosamund knew how possessive of his territory was Cynric, Wynnsef's marshal. The notion of a woman—and a nun into the bargain—helping there would doubtless stir the stodgy old dear heart to an apoplexy.

"I and the people of Attewell would be grateful if you would help me tend their sick this day," she said.

She was rewarded with a sunny smile that lacked only a couple of teeth. "Oh, yea, my lady," Sister Dameta exclaimed. "I would be delighted to help."

"The mere sight of you will lift their hearts," Edeva assured Sister Dameta.

"I—I shall pray for them," Sister Dameta vowed. "And I will do whatever you need me to do, Lady Rosamund."

As the three of them headed for the stables, they gradually acquired Sister Octavia and Sister Mary for their enterprise.

At the stables, a lad was dispatched to find John in order to alter the information Rosamund had sent him before breakfast. Instead of just her, there would be five women riding to Attewell. Would he please arrange to have however many men he wanted to accompany them meet them at the main gate?

Faced with finding steeds for four unexpected women, Cynric grumbled and harumphed.

"I would be content with a donkey, Master Cynric," Sister Dameta meekly offered.

"Are you implying, Sister, that I, marshal of Wynnsef's acclaimed stables, cannot find good mounts for four brides of Christ?" he replied, clearly affronted.

Nearly his equal in size and strength, Sister Dameta, tongue-tied with embarrassment, shook her head.

Sister Mary, who did not suffer from timidity,

stepped forward and nearly set the tip of her nose to his. "You know well that was not what she meant—or you would if you had even an ounce of the sense Our Lord gave the lowliest worm. She was *trying* to be accommodating."

Cynric's eyes flared open with surprise, then rapidly narrowed with indignation. "*Worm?* A worm, is it? I—"

"Cynric," Rosamund said softly.

Abruptly he broke off. With a hard glare at Sister Mary, he stamped off, muttering to himself.

"Sister Mary, your defense of our Sister Dameta is commendable, but perhaps you would have been just as effective if you had not implied the man did not have the wit of a worm," Sister Octavia pointed out in a quiet voice.

Sister Mary folded her arms over her bosom and thrust her hands into her wide sleeves. "I doubt that."

Rosamund decided that retreat was the best form of diplomacy in this instance. "Come, ladies. Let us enjoy the pleasure garden while the horses are readied."

That met with everyone's approval, and Rosamund sent a wide-eyed lad to inform Master Cynric of their whereabouts.

Eventually, the horses were saddled and delivered to the garden gate. The baskets were tied to La Songe's saddle.

What had been intended as a customary call on the village's ailing was rapidly turning out to be a pageant, Rosamund thought. Still, these women were displaced and idle because of Abbess Matilda's concern for Rosamund, who was trapped here, unchaperoned, in the daily company of that potent brother of shadows, the Moon Lord. If the abbess remained, but sent the nuns home, she would also need to send most of her men as escort. Rosamund suspected Abbess Matilda had chosen for her nuns to remain at Wynnsef in order to keep all her knights and men-at-arms here. It would

be advantageous to find oneself in a position to give
aid to whichever lord of Wynnsef looked most likely
to win. The lord of Wynnsef—whoever that turned out
to be—would be a powerful ally for Hembley Abbey.

When the women arrived at the gate, they found
John himself there, but no sign of the rest of the
escort.

"My Lord Tancred has given orders that the ladies
are to remain within the safety of the castle," he said.

The ill of Attewell had already been forced to wait
longer than they should have for her skills and
medicaments.

Rosamund met John's gaze squarely. "And did
Lord Tancred say why he wished us to remain in the
castle?" she asked softly to conceal her anger over
Tancred's high-handed manner.

John, who knew her too well to be fooled by her
quiet, arched an eyebrow. "He, Lord Kadar, and several of the knights rode out in two patrols this morning. Brigands struck Cloptune last night."

"How bad—"

He indicated that she should direct her horse aside
with his so that John might speak privately with Rosamund. When they were out of earshot of the others,
he said, "Several cottages burned. Three women
raped. Four men wounded, two dead. The brigands
made off with most of a flock of sheep and some
coin."

Rosamund's stomach clenched. Cloptune was a
small village. That kind of damage would be a stag-
gering blow.

"Then we shall go to Cloptune," Rosamund said,
determined. "They have need of us there."

"Lady, Lord Tancred is right. It would be too dangerous for you to leave the castle now."

She lifted her chin. "We will take an armed escort
with us."

"Jesú. You know we could come under attack by
Lord Arnaud or by Lord Godfrey at any moment. We

cannot spare the men for a nonessential purpose. Your cause is worthy, my lady, but not essential."

Rosamund stared at him. "If my brother arrives, John, I expect you to throw open the gates and let him in."

John sighed. "It has gone beyond that. If I tried to open the gates to Lord Arnaud, I would be killed in an instant. My men—your brother's men—have sworn to Lord Tancred. They are his men now, my lady. Even I am his man now. You are as dear as a daughter to me, and I would die to protect you." He did not need to speak the words for Rosamund to hear them clearly: "I will not fight for your brother."

"John," she said, in a voice gone tight with fear and anguish. "John, how could you?" She had known he was now Tancred's man, but it was not until this moment that the change became real.

"You are my concern, my lady. You and the castle that was your father's. Arnaud cannot continue to hold it. You know he cannot. He is lazy. Irresponsible. He will eventually lose to Lord Godfrey, and then all *will* be lost." John shook his head. " 'Tis better that a man, one of honor and a true leader, rule over Wynnsef. You will have a chance to enter Hembley Abbey, as you wish. Or to wed. If you choose."

"Wed?" she echoed, astounded.

"It is not too late, my lady."

To have a family, children . . . Resolutely, she shut off those thoughts. She had made a decision. For her, the right decision.

"Yea, John," she said tonelessly. "It is."

"As you will, Lady Rosamund. But there is yet time to think on it, for you will not leave the castle now."

"I never thought I would see the day when you betrayed me," she told him angrily, her heated words a cover for her deep hurt.

The grizzled warrior looked away, and Rosamund knew that she had wounded him. Even her fury was no match for the strength of her remorse.

"Lady, you have never had a more loyal friend than I am to you. Would that you could see that."

"He is my brother," she said, hating the pleading note in her voice. "He is Father's firstborn, and he deserves your loyalty, too. Contrary to what Lord Tancred says, Arnaud is not all bad."

"No one is, my lady."

"No one knows him as I do," she insisted. "If you did, you would see he has good qualities."

"All in Wynnsef know his good qualities, Rosamund," John said, his voice gentle, his weathered face a mask of sympathy. "It is you alone who has refused to see those qualities of his that are not good."

Rosamund pressed her lips together. She looked skyward, determined no tears would fall from her brimming eyes. Inhaling sharply, she held her breath, then sharply released it. "You know how Papa was with him, John. Arnaud could never seem to please him. And he tried, he truly did try. He wanted Papa's approval so very much. I think—" She swallowed hard. "I think I must have stolen all of Papa's love, for he had none for poor Arnaud."

John sighed. "Sometimes a man has a child that is just hard for him to love. I know Thomas tried. He *wanted* to care. And he did. But Arnaud was so whining. Worse, he never acquired your father's love for the land. But you did. You've always had a strong bond with it. Then there were the reports from the lord Arnaud fostered with."

"What reports?"

Frowning down at the reins in his hand, John said, "Arnaud was a bully. And a sneak. It shamed Thomas, who had tried to teach Arnaud the ways of an honorable man."

"Yea, he did!" Rosamund exclaimed, unable to bear the thought that someone might believe her father remiss in those duties. "Before Arnaud went to foster, Papa kept him at his side often, trying to teach

him, by example, his responsibilities to his family and
to his people."

A faint smile touched John's stern mouth. "I remember you always tried to go with them." The smile
faded. "And I remember Arnaud had no interest in
learning about those responsibilities. You learned in
his stead. I think that won your father's heart."

"And now you will not allow me to tend those in
need. They are our people, John, and they've been
attacked."

"Lord Tancred is right. It is unsafe for you outside
these walls. But when he returns I will plead your case
myself, if I must. It is the best I can do, my lady. I
will not risk you or the sisters when I know right well
there is danger."

Rosamund opened her mouth to protest, but was
interrupted by the blare of a trumpet from outside
the gates.

One of the patrols had returned.

FIFTEEN

Kadar and his men escorted the wagon bearing the injured villagers into the castle.

The fact that the wounded villagers had been ferried to the castle by Kadar's patrol was in itself somewhat unusual. Knights did not concern themselves with the peasantry, who, on most estates, saw to their own injuries.

Still mounted on their own horses, Rosamund, Edeva, and the nuns followed the motley party into the inner bailey, where the stable lads ran to take the reins. Kadar gave a curt order, and only the steeds of the women were taken off to the stables.

He bowed, giving that strange, graceful salute of his to Rosamund and those of her group.

"Where is the other patrol?" Rosamund inquired, when what she really wanted to ask was "Where is Tancred?"

"I give you greetings from Lord Tancred," Kadar said, his eyes flickering to Edeva, then back to Rosamund. "It was his wish that those injured by the brigands be conveyed to you." If he was annoyed at being given such a lowly task, he showed no evidence of it. "We encountered them trying to make their way to you, my Lady Rosamund. Nothing would do but that you see to their injuries. It would seem that the Green Witch of Wynnsef is in truth an angel with the healing touch." A smile lurked around the weary corners of his mouth.

"I am neither witch nor angel," Rosamund said, feeling her cheeks grow warm.

He inclined his head, then regarded her through his lashes. "God knows all, lady."

"Yea, He does, Lord Kadar," Edeva said softly.

The ebony gaze cut away to fix on the young woman who stood next to Rosamund, garbed in a novice's white garments. "You will assist Lady Rosamund, Sister Edeva?" he inquired gravely.

Rosamund felt as if she had seen Kadar transform before her eyes. Where was the charming exotic? The courtly foreign knight? Here in his place stood a tall, handsome man clad in mail fashioned with only a few details that smacked of another land. Gone was the ever-present glint of humor in his eyes.

"Yea, if she will accept my help. But . . ." She hesitated. "I am not a nun, Lord Kadar."

"Not yet, perhaps."

"Not ever," she said so quietly Rosamund scarcely heard her.

Kadar heard.

How Rosamund knew that, she could not say, for he made no comment. His expression seemed not to change. Perhaps it was the steady gaze, as dark as Edeva's own, that lingered just a breath longer than it might otherwise on the woman in white.

Without another word given between them, Kadar took his leave of Rosamund, and swung back into the saddle. Wheeling Zahir around, he led the patrol back toward the gates and the rippling fields and forests of Wynnsef beyond.

Edeva continued to gaze where he had gone, for minutes after he had passed from the sight.

"What did you say to him, Edeva?" Sister Octavia asked. "He seemed most strange when he left, even for a foreigner."

"Sisters, there are patients to attend," Rosamund

said, briskly, unwilling for Edeva to be questioned when she seemed so oddly preoccupied. Rosamund intended to pose her own questions to her later, in private. "I would appreciate your aid in this matter."

"Oh!" exclaimed Sister Dameta, looking about. "These poor souls!"

The injured were swiftly brought into the great hall, where Rosamund, assisted by Edeva, set to work over their wounds, and the good sisters over their wounded spirits.

"Lord Tancred" and "Lord Kadar" were much on the lips of each grateful patient, their names spoken with reverence.

"Lord Tancred, he did promise to furnish us the materials to rebuild those houses what was burned," one man said.

Surprised, Rosamund paused as she applied a comfrey and marigold poultice to the burns on his arms and back. "Did he?"

"Aye, lady," another fellow volunteered. "Said as how it was his fault in not protecting us from those whorin' bastards—beggin' yer pardon, my ladies. Them last be me own words, not his."

"And Lord Kadar will doubtless do as he has done since his arrival," Father Ivo said, as he arrived to check on these members of his far-flung flock. Only the gift of a horse that Rosamund had managed a few years ago allowed him to see all of them on a much more regular basis than when he had been making the trek on foot between villages and the more isolated farms.

"And what . . . would that be . . . Father?" one of the women asked faintly from Sister Octavia's strong arms, where she appeared to feel safer than she'd felt since the night before.

"Lord Kadar contributes generously—if quietly— to the tithe barn and to our alms. I thought I would mention that here because I much dislike some of the comments I have heard about him. True, he is a Saracen—"

"He believes in the same God we do, Father," Rosamund said.

That brought exclamations and murmurs of surprise or doubt throughout the great hall, from those who had little contact with Kadar.

Father Ivo's eyes widened. "Does he? Does he indeed? How extraordinary."

"Lady Rosamund," said a man whose sword slash Rosamund had already stitched and bound. "What is Lord Kadar lord *of*, exactly?"

At this, even Edeva turned to her. The buzz of conversation in the great hall had quieted.

"I cannot say," Rosamund confessed. She sought out one of Tancred's men who had helped to seize Wynnsef.

Such a knight sat assiduously sharpening his sword in a patch of light from one of the high windows. Rosamund did not know his name, so she rose to her feet and walked over to address him.

"Chevalier," she said, "can you tell us what Lord Kadar is lord over?"

He looked up at her. "Lady," he said respectfully, "that is a question you must ask Kadar. It is not for me to answer."

Puzzled, she inquired, "Do you not know?"

"He is a private man, my lady. Did he wish everyone privy to his affairs, doubtless you would now know. Because you do not, I will leave it to him whether or not to answer your question."

Well, I guess I have been put in my place, Rosamund thought, embarrassed.

She returned to her patient and went back to work. "And there we have it," she told the others, who waited for the answer. "If Lord Kadar wished us to know of what he is lord, we would know."

As everyone went back to their tasks, it occurred to Rosamund that as far as she could remember,

Kadar had never indicated that he should be addressed as a lord.

Supper time came, and still there was no sign from the two patrols, no word of what they had encountered in their search for the bandits. The meal was kept warming in the kitchens, until finally Rosamund gave the order to serve. Everyone was hungry and the food would soon be unfit to eat.

As the dishes were brought out and the diners served, the mood in the great hall was subdued. Everyone knew that some bandits were naught but lordless knights—armed and trained warriors. Such men would be deadly foes and desperate not to be caught, for hanging would be their fate.

Unhappy with her thoughts that dwelled fretfully on Tancred's danger, she called for diversion—the only one available at Wynnsef. Will went to his ususal place, and quietly strummed a few chords on his lute.

The abbess shot Rosamund a wry glance. "Oh, this shall lift the strange mood of this hall." She shook her head. "I do not understand why all here are so dull over the patrols' delay. Tancred has not been here so long he has had time to truly matter to the people of Wynnsef."

Rosamund gazed out over the sea of faces in the great hall. "Most here are his men," she murmured. But in her heart she knew Abbess Matilda was wrong. In less than two weeks, Tancred *had* come to matter to the people of Wynnsef. They had found a lord they could respect, a lord from whom they would receive just treatment.

A tiny worm of jealousy nibbled at her. She had worked hard on their behalf. *She* had given them just treatment. Or as much as she could before Arnaud interfered. Always he kept an eye toward profit. It mattered little to him that villeins went without food, unable to find the time to tend their own crofts because of his demands, or that their fields were less

fertile because he had insisted their sheep or cattle
graze in *his* fields, thereby fertilizing his land. Or that
they were miserable with cold in the winter because
he decided to charge more for the right to gather dead
wood in his forest—more than they could pay. Still,
in that he was no worse than many lords. And she
had always *tried*.

In the end, however, Arnaud was distrusted, she
was often blamed, but along came Saint Tancred, and
it was suddenly hosannas in the Highest!

Will began to play a tune. It was an unfamiliar melody, but what riveted her attention was the skill with
which he played it. His slender fingers moved more
effectively across the strings. He seemed to possess
greater confidence.

At that moment, Will looked up and saw her watching him. Was that uncertainty in his gray eyes?

She smiled warmly and nodded her approval. His
answering grin glowed like the sun.

He moved into a familiar ballad about unrequited
love. His voice still cracked once in a while. Rosamund looked around the chamber, and saw that she
was not the only one who noticed the change.

"The boy may make a troubadour yet," Abbess Matilda observed.

A weary servant approached Rosamund. "Lady Rosamund, Marcus does believe he has found a rat's nest
in the upstairs linen cabinet. He is not certain, though,
and asks that you to come judge."

"Am I the only one in Wynnsef who can recognize
a rat's nest?" she asked, feeling every bit as tired as
the poor servant looked. As soon as the words were
out, Rosamund regretted them. "Never mind, Gerta.
I'll go see what Marcus has found."

Rats, she thought as she trudged up the spiral stairs
to the floor above. Just what she needed. In the linens,
of all things. Rats could go through those like a warm
knife through butter.

It turned out that Marcus had in fact found a rat's

nest, but it didn't appear to be one still in use. The nasty thing should have been cleaned out ages ago, after the last all-out campaign to rid the castle of rats. After Marcus disposed of the old nest, the two of them searched the entire floor for evidence of current rodent occupancy.

The entire floor, that is, with the exception of the solar—Tancred's chamber. Which took up much of the second floor, other space being utilitarian in nature.

After they had satisfied themselves that there was no evidence of infestation in the area they could search, Marcus bade Rosamund happy dreams and hastened off to his own pallet. As she watched the spry, elderly man disappear down the stairs, she caught her bottom lip between her teeth. She needed to be absolutely certain that there were no rats on this floor. It would never do if she had left a stone unturned, only to later discover that a family of rats had been hiding there. Soon those rats would have repopulated this floor, then the one above, with not only the chapel and Brother Felix's quarters, but the abbess's chamber as well. In no time, a keep could swarm with the destructive creatures. From here, they would spread throughout the castle like wildfire. It would be disastrous if they were to infest the storage chambers, or overbalance the never-ending battle to keep the granaries from being overrun.

She needed to inspect Tancred's chamber to make certain it did not harbor the vermin. In the name of efficient housekeeping, of course.

As she stood deciding, she was aware of a particular door directly behind her.

Slowly she turned. It looked as it had always: heavy oak with an iron latch handle. The solar had been her parents' chamber. Then her brother had moved in. What lay inside now? What kind of room would Tancred inhabit? Would the chamber be as Spartan as a monk's cell, his acclaimed standards being so high, so honorable? Would it be filled with weapons and other instruments of a warrior's calling?

Rosamund worried her bottom lip as she stood there, studying the door. She really ought to look inside. For rats.

Straining to pick up any nearby sounds, she heard only the silence of a sleeping keep and the small pops of flame consuming resinous wood as the torches burned in their blackened wall brackets. Slowly, she reached a hand out to the latch.

With a small *clink* the latch lifted. Under her hand, the door swung open. Her heart began to gallop as she stared into the tenebrous room. She stood rooted there for more minutes than she cared to count before she lifted the torch outside the door from its bracket. Then, drawing in a long, heartening breath, she entered the Moon Lord's chamber.

It was as if she had stepped into another world.

Richly colored tapestries with strange, graceful designs covered the walls. Instead of rushes, thick wool tapestries also covered the wood-planked floors, which struck Rosamund as a sinful misuse of the beautiful things. The great bed her grandparents and then her parents had shared was now hung with damask draperies that shimmered in the dancing light of her torch. Within, a coverlet of golden fur from great beasts unknown to her covered the bed. Beside the bed stood a tall silver stand looking like an exotic candlestick but its graceful shape supported, instead of a thick candle, a silver, pierce-worked censer.

The only other censer she had ever seen was that used in chapel, and it was much smaller and attached to a chain. Indeed, she had never heard of anyone not connected with saying Mass actually *using* one. Incense was for church. So why would someone want a censer in his bedchamber? Her nose wrinkled against the memory of the incense used in chapel. It always made her sneeze. Not one of those tiny, dainty sneezes, such as the ones Helvise gave when her nose tickled. No, Rosamund's sneezes were loud and violent enough to raise the lead-covered roof of a keep, drawing the attention of all present. A mortifying experience, but one as regular as the rising of the sun.

Odd. Her nose didn't tickle *now*. After a quick, guilty glance at the half-open door, Rosamund leaned toward the exquisite censer and sniffed.

A peculiar scent filled her nostrils. Strangely heavy, it possessed a faint musky note to it. Certainly she had never smelled anything like it in chapel. Her eyebrows drew together as she tried to identify the herbs or spices that might have gone into its making. After inhaling deeply several times, something, some mysterious element of it, still eluded her. When she closed her eyes to concentrate, the room dipped to one side. She opened her eyes, disconcerted. Clearly she was more fatigued than she'd realized.

Intrigued, tempted, she hesitated, then lit one of the many tapers set about the room. Going to the door, Rosamund stuck her head out. She saw no sign of anyone. Again, silence met her ears.

Odd, how Tancred's image kept floating to the surface of her mind. Although she knew she shouldn't, Rosamund fretted over Tancred's failure to return. He might be a king's champion, but brigands were notoriously devious. Rogue knights were even more dangerous; they were not only desperate but mounted and armed.

She blinked. Had the furniture moved? Rosamund stared hard at it, but nothing stirred.

Perhaps John had received word from him. All she wanted to know was that Tancred was unharmed. She tried to recall if John would still be on duty at this late hour, but her mind stumbled over rosters and times. Guard duty wasn't really her area of authority.

She decided to take a chance that he would still be up. He would know not to reveal to anyone her questions regarding Tancred. *Not* that she would be making any significant queries.

Taking up a torch, she hastened down the stairs, and out the doors leading to the kitchens, the buttery, and the pantry. She made for the gatehouse, though her path refused to remain very straight. As she approached, she listened for male voices or the sound of bone dice tossed on a tabletop. Instead, she heard only a tuneless rendition of Will's first composition, a song about a falcon. The voice was not as deep as John's. She could not recognize it. Taking a chance, she tapped on the door and then peered inside.

A young man-at-arms clad in the usual conical helmet and metal-bossed leather gambeson, looked surprised to see her. And why shouldn't he be? The fellow was one of Tancred's, and she had not come near this place since his master had won control of Wynnsef.

"Lady Rosamund! Eh, *bon nuit* to you, my lady. How may I serve you?"

Now that she was here, she felt foolish. While the evening air wasn't cold, it was considerably cooler than her body, which felt unaccountably flushed.

"I, uh, I wondered if you have received word yet from Lord Tancred? About the patrols," she added quickly.

He regarded her with large brown eyes that were entirely too world-weary for such a boyish face. "Nay, lady. We've heard naught."

"Do you know if he—if *they* will return this night?"

"Nay, Lady Rosamund. If word should be received, shall I send to you?"

How must she appear to this stripling with a veteran's soul? An unwed lady going alone to the castle gatehouse, in the middle of the night, to ask after her captor. *Think, Rosamund, think. Cover your unseemly behavior with a plausible excuse.* But tax it as she might, her brain refused to obey.

Under the guard's patient gaze, she grew uncustomarily flustered. She decided that retreat was her best action.

"Yea," she muttered as she gathered her skirts. "Please do."

She plunged back into the dark, glad for what concealment it afforded, wishing her torch were not quite so bright.

When she arrived in her room, she remembered that she had forgotten to close Tancred's chamber door. She had lighted a taper, but failed to put it out.

Rosamund rubbed her forehead with one hand. Sweet Mary, she was so woozy. All she wanted was to lie down and sleep. Strange. Worry usually kept her awake.

Absently, she lit the braziers as she struggled to think the situation through. If she did not return to Tancred's chamber to put out the light and close the door, there might well be difficulties later. Were he to return in the night, he would know that someone had gone into his chamber, and tomorrow might find servants being interrogated. She couldn't very well allow some hapless maid or even Marcus to be accused of trespassing in the master's private quarters. Rosamund would have to own up to it, and wouldn't *that* be awkward?

She put out the torch and then lighted a small candle, intending to relight the torch once she set it back in its bracket outside Tancred's door. With a heavy sigh, she left her room as quietly as possible, aware of the nuns that slumbered nearby.

On cat feet, she hurried back across the courtyard that separated the old keep from the new. Retracing her path through the passageway that passed between the kitchens and the great hall, she avoided the sleeping servants and slipped up the steps to the second level, the dark mantle she'd donned in her room flowing around her. A furtive survey revealed no one to her, and she replaced the torch, tipping the flame of her taper to it until it caught on the wood.

The door was as she'd left it—standing halfway open. Inside, the candle she'd forgotten was burning cheerfully. As she reached out to snuff it, her gaze was drawn to the censer, as if by a magnet. She had also forgotten to replace the pierce-worked cover. She frowned. It wasn't like her to forget so many details.

The incense looked like a lump of blackened resin in the elegant silver dish. What *was* that stuff? She thought she'd identified frankincense, which she'd smelled in the chapel on holy days, and the floral fragrance of cabbage rose, but there were other scents she could not identify, some spicy, but one that was intensely sweet, almost cloying.

She walked to the censer where again, she inhaled deeply. A pleasant warmth rolled through her body. Hmm. Definitely frankincense. Rose. Perhaps mint. What were those others? Had she never smelled the ingredients before? This was maddening!

Perhaps if she burned the incense—just for a moment, a very short moment—she would be able to identify the other ingredients and let the matter rest.

Touching the yellow flame of the candle to the lump of resin, she watched. At first the incense resisted. Then, slowly, it caught. She exhaled softly on it until she saw a line of red ember on the resin. When a thin, lazy thread of smoke wafted upward, she leaned over and breathed in. The delicate tissues of her nostrils tingled as the aromatic air passed through.

Rosamund blinked, trying to focus. 'Twas the most unusual feeling. Her eyes drifted closed. There it was again—that sensation of . . . floating.

With a thump, she sat down on the side of the bed beside the censer. Floating. That was a good word. Either she was floating or the chamber was. It didn't seem to matter which.

Gradually, her perceptions of the things around her shifted. The golden fur of the coverlet grew more brilliant. Beneath her palms, each hair felt thick and coarse. If she smoothed her hand one way, the shortish hairs bristled up. If she smoothed her hand in the opposite direction, the fur lay down, glossy and sleek.

Opening her eyes, she almost gasped with awe at the entrancing intensity of colors in the sumptuous tapestries and carpets surrounding her. For a while, she just sat there gazing at them.

"When Ranulf told me you had asked after me, *ma chère*," a deep, masculine voice said from the doorway, "I had no idea you were so impatient for my return."

Rosamund turned. It seemed to take forever before she could clearly view Tancred. She smiled dreamily. "Are you well?"

He frowned. Then he strode into the chamber, his boots muted by the rich floor coverings. His hair was damp, as was his naked upper body. He wore only his braies. Leaning down, Tancred brought his face close to hers. He peered into her eyes.

She went cross-eyed trying to keep him in focus in the wavering glow of the two candles.

"Jesú," he muttered. He snuffed the burning incense. As he did so, she flopped backward onto the fur coverlet.

"What possessed you to enter my chamber, damoiselle?" he demanded as he grasped her upper arms, drawing her back into a sitting position.

She widened her eyes, trying to align the images of his face. "Rats."

His scowl deepened. "Rats?"

She was sure she nodded only slightly, but her head seemed to bounce like an inflated bladder. "Yea, m— m—my lord. Rats. Nasty creatures, rats. They get into everything."

"Unlike a certain lady I know," he said dryly.

"Well. Marcus and I searched this floor after he found a nest." She shook her head. A mistake. The world swooped sickeningly. "But most of this floor is the solar, you see. *Your* chamber. Lord a—a—and master. Couldn't have rats in here, now, could we? Next thing you know, they would be upstairs in the abbess's chamber."

"Ah. So now we get to the true reason rats concerned you."

Was that a smile lurking behind those splendid lips? Rosamund leaned fractionally closer and peered at them. "Are you smiling?" she asked, suspicious.

The corners of his mouth twitched. "Me? Certainly not. I'm much too vexed to smile."

His jaw was shadowed by new beard. Her brow wrinkled. "You have not shaved." Then she remembered that he had been tracking brigands since morning.

"Did you catch the brigands?"

"Most of them."

"Oh, forgive me. I'm in your way. You . . . you must be exhausted." Instead of rising from the bed, she ran her hands over his wide, bare shoulders, feeling the smooth subtleties of muscles and bone beneath his supple flesh. "Are you unharmed?"

"Yea, *ma églantine*," he said, his voice oddly hoarse. "I am unharmed."

Rosamund felt as if she were spiraling down into the liquid silver of his gaze. Without knowing why, she gently brushed her fingertips over his beard. "I feared for you, Tancred," she murmured.

It was true, so very true. She had worried since she had learned of his mission. She didn't understand why she had told him, though.

He covered her hand with his larger, stronger one. Lowering his head, Tancred caressed her palms and fingers with the plush feel of his new beard. "I know."

As if catching himself in some forbidden act, he let go of her hand. "Listen to me, Rosamund. You are feeling the effects of the incense. It releases your normal restraint—"

Her lashes lowered as she surveyed his powerful body. The dark, crisp curls that bisected his deep, ridged chest narrowed as it descended into the waist of his braies. He smelled of sun-warmed well water and elemental male. "I feel things," she told him languidly. "Strange, delicious things."

A muscle in his jaw jumped. " 'Tis the incense. It makes one . . ." His voice died as she leaned toward him to set one fingertip upon his full upper lip.

He went still.

Giving that strong bow her full attention, she slowly glided the pad of her forefinger along the voluptuous curves.

Abruptly, Tancred caught her hand in his, removing her finger from his lip. He took a deep breath and exhaled sharply through his nostrils. "This incense makes one more aware of one's . . . body."

"You have just breathed the incense," she pointed out. "Do you not wish to touch my lip?" As if by her wish she commanded his eyes, his gaze fastened onto her mouth.

"I have breathed this stuff often," he replied gruffly. "Too often. I have developed some resistance. You have none. Come, I must return you to—"

"Touch my lips, Tancred. No one ever touches my lips," she complained softly.

"Be glad of it, little nun. 'Twould only make you unhappy." He pulled her to her feet.

She looked up at him. "I am not a nun yet," she said. Why would he not touch her lips? She would happily touch his again.

He gazed down into her face, and she caught a brief glimpse of hunger quickly shuttered away. "No," he said, lowering his head, his voice sinking to a rough whisper. "You are not." Lightly, softly as the breath of a butterfly, he brushed his mouth across hers.

Sensation sparkled over her parted lips. When she remained breathless and still, wrapped in the gossamer of wonder, he touched his mouth to hers again, this time lingering to gently pluck her bottom lip between his own, then settling over to kiss her with slow, thorough possession.

Oh, had anything ever felt so fantastical? Like faerie

dust and summer honey and crystal mead all rushing through her at once, whirling in her mind, glimmering through her body in an aching, thrilling stream.

Following her need to get closer to him, Rosamund slid her palms up his firm chest, to his wide shoulders and up the strong column of his masculine neck. She buried her fingers in the damp silk of his hair. "Again, please."

Beneath the black fringe of his lashes, his eyes were startling rims of silver encircling gleaming black pupils. He made no move to kiss her again, his body taut beneath her arms. "Greed is a sin, little nun." His voice was harsh, as if it rose from a parched soul.

She rose onto her toes, sliding her body up his, at first for balance, then because it felt good. She sought to reach his mouth with hers. "Then, my lord, I am a sinner."

SIXTEEN

He remained unbending, keeping his head facing sternly forward, his eyes fixed on the wall. Determined, she curled her fingers into his hair, towing his head down, bringing his face closer to hers. It mattered not to her that his fierce, beautiful face convulsed with an expression of anguish.

"No, Rosamund," he whispered harshly.

Even as she heard his words, she sensed that he had lost to her. Some strange, ancient, element within her rejoiced.

Tancred dragged her more fully against his body as he took her lips in a searing, openmouthed kiss of claiming. Joy swept through Rosamund with the force of summer wildfire, and when his tongue sought hers, she stroked it with her own, twined with it in an untamed mating.

His warrior's hand found her breast, strong fingers conforming to the full contour of its outer curve. She pressed into his palm and heard him growl deep in his throat. His thumb slipped over her tight nipple, launching a shaft of lightning through her. How could such a simple touch have such a powerful effect, she wondered dazedly.

His lips trailed kisses along her temple, behind her ear, down her jaw. One hand stroked her back, riding up and down her spine. It moved with a slowly increasing pace as his mouth wooed her, charmed her, tempted her.

The hand inched a little lower, to her waist. Below her waist. It slid over the nascent curve of her buttocks. Each splayed finger made its own warm impression. Then his palm crested that curve. It cupped her, easing her hips closer to his. Through her light woolen garments and the linen of his braies, Rosamund felt the rampant ridge of his arousal.

A candle went out.

For the first time she noticed the increased tempo of his breathing. He placed his hands on her shoulders, and gently, but firmly, moved her farther away from him.

"Mayhap 'tis only a candle," he said, his voice rough. "Or mayhap it is a small act of God reminding me that what we're doing is wrong."

No! He was mistaken. What they were doing was right. It felt so very right. "Tancred—"

"Best I see you to your chamber. On the morrow, you will have an aching head from the incense. I would not have you suffer more pain than that. Rosamund," he went on quickly when she drew breath to object, "tomorrow you will feel different about this. You will resent me for the embarrassment you will feel. I would not have you hate me more for taking something precious from you." He moved to touch her cheek with the back of his fingers, but seemed to catch himself. He let his hand drop to his side. "I am well enough acquainted with you, *ma églantine*, to know you are no easy woman. If ever you give yourself to a man it will be because he means something to you."

He was wrong, she thought as he escorted her back to her chamber, taking care that they were not seen.

She resented him now.

The following morning Rosamund felt as if she had slept with her head in a kettle, and a score of Satan's imps had spent the night banging on it with clubs. Just when she believed she could not feel worse, she remembered how she'd all but ravished Tancred.

She couldn't face him yet, she thought, panicking. She could *not* sit next to him through the meal, visible to all, while she could almost see his lips forming the word "harlot." So she sent word that she was unwell and then hid in her chamber, half certain he would demand her presence in the great hall.

Far from dragging her out of hiding, he instructed the kitchen to send breakfast to her room. Edeva arrived only minutes after the tray.

"I expected to find you at death's door," she teased as she sat down on the edge of Rosamund's bed. "Instead I find you as lovely as ever."

"I don't *feel* lovely." Rosamund wanted to confide in her friend, but she could not bring herself to utter the shaming words. So she ate in near silence, trying to listen to Edeva, yet distracted by the memory of what had passed in Tancred's chamber. And that incense . . .

"And then the donkey said to me, 'Edeva, you can say anything at all because Rosamund is not listening to you.' "

Rosamund blinked. "A donkey said what?"

Edeva released a long-suffering sigh. "Have you heard anything I've been saying? Besides the donkey speaking, that is."

"I apologize," Rosamund said, contrite. "My head feels thick and dull. But I want to hear what you have to say. I'll listen better, I promise."

Edeva leaned closer to scrutinize Rosamund's face. Fearing her guilt would show in her eyes, Rosamund's gaze slunk down and away.

"You are a trifle paler than usual," Edeva observed with a slight frown.

"I'm well enough," Rosamund said. " 'Tis only that my head is pounding."

Laughing, Edeva shook her head. "What a terrible liar you make."

Rosamund chewed her bottom lip, glowering at what was left of the manchet loaf.

"It must be something most terrible," Edeva said softly.

"It is."

"Please don't make me have to try to trick you into telling me. You've always been too clever for me, and I find it quite depressing."

"I'm a fallen woman," Rosamund blurted. "No self-respecting abbey will want me now. No self-respecting man would want me. Indeed, *I* do not much like me!" She pressed her fingertips to her temples. "And my head throbs most foully."

She poured out a confession of what had taken place the night before, fearing that Edeva would form a disgust for her, but needing to get the tawdry matter out in the open. When she finished, she stared down at her hands lying on the coverlet, waiting on Edeva's rejection, hoping that it would not come.

"Rats, eh?" Edeva said. "For certes, I would not have thought of that excuse. Perhaps it will work on Kadar."

"It was not an excuse," Rosamund insisted. Then, "I have noticed you are paying Kadar a goodly amount of attention. And why did you tell him you are not a nun and will not become one? The convent is your protection, Edeva, the sisters your family."

Edeva clasped Rosamund's hands in her own, as if she needed corporeal contact with a friend. "And none are dearer to me. I do not doubt their love. But I do not fit there. I am like . . . I am like a bramble grafted onto a lily. They all try to help me. They even make excuses for my failures, hoping to help me fit more smoothly into their life in the abbey. But I have lived there many years now. Certainly long enough to know." She sighed. "Somehow, I always manage to be the stone dropped into the abbey's tranquility."

Her dark eyes glistened with unshed tears. "I want to be like Sister Octavia or Abbess Matilda, but I can never seem to manage for long."

Rosamund lightly squeezed Edeva's hands, seeking to console the pain she had never suspected. "You are who you are, and I would not change that for all the world on a silver plate."

Edeva's mouth trembled. She smiled but it quickly faded. A tear escaped her eye, and rolled down her cheek. "My mother was a Gypsy, did you know that?"

Rosamund shook her head.

"The terrible family secret," Edeva said lightly, but her casual tone could not fully cover her hurt. "It was a love match that infuriated my father's family. My mother's family left her behind in disgust when she accepted my father's offer of marriage. But my parents were deeply attached to each other. I was their only child." Her smile was genuine this time. "Life was so good for the three of us. My father's relations, of course, were offended that their eldest son's sole child was so dark. Like a Gypsy."

Rosamund ached for her. "What silly folk."

Edeva's smile faltered. "When my mother died, it was the end of my world. It was also the end of my father's. After that, he cared about nothing. If he could have followed her into the grave, I believe he would have done so gladly. Then his family swarmed in, and his mother sent me to Hembley Abbey. Later, I received word that he had been wed to a proper lady." She swallowed. "I have always pitied her. All she got was a husk."

Rosamund felt a great deal less sympathy for Edeva's father than she felt for Edeva, who had been a grieving child when she'd been carted off to a distant abbey. Neatly and respectably disposed of. And her father had allowed it.

"Kadar is out of place, too," Edeva said. "While anyone can see that he and Lord Tancred are bound by affection as strong as any brothers', Kadar will never be enough like the other men to be completely at ease."

She met Rosamund's gaze squarely. "I want him, Rosamund. I have never wanted a man for my own. Not this much. I *know* that I am his match. I would understand his loneliness. I think he could understand mine." She gave Rosamund a wavering smile. "He likes my dark looks."

"Edeva, what do you even know of the man?" Rosamund asked earnestly, worried by this revelation.

Edeva lifted her chin. "I know that he is intelligent and that he is honorable."

"Yea, two good qualities, but he could be brutal—"

"He is not. I have watched him, asked about him when I could . . . without being too conspicuous. I know that he has a good heart. Did you know that he is tutoring Will with his lute? Kadar plays the instrument beautifully."

"He does?" That came as news to Rosamund.

"Lord Tancred asked him to tutor the lad because he knows how proficient Kadar is with the lute."

Rosamund blinked. "He did?"

Edeva nodded. "Have you not noticed how much better Will plays the lute these evenings?"

She had. "Lord Tancred sought out Kadar and asked him to teach Will?"

"Did I not just say as much?"

"Perhaps it was Kadar's idea," Rosamund suggested. She wanted the truth. *Needed* the truth.

Edeva chuckled. "Oh, no. Kadar would not do that. He does not wish anyone to know he plays the lute, so please say nothing about it."

"His secret is safe with me," Rosamund muttered bemusedly. "How did you come to learn this?"

Edeva's smile lighted the chamber. "Kadar told me. I thought I would never succeed in coaxing him to talk with me. You know how he becomes like a stone and is so somber when I am around. I believe I've finally managed to convince him that I don't bite. He is still overly formal with me, but that will change when he falls in love with me."

Rosamund regarded their joined hands. "Have you . . . Edeva, have you considered that he is not a Christian and not likely to become one? I have seen him at his devotions. He is most tranquil, then, I think. I've never seen anyone here ridicule him for it, but I can only believe that someone has, mayhap more than one. Still, he openly observes his faith. I cannot believe he would convert, not even for love of a woman."

"I would not ask it of him," Edeva said firmly.

"Edeva, you are not thinking of denouncing your faith?" Rosamund asked, shocked. That was unthinkable. Besides, the Church was harsh with those they considered heretics. The term "heretic" seemed dangerously pliant in the Church's hands. "You would be in peril. Even Kadar is not truly safe."

"I am interested in learning more about his beliefs. That does not mean I will tamely embrace them as my own. But I do not accept that we know everything about God or His will. Perhaps I shall learn something interesting from Kadar."

She peered more closely into Rosamund's face. "How is your head?"

"Better. It was either drinking that caudle or your news that made me forget it."

Edeva laughed.

Rosamund rose from her bed. She went to the ewer, poured some of its cold water into the basin, then washed her face. "I believe I've discovered who cries out in his sleep and wakes Abbess Matilda. I may be able to solve his problem, which will also solve hers."

Edeva's eyes grew large. "Lord Tancred is the one?"

"How did you know?"

Edeva chuckled. "You hide from him for some reason."

Pulling a tunic and a kirtle from the chest at the foot of

her bed, she quickly began to dress. Without being asked, Edeva assisted her.

"Well, I am not certain, so tell no one. He burns a strange sort of incense to help him sleep," Rosamund explained. "It does not work as well for him as it once did. He told Abbess Matilda that the man whose shouts have awakened her is afflicted with night terrors." She paused as she pulled on her hose to look at Edeva. "Night terrors would keep a man from sleeping properly, perhaps make him cry out."

"Yea, they do. Occasionally, patients in the abbey's infirmaria have night terrors. They scream and thrash until they are awakened. 'Tis enough to break one's heart."

Rosamund pushed her foot into her shoe. "I should think that being captured and tortured by an enemy might be enough to give any man night terrors."

"It would indeed."

"So, if Lord Tancred needs a strong sleeping draft, one that does not give him an aching head, I will turn my hand to it." She looked out the window. "The meal is over. I can go to the herbarium without being noticeable." The courtyard she must cross was busy now.

Rosamund eased out the door, Edeva following close behind her.

"How will you convince him to drink your potion?" Edeva asked, hurrying to keep up. "Word has already spread about how quickly Lord Tancred turned it down for one of his men. Who is really Lord Tancred."

Rosamund swiftly descended the stone stairs. "I do believe Lord Tancred is suspicious of my vaunted green magic."

"You said you had no such magic," Edeva pointed out.

"And I do not."

They wended their way through the castle grounds and then hurried down the kitchen and physic garden paths until they finally reached the cottage that served as her herbarium. Once inside, Rosamund set to work.

"It must be strong," she muttered as she worked. "It must do what that incense cannot."

"Do not forget the unpleasant effects of that incense. Your head?" Edeva said as she inspected the contents of a jar. She sniffed and made an approving sound, then stoppered it and replaced it on a shelf above a work table.

Reminded now of the effects of that incense, it was not of the headache that Rosamund thought. Anything that could strip away a lifetime of decorum was dangerous indeed.

It was frightening to discover how easily her defenses had collapsed. Not only had her defenses gone down, her offenses had clearly come up. Indeed, she had been so offensive that it made her cringe at the thought of facing Tancred at supper. Rosamund took a deep breath, then huffed it out. Well, she would live through it. She had lived through worse.

Finally she regarded the results of her labor: a dark brownish-green that filled a small pot. This potion should bring Tancred healing sleep. Unlike the incense, the herbs she had used did not drastically lower one's restraints, nor did they leave one feeling heavy-headed and dull the following morning. If he did not appreciate the green flavor of the mixture, why, then he could stir it into a cup of brakott—sweetened and spiced ale.

If he would.

If he would even consider taking it.

Rosamund sighed as she added more valerian root to the preparation. He *needed* this potion.

Her hands paused.

"What is it?" Edeva asked.

"I know of a way to make certain Lord Tancred takes this sleeping draft."

At the last meal of the day, the cup bearer brought the lord of Wynnsef brakott.

Tancred regarded the contents of his goblet. "Are we out of wine?" he asked.

"No, my lord," the bearer replied.

Watching from just within the passageway to the kitchens, Rosamund decided it was time for her to make her appearance. The way Tancred looked into his cup told her this might not go as smoothly as she had hoped. Swiftly she crossed the space between the passageway and the dais.

Abbess Matilda sipped from her cup. " 'Tis quite excellent," she told Tancred, as rehearsed. "I should have expected that any brakott produced here would be superior to the ordinary stuff."

"Is there a problem, Lord Tancred?" Rosamund inquired politely as she slipped into her chair, just as if she had not twined her arms about his neck last night.

His eyebrows drew down, but he met her gaze. "Not a problem, precisely. Why are we being served ale instead of wine?"

"Are you such a creature of habit that you wish to drink the same thing every day? I developed a new *recette* for brakott, and since there was an exceptional batch of ale available, I thought to try it out now. You know what a short while ale does keep."

"So you plan to test this new variety of brakott on us?" Finally, his gaze swung to her, clashing with her own.

He was looking for a fight.

Rosamund did not intend to give him one. "No, I have already tested it. I like it well, as do all else who have tried it. Even my lady abbess finds it pleasing, and her tastes are highly refined."

"And mine are not, is that what you mean?"

"If that is what I meant, Lord Tancred," she replied mildly, "then that is what I would have said."

She slipped the flagon she carried, out of sight amongst the folds of her skirt, onto the table as she held Tancred's attention with her eyes. "You have not even tried the brakott, but if you prefer to have wine, then I will have Dunton open a new cask just for you." She turned to the cup bearer. "Please ask Dunton to open the Burgundy, then bring some to Lord Tancred." This was as close to a battle as she would give him, for it served her purpose.

He snapped up the bait. "No," Tancred said to the cup bearer. "That will not be necessary. I'll drink the brakott."

With a furtive gesture, she shooed the cup bearer away. Gratefully, the boy escaped.

Rosamund welcomed her mission of getting the sleeping potion down the stubborn Moon Lord's gullet; it distracted her from the jangling nerves that came of remembering she had shared with him breathtaking kisses last night.

The meal progressed, with Tancred brooding in silence while Abbess Matilda and Rosamund carried on polite conversation around him. When he finished his first cup of brakott, she poured him one from the flagon she had brought—the one containing the sleeping draft.

It had been necessary to confide her plan to Abbess Matilda earlier because Rosamund knew it would have been impossible to keep the special flagon available to Tancred, yet out of the abbess's sharp-eyed notice. In explaining how she knew the identity of the man suffering the night terrors, Rosamund had omitted some of the facts, which was something else she would need to confess to Brother Felix when all of this was over. At this rate, she would need an entire day just for confession.

Tancred was a large man, and Rosamund estimated that it would take two cupfuls of the dosed brakott for the potion to have its effect on him.

Her estimate proved wrong. He poured himself a third cup before she could stop him, but still she saw no signs of drowsiness. Disappointed at her failure to help him, she managed to replace the flagon of the "special" brakott with the ordinary stuff.

The evening wore on, with Tancred saying little. It was not until the honeyed pears were served that Rosamund and the abbess succeeded in coaxing Tancred into discussing what had passed between the patrols and the brigands.

"You said that you had apprehended most of them," Rosamund said. No sooner had she said that than the memory of where she and Tancred had been when he had told her that flooded her mind. Her cheeks heated. "How did you capture them?"

"We did not capture them. We killed them," he said bluntly.

Rosamund and Abbess Matilda sat in stunned silence for a moment.

"They knew that either way they were dead men," he continued, perhaps sensing that his words had been too harsh. "They refused to surrender to us, though we gave them the chance. I suppose they preferred a quick death rather than strangling at the end of an executioner's rope." He finished off the last of the second cup of dosed brakott. "Some were rogue knights. Most of them were starving men-at-arms who could find no lord."

"Men-at-arms who could find no lord? There is always need for them," Abbess Matilda said.

Tancred watched as Will went to his customary stool in the middle of the hall. "This is no demand for a fighting man who is missing a hand, an arm, or a leg, my lady abbess."

Rosamund knew that the life of a warrior was good only as long as he was hale, hearty, and employed. Even if fate spared him loss of life or limb, eventually age would steal his swift response and supple grace. Unless, by that time, a knight had been able to accumulate a goodly sum from tourneys, wed an heiress, or secure an estate, he faced a wretched existence of poverty. To men-at-arms, the avenues for elevation were even more limited.

Will started with a favorite in the hall, a jaunty song

about a cuckolded miller. His fingers moved nimbly over the strings of his lute, adding flourishes his playing had lacked before.

"Will's skill with the lute has improved remarkably, don't you think, Lord Tancred?" Rosamund inquired, her heart warmed by the thought that this knight had persuaded a friend to help the lad improve his musical skill—and had said nothing to anyone about it.

"Yea." Tancred smothered a yawn.

Rosamund sighed quietly with relief. The potion was working after all. Soon his eyes would grow heavy, and he would retire to his chamber for the night.

At that moment, Will lifted his voice. "I humbly wish to dedicate this, my first *chanson de geste*, to Lord Tancred, my generous patron."

And adored hero, Rosamund thought, smiling. Justly so. Tancred had allowed Will to accompany him on more than one occasion. Arnaud's horror of imperfection had caused him to spurn the lad, refusing to allow him within sight.

Will played a lovely melody of his own composition as an introduction to the song, priming his audience for the forthcoming story of knightly honor and feats of bravery. Rosamund had felt honored when Will had nervously asked her opinion of the *chanson* before he risked playing it for his hero. For a troubadour's first major effort, Rosamund thought he had done extremely well.

She sneaked a glance at Tancred. Although he objected to those other already existing songs about him, she felt certain he would be touched by Will's labor of devotion.

Sending his voice soaring—always a risk—the notes hit true, and Will launched into his composition.

Tancred fell forward onto the table with a thud.

Rosamund glared at him. "My lord, how could you?" she hissed. "You will crush the lad's feelings!"

Tancred did not stir.

Rosamund's heart leaped into her throat. "Holy Sepulcher," she muttered. Quickly she placed her hand under his nostrils. He was breathing.

Shouts rose from some of his men. Knights bolted from their seats, leaping onto the dais.

"He is dead!" one exclaimed.

Chaos erupted then. Women cried out as they were buffeted in the unruly crowd. Benches crashed to the floor. Wolfhounds barked. A din of alarmed voices escalated.

"He is not dead!" Rosamund insisted. "He lives!"

In the panic, the men did not seem to hear her.

One of the knights lifted Tancred's empty goblet to his nose and sniffed. He spat a venomous oath. "Our liege lord has been poisoned!" he cried. Then he turned to glare at Rosamund. "I say the witch did it!"

SEVENTEEN

From the window of the state bedchamber, Rosamund watched the sky grow pearly gray with the promise of dawn.

"You have not moved from that spot since those fools imprisoned us," Abbess Matilda said from the massive curtained bed. She stretched and yawned.

Rosamund made no reply as she picked out a trace of rose in the sky.

Edeva ceased her pacing for a moment. "They should have released us by now. After all, Rosamund said he lived."

Even sunk in her deep cocoon of misery, Rosamund dully read the silence that followed. It was in all their minds, made more terrible by the uncertainty: *Tancred had died in the night.*

She had lost patients before. It was not rare that wounds or afflictions were beyond her power to cure. Even so, after she had done all that she could, she always grieved.

Never had she killed anyone.

Never, that is, before last night.

She had made the potion strong, for it had seemed to her that it needed to be if it was to do what even the powerful incense could not. Still, she had used care when measuring each ingredient.

Of its own accord, her hand went to the breast of her kirtle under which lay the crimson silk pouch, and

the precious token it contained. She had stitched the
pouch to a ribbon the morning after she had shared
kisses with Tancred. It would have been so easy for
him to have taken her. She had all but lifted her skirts
for him. Even through the fog of incense, she could
see that he had wanted her. Despite that, despite her
unseemly cajoling, he had not taken advantage of her.

The strength of his honor had caused her to consider. Alone, in the dead of night, she had examined
her heart. What she had found there had shaken her.

Even now it threatened to shatter the tenuous foot-
hold she had painstakingly carved in the precipice of
life. Yet she was not without her own honor. She knew
her duty. Accordingly, she would not acknowledge her
true feelings about Tancred to anyone. As Edeva and
Abbess Matilda had slept, Rosamund had wept silent tears.

Rosamund would have been the last person in England to desire Tancred's death. She had meant only
to help him, to give him some relief from the torment
of his dreams. Still, no one had come to this chamber
where Abbess Matilda, Edeva, and Rosamund had
been confined by Tancred's men, and so, as hour
trailed hour, the question had run through her mind
a hundred—no, a thousand—times. Had she murdered Tancred?

As the sun rose above the east curtain wall, Brother
Felix was admitted into the room. Alas, he could tell
the women nothing, for Tancred still lay unconscious
on his bed in the solar, as he had since the knights
had carried him there. The four of them celebrated
Mass together, then the good brother was let back out
of the room.

Breakfast was brought to them. When Rosamund
would have turned away, Abbess Matilda scolded her
until she managed to choke down several bites. Then
the abbess had gently stroked Rosamund's stiff shoulders in wordless solace.

Neither Edeva nor Abbess Matilda reproached Ro-

samund for their own confinement—the punishment
they suffered because of her. Mayhap the guilt she felt
would have been easier to bear if they had.

Together, they knelt and prayed.

That was how Kadar and the guards found them.
"Lord Tancred has awakened," he said, his dark,
handsome face impassive. "He commands you attend
him."

His gaze lingered on Edeva, who lifted her chin and
gave him a cold glance before looking away.

Another shadow on her conscience, Rosamund
thought as the tall knights escorted them down the
stairs to the solar—the destruction of Edeva's
happiness.

At least Tancred lived, and for that she sent up a
silent, joyous prayer of thanksgiving.

Upon seeing them, a man-at-arms opened the door
to the solar. Inside, Tancred sat in a carved, Roman-
style chair. His hair was still wet from washing. He
had shaved and changed his garments. Beneath his
eyes, the usual smudges of fatigue were gone. When
he saw the women, he rose to his feet.

With anxious eyes, Rosamund studied his color and
found it excellent. From all appearances, Tancred had
enjoyed a long, restoring slumber.

He invited them to sit. Abbess Matilda chose to
stand, and Rosamund and Edeva took their lead from
her, also remaining on their feet.

Tancred had not felt this well in some time. He had
learned to function despite the disturbance of the
night terrors, for it was that or perish. He had forgotten what it was to sleep the whole night through.

Upon waking, he had been surprised to learn that
his men held Rosamund, the abbess, and Edeva in the
state bedchamber. It seemed his men had feared he
had been poisoned by the Green Witch.

Now he allowed himself the luxury of looking at
Rosamund. She was so very beautiful to him. He re-

gretted the half-circles of sleeplessness that resembled bruises. At that moment, she moved slightly, and the sunlight coming through the window caught the faint, silvery tracks of tears on her cheeks. His heart clenched at the sight.

He steeled himself to reality. She would forever remain beyond his reach. She was destined for the convent. He was destined to bring death to her brother.

"I have been told that you sought to poison me, Rosamund Bourton. What have you to say for yourself?"

Abbess Matilda made a sound of disgust, but otherwise held her tongue.

"Had I wished your death, Lord Tancred, you would be dead," Rosamund said, echoing words of his from another, more innocent, exchange. "It was my intent to help you to find restful sleep, nothing more."

"So it was a sleeping draft that you placed in my brakott."

"Yea, lord. Nothing more sinister than that."

He lifted a single eyebrow. "And yet I fell unconscious at table." Just thinking about how weak and foolish he must have appeared to everyone in the hall embarrassed him.

Her silken cheeks grew a charming shade of pink. "I knew that I must make the potion strong in order for it to work for you. I . . . may have miscalculated *how* strong the draft needed to be."

Tancred felt refreshed and alert. "Did you devise this potion yourself, Lady Rosamund?"

"Yea, I did. These ladies are innocent."

He fixed her with a stern gaze. "Why did you not simply offer to give me this sleeping potion, instead of sneaking it into my cup?"

She met his gaze squarely. "If I had, my lord, would you have taken it, knowing that it had come from my hand?"

Too clearly, he recalled her earlier offer to make a sleeping potion for the "man-at-arms" he had told

Abbess Matilda was responsible for the nightly commotion. Tancred had quickly, bluntly turned it down.

"Perhaps not," he admitted gruffly. "Still, that does not excuse your act of slipping something into my drink. Were you one of my men, I would flog you myself."

"Your men have all sworn oaths of loyalty to you, Lord Tancred. I have not."

Nor, he knew, would she ever speak that one oath of lifelong loyalty he would give his blood to hear from her sweet lips—the vow of a woman to her husband.

"None of this would have been necessary had you not been so stubborn and superstitious, my lord Tancred," Abbess Matilda informed him crisply, her hands tucked into the loose sleeves of her brown kirtle.

He turned a cold gaze on her. "Madame, you are here on my sufferance and only because I, like you, have a care for Lady Rosamund's good name. Should anything of this sort occur again, however, you will no longer be welcome at Wynnsef Castle."

Abbess Matilda regarded Tancred evenly, her ageless, elegant face calm. "Does the truth anger you?"

"Deceit angers me. You would do well to bear that in mind."

"It was my idea," Rosamund interrupted, unwilling to let his displeasure fall on the innocent, fearing that he might offend the abbess enough to incite the Church against him. "It was my fault."

Tancred glanced at her. "I know."

"Then why—"

"Complicity, Lady Rosamund. Without the aid of Abbess Matilda or Lady Edeva, you would have been hard-pressed to succeed in your plan—as well-intended as it perhaps was." Tancred looked at the abbess. "My lady abbess, your calling requires forgiveness. Mine requires . . . caution." Their gazes held for a long moment. Then the abbess silently inclined her head.

As the three women left the solar, Kadar caught up with Edeva. The abbess went down the stairs, unaware of Kadar, but Rosamund halted some distance from them, unwilling to leave Edeva alone with the Saracen, uncertain of his intent, yet suspecting that he meant no harm.

His glance at Rosamund made it clear he would rather she were not present, but when she made no motion to go, he turned his attention to Edeva.

"I deeply regret having to detain you as I did," he told her in a low voice. Even Rosamund could see it was important to him that Edeva accept his apology.

Showing a hesitancy Rosamund had never before seen in her friend, Edeva searched his face.

"I would never harm you," he added earnestly when Edeva did not reply.

"I know that." Her voice was soft.

"Never did I believe you would seek to murder Tancred," he declared.

"I know that, also."

His handsome face brightened. "You do?"

Cheeks glowing dusky rose, Edeva nodded. She lowered her lashes. "Although I am not well acquainted with you, I know you are a good man. A brave and noble man."

Deep color moved up Kadar's neck, but he beamed like a lunatic. "I . . ." He caught sight of Rosamund and seemed to remember he was not alone with Edeva. He cleared his throat. "You do me great honor," he finished. His hands opened and closed in a restless gesture.

As if she could read what was in his mind, Edeva offered her hand to him. Swiftly he accepted it. Despite Rosamund's presence, he pressed a lingering kiss to the back of her hand. His head still lowered, he lifted a dark, soulful gaze to Edeva's. "I am your servant to command, my lady."

"You are very kind, Lord Kadar," Edeva said, the

tone of her voice speaking more than Rosamund
thought wise.

"We do not wish to keep Abbess Matilda waiting,
do we, Edeva?" she said briskly, feeling like an ogre
for interrupting this rare moment between these two.
Still, it did not take an oracle to interpret those moon-
calf looks they had shared. Best to allow them time
to consider the consequences of continuing in this
direction.

As Rosamund ushered Edeva down the stairs, she
felt vastly relieved that she had not harmed Tancred.
It was clear to anyone who looked that he had, in
fact, benefitted from her sleeping draft.

She also felt relieved that no action had been taken
by Tancred against any of them.

This was the *last* time she tried to help that usurping,
ungrateful man.

By the time the moon rose, Rosamund was in sore
need of the tranquility her garden offered. The day
had been filled with the strangest behavior from Tancred's men. They were especially courteous and
thoughtful to her. When she saw her brother's men—
now sworn to Tancred—she could feel only guilt. She
had betrayed her brother. She had been *kind* to the
enemy.

She had fallen in love with the enemy.

So she slipped through the dark, now, with only her
candle for light, its flame protected by her cupped
hand. The heavy, iron-studded door opened to her as
quietly as ever. She locked it behind her.

She went to a turf bench, where she sat, drinking
in the soothing night sounds. She waited for the feeling of peace to steal over her as it always did. There
was only the music of the water flowing down the
fount, the faint rustling of the leaves stirred by a soft
breeze. Breathing deeply, she took in the scents of
moist earth, of thriving plants, of burgeoning flowers.

Oh, if only she could live here. No more Arnaud.

No more enduring his resentment, no more bearing her guilt. No more struggling to make Wynnsef profitable enough to pay for his pleasures and scutage without sucking the peasantry dry.

The convent would be like this garden. Everyone would have a task. No one would be taxed beyond her abilities. Harmony. Peace. Like this special place.

She heard a soft metal scraping at the door. Turning her head, she watched as it opened.

Tancred stopped short as soon as he saw her. "Don't you ever come here by day?"

Rosamund remained sitting on the turf bench, leaning back on her hands. "When? When would I have time to come here during the day? There is always something that must be done. Every minute is filled."

He closed and locked the door behind him. "You would have more time if you didn't spend it making potions."

She chuckled bitterly. "Oh, I've certainly learned my lesson there. No more potions or tonics or . . . anything. I have patients enough who seek my aid. I'll not waste my precious time or effort on those who refuse my offers. Indeed, I'll make no more offers."

"No more offers." He strolled to a trellis supporting the lush new tendrils of honeysuckle.

"None." The word was short, clipped, final.

He coaxed a tender tip around the end of a forefinger. "What if someone asked you?"

"Asked me?" Rosamund found herself unable to look away from his gentle movements. "It's not enough."

He paused. "Not enough?"

"I have been imprisoned and shamed for aiding someone who clearly needed what I could willingly give, but who would not accept it from me. No. A mere asking would no longer be enough. I must know that what I give is truly desired. More than that. What I give must be *needed*. Urgently."

Tancred turned to face her. His face was a dramatic

mask of silver and onyx. "You are saying that you must be . . . begged?"

Restlessly, she stood and then wandered over to the fount, where she inserted the candle into its slot. "Yea, my lord. I suppose I am. Mayhap I weary of being undervalued."

He went to a wild cherry tree, where he idly breathed in the fragrance of the blossoms. "We are all undervalued at one time or other, damoiselle."

She lifted her head to look at Tancred. Yea, he was truly the Moon Lord, for as beautiful as he was by day, his beauty grew more powerful, more mysterious beneath the moon.

"Not so consistently, Lord Tancred. But no more. I am quit of that role in this life. I am a woman, not an ox or a donkey."

A pale flash told her he smiled. "No one would mistake you for either."

"Yet I am treated little better."

"I think not," he said sharply.

"Good night, my lord," she said, snatching up her candle. She moved swiftly toward the door.

Tancred moved swifter still. He caught hold of her arm.

She tried to tug free, but his grasp, while not tight, was iron-strong. "Unhand me," she commanded.

To her dismay, he not only refused to release her, he slowly drew her closer to him.

"No closer. Please," she beseeched.

He gazed down at her, his face shadowed, unreadable. "I am sorry," he said softly. "I would they had not confined you."

His fingers brushed the edge of her veil back, making her vividly aware that she had not worn a wimple as she felt the warmth of his skin against her temple. Her heartbeat quickened. "That is an apology," she informed him in an absurdly breathless voice.

"Yea. It is."

This close, the details of his face grew clearer. Rosamund wondered crazily if Apollo had ever been so comely. She doubted it. With a will, she concentrated on resisting him. Why wasn't it easier? There was no incense in her garden.

"That is not enough," she said.

"For blessed sleep you would have me beg?" he murmured, his breath glimmering across her cheek.

"Plead."

"Plead then. You would have me plead?"

"O-on your knees. For I offered my aid freely, but you sp . . ." Her voice died as her mind drifted, attuning itself to the pattern of his breath caressing her, to the beat of his heart. Catching herself, she cleared her throat. "You spurned it."

"I want you to continue to make the sleeping potion for me," he murmured, lightly nuzzling her jaw with his nose. It tickled.

"How cheaply you think I can be bought," she retorted. Despite her renewed resolution, her voice retained a tenuous quality that she feared would tell him how much power he wielded.

"Not cheaply."

She scowled, piqued by his confidence. "And not bought!" She jerked free of him. The candle went out.

She hurried to put the fount between them. "I am not clay in your hands, to be stroked and molded to your whim."

Tancred sighed. "No. Nothing so pleasurable as that."

"Oh!"

"Go sit on that bench, damoiselle."

Her eyes narrowed with suspicion. "Why?"

"If I must grovel, at least allow me to do it my way."

"Plead."

He ignored her correction. He pointed. "The bench. Go."

She considered for a moment, examining the situation from various angles, before deciding she was safe enough. Sidling away, keeping her distance, she went to the turf bench he indicated. She sat.

When he started toward her, she sprang to her feet. Abruptly he stopped. "Lady Rosamund," he said, his voice rife with impatience, "I promised you one month before any Wynnsef woman would be ravished. It has not yet been that long." As she sat down again, he muttered under his breath, "Of course, I never said I would never strangle a Wynnsef woman."

"I heard that!"

"Good." He reached her. Placing his hands upon her shoulders, he pressed her to sit back down again. "Now stay there."

The nerve of the man! she thought indignantly. Did his arrogance know no bounds?

To her astonishment, he went to one knee before her. He caught her hands in his, but she was too surprised to pull them away. He placed them against his solid chest. Beneath her palms, the fine wool of his black-and-silver surcoat felt smooth. Smooth and warm.

"Rosamund Bourton," he said, "I beg you to continue making me the sleeping potion. Not quite as strong as that first, if you please. But you were generous to make the first offer, and I was wrong to turn it down."

She looked down into his somber face, stunned.

"Will you find forgiveness in your heart for an ungrateful wretch?" he asked in a quiet voice.

Well, he was not the first to be suspicious of her abilities, she reluctantly admitted to herself. He was not the first to react to her this way. He was not even the most blatant. And he had intended no cruelty.

Some had. One had. It was his weapon. Papa had admired her gift with green growing things, with finding their needs and their powers. It was her bond with the land, and thus their strongest bond in common, hers and Papa's. Arnaud had been excluded. He possessed no innate tie, no empathy with the earth. While he might see and hear and speak, while his limbs and skin might be perfect, he lacked an essential sense. 'Twas not something that could be learned, for Arnaud was bright enough, and both she and Papa had tried to teach him. The lessons had only made poor Arnaud's frustration worse, until he had refused to acknowledge that any such tie to nature could exist. All the while, his anger had grown.

That poison did not fester within Tancred. He might have been uneasy with her gift, with the exaggeration of it that came through the stories told by the local folk, but he had not meant for her to be hurt. She felt it there in the unwavering clasp of his hands, in his steady gaze.

Did she have it in her to make him suffer when it was within her power to give him the healing gift of sleep?

He was the enemy. *The enemy.*

Yet she could not hate him. Not anymore.

"I will make you the sleep draft," she said. A smile teased her lips. "Not as strong as the last."

One corner of his wide, sensual mouth lifted. "Thank you. I cannot tell you how much better I felt this morning when I woke. I have never liked that incense. It clouds the mind."

That is not all that it does, she thought, flushing at the memory of lacing her fingers into Tancred's hair, of pressing her body to his. Most of all, she recalled the kisses. Vividly.

To her surprise, he sat on the daisy-dusted lawn, leaning his back against the bench, one shoulder close enough to her knee to warm it despite the mild spring cool.

"Why did you never wed?" he asked, looking up at her.

The question was impertinent, yet somehow she did not feel offended. "My father needed me. He never got over my mother's death and couldn't bear for me to leave home. Arnaud promised him on his deathbed that a suitable marriage would be arranged for me, but . . ." She shrugged, unwilling to cast her brother in an unpleasant light to the man who had stolen his heritage.

The heritage he had failed to safeguard, a small traitorous voice said from a dark corner of her mind.

"It is not too late," Tancred said.

She gazed down into his moon-filled eyes. There she thought she saw worlds of possibilities, but she knew it was only her imagination "It is. Much too late."

Rising, she walked to the tunnel arbor. The cycle of life was endless, she thought as she slipped her hand beneath a newly opened grape leaf, its delicate edges still slightly curled. The arbor was enclosed with new leaves. Buds on the rosebush were unfurling, now recognizable as flowers.

"Why is it too late?"

His voice came from behind her, and she tensed, afraid to feel his breath upon her skin, yet longing for the small miracle of that intimacy. A miracle that was part of the cycle of life.

A part that a nun must deny herself.

The deep, aching pain that realization brought her propelled her a few steps along the flower bed as she struggled to cope with it. Her breath came swift and shallow, like that of a wounded animal.

Why was acceptance so difficult now? So grievous? She had already acknowledged that hers would be a cloistered life. Her mouth spasmed in a brief, painful smile. The serenity of that prospect had, for years now, appealed to her. It was a far better way of life than the one she had led since the death of her father. Worked beyond her strength, ridiculed and criticized. Going into a convent would work no harm against her brother, yet there would be escape from him.

She turned her head slightly, glimpsing Tancred from the corner of her eye. How marvelous he looked in the moonlight. Any woman would want him. Likely,

many already did. Ladies of great fortune. Heiresses.
Young heiresses.

Tancred was not for Rosamund. There could be no
tranquility with a man such as him, no peace. Work
and heartbreak, that would be her lot with him. She'd
already received a sample of his caution. What would
be her fate next time something unexpected happened? Indeed, she took a risk even making more of
the sleeping draft for him. She was the Green
Witch. Suspect.

"What is it, Rosamund?" he asked.

"Nothing."

He stalked over to her, a predator coming after
his prey.

Yet when he rested his hand upon her shoulder, it
was a gentle touch.

"What is it, *ma églantine*? You tremble."

Ma églantine. My sweetbriar. The words were a dulcet breath against her veil.

She shook her head, trying halfheartedly to dispel
the magic he wove around her with his nearness, when
the mere thought of him entered her mind.

Her tongue-moistened lips went dry with panic.
"Tell me," she said, reaching for the thing most likely
to drive him away. "Tell me how you came to bear
that brand?"

He went still. She cringed against the pain of hurting him.

Slowly, as if unwilling feet bore him, he went to the
fount. There he cupped his hands, catching the crystal
water. Lifting it to his mouth, he drank, his eyes lowered, the muscles in his strong throat flexing with each
swallow. When he finished, he ran his wet hands over
his face, causing it to glisten, as if sprinkled by
faerie gilt.

She had wanted to drive him away, and she had
succeeded, but it brought her no triumph. Instead, she
felt hollow inside, as if her chest might cave in for
lack of inward support. Absently, she lifted the open-

ing bud of a plant a pilgrim had brought her. Bright
yellow in the daylight, it now lay pale in her paler
hand.

Did Tancred despise her? She thought that should
not bother her, but it did.

"I was branded," Tancred said in a quiet voice,
"while I was held captive in Bâb Al-Muhunnad,"

Eighteen

"Oh." She had thought as much, but hearing the words from him made the brand that rode his cheekbone more personal and the cruelty of it more immediate.

He remained by the fount, allowing the water to run over his hands. Taking a long breath, he eased it out. "Yasir, one of Sabih Ibn Qasim's officers, took a . . . liking to me."

She barely heard that last, so faint were the words. "Liking?" The word confused her. Did not the Saracens in that fortress hate the Christians?

Tancred looked down into the water. In the light of the moon, his face tightened. "He wanted me as . . . as a man wants a . . . woman."

Stunned, she stared at Tancred. No one could ever mistake this man for being anything other than a powerful, potent male.

"Was he *blind*?" she blurted, incredulous.

One side of Tancred's mouth curled briefly upward. "Not blind. Perverted. Yasir's private ways disgusted even Sabih Ibn Qasim, whose hatred of Christians was unrivaled."

She could not bring herself to ask if the officer had managed to have his way with Tancred. She was not certain she wanted to know.

Tancred scrubbed his palm against a stone leaf on the fountain. "When we were brought into the castle,

Yasir claimed me as his personal spoils. His slave. I did not know what he intended, for at that time I did not yet speak the language, nor did the other crusaders with me. He had his men pull me out of the starving group of captives I arrived with. I was taken to his . . . *harem*."

"*Harem?*"

He did not look at her. "In that part of the world, it is the place where the women of a household are kept in seclusion, away from the eyes of men other than husband or master. The word is also applied to the women who live there. Yasir kept a *harem* of men."

In the silvery glow of the moon, she saw Tancred swallow. "You need not say more," she told him, unwilling for him to suffer, yet frozen to the place where she stood.

He shook his head. "You have looked at this brand many times. Everyone does. Only those who survived Bâb Al-Muhunnad and Kadar know how I received it. And now you will."

She nodded.

"No language was necessary for me to know I was in direst danger once I saw the men who lived there. Handsome men, all. Well made, but for the scars and new wounds on their buttocks, their cocks, and coillions." Tancred rammed his fingers through his hair. "I could clearly see these marks. All any of them wore were robes of sheerest gossamer."

Rosamund recoiled at the lurid picture that conjured.

His hands gripped the edge of a stone leaf on the fount, but when he spoke, his words were low, nearly monotone. "Some of them had been castrated. They had no cocks or coillions. And the only hair any of them possessed was on their heads. Like Saracen women, every bit of their body hair had been removed."

"Sweet Mary," she breathed, sickened at what had been done to the men. "Were they all crusaders?"

"No. I discovered later there was only one other crusader among them. They came from many lands. Most had been purchased as slaves, but some were captives."

It horrified her to think the fate of those unfortunates had been shared by Tancred. Then vivid memory streaked into her mind. She had already witnessed firsthand that he remained magnificently whole, and that he bore no unsightly scars on those eminently noticeable areas of his body.

As if he could read her thoughts, Tancred gave her a grim, wolfish smile. "I fought him. Every chance I got, I struck out at him. I am a large man, but Yasir had giant eunuchs to do his will. I fought them, too. Yasir became furious and had me hung upside down. His slaves beat the soles of my feet with rods until I fainted from the pain."

Rosamund had never thought of the bottom of her feet being particularly sensitive, but as she listened, she realized that they were tender. Her experience in the well recalled the misery of hanging upside down. Her head had felt as if it would burst. She had no doubt that she would have passed out long before Tancred ever did. What pain there must have been in order to cause such a man to faint.

"I feared I would never walk again," he continued. "And crippled, I was easier prey. Or so Yasir thought. I managed to knee him in my struggles. After his giants beat me unconscious, he left me alone for almost a month. When my feet were healed enough, I tried to escape. I made it out of the *harem* and past Yasir's quarters. I got as far as one of the main courtyards in the fortress. As his creatures were closing in on me, I shouted a challenge for personal battle at him. Sabih Ibn Qasim was within hearing, but he did not understand French. By the time he'd had my challenge translated, I had been dragged to a whipping post, and Yasir was himself applying the whip to my bare back. Later, I learned that he wept as he did it." Tancred wiped his wet hands over his face again. "I pitied him then. Poor sick bastard. It had been easier just to hate him.

"Yasir had me carried back to his quarters. He tended my back with great care. Then he heated the ring he wore and branded me his. If he couldn't claim me the way he wanted, at least he could in this manner."

"Jesú," she whispered, thoroughly shaken. She crossed the distance between them with swift steps. Refusing to examine her folly, she embraced him.

Instantly, his arms came around Rosamund. Tancred held her tightly against his body, and she discovered that his heart was pounding. Dredging up this black past came with a painful price.

"Sabih Ibn Qasim insisted Yasir accept my challenge for a personal battle," he said, his cheek pressed against her hair. He made a sound that might have passed for a chuckle had it borne the faintest trace of real amusement. "Either way, he won. He would rid himself of an officer who disgusted him, or another despised Christian would die."

"Shall I take it you won that battle?" Rosamund asked, wishing she could soothe away for him all memory of his captivity. Was it any wonder nightmares plagued him?

He gently brushed back from her temple a tendril of hair that had escaped her plaits. "Yea. I slew him and pulled that cursed ring from his finger. Then I was thrown into that dark hole, but they did not take the ring from me."

"Do you still have it?"

He shook his head. "I smashed it between two rocks and buried the fragments in different places. I keep the brand as it is on my face as penance."

She lifted her head to look up at him. "Penance? You? After he . . . *harmed* you! He fought you, did he not? You both had swords?" Tancred murmured assent, and she went on. " 'Twas not even a truly equal fight, for you had been brutally treated, while he had not. No," she told him firmly. "God spoke in that battle."

Tancred pressed a soft kiss on the veil at the crown of her head.

That did not count, she told herself as butterflies swooped in her stomach. *He did not touch skin*.

"Did God speak when crusaders killed women and children? They were helpless. Sometimes, they were even Christian. The Church says they are heretics. But does God? I envy those whose faith is so strong that there is no room for question. They sleep the sleep of the righteous. I do have doubts, and for them I do penance." He rubbed his thumb over the brand. "A small punishment for the arrogance of uncertainty."

"Perhaps it is the memory that is the true punish-ment." A terrible one, it seemed to her.

"Mayhap you are right," he said softly.

A nightjar sang in the silence.

"Is . . . is that why you've taken the moon and stars as your blazon?" Rosamund asked.

"It is."

"And it is why you have been named the Moon Lord."

His fingertips stroked her shoulder. "No. I am called the Moon Lord because night is when I'm to be feared the most." She felt his lips curl into a smile against her temple. "Or so it is said."

She could easily believe that he was most dangerous when the moon ruled the sky. It had been nighttime when he had taken Wynnsef. "How came you to take castles by night? How did you learn to use such stealth?" There were always sentries posted on the wall walk. Even though Wynnsef had been desperately undermanned, no one had seen or heard Tancred or his men until it was too late.

He did not answer immediately, and she thought

she might have asked one question too many. Tancred fascinated her. She wanted to know everything about him, but she knew he was a private man.

"The way of things in Outremer are not simple," he said. His voice was low and haunted. "It is more than just Christians fighting Moslems to free Our Savior's land. There are many factions with conflicting interests. Among those involved are men who employ stealth to strike at their enemies. *Hashishiyun.* The Assassins. After a bizarre fashion, they are allies of the Templars, but no one knows to whom they are truly loyal. Their discipline is severe and their methods cunning. It was from them that I learned my skills, though several times it nearly cost me my life." He shrugged one shoulder, as if to shake off further discussion.

Rosamund had no wish to detain his thoughts in that harsh and terrible time.

They stood there in each other's arms for a while, wrapped in the quiet of the garden, serenaded by the gentle music of falling water and the wistful *churr* of a nightjar. Rosamund rested her cheek against Tancred's chest, her head tucked beneath his chin. She listened to the strong rhythm of his heartbeat and basked in the warmth of his embrace. It came to her that for the first time in years, she felt content. Protected.

Every woman should feel this way, she thought. But when she wanted to turn her face and press a kiss to his chest, she knew she enjoyed his embrace far too much.

As if sensing her unrest, Tancred curled a forefinger and nudged her chin up with his knuckle. He brushed his lips across hers once, twice, then settled to share with her a kiss of such yearning tenderness, she thought her heart would break. Once she had dreamed of just this. Of finding a man who could kindle in her the feelings and sensations that awoke to Tancred's touch.

Things had changed.

She had watched her friends wed and have children. For years, she had daily labored long, grueling hours, doing the work of a chatelaine and a seneschal because her brother would not part with the coin for the later, and she had been long-trained as the former. Her emotions had been battered by her own dashed hopes, her brother's animosity, and the caprice of nature and circumstance.

Finally, she had come to a decision. She would be a nun. In a convent she would find peace and order. There she could lose herself in the blessed serenity. Rosamund would become just another, ordinary slat in the mill wheel. Decisions would be made by someone else.

She felt worn and empty most of the day, every day. Now came a man who made her feel alive. But he had stolen what belonged to her brother. Her only brother. Her only family.

The door to the convent remained the only one truly open to her.

Rosamund bowed her head. Closing her eyes, she took a deep breath and summoned her willpower, praying for help in case that wasn't enough. Then she lifted her face to meet Tancred's questioning gaze.

"We both know," she said, her voiced threatening to break, "that the only way open to me is the convent. Please, Tancred—" Her throat closed, and she pressed her lips together, struggling for control. "Please, don't make this harder than I can bear."

His face grew shuttered, but even in the dim light, Rosamund saw the bleakness in his eyes.

She left him standing there, alone in the walled garden, and knew that each of them, in his own way, was a prisoner.

For the next several days, Tancred spent his time in sword and lance practice, working with his men, and in patrolling the land belonging to Wynnsef. Rosamund wondered if he had heard that her brother was on the march, or if this was usually what he had done before taking Wynnsef. She knew that he avoided her, as she did him. At meals they scarcely looked at each other and spoke even less. It left her feeling desolate.

She threw herself into the demands of administration that came with being seneschal and those of being chatelaine, trying not to think of Tancred, of his kisses, of his kindness, of their time together in the garden. But he came to her in the night. In her dreams she once again experienced the golden thrill of his lips, the sweet, intoxicating intensity of his caresses. The deep, midnight smoke of his voice curled around her like warm vapor. Like a sweet mist. Like exotic incense.

She woke from these visitations filled with a deep, haunting ache of loss. Invariably, she would think of his patience and generosity with Will and recall how he had given her the place of honor in her own household that Arnaud had denied her, and the tears would roll down the sides of her cheeks to dampen her pillow. A few hours of restless sleep was all she got each night.

As she had agreed, she made the sleeping draft for Tancred to take each night. Despite that, he did not look as if he slept much.

This morning, she retreated to her herbarium, where she had a balm to finish making. It was here that Edeva found her.

"I don't know what has passed between you and Tancred, but 'tis obvious to all that both of you are unhappy," she scolded.

Rosamund's cheeks heated. Surely she had not been so obvious. "You exaggerate," she said. "It's noticeable to you, but that's only because you are my dear friend."

Edeva inspected a small marble pestle sitting in its marble mortar on a worktable. "I *am* a dear friend, and that is why I have come to take you away from this place for a few hours." She moved to Rosamund and touched her arm. "It hurts me to watch you pretend that Lord Tancred does not own your heart. And he is as bad as you, though it is clear to everyone that you two love each other. It would be a good match. You would not even have to leave Wynnsef. Tancred does plan to engage a seneschal, Kadar has mentioned this to me."

Rosamund looked up from her work. "Kadar?"

"Yea." A dreamy expression came over Edeva's face. "Is Kadar not the most handsome, charming—" She seemed to catch herself. She straightened abruptly. "He and Lord Tancred are most protective of each other."

A ghost of a smile curved Rosamund's mouth. "So I have noticed. I find such loyalty endearing."

Edeva smiled brightly. "So do I. But it is my loyalty to you that has brought me here this fine, sunny morn. The day is much too lovely to spend it hiding in this moldering hut. Is there not something you need to pick in the forest? Mushrooms, cats-paw, or something of the like? There are flowers in bloom, Rosamund. They are crying to be picked. I will weave you a circlet, and you can make me one. We'll dabble our feet in the stream and listen for cuckoos. Sometimes they arrive early, you know."

Although Rosamund knew that she shouldn't, not with the amount of work there was to do, the picture Edeva painted was too tempting to resist. Its central attraction was the distance it would place between her and Tancred, and its value as a distraction.

In less than an hour, the two of them, accompanied by a knight and a handful of mounted men-at-arms assigned by John, were well on their way to the forest. Once away from the castle, Rosamund found it easier to share Edeva's eagerness to fill their baskets with bluebells and primroses. On the way, they stopped to pick speedwell flowers, which they laughingly presented to the members of their escort. The men smiled indulgently, obviously pleased to be given this duty on such a fine day.

It was much cooler in the shade of the woods, where the ground was covered with rich green moss, a few remaining primroses, vivid violet bluebells, and shy, white-flowered wood sorrel.

First Rosamund and Edeva searched out mushrooms, careful of the ones they picked, then moneywort from along the banks of the stream. That finished, they set about picking flowers. When they had enough, they wove them into festive circlets, as they dangled their bare feet in the stream.

"I have discovered why Kadar accompanied Lord Tancred out of the Holy Land," Edeva said. She smiled smugly.

"Oh?" Rosamund wished that she did not care why, but she did. Edeva wasn't helping by serving that curiosity.

"You know you are interested," Edeva said. "You love Tancred. He loves you—even Kadar knows that. And you know how unobservant men are in such matters."

Rosamund slid her gaze from the flowers she was weaving to Edeva. "What more did Kadar say of Tancred's feelings?"

Edeva shrugged. "He would not discuss it more, save to say that he felt certain Tancred has feelings for you. I told him I believed you had feelings for Tancred."

"My thanks, Edeva," Rosamund said sourly. "I prefer not to appear pathetic if I can avoid it. I plan to enter Hembley Abbey. Tancred will find a nice heiress to wed. In time, we will forget. He will have sons to train. I will have prayers to say."

Edeva laid down her partially completed circlet and clasped her hands over her kirtle-clad knees. "The convent is not the place for you, Rosamund. You will never be happy there."

"It is all that is left to me, Edeva. Would you strip me of my last hope?"

"Wed Tancred."

Rosamund traced the curled edge of a bluebell. "I cannot. He has stolen Wynnsef from Arnaud. If my brother fails to win back my father's legacy, he will be naught but another landless knight. Unlike Tancred, there are no *chansons* of his many brave deeds. I am not even certain he still holds the favor of the king. Arnaud might be reduced to beggary or brigandage. Do you truly believe I could wed the man who has done this?"

"Even after what Abbess Matilda said she learned from Lord Quorley?"

"Hearsay." But what she had heard about Arnaud's treachery bothered her.

Although she would never admit it aloud, she knew Arnaud had no love for King Richard. He nurtured a grudge against his liege lord for a slighting remark Richard had made during an exhibition fight years ago. The king valued bold courage. Arnaud was too cautious for his tastes.

Rosamund had heard her brother bitterly recount the incident until she wanted to pull out her hair. At least Arnaud had shown the sense not to speak of his grudge within hearing of anyone except her. Yet when she had failed to raise sufficient coin to pay the scutage, Arnaud's full fury over the necessity of accompanying his liege lord out of England had broken free. In the end, he had managed to rein in his temper sufficiently to put on a brave show and lead his retainers away to join King Richard's host.

Now Arnaud had been thwarted again. His lands, his castle had been taken, and by one of the king's chosen. This time, there might be no controlling Arnaud's rage. Rosamund knew her brother well. He would retake Wynnsef . . . or he would destroy it.

For Tancred, holding Wynnsef would likely be his best chance at building a respectable, stable life.

She told herself that a few kisses could never take the place of the lifetime of loyalty she had shared with her brother, yet even as she tried to convince herself, she knew that there was more, much more, than kisses between her and Tancred. Still, she was no moonstruck girl to believe anything could come of it.

In the end, she feared there would be blood spilt between Arnaud and Tancred. The only control she had in what happened between these two men, both so important in her life, was her refusal to aid in the destruction of either. The only way to do that, was to enter Hembley Abbey.

Rosamund sighed. She would enjoy this day, and then tuck it away in her memory as a small treasure. Among the birches with their tender emerald leaves, and the massive oaks, the wild cherry trees were still a-froth with white bloom, and the crabs appeared like pink and white clouds with trunks.

Leaning back on her arms, she closed her eyes.

"You've not listened to a word I have said," Edeva complained.

"I am listening," Rosamund replied, smiling. "I have not heard one cuckoo. Perhaps they are not here yet."

Even with her eyes closed, Rosamund was aware of the men-at-arms ranging a short distance around them. In the mysterious quiet of the woods, even male murmurs took on piercing lives of their own.

"Here," Edeva said.

Rosamund felt something placed on her head. She opened her eyes, but had to take it off before she could see it. She laughed with delight. " 'Tis beautiful, Edeva," she said, admiring the circlet of bluebells, wood sorrel, and anemones.

"Where is mine? You have been daydreaming."

Quickly, Rosamund finished the little left to weave. "Your crown, my lady," she said, presenting the circlet to Edeva.

They decided that it would never do to wear such

gorgeous crowns over veils, not on such a glorious spring day, and most certainly not in the woods. So off came veils and wimples. Feeling silly and youthful, they loosed their hair from their plaits, letting it stream down their backs to their hips. It would sweep up bits of grass and leaves as they basked on the bank of the stream, but that mattered not.

"I hear a jay!" Edeva exclaimed as Rosamund placed the delicate wreath of flowers perfectly on her friend's dark crown.

Some of the men chuckled, clearly enjoying the weather and the women's gaiety.

"A jay is nice," Rosamund declared. "But it is not a cuckoo." She held still while Edeva adjusted her own circlet to a more perfect position.

For minutes at a time, Rosamund was able to keep thoughts of Tancred at bay. When they intruded, and her throat tightened, she forced herself to smile. Edeva did not often leave the shelter of the abbey, and Rosamund would not cast a shadow on this time for her. On this time for either of them, for Edeva seemed determined to have Kadar for her own. To do that, she must leave the abbey behind.

With so many flowers still in their baskets, they set about weaving circlets for their escorts.

Aware of Edeva's affection for Kadar, Rosamund said, "You were about to tell me why Kadar stays with Tancred." Her throat closed on his name, but she managed a smile.

Edeva's fingers stopped their motion. "Rosamund," she said in a low voice not meant to be heard by any of the nearby men-at-arms. "Tancred loves you. You know he does. Anyone who sees you together knows he loves you. And that you love him."

Rosamund drew back, as if that short distance could protect her heart from the laceration Edeva's well-intentioned words performed. "Please, do not do this, Edeva," she said, her voice uneven.

"Kadar says . . ." Edeva looked as if she'd remembered something. Abruptly, she abandoned whatever it was that she had been about to say.

Because Kadar was so clearly Tancred's closest friend, Rosamund found her interest captured, "What does Kadar say?" she asked, despite all good sense.

Edeva seemed to find the circlet she was making vastly absorbing. "It upsets you. I'll not speak of it further."

Rosamund suspected that Edeva was avoiding her gaze. "I would hear what Kadar said."

"Only that he can see you have captured Tancred's heart."

There was something more here. "And?"

Edeva kept her gaze on the flowers she wove. She cleared her throat. "And . . . Kadar told Tancred that he—Tancred, that is—should wed you."

Inside her chest, Rosamund's heart began to beat more swiftly. "And?" she prompted softly.

Still not looking at her, Edeva waved a hand, indicating that the rest was of no importance.

For a long moment, Rosamund regarded Edeva. Why this sudden reluctance to expound on *anything* Kadar the Magnificent had to say? Edeva had not found anything else he'd uttered to be of less than apocalyptic significance.

When Edeva finally spoke, it was in a small, unhappy voice. "Tancred said no."

Rosamund stared at her, struggling to catch her breath, hoping that her heart's blood did not pour over the flowers on her lap, for she felt as if a sword had been thrust into her chest.

"Oh, Rosamund," Edeva whispered raggedly, grasping Rosamund's slack hands. "I am so stupid! I forgot what Tancred had said. I'd remembered only that even Kadar could see you and Tancred belong together. Please, *please* forgive me."

Rosamund managed to make her fingers work and gave Edeva's hands a small squeeze intended to pass for reassurance. A few minutes more, and she could almost breathe normally again.

It was her heart that would never be the same.

She noticed tears rolling down Edeva's cheeks, and her own tears came perilously close to spilling. "Oh, no, dearest friend," she said, "it is not worth weeping over. You've not inflicted any lasting damage. See? I'm quite whole."

"No thanks to me. In truth, Rosamund, I want you to be in love and happy."

"You are in love and happy. That must be enough for both of us. Would you want me to pine for a man who does not want me?"

"No. But he *does*—"

"Tell me why Kadar accompanied—Tell me why he came to England," Rosamund said. She completed a wreath, and began a new one.

Edeva sniffled. "Lord Tancred saved Kadar's mother and sister."

"Indeed?" Rosamund prompted automatically, trying to concentrate on the brilliance and delicacy of the blossoms she wove.

"Yea. He single-handedly, and at great risk to himself, prevented them from being ravished by the enraged crusaders who attacked their caravan traveling from Damascus. Tancred did claim the women as his share of booty, forgoing the gold, silk, and spices the other crusaders took. Then Lord Tancred—a mere knight at that time—escorted the women to their destination, their home, not far away. Kadar's father is a caliph, a man of wealth and importance. He was astonished by Lord Tancred's courage, by his generosity in saving the women of an enemy. Kadar's father offered Lord Tancred riches and position, which he politely declined. Oh, you should hear Kadar tell the story! Tancred gave all credit to his training by his foster fathers."

Edeva dabbed at the remnants of her tears with her sleeve. "Then Kadar's father noticed the brand on

Tancred's cheekbone. That circle with the two stars is the family emblem of one of his relatives. At once, Kadar's father knew who had inflicted it on Lord Tancred. A close blood cousin, it seems. Well, that made matters worse. Not only had Lord Tancred risked his life and lost his rightful booty to save Kadar's mother—his father's favorite wife—and Kadar's sister, but a blood-kinsman had tortured Lord Tancred. Kadar's father was greatly distressed. The honor of the family was stake."

"Indeed." Rosamund could not see how. Yasir had been demented. It was the only explanation for his twisted behavior. Tancred had slain him in battle. "Did Kadar's father know that Tancred had done battle with that kinsmen and . . . triumphed?"

"He did, but 'twas not enough to satisfy honor."

There was truth in that. Yasir's death could not simply eliminate what he had inflicted on Tancred. The memories of that pain and shame might haunt him all his days.

She nodded. "A wise man."

"Kadar's father placed on him a sacred trust. Kadar is bound by an oath to stay with Tancred and protect him, until he returned safely home—which it seems he has done—and until he saves someone Tancred loves—which he has not."

Rosamund's eyes widened. "But such an oath might well take a lifetime to fulfill," she exclaimed. "It is too harsh!"

Edeva lifted her shoulders slightly and allowed them to fall. "Kadar says it was an oath he took with full knowledge. His mother and sister are precious to him. Tancred has become as dear as a brother. But . . . the only person Tancred has loved since Kadar made that oath is you."

Rising to her feet, Rosamund brushed grass and bits of twigs off the skirts of her kirtle. "Is Kadar eager to be released?"

Edeva stood up, too. "He does not seem to be. He

has said naught of any desire to return to his own land."

"I am certain Kadar will one day have his opportunity, but it will not involve me." She forced herself to smile, longing to recapture those moments when there had been only the flowers and this spring day. Even as that thought passed through her mind, she realized the sky had grown darker, but it was difficult to see much of it through the canopy of new leaves and blossoms.

She crowned the conical helmet of one man-at-arms with a flowery wreath. "Your reward for your patience, Ranulf," she said.

The young man blushed even as he grinned. "I thank you, my lady. It fits my helm perfectly."

She laughed. "Yea, it does."

Each man in his turn received a circlet of flowers. From the jugs she had brought on the back of La Songe and then set in the icy water of the stream, Rosamund and Edeva poured each man a horn of cool ale and one for themselves. As they quaffed the refreshing liquid, the breeze grew stronger.

Edeva straightened suddenly. "I heard one!"

Metal rattled as men-at-arms quickly reached for their weapons. "One what, Lady Edeva?"

"A cuckoo," she replied brightly. "Come, Rosamund, we must find it." She whirled and ran.

"My lady, we should go," one man shouted after her, his voice ringing through the trees. "The clouds—"

But by then she had already disappeared into the dense, dark forest.

Two men-at-arms took after her.

Concerned, Rosamund pursued her, calling her name. "Edeva, come back! We must return to the castle."

"It *is* a cuckoo," Edeva's voice echoed back. "I can see it."

Raindrops began to splat against the leaves around

Rosamund, occasionally falling on her. She followed the direction of Edeva's voice. "You must come back. It is time to go." The gray sky rapidly grew darker.

Far in front of her and behind her, Rosamund heard the shouts of the men-at-arms. The sun vanished behind heavy black clouds. Dead twigs jabbed the tender soles of her bare feet. Her toe caught in a tree root and she stumbled. "Edeva, we are coming for you. Stay where you are, do you hear me?"

If she did, she could not have told Rosamund, for at that moment, a deluge from the sky drowned out everything but its roar.

In the dark, Rosamund hunkered down, planning to wait until the worst of the storm abated and the knight or the men-at-arms caught up with her. She worried that Edeva might not do the same.

The legs of a horse came into her line of vision, then a wet masculine hand. Thankful that their escort had found her, she took the hand, but as she placed her bare foot onto his foot in the stirrup, she noticed that the condition and quality of neither his shoe nor mail chausses were up to that of Tancred's and Arnaud's men.

Alarmed, Rosamund tried to pull free, but the large hand holding hers tightened its grip. As she was hauled, struggling, onto the saddle, she turned enough to look into the gap-toothed leer of a complete stranger.

NINETEEN

From the wall walk, Tancred saw his men riding toward the castle. The rain had stopped, but the lowering sky promised more to come. His brows came down.

"John, did you not say you had sent six men with Lady Rosamund and Lady Edeva?"

John Willsson stepped beside him, following Tancred's gaze. "Yea, my lord, I did. I preferred that either you or Lord Kadar accompany them, but you had ridden to Cloptune, and Lord Kadar had gone to Attewell to speak with Uehtred as you requested. I sent Warin of High Odom, sire. He is a good man. A seasoned fighting man." He named the others he had sent, all dependable warriors.

Tancred turned to acknowledge John's dedication to Rosamund. "Thank you, John."

"I'd not let her come to harm, could I help it," John said, his voice low and even. "Nor Lady Edeva."

"No. Of course you would not. But there are only four riders now." They were still too far away for Tancred to determine their sex.

Beside him, Tancred felt John go tense.

Turning on his heel, Tancred called out orders for certain armed knights and men-at-arms to mount up even as he strode down the stairs into the courtyard. Without a word from him, his squires scurried to equip and saddle Vandal, to bring Tancred his gambeson and arming hose, his mail and helm. One lad rushed to retrieve his lord's lance, shield, and mace. His sword he always wore. Until the matter was settled with Arnaud none expected him to relax his watch for either Wynnsef or himself.

In minutes, he mounted his destrier and led the other knights out of the castle. When he drew close to the hard-riding horsemen approaching, his blood froze.

Rosamund was not among them.

Soaked and bedraggled, the hem of her skirt caked with mud, Lady Edeva looked as if she been weeping.

From behind Tancred's band came the thunder of a single horse. With a jingle of tack, and a horse's deep grunt as it dug into the moist earth to make an abrupt stop, Kadar arrived. Despite the ventail of his coif that covered the lower portion of his face, and his helm's nasal, Tancred could clearly see his friend's initial relief at finding Edeva.

"Rosamund?" Tancred barked to Ranulf, eyeing the flower circlet on his conical helmet.

The other men noticed his glance and snatched off their own, likely forgotten, flowery adornments.

"She was separated from us when the storm hit," the young man replied stoically. "Chevalier Warin sent us to bring back reinforcements while he and the other men continue to search for Lady Rosamund."

Edeva sobbed. "It was my fault, my lord. I ran heedless into the forest to see the cuckoo, and Rosamund came after me. The sky was growing dark so quickly . . ."

To Tancred's surprise, Kadar guided his horse over to Edeva's. Never before had Kadar openly shown his preference for this woman.

"You are unharmed?" the Saracen asked her, reaching out to gently brush a dark, wet lock of hair from her cheek. "Have you any idea where the lady Rosamund might have gone to? Is there shelter anywhere? A woodward's hut, perhaps?"

Edeva shook her head. "N—not that I know of."

Tancred looked to Ranulf, who had no answer. Frustration boiled up inside him, the need to take action, to reach Rosamund and find her safe *now*.

A man spoke up from the back of the small group, one of the few men-at-arms who had been left to defend Wynnsef by Rosamund's brother. "Lord Arnaud tore down any shelters built in the woods," he said. "Too convenient for poachers or brigands."

Tancred turned to Kadar. "I know Lady Edeva would prefer you accompany her back to the castle. The rest of you," he continued to the others, "come with me."

"Tancred, I have my oath to fulfill," Kadar objected. "As much as I wish to accompany Lady Edeva, it is with you I must go."

Tancred gritted his teeth against impatience. "Go with her, Kadar. When she is safe, bring ten of the men with you—you know the ones—and ten more, all to the forest. We will need more than these few men to search that vast place." Without giving Kadar time to argue, Tancred kneed Vandal and was instantly charging toward the dark woods in the distance, his men riding in his wake, the hooves of their mounts pounding the earth.

It was nearing twilight when they arrived at the place where Rosamund and Edeva had dangled their bare feet in the stream. Driven by his fear for Rosamund, Tancred did not set up camp to wait until morning, when they would have had full sun. They still had a few hours of light, and he was determined to make the most of them.

The rope cut painfully into Rosamund's wrists as she tried to work the binding loose. So far, her efforts had proved futile, but until she could free her hands, she could not unfasten the rope they'd wound around her neck like a collar, then tied to the trunk of the tree at her back.

The brigands who held her captive sat around their campfire in the middle of the clearing, confident in the security of their domain. From where she sat on the damp ground some distance from them, she could see the entire camp. It consisted of a few ragged tents, some lean-tos that looked as if there might have been a little skill involved, and the picket line to which there were tied precisely ten horses.

Rain and the wet ground had thoroughly soaked her light woolen kirtle, and she shivered with the advancing cool of the evening. Still, she tried to keep count of the number of men she saw through her one good eye. The other was swollen shut. The tip of her tongue flicked over her split bottom lip. When she had struggled to escape, her abductor had struck her several times.

Through her hunger and thirst, she tried to concentrate. A little earlier, four men had stalked off into the forest, bearing their weapons. Rosamund thought they might be sentries, for they had not returned. That left eleven men sitting around the fire, some occasionally casting glances at her, which made Rosamund nervous.

Once she'd been dumped into the camp, the men had not harmed her more than to cuff her a few times and shove her hard enough to send her stumbling to the ground, which had brought some of them amusement.

Now they passed a few jugs of ale around, and she had detected a worrisome change in the quality of their speech, a more boisterous volume to their laughter.

Her apprehension mounted. She kept working at her bonds.

Rosamund prayed that Edeva and Tancred's men had escaped. That they sent aid. And that the aid arrived *soon*.

Rosamund had already told these brigands her identity and that she was chatelaine of Wynnsef. She'd ardently hoped they would decide to keep her safe for ransom. She'd silently hoped that someone in Wynnsef could or would pay for her freedom. Her hopes had come to naught. The brigands had laughed at her again, but this time the nasty, gloating sound had knotted her stomach with anxiety.

It began to rain again. Rosamund huddled against the oak's trunk in wet misery, hoping that the chill wet would dampen any ardor her captors might feel. Judging from the foul curses she heard coming from around the campfire, the rain did nothing to help tempers.

When the downpour persisted, drumming harder and harder, the men disbursed, going to their wretched tents and lean-tos. The largest of the lot, the man she'd concluded was their leader, was the last to rise from his place by the now extinguished fire. He walked toward her.

Rosamund tried to control the pounding of her heart. She gathered her feet under her, but her tether made it impossible for her to stand.

Dim moonlight sliced through the high canopy of leaves, slanting through the dark and pouring rain like watery silver swords.

Crouching, she regarded the man warily.

He stood over her, his fists on his hips. "The picture of a fine lady," he said in a sober voice. He reached for her tether and cut the knot with a knife. "You're mine first."

Cold and fear clutched at her ribs, and she shuddered. "What do you mean?" she asked, rain dripping off her nose, her chin.

He jerked the rope, and it raked the tender flesh of her neck, forcing her to quickly stand or choke.

"I mean that I'll swyve you first." He started toward the largest lean-to. "And when I'm finished, I'll give you to the next man."

Horrified, she struggled against the pull of the rope. "Ransom me—"

He whirled, grabbing a handful of her hair and jerking her up against his body, forcing her head back so that she could see his angry face. "Your only value to me is for revenge. Everyone knows you are Tancred de Vierzon's woman. He may not have taken you yet, but even Saint Tancred"—he sneered—"will weaken eventually."

"R—r—revenge for what?" she stammered, hating the cold and rain that weakened her, hating the frailty of her woman's body, when she wanted so badly to strike out, to *hurt* this beast and his ilk that wallowed in their shelters here.

"That bastard killed my brother. He killed my comrades."

"You're brigands. You murder and steal. If the sheriff were to catch you, you would hang."

He shook her, sending fiery pain through her scalp. "Bitch! You dare judge us, you who have a home and plenty to eat?" He grabbed hold of her kirtle and tore away its right shoulder, baring one breast and the pouch of crimson silk she wore suspended by a ribbon around her neck, under her clothes.

From the corner of her eye she saw a tall shadow separate from a tree trunk.

"What have we here?" her tormenter asked, reaching for the pouch, sliding his hand roughly over the pale skin of her breast.

Suddenly, his head jerked back, his eyes wide with surprise. A blade flashed in the moonlight. In the blink of an eye, it moved across the brigand's throat. Dark liquid poured from the gash.

Startled, he released her. He turned in time to see a tall shadow-figure step around him to grasp Rosamund's arm.

"Come," Tancred said in her ear. "To the horses."

The brigand fell to the ground. He arched up, gurgling softly.

"Don't look," Tancred murmured, moving to block her view. He cut the rope that bound her wrists, then, his strong hand at the small of her back, he swiftly guided her to the horses. "Can you ride without a saddle?"

She felt she could do whatever it took to follow him out of that place. "I will."

He lifted her onto the back of the best-looking of the tethered horses. Then he mounted behind her and took the reins.

"We'll take no chances now," he murmured beside her temple.

The death throes of the fallen brigand was apparently enough to wake a man from the closest tent. The fellow stumbled out, almost tripping over the body.

Behind Rosamund, Tancred moved suddenly. She heard a soft thud as a knife found its target in the second brigand's throat. The man crumpled to the earth.

Tancred turned the horse, and as they left the clearing, heading back into the forest, Rosamund saw several shadows melt away from the dark of the trees, moving silently to converge on the brigands' shelters.

The rain stopped. She and Tancred rode through the silver-slashed maze of midnight giants in silence. She pressed back against him, seeking warmth, drawing reassurance from the uncompromising strength of his body.

When finally they burst from the forest, a dozen riders fell in around them. The whisper of the wind, hooves thudding against wet turf, and the creak of wet leather were the only sounds.

No trumpet sounded to alert the castle that its master approached. There was only the movement of shadows outside the towering gate, then the clatter, thud, and clank as the drawbridge was lowered, the portcullis raised. The hollow thunder of horses' hooves as the rescue party crossed the bridge into the safety of Wynnsef Castle.

Torches burned in the inner bailey. Sleepy stable lads ran to take the reins of the horses.

Tancred slipped down from the back of their mount. He lifted Rosamund down, but instead of setting her on the ground, he swung her into his arms, then strode toward the old keep. No one said a word, or even seemed to notice.

"You can put me down, Tancred," Rosamund said. "I am capable of walking." But it felt so good to be cradled in his strong arms, resting against his solid chest.

He made no answer. He simply kept walking.

"Truly. I can walk."

"Quiet, woman."

She blinked her one good eye in surprise. Never had she heard him use such a tone of voice. Hard, fierce, with a strange, unidentifiable under note.

Uncertain whether she should be angry or worried, Rosamund's weariness finally won out. She wilted against him.

Instead of taking the stairs up to her chamber, he stalked down the steps, into the warren of echoing, vaulted chambers filled with hides, wine butts, iron ingots, and myriad other items, among them, a bathing chamber. It was there he brought her.

Servants hurried in and out of the pavilion with steaming buckets.

"Leave us," Tancred told them curtly, and they did, scurrying away toward the stairs and freedom.

Rosamund looked around. There were linen drying cloths, some folded garments, and a great fur, folded neatly, its underside the only thing exposed.

Tancred set her feet on the floor.

She frowned, then winced at the pain. "I know you must feel chilled and dirty, my lord, but surely I cannot be expected to attend your bath now."

As her echoing words finally faded, there was only the crackling of the flames on the hearth to hear.

Tancred drew from his matte black belt another knife, only slightly smaller than the one he'd thrown into the brigand's throat. Her eyes widened.

He ignored her reaction, carefully cutting the tether from her neck, his fingers warm and gentle against her skin. He flung the rope into the fire with barely suppressed violence. His nostrils flared as he stared at her abraded skin.

Tancred's gaze lifted to her split lip, then to the aching place on her cheek that was doubtless swollen and bruised. With infinite tenderness, he cradled her temples between his hands and kissed the unharmed half of her mouth, taking care not to hurt her.

Her fingers curled around his wrists, her eyes fluttered closed. Despite the warmth of the fire, she shivered.

"When I learned that you had not returned from the forest," he whispered, his gaze entrancing hers, "I thought I might go mad."

Her heart lifted at the words. Tancred had feared for her. And he had come for her, delivering her from certain degradation and death.

He eased the rag that was her kirtle from her arms and torso, allowing it to drop into a sodden pile at her feet. Her chemise was plastered to her body, its thin linen concealing nothing from his eyes. Rosamund knew she should feel self-conscious, but she discovered that she wanted Tancred to see her body. Only Tancred . . .

He slipped the flimsy garment off of her, leaving her with only the silken pouch hanging by its ribbon between her breasts.

"What is this?" he asked. "Some saint's thumb bone?"

She smiled, then winced, and a shadow flickered across his face. "Open it," she bade him.

He untucked the delicately embroidered flap, then dipped his fingers inside—

—To withdraw the silver disk set with the single, perfect moonstone.

He looked at it for a long moment. Then she saw

his throat work as he swallowed. His hand closed over it, clenching into a fist. His eyes squeezed closed.

"You carry this with you," he said hoarsely.

Shaken by the strong emotion she witnessed him trying to rein in, Rosamund hesitantly reached up and smoothed her fingertips over his cheek. "Always."

He placed the disk back into its envelope, then pulled her to him and held her close for a long moment, his hand tangled in her wet hair. Abruptly, he took her up into his arms and then moved to the tent, ducking through the flap. Humid mist swirled around them.

He set her into the tub of steaming water. On the small table close to hand, she saw that a vermeil flagon and two goblets had been arranged. There was also a ball of Italian soap.

Her heart skipped a beat when he ducked back out of the tent, but he was back almost as soon as he was gone. He held a small jug and some small squares of linen. As soon as he unstoppered the jug, she knew what it contained: verjuice made from apples. And she knew what it was for.

He moistened a cloth square with the verjuice, then, with great care, applied the verjuice to the cut on her lip. It stung, but she refused to show her discomfort. She knew it would make him unhappy to hurt her.

"I fear it has been too long for your eye," he said. "Leeches will not help now. The color and swelling must run their course." He pressed a soft kiss to her forehead. "It will be gone in a sennight or two, as will this bruise on your cheekbone. Did the man I found jerking your rope do this to you?"

"No."

He muttered a curse.

"He went out to sentry duty."

Tancred smiled savagely. "Then I have avenged you."

"You killed four sentries?"

"Yea."

"Oh." She wasn't sure she wanted to know more.

He picked up a different jug, testing its contents with his fingers. "No one takes from me what is mine."

Rosamund could not understand why Tancred's possessiveness pleased her. Perhaps because it was new to her. Perhaps she had never expected a man to feel that way about her. Certainly no man she had wanted so very much in return.

Tancred poured the warm water in the jug over her head with a clement hand. Then he washed her hair, applying the luxurious soap until it lathered. Slowly his strong fingers massaged her scalp, working the creamy froth until a thick droplet fell onto her bare breast.

His fingers stilled, and she knew that he watched it. Gradually, warmed by the heat of her skin, the creamy foam liquified. Slowly at first, then with gathering momentum, it slid downward until it trembled on her pink nipple. Aware of Tancred's focused attention, alive to the faint sensation of the slipping droplet, her nipple hardened.

In the silence of the pavilion, she heard the sound of his quickened breathing.

The whisper of clothing falling to the floor swiftly followed.

She turned her head slightly and saw, at close hand, a length of long, muscular leg, short black hair over fair skin. She looked up, and her mouth went dry. Tancred stepped into the water with a natural grace, the display of rippling sinews impressive.

He sat down, facing her, then leaned over the side of the tub to lift another jug of water. This he poured gently over her head, sleeking the soap out of her hair with his palm.

"Your hair is lovely," he said. " 'Tis like sunlight through the petals of buttercups."

He was so close, so beautiful. So baffling. So male. Awareness of him, of his magnificent body, of her own tremulous, soaring, emotions spiraled through Rosamund.

"What?" she asked, her voice shaky. "Not spun gold?"

His white teeth flashed in the shadow of his new beard. "That, too." He set aside the empty jug, then lifted a lock of her hair to his lips.

Shyly, she reached out to run her palm down the side of his columnar neck and over one broad, smooth shoulder. So powerful yet so elegant. How easy it might be to forget the years of loneliness, the hurt.

He turned his head away. "Do not look at me like that, *ma églantine*. I am not worthy. I am . . . unclean."

Her hand hesitated on him, but she kept it where it was. "Unclean?"

"I have been desired . . . by another man."

"Other than Yasir?"

Slanting black slashes drew down. "*No*. But he . . . touched me."

Her hand sought him under the water. "He touched you . . . here?"

His rampant arousal was unmistakable. It felt like nothing she had ever touched. It far exceeded the length of her palm. So hard, she thought astounded, yet so like silk.

Tancred sucked in his breath. Sternly, he kept his face averted. The muscles of his jaw bunched. "Yea," he answered between gritted teeth.

Her power over him was a heady elixir that eddied through her blood. She moved closer to him, aware that while his face remained turned away, beneath those lowered lashes, his silver eyes watched her breasts.

"Did you like it when he . . . touched you?"

He ground out his answer. "I killed him."

"Yea. You did," she reminded him. How could he believe that Yasir's twisted attentions had left him tainted? But then she remembered the horror of his ordeal and how young he must have been at the time.

"Do you like it when I touch you, my beloved?" she whispered in his ear.

Her fingers moved on his hard, fulsome flesh, following nebulous instinct.

His breath grew short and sharp. His head tilted back. "Yea. Oh . . . God . . . *yea*. I do like it . . . when you . . . touch . . . me." The last word was little more than a groan, rising from deep in his chest.

Rosamund found his response to her touch exhilarating. "Hear me, Tancred de Vierzon," she told him in a low, intense voice. "I am the Green Witch, and I cast a spell on you now as I grasp you in my hand. You come to me pure. You fair shimmer with the glow of manly goodness and chastity. Though others desire you only *I* shall bring you pleasure. Only I shall touch you at all."

Suddenly, Tancred sent her sprawling beneath him, her back pressed against the wall of the tub. He caught her hands in his. "The Green Witch, is it?" he asked between the kisses he pressed to the uninjured side of her face. "The only Green Witch I know puts me to sleep every night."

"Oaf!"

He laughed, easily clasping both of her struggling wrists in one hand, while he pushed her hair away from her neck with the other. As he lowered his head to kiss that bare length, he frowned and drew back slightly. "How came you by this bruise on your neck? It is far older than those of tonight."

She cast him a pettish look. "*You* did that, ungrateful man, the first time you insisted I act your slave while you bathed."

"I marked you?"

"You need not sound so smug. Any dolt can make a love bite."

He nuzzled the curve between her jaw and shoulder. "Yea, but only this dolt had better be the one to bite your neck."

She giggled, intoxicated with her love for Tancred

and the realization that he returned it. "It tickles.
Stop."

He nibbled behind her ear. "I never want to stop.
You climbed into my blood the day you stood on the
wall walk, tilted up your chin, and denied me entrance." He leaned back to look at her. "In every
flower I see your face, your angel's smile. Every leaf
is your hand, raised heavenward, asking for prosperity
for your people, but naught for yourself."

She ducked her head, feeling monstrously ugly with
her blackened, swollen eye, her bruises, and her cuts.
"You make me sound a saint. I am far from selfless.
I want things."

With the gentle nudge of his knuckle, he brought
her head back up. His gaze seared hers into immobil-
ity. In her stomach, a thousand swifts took flight.

"I want things, too," he said. His voice was deep
and as dark as midnight, filled with promising
shadows.

Helpless to look away, she saw the onyx of his pupils expanding, the silver of his irises growing slimmer,
until they were but shining rings. "What . . . things?"

His hand stroked her throat. "Things only you can
give me." His fingertips brushed the tops of her
breasts, skimming downward, across the edges of more
deeply colored flesh.

Beneath him, engulfed in warm water and searing
sensation, Rosamund shuddered with the force of her
desire. Against her bare thigh, she felt him grow
larger, harder, hotter still.

He tenderly kissed her mouth, stroked her tongue
with his. When finally he released her hands, they
found their way into the heavy silk of his raven hair.

He sat up, and she made a small noise of complaint,
until she felt his arms go under her. When he stood,
he took her with him. Together they rose, water surg-
ing off their bodies.

When he left the tub and then the tent, disappointment claimed Rosamund. She was certain he planned

to take her to her bedchamber and leave her, high-minded knight that he was.

He set her down, and picked up a garment from the bench. She swallowed hard against the tide of disappointment. Quickly, he thrust his arms into the sleeves of a shimmering black silk robe. He then took up the large fur. When he shook it out, she saw that it was the strange golden fur coverlet she had seen on his bed. Now she saw that it was several furs skillfully joined.

To her surprise, Tancred wrapped the luxurious coverlet around her, fur side against her bare skin. Then he lifted her in his arms again.

He took her to his chamber. There he laid her on the massive draped bed and unwrapped her.

"I feared you would leave me in my room," she confessed between the kisses she pressed to his mouth, his cheeks, his eyelids.

"Not likely," he rumbled, as he dropped his robe on the floor and joined her on the bed. He skimmed the length of her torso with callused palms. "This is your chamber now. Our chamber."

Their love was sparkling nectar that filled her, washing away years of echoing loneliness. As they learned every plane and curve of each other's body, she committed to heart every beloved resonance in his voice, every shift in his expression, and the nectar surged into a tide that overpowered any other claims or considerations. There was only now. Only Tancred. Only the wonder of no longer being alone.

When finally Tancred slid between her thighs, taking his weight on his forearms, she was ready, oh, more than ready.

He guided himself into her waiting body, his lashes lowered and his nostrils flared, yet he remained gentle, even as he took her maidenhead. With hands that conjured breathless magic and lips that coaxed and lured her, he brought her back to feverish desire, and she accompanied him willingly. So very willingly. Never before had she been so at one with another soul.

Passion swept her up and she reached for bursting stars even as she felt Tancred's seed flash hot and sure within her. It was only afterward, as they lay quiescent in each other's arms, that realization came to her.

As long as they had each other, they were no longer prisoners.

TWENTY

In the nascent dawn, Rosamund stretched content-
edly, glorying in the warmth of Tancred's nude body
lying beside her. Unable to bear minutes without looking at him, she turned her head on the pillow.

His dark hair was tousled from her fingers the many
times he had made love to her over the course of
the past miraculous night. Even relaxed in sleep, his
eyebrows were slanting slashes. His black lashes were
incredibly thick, luxuriously long, and they curved
upon his high, broad cheekbones. She had always
thought his straight nose particularly elegant. His angular jaw was shadowed with the night's growth of
beard. And his mouth . . . Ah, his mouth. Unable to
resist, she rolled onto her side and gently traced his
wide, sensual mouth with the tip of a forefinger. What
marvelous things his mouth could do. How beautiful
and unconventional it was with its top lip slightly fuller
than the bottom. A man's mouth. A lover's mouth.

His lashes lifted fractionally. Beneath them she
glimpsed those silver eyes that missed nothing. Since
his arrival, she had witnessed them turn as cold as
winter, but last night they had glowed with tender fire.

"Good morn, my lord," she said softly, placing her
hands possessively upon his chest then resting her chin
upon them.

Last night, everything had changed. In her wildest
imaginings, she would never have suspected how close

she could feel to another person, much less this fierce
knight. Each claiming had brought more than a joining
of bodies, more than a shattering crescendo of pleasure. There had also been profound communion, a
twining of souls.

"So it was not just a dream brought on by your
potion," he said softly.

"My potion does not bring dreams, sir," she informed him with cheerful impertinence.

His mouth curled upward, lighting eyes, his face,
and reminding her of his youth. For all of his military
experience, he was not but five or seven years older
than she. The force of his presence and the way other
men looked to him for leadership made that easy to
forget.

"No? Then how can I explain these most ardent
dreams I have had concerning you?"

His admission delighted Rosamund. "Have you had
them only since you began taking my sleeping draft?"

His large hand came to rest on her bare shoulder.
"No."

She could see the heat gathering behind his gaze.
"Ah," she murmured. "There you have it. 'Tis not my
potion at all, but your own carnal thoughts."

His other hand drifted to her hair, which tumbled
over her shoulders and back. "Is that bad?" He shifted
the weight of his body somewhat. Powerful muscles
rippled beneath smooth skin. His adjustment brought
her thigh into direct contact with his impressive
erection.

"Not as long as you have them with me," she
purred, sliding her hip against him in a sensual stroke.

He inhaled sharply. "Come here, wench." Abruptly,
he rolled her over onto her back, bracing himself
above her on his elbows. He nuzzled her ear. "I have a
particularly wicked thought I want to share with you."

She laughed for the sheer joy of it, her heart filled
to overflowing.

"Oh, ho! Funny is it?" He kissed her. His gaze

moved to her lips. "How came you by this little scar, *ma églantine*? Here, by your mouth. I have often wondered." He stroked it with his thumb. "Did a drying rack for your herbs fall on you?" he teased.

Shame filled her and her gaze slid away from his. The temptation to lie fluttered through her mind, but she knew that it was not in her to lie to Tancred. Not now. Perhaps never again.

"Arnaud," she muttered. She felt his muscles go taut. "The crops were poor. There was not enough gold to pay scutage."

"He *struck* you?" Tancred demanded, his voice low and harsh.

From long habit, she rushed to her brother's defense. "I did fail him. 'Twas my responsibility—"

He touched his index finger to her lips, stopping her excuses. "Hush. Arnaud has no place between us. This is our time. And this scar, this infinitesimal imperfection is made perfect by its association with your most exquisite face." He brushed his lips over the scar. "I fear you make the angels jealous."

She kissed him then, slanting her mouth over his. With all her heart she poured forth her appreciation, her delight, her love. And he returned it in kind.

Gradually, the kiss slowed, deepened, grew more erotic.

His lips warmed her senses as one hand tangled into her mane. His other hand masterfully caressed her breasts, then moved down to slip between her legs. With a greedy moan, she opened her thighs.

Someone pounded on the chamber door.

Tancred ignored the intrusive clamor. His fingers deftly, delicately opened her, to find her moist, ready . . .

A fist banged repeatedly on the door. Ranulf's voice called out, "My lord, forgive me, but I bear important news."

With a heavy sigh, and a quick kiss of apology, Tancred rolled off the bed and strode to open the door, keeping it closed enough to insure their privacy.

Rosamund suspected that by now, just about everyone in Wynnsef must know she had spent the night in Tancred's bed. The way he had carried her off after saving her in the forest, the servants who had seen him carry her into the bathing chamber, servants who had not found her in her own chamber—in the close quarters of a castle community, few secrets could be kept.

"Yea, Ranulf," Tancred said, "what is it?"

"My lord, Arnaud Bourton and his forces approach Wynnsef."

"How long before they arrive?"

"They are expected by None, sire."

"Thank you, Ranulf. Alert the men. Send the messenger to Arnaud. I will be with you directly."

Tancred quietly shut the door. He stood there a moment without speaking. Then he looked at Rosamund, who sat frozen on the bed, the fur coverlet held over her breasts.

Too soon, she thought, anguish tightening in her chest. *Too soon.* Why could Arnaud not have arrived just a little later? She was not ready yet to return to loneliness.

"I will call for Brother Felix," Tancred said. "He will marry us."

She shook her head as she climbed off the bed. Distractedly, she looked around for her clothing.

In three long strides, Tancred reached her. He took her arm and turned her to face him. "I want you to be my wife, Rosamund."

Again she shook her head, fighting back tears. Remembering she had been naked but for the fur coverlet, she stooped to pick up Tancred's silk robe.

"Why do you shake your head?" he demanded. "I believed you wanted me for your husband. Was I wrong?"

Breathing hard, she struggled through the simple

task of donning the garment. It was ridiculously large on her.

Tancred placed his hands on her shoulders, making it impossible for her to pretend that all she had to do was get back to her bedchamber.

"Answer me, Rosamund," he said, his voice low and tight. "Do you wish to be my wife?"

Reluctantly, she raised her gaze to his. Her heart shuddered with the force of her longing. "Yea, Tancred. I do wish to be your wife. More than you will ever know."

Gently he drew her into his arms. He cradled her against his body. "I know this is difficult for you, *ma églantine*. Sacred Rood, you must feel as if you're trapped in the middle. For your sake, I would not have it so. But there is no other way from this. I have known that I would face your brother since my time in the Holy Land."

Rosamund leaned against Tancred, drawing strength from him. It flowing into her through his embrace, but even more through his words. Fate and King Richard seemed determined to keep them apart. Fate had placed Arnaud and King Richard at odds, and King Richard had promised Wynnsef to Tancred, a landless knight hungry for a place of his own. But Wynnsef had been promised to him only if he could take it.

He had done just that.

And now Arnaud would either take Wynnsef back or destroy it.

"He will fight you," she said tonelessly.

"Yea. He will."

"He is my brother, Tancred."

"One who has treated you ill, beloved. He does not deserve your loyalty."

She pressed her hands lightly against his chest. He resisted her gesture for a moment, then dropped his hands to his sides.

"I love you, Tancred, but I cannot wed you under these circumstances. I just . . . cannot."

"So you will ignore what we have shared. You support him."

She had been wrong. Last night had changed nothing.

Rosamund walked out the door to return to her own place. Before her stretched years with a bitter brother. Behind her, she left more than Tancred.

She left her heart.

At a slow, almost leisurely, pace of hours, Arnaud's men surrounded Wynnsef. First the appalling mass of foot soldiers and mounted knights arrived. Tancred smiled grimly, knowing that as that swollen host trudged through the forest they had suffered unexpected losses from archers hiding in trees and traps concealed by the bracken and woven mats made to look like humus. Their shouts and cries and the reports of the returned archers had assured him of his many small successes.

The creak of wheels preceded the baggage train as it rolled into sight. On three of the wagons, the timbers that would be assembled into siege machines were plainly visible. As the train came to a halt on the meadow across the moat, men swarmed over the wagons like ants on a mound as they unloaded trunks and casks and baskets first, then, within the hour, the parts of the machines. The first pavilion to go up was Arnaud's. No one could mistake that garish scarlet and yellow.

He had still not given his answer to Tancred's challenge for personal combat.

From an arrow loophole, on the wall walk, Tancred regarded with cold anger the fluttering banner over the largest tent in the camp across the moat.

"He will not hurry to answer your challenge," Kadar said. "He knows it means his death."

"The whore's son likely uses the excuse that a baron need not accept the challenge of a mere knight."

Kadar smiled. "Ah, but I am certain he would like

to try. Alas, he cannot do that, unless no one else read the message. You are a champion of your king. As such, a challenge from you might be seen as a challenge from your king."

"Apparently Arnaud's immediate cowardice outweighs his future with Richard."

The spring breeze caught Kadar's mantle, sending it out in a billow of rich blue wool and glossy sable. "Your king, did he not leave the decision in the hands of Allah?"

"He did. Still, a baron is not so high as a king. Arnaud's vassals will not be easy with a liege lord who fears to defend his own honor. Arnaud is not so high in favor that he can afford to ignore my challenge."

The challenge that, if accepted, would forever seal Rosamund away from him. A dull, empty ache in the area of his heart had become his inseparable companion since she had walked out of his chamber this morn. Knowing that nothing could bring her back to him, no matter who triumphed in the coming conflict, gave him no relief.

"And if he does ignore it?" Kadar inquired.

Tancred smiled grimly. "Then, my friend, we shall use all that I have learned from the *Hashishiyun*. The night shall be our boon companion."

White teeth flashed in Kadar's dark face. "Perhaps Bourton has not learned why you are called the Moon Lord."

"Perhaps he has learned nothing at all."

Kadar laughed. "It seems he has not."

As they watched, a man left the large tent. He mounted a horse caparisoned in a mail bard tethered outside. Turning the beast's head away from the tent, he rode straight for the castle. Minutes after he reached the gate, Tancred was brought a message.

He examined Arnaud's seal, then broke it open. A corner of Tancred's mouth curled up when he read the small fold of parchment.

Bourton wanted a meeting.

The sun was on the wane when Tancred, Kadar, Bernard, and Osbert rode out through Wynnsef's front wicket gate to meet Arnaud and three of his men at the agreed-upon point halfway between the castle and the front line of Arnaud's forces.

Arnaud's sullen appearance and the tight, blank expressions of his advisors—senior vassals by the looks of them—spoke volumes. Tancred glanced at Kadar, who lowered his eyelids slightly and lifted them again, signaling that he, also, had noticed the tension between Arnaud and his vassals.

Tancred would have wagered that Arnaud was not there by his own desire, but rather had been pressured by his advisors to meet with his challenger in person. For all they knew, Richard might have dispatched men to ride to aid Tancred. Like hounds, landholders kept their noses to the wind, and by now these men would have smelled the king's abandonment of their overlord. To which side Richard's favor ultimately fell was a matter yet to be decided, and none wished to be caught awrong when the ax fell. Their fortunes depended upon it.

"Is my sister well?" Arnaud asked as soon as the chill courtesies had been dispensed.

His inquiry surprised Tancred. Then he remembered the many reasons this man had to hope his sister continued in good health. "She is," Tancred said coldly. Rosamund's loyalty was too precious to be squandered on the likes of this squirming creature. Arnaud did not appreciate the magnitude of the gift . . . and that indestructible fidelity remained forever beyond Tancred's reach. She had made that achingly clear.

"Will you send her to me?" Arnaud asked.

Never would Tancred return Rosamund to this whore's son who had used her so ill. Too clear in his memory was the cause of that small scar near her lovely mouth. Yet that unforgivable abuse was just the honey on the cakes of Arnaud's pettiness toward his sister. His steadfast sister.

"No." Tancred's gaze bored into Arnaud's. "She is safer with me."

Arnaud's blue eyes flashed with anger. "You dare hold her hostage?"

Tancred loved this woman who possessed more courage than her cur of a brother could ever aspire to, and, by the Cross, he would die to keep her safe. She could refuse to become his wife, but she could not keep him from loving her.

"In *my* household," he replied with deadly quiet, "Lady Rosamund is treated with honor."

Arnaud flushed and looked away.

Tancred's mouth curled in contempt. "Your treachery in Outremer killed my foster father and many other excellent men, Arnaud Bourton. The rest of us were taken and tortured. Most died. For this alone, I would challenge you to personal combat. By King Richard's will, the outcome of this battle will decide the rightful master of the honor that contains Wynnsef, among other estates."

Arnaud's head snapped back. "You traitor's spawn!" he cried. "You upstart nithing! Who are you to challenge *me*?" The note of hysteria that rode his voice made his insulting words ineffective. More than one of his advisors reddened.

From beneath lowered eyelids, Tancred regarded this loathsome creature that claimed kinship with fair and fearless Rosamund. "I may be a traitor's son, Arnaud, but you are a traitor. Had we been able to find your Turkish lover, or if Sevigny had lived through Bâb Al-Muhunnad, we would not be having this conversation. Your head and various other parts of your worthless carcass would already have been rotting on pikes in different parts of the kingdom."

Still Arnaud did not accept the challenge.

God's eyes, what did it take to make this coward defend his name, for he surely had no honor? Clearly he planned to hide behind his host and direct them to do his fighting for him, but Tancred did not desire to squander the lives of his men.

Disgusted, he eased Vandal slightly closer to Arnaud. It told him much that none of Arnaud's men sought to stop him. In one swift motion, he swept out his leather glove to sharply strike Arnaud's cheek.

"I challenge you to personal combat, Arnaud Bourton. Do you accept?"

Arnaud's destrier danced nervously, and he was forced to see to it. Even when he had succeeded in calming the beast, he did not answer, nor did he meet Tancred's gaze.

"Do you accept?" Tancred repeated more forcefully. By the Rood, he would not leave until he had an answer.

In the taut silence, one of Arnaud's men spoke. "He accepts."

The others nodded, closing ranks more closely around their cowardly liege lord. From the narrowed eyes and clenched jaws, Tancred did not think they moved to protect their lord as much as to prevent him from fleeing.

Arnaud grew pale.

"Yea, he does accept," said another of his vassals.

Arnaud managed finally to rise to the moment. He straightened in his saddle. "You have your answer, Tancred de Vierzon."

The time and arena were established with a few terse words between Kadar and one of Arnaud's vassals, then the two parties returned to their camps.

As Tancred rode through the wicket gate, ducking his head under the arch, he realized something was missing from the satisfaction he had expected to feel now. He caught himself as he started to turn his head to look for Rosamund on the wall walk.

A woman's cry pierced the strained silence in the bailey and rose to a keening wail. Tancred felt as if a knife had been thrust into his gut and twisted.

Ragged sobs echoed against the stone walls, tearing at him. Gradually, they subsided into silence.

At dawn the following morning, after years of waiting, Tancred would have his revenge.

The wind tugged at their veils as Rosamund, Abbess Matilda, and Edeva stood at the battlement. They watched as the two men and their advisors conferred below them, at a point midway between the castle and Arnaud's camp.

A hollow ache filled Rosamund as her gaze hungrily drank in the sight of Tancred. From this distance, and attired in his mail and helm, he looked much like the other men, yet she picked him out immediately. His height and his confident carriage set him apart. That and the black surcoat with its blazon of silver moon and stars.

Then there was Arnaud. He, too, wore mail and helm, sat astride a large destrier and came attended by his senior men. She saw only reluctance in every line of his body, in every motion. She bit her lip against the painful pity she felt for him. Though senior to Tancred by at least five years, he lacked the experience his enemy had acquired at such high cost. For the most part, he had avoided battle, unless he had something to gain and the odds were heavily in his favor. Only now, Rosamund realized that her brother had just played at being a knight. He had always been more interested in hunting and hawking.

Tancred, on the other hand, had taken his profession with deadly gravity. Stripped of his heritage, it was all he'd had.

Silently, she grieved for the loss of him. She felt thankful for the night of wonder and joy she had shared with him. She would always have the memory, a sparkling treasure to recall in still, solitary moments. Though she abided in an abbey, this memory she would keep . . . along with the silver disk set with the single, polished moonstone.

She had said as much to Abbess Matilda, when she
had gone to her for confession just after she had
bathed and dressed this morn. Her refusal to part with
the memory or the moonstone had been patiently acknowledged by the abbess, who, it seemed, possessed
greater wisdom in the ways and hearts of men and
women than one rustic lady of nineteen years could
have foreseen.

As they watched, now, Tancred guided his mighty
black destrier forward. Why did Arnaud's vassals not
move to prevent his coming so close to her brother? she
thought, alarmed, leaning forward in the stone crenel.

Tancred's arm flashed out. She gasped as he struck
Arnaud hard across the face with his glove. Dully, she
recognized by the advisors' lack of action, that they
did not support her brother.

Shortly after that, the two groups parted with the
air of something having been settled. But what? No
one would tell her, and she shied from believing what
logic suggested.

Her question was answered only minutes later. The
news spread through the castle like wildfire. Arnaud
had accepted Tancred's challenge. They would join in
personal combat at dawn. Their battle would decide
the fate of the honor that included Wynnsef. It would
also leave one man dead.

Rosamund turned to Abbess Matilda in panic.
"They cannot do this!" she cried. "Arnaud is no
match for Tancred!"

Abbess Matilda drew Rosamund to her. "It is beyond our power to prevent, my child. When the king
gave Tancred the right to fight for Wynnsef, he did
not refuse him the option of personal combat. And
there is the matter of the accusation of treachery
against your brother. The Earl of Quorley informed
me in his latest letter that Arnaud's Saracen woman
was located by King Richard's agents. She admitted
to learning the garrison's passwords from Arnaud, and
then passing them on to one of Sabih Ibn Qasim's

men. I fear that, even if your brother was not an outright traitor, his weakness for this woman and the fleshly pleasures she offered him still resulted in the destruction of King Richard's garrison at that crucial place. Far better for Arnaud to perish by Tancred's sword than to be taken by the king's men and subjected to a traitor's death, for that shall surely be his fate if he does not die tomorrow."

A horrified sob escaped Rosamund, and she pressed her fist to her mouth. "It cannot be true," she objected chokingly. "Does . . . does Tancred know this?"

"No. For him, this is an affair of honor, revenge for the death of his foster father." Abbess Matilda's ageless face wore an expression of gentle compassion. "I regret that this must be, my daughter. We both know Tancred will be more merciful than King Richard's headsman."

The blood drained from Rosamund's face, leaving her feeling numb. She stared at the abbess, stunned into silence.

Her beloved was to become her brother's executioner.

Rosamund could bear no more. A raw, wordless cry of anguish tore its way up out of her lungs, raking her throat. There on the wall walk she sank to her knees, fists pressed to her face. She rocked in an agony of grief. Sobs wracked her body.

The abbess and Edeva moved to protect Rosamund from the eyes of the curious. They were swiftly joined by John, who lifted Rosamund in his arms. He bore her away to her chamber, Abbess Matilda and Edeva sweeping behind him. Aefre headed for the herbarium to fetch the sleeping draft.

Tonight, more than one soul would have need of soothing.

Tancred heard about the incident on the battlement when he returned from the stables, where he'd settled Vandal. Christ Jesus, but he had much to atone for.

He paced the bailey. He wanted to go to Brother Felix. That would be easier. But he knew he could not take that course.

He sought out Abbess Matilda, finding her at prayer, alone in the chapel. The light of dusk caused the panes of costly glass in the single window to glow. White candles set about the small chamber gave off the comforting scent of beeswax, mingling with the hint of incense that lingered in the still air. Their soft glow formed small oases of golden light. The slim, kneeling figure of the abbess seemed perfectly in place.

Tancred stood in the doorway, longing for peace. But he knew that peace was like the pools of candlelight in this shadowed chapel; it came in moments, hours, small unexpected glimmers in the dark. In his life, it had never lasted long. As he waited for the abbess, heart-sore and turbulent, he thought his soul was turning to ash.

As if sensing his presence, Abbess Matilda slowly lifted her head, but she did not turn. "Tancred de Vierzon?" she asked softly.

He stood behind her. Her recognition of him unsettled him, yet at the same time assured him that he had been right to come here. "Yea, my lady abbess."

She rose, then, and went to him. He still wore his mail, though he carried his helm beneath his arm. As she waited for him to speak, he sensed no impatience in her.

"First," he said, "I ask your forgiveness in confining you to your chamber last even. I was reckless and filled with hope that I could make Rosamund of Wynnsef my wife."

"Only a fool would not have seen your fear for her. Only the blind would have missed your love for her. For penance, you will build another wing onto the infirmaria at Hembley Abbey."

Tancred clenched his teeth, but nodded. It would not be impossible if he retained Wynnsef. If, perchance, he lost the battle tomorrow, his legacy was not rich enough to pay for candles for the infirmaria, much less a new wing. "You must have great confidence in me."

She slipped her hands into her sleeves. "I do. I believe you have confidence in your own abilities as well. Perhaps later I will even share a bit of news with you, but not now. Is that all?" she inquired.

"I ask that you hear my confession," he said humbly.

For a long moment, she studied his face. "You are certain you do not wish Brother Felix to hear it?"

"Yea, my lady abbess."

Again she seemed to take his measure. Then she turned and quietly closed the chapel door. "Very well."

Tancred kissed her ring, then knelt before her. He bowed his head.

"Bless me, Mother, for I have sinned . . ."

At dawn, Tancred and Arnaud each received last rites. Then, bearing sword and shield and clad in mail and helm, their long surcoats fluttering in the early-morning breeze, the two men stepped into the battle arena—an area staked out on the grassy meadow.

They circled and circled. Arnaud seemed unwilling to participate, almost to be fleeing his opponent. Finally, Tancred struck the first blow. Arnaud managed to bring his shield up just in time, but he staggered under the impact. Then he swung his sword at Tancred.

Tancred dodged the strike. He sliced the air with his own deadly blade.

Arnaud deflected the sword, but just barely. The edge of his shield came away looking chewed. Tancred struck aside Arnaud's return blow.

The battle wore on, the only sounds on the crowded meadow a cough here, a murmur there, and the thud and clang of metal against bossed wood and metal against metal.

With each heavy blow, Tancred's anger bubbled more and more free of his restraint. Why was he giving Arnaud so many chances? The coward had kept Rosamund a prisoner of Wynnsef. He had killed Eudes!

Eudes, whose gruff kindness had eased the battering and loneliness inflicted by the other pages on a traitor's son. Eudes, whose patience had seen the gradual inculcation of painfully high standards in his foster son. Eudes, whose unspoken love of Tancred had shown through in his actions. The memory of his smile. The sound of his deep laughter. All these things poured through Tancred, tearing at him, taunting him for not having already brought Arnaud Bourton to justice.

Rage boiled through his veins like molten iron. As the two men circled each other, shields ready, sword-arms poised, Tancred saw Arnaud as everything an honorable knight was not. He worked his sweet sister as he would the meanest hireling, humiliated her before her people, and mishandled her. He had betrayed his comrades to the direst of enemies. With every lash of Yasir's whip, with every sickening caress of his hand Tancred had thought of Arnaud.

Treachery. It filled Tancred's life and poisoned anything—any*one*—good that found him.

And he was sick of it. The wrath in him burned hotter.

Tancred's father. King Richard. Arnaud Bourton. Betrayers all.

But Arnaud was not as fortunate as Tancred's long-dead sire or the faithless but distant Richard. *He* was to hand. *He* would pay. Dearly.

He would pay for them all.

Tancred's fury drove him with merciless force. Sweat ran into his eyes as his blade rained blows on

Arnaud's sword and shield, until that man could barely lift either.

Damn Arnaud . . . damn Richard . . . damn Father . . . damn them . . . all to . . . *hell*!

Finally, his mail stained red, Arnaud stumbled to one knee. Slowly he toppled. He lay in the dust, still, save for his heaving chest.

Swiftly, Tancred stepped in to deliver the killing blow.

"I sub . . . mit!" Arnaud panted. "I . . . sub . . . mit."

Blood pounding in his ears, gripped by unreasoning rage, Tancred raised his sword.

"Mercy!" Arnaud cried.

The single word penetrated Tancred's stormy brain as he grasped his sword to drive it into Arnaud.

Mercy.

Tancred had received no mercy from his father. None from Yasir or Sabih Ibn Qasim. Little from King Richard. Eudes and the others, they were dead because of this sniveling creature at his feet. Mercy, by God.

Eudes. What would his foster father have said to a traitor begging mercy? Eudes had taken mercy on Tancred. Eudes and one other person.

Rosamund. She had given him much. Lessons. The peace of sleep. But most of all, even knowing what he was, she had given him her love. If he killed her brother, she would give him her hatred.

He could not live with that.

Breathing hard, Tancred stepped back and lowered his sword.

A cheer went up among his men. Wynnsef was his.

Tancred wiped his sword and sheathed it. His blood still ran high, and his hands shook as he dragged off his mitten gauntlets.

Swiftly, Kadar strode to his side. Laughing, the Saracen embraced him. "You have won, my brother. You are master of Wynnsef!"

Tancred did not wish to examine the dark miasmic

feeling of defeat that filled him. He ought to feel triumph. Vindication. Instead, all he felt was . . . emptiness.

Suddenly Kadar stiffened. A soft groan broke his lips.

Still dazed from his battle, Tancred blinked. "Kadar?" From the corner of his eye, he saw Arnaud jerk back, then withdraw several steps.

Kadar sagged in Tancred's arms. Tancred felt warm liquid flow over his fingers. Alarmed, he bore his friend gently to the ground.

A cry of exultation made him look up just in time to see Arnaud lunge toward him with his bloodied sword.

Shielding Kadar, Tancred rolled out of Arnaud's path, and then jumped to his feet. Before he could finish drawing his sword, Arnaud's blade pierced his shoulder. Pain burned through him, but he drove his own weapon home, beneath Arnaud's arm, where the mail did not reach.

Wrenching his blade free, he stepped back to regain his balance. This time he did bring his sword down for a killing blow. He watched the life go out of Arnaud's eyes.

The body thudded to the dirt as Tancred turned back to Kadar. Edeva bent over the fallen Saracen. John examined the wound to his back. He looked up at Tancred, his expression grave.

No! Violently denying the possibility of death, Tancred knelt by his friend. "Kadar," he called softly. "Kadar, my brother, can you hear me?"

Kadar's eyes fluttered open. "Yea. I hear."

Hot tears clogged Tancred's throat. "If you are to fulfill your oath to your father, you must live."

Kadar tried to focus his eyes. "I do not . . . understand."

"If you are to save someone I love, you must live. Only you can do this thing, do you hear? For I love you, my brother. Without you, I shall be lost."

Edeva nodded, her cheeks wet with tears. She made

an attempt at a smile as she stroked Kadar's hair. "You must live, my love. Then you will have fulfilled your oath, and we can wed."

"How . . . can . . . I . . . refuse?" Kadar's voice was little more than a whisper. His eyes drifted closed.

Rosamund tended Kadar in the Great Hall for the full phase of the moon. In that time she had the aid of the abbess, the nuns, and anyone else who thought she might need something brought or carried away. Edeva remained ever present, refusing to leave Kadar's side except for the most pressing necessities. Tancred came to sit beside his cot in the morning, and every evening. During those times, Rosamund quietly excused herself to flee to the kitchens, which were within shouting distance if she was needed, but well away from Tancred. Her heart could not bear to be in his presence, could not survive long the sight of his beloved face and know that he could not be hers. It was not right, it was not. She burned with shame that her brother had behaved so cravenly, yet . . . he *had* been her brother.

Turmoil battered her heart, wearied her brain. She wept often. Too often, she felt certain. Tancred seemed more reserved than usual, but she saw no evidence of *him* making mad dashes to the pantry to sob into a drying cloth.

The long hours nursing Kadar finally took their toll, sending her into a blessed state of numbness.

Kadar lived through the delirium and the fever—a miracle Rosamund attributed to the prayers and good wishes of the inhabitants of two villages and Wynnsef. Her own prayers accompanied theirs, but she doubted they could compare to the potent supplications of Edeva and Tancred.

When it was safe to move Kadar, the abbey's wagons were readied and a litter constructed for him. He would make a swifter recovery at Hembley Abbey, which offered better facilities for the care of the injured and sick.

At first there was some small flutter among the nuns regarding the fact that Kadar was a Saracen. Certainly he was a brave knight, a generous man, but he was an unbeliever. Was it permitted to take such a person into their infirmaria? Into the hospitium? Brother Felix and Father Ivo quickly put that concern to rest. Kadar was one of God's children. If He, in His infinite wisdom, had seen fit to create a Musselman, who where they, the servants of God, to refuse him aid?

Abbess Matilda, who was better informed on matters of Church policy, but also on the exigencies of managing an abbey, merely stood silent, her hands in her sleeves. By the time the nuns realized that she had not spoken her piece, she had ordered Kadar be settled onto his litter, then climbed up onto the lead wagon's seat. This time, she accepted the hand Tancred offered with no protest, merely inclining her head to him in elegant acknowledgment.

Edeva and Rosamund rode on either side of Kadar's litter, that was suspended by ropes from poles affixed to the saddles of two horses ridden by men-at-arms.

Tancred dispatched a large escort of his men to accompany the caravan, despite the annoyance of Hembley Abbey's captain.

As she rode out through Wynnsef's gate, Rosamund turned in her saddle to look upon that noble castle for the last time of her life. Knowing herself to be unwise, she found herself searching the battlements for Tancred. When she found him, her heart squeezed painfully. He met her gaze, watching as she rode away, out of his life forever. She swallowed heavily. Would he miss her? Would he think of her whenever he went into the walled garden? Tears filled her eyes, blinding her. She turned to dash them away.

When she looked back toward the castle, Tancred had gone.

*   *   *

Rosamund submitted herself to the Abbess Matilda's regime, trying to find comfort in the eternal sameness of each day. Order and peace were what she had wanted, and she found them here in overly great abundance. Hour after hour. Day after day. Month after month.

Once, Tancred came to visit Kadar. He paid his respects to Abbess Matilda, sat by his friend in the shade of the hawthorn tree where Kadar was now allowed to take the sun for a while each day. They talked and laughed. She could hear their voices from the herb garden where she had been assigned to work, though she could not see them. Tancred conversed with Edeva, who seldom left her beloved's side, and spoke pleasantly with the nuns who nursed Kadar.

He did not ask to see Rosamund.

That night, she prostrated herself before the cross in the chapel. Her tears wet the stone floor against which her forehead pressed. She prayed for forgiveness. She prayed for guidance. She prayed for Tancred's health and safety. In the dark, lonely hours of the morning, exhausted by grief and confusion, Rosamund uttered the simplest of all her supplications.

Thy will be done.

Perhaps God heard at least that one prayer, for at Matins, she learned that Tancred had ridden away from the abbey before dawn.

Rosamund tried to be thankful for his leaving, reminding herself that he had killed Arnaud. He had slain her brother. In response, her innate honesty rose to assume the image of a mirror. What she saw in her reflection distressed her greatly. It shattered a lifetime of blind loyalty, for finally she was forced to admit that blind loyalty was all that she had managed to keep for Arnaud. Her love had eroded away years ago, worn to dust by his petulance, his dishonesty, his insults and her captivity. He had been dishonorable to the end, forcing Tancred to end his life.

She mourned her brother then, for the unhappy soul he must have been, but for the first time, she admitted to herself that he'd had a chance for happiness. If anyone had been given an opportunity for a full and contented life, it had been Arnaud.

True to his oath, Kadar recovered. Rosamund felt certain Edeva's glowing love had been the true source of Kadar's astonishing recovery. Although she was happy for them, she was sad to see them leave. Shortly after, their letter arrived from Wynnsef to announce that they had wed.

Along with that news came a letter from Tancred's seneschal. Rosamund was summoned to the abbess's lodging. As her eyes moved over the single page, she learned that Tancred had released from the honor the estate of Belleborne as Rosamund's dower property. It would go to the abbey when she took her vows.

Her eyes widened. Tancred had withdrawn from Wynnsef, leaving it fully garrisoned with men chosen by John. She thought at first that he might have gone to one of the other estates in the honor, but as she read, she learned that he held the honor for her, acting as her self-appointed guardian. He had gone to seek his own fortune elsewhere.

She looked up. "I do not understand. Wynnsef meant all to him. It and the rest of the honor raised him to the position of baron—a grant directly from the king." Over her brother's dead body. "Without it, he is aught but a landless knight. Why would he do this?"

Abbess Matilda regarded her for a moment. "Are you truly unable to guess?"

Rosamund heard his deep, night-shadowed voice in her mind once again.

I want things, too. Things only you can give me.

I want you to be my wife, Rosamund.

We both know Tancred will be more merciful than King Richard's headsman.

He had been betrayed twice in that place.

She swallowed hard. "I believe I know why."

"Tancred de Vierzon is an honorable man."

"Yea, he is," Rosamund said hoarsely.

For a few moments, silence filled Abbess Matilda's spartan lodging. Then she said, "Tell me, daughter, do you still keep with you that silver disk with the moonstone?"

"I do."

"And do you still refuse to give it up?"

Rosamund fingered the rectangle of thick parchment. She nodded.

"What did you keep of your brother's?" Abbess Matilda asked in a gentle voice.

Lifting her head, Rosamund met the gaze of the abbess. "Memories," she said.

Her penance.

TWENTY-ONE

The two small braziers in Abbess Matilda's modest receiving room did little to dispel the damp November cold. Rosamund tucked her hands into the sleeves of her simple white kirtle, her palms and fingers icy against her arms.

"I cannot say that I am surprised to see you here, Rosamund," Abbess Matilda said, sitting at her writing table. "I confess, I expected you sooner."

"Sooner?" Rosamund had just arrived on time to this appointment she had requested.

Abbess Matilda smiled gently. "You have come to tell me that you do not believe you are suited to be a nun, have you not?"

Rosamund flushed. "Am I so transparent?"

Abbess Matilda motioned her to the chair beside the table. "No, my child, you are not. 'Tis merely that I have observed your efforts these past eight months. We all have. You have worked hard to become one of our community."

Rosamund frowned down at her joined sleeves without truly seeing them. In her mind's eye, all she saw were scenes from months of struggle, confusion, disappointment, and, at last, realization. "I have tried . . . so *very* hard."

After so many years of being in charge, attempting to become just another slat in the mill wheel had proved far more difficult and unsatisfying than she had anticipated. She had thought that she wanted her burden of responsibilities to be lifted from her shoulders, but when it finally had been taken away, she'd discovered that they had given her a sense of worth. She had also made the somewhat unflattering discovery that she *liked* being in command. There was such a thing as having too much peace and tranquility.

"You have many of the qualities needed to make an excellent abbess." Abbess Matilda's smile deepened. "I think I knew that from the beginning. I saw a good deal of me in you. You are a natural shepherd, Rosamund. You have a certain force of character that makes others take notice. You have a way of getting things done quickly and efficiently." She sighed. "Had you come to Hembley seven or eight years ago . . ." She shrugged. "We are God's to command."

"I shall miss you and the sisters," Rosamund said softly.

The abbess rose and held out her hands to Rosamund, who grasped them, her throat tightening with emotion.

"I will miss, you, also, my daughter."

Rosamund returned to Wynnsef Castle. Many did not understand why Tancred had left his only chance for stability, but they did not know all that had been involved. She did what she believed he would want her to do—she did not speak of the matter.

Before he'd left, Tancred had engaged a highly competent seneschal, who, upon his first meeting with Rosamund after her arrival from Hembley Abbey, had introduced himself as Neville of London.

"Lord Tancred told me that I must say this to you," the short, slim man had explained, clearly not understanding why.

She'd also discovered that Tancred had left orders that every plant within the castle must be carefully tended. Many of them had died, of course, but most had lived. Within the walled garden, where the water channels fed the beds, everything that was not choked by weeds thrived. Now that spring was come, she went there often.

Sleeplessness often drove her to the wall walk at night. Looking out over the darkened land, she wondered where Tancred had gone. Had he forgotten her? John stayed much by her side at these times, never asking questions. She treasured his friendship.

During the day, Saer of Grimfield, her seneschal, tended to the accounts and much of the administration of Wynnsef and the other estates of the honor, freeing Rosamund to concentrate on the duties of an heiress and chatelaine. For all that she longed for the sight of Tancred, she still had the people to consider. So she worked, welcoming the distraction from her aching heart.

As she sat spinning in the great hall, listening to Dunton bickering with Jack the pantler, Piers strolled casually across the hall to sit down on the bench beside her.

She lifted an eyebrow at the boy. "What of your lessons with Brother Felix?" she asked.

He cast her an innocent look. "He dismissed us. Some of the older boys behaved as fools, and he said spring fever had taken them." He cocked his small head. "I think Brother Felix was taken by it, too. He keeps looking out the window, and you know the fruit trees in the garden are all abloom."

Everyone in Wynnsef knew how Brother Felix loved the white frothy blossoms of the fruit trees in the spring. Indeed, the common garden was experiencing much usage these days, Rosamund conceded. She had seen not only young maids casting glances at the vigorous lads showing off for them, but older married women strolled upon the daisy-flushed lawn with their husbands, giggling together as if reliving that first flush of youth. In the mews, one of the falcons had laid two healthy-looking eggs. Lambs frolicked in the fields, and puppies squealed in the kennels. At times it

seemed as if every female in the castle had an attentive mate. Every female but Rosamund.

"I am come to cheer you, my lady," Piers piped.

She smiled at his earnestness. "You are very kind,
Master Piers, but what makes you believe I need
cheering?"

"You don't smile much anymore," he told her.

She stared at him in surprise. "I'm smiling now,"
she pointed out.

"Yea, but it is one of the few smiles you've had,"
he replied solemnly. "And you never laugh. I want
you to be happy always, my lady."

She stopped her spinning to tousle his bright hair.
Life had not been kind to Piers, taking his father when
he was but a babe. How did he keep his sweet nature?
Was it some secret of childhood, a resilience one lost
as one stared the ancient age of twenty in the face?

"Well, Piers, there are times when it is difficult to
be happy," she said gently.

He reached out a small hand to pat her arm reassur-
ingly. "You are sad because Lord Arnaud died, aren't
you?" he asked, sympathy coloring his childish voice.

Rosamund regarded the woolen thread she held between her fingers. "Yea, Piers, I am."

"And because Lord Kadar was hurt."

"Yea. He is a kind gentleman, and he was ill for a
long time."

Piers nodded thoughtfully.

Rosamund resumed her spinning.

"And because Lord Tancred left, huh?" he said.

Her throat tightened. "Yea. And because Lord Tancred left."

"He is a great lord, is he not, my lady? I liked
Lord Tancred."

She nodded. Out of the corner of her eye, she saw
that Will had quietly taken a seat next to Piers.

"Quiet about Lord Tancred," she heard him ad-
monish Piers in a low voice.

"Why?" the younger boy asked, his large blue eyes wide.

" 'Cause she loves him, dolt, and now he's gone."

"Oh."

She pretended not to have heard. "Hello, Will. Piers says Brother Felix ended today's lessons early because some older boys were misbehaving. I trust you were not one of them?"

"No, my lady. Besides, you know Brother Felix has spring fever. He has never ended lessons before just because the lads weren't quiet."

She had to chuckle at that. Will was quite right. The good monk did not tolerate misbehavior, though there was little of it.

"I composed a song for you, Lady Rosamund," Will said. "Would you like to hear it?"

So, she thought, he was trying to cheer her up, too. How downcast she must seem to everyone. She must make an effort to seem gaier and more congenial.

"I certainly would. 'Tis not every day a lady has a handsome fellow compose a song for her."

Will just happened to have his lute with him. Piers watched the older lad fuss with tightening a string as if he'd never seen anything so fascinating.

Ah, to be so easily enthralled again, Rosamund thought fondly.

Then Will struck a chord. The notes strummed true, a pleasant blend of sound. He had improved upon the lute so much since Kadar had tutored him. Will began to sing, and she nodded her encouragement. The melody was lively, the words . . . well, the words would become more refined as Will grew more skilled, more sophisticated. Still, it was a charming song. She set aside her spinning and lightly clapped her hands in time with the song's rhythm.

Piers followed her example enthusiastically. As he nodded his head from side to side, the light from the open door shone on his golden blond curls and gleamed in his eyes the color of bluebells.

Yearning pierced Rosamund like a knife. Oh, for a
child of her own—Tancred's child! How she longed to
see him grow tall and strong as his warrior father.
What joy it would bring to watch the two of them
together. Would he have been fair like she or beautifully dark like Tancred?

Such a child would never exist. She would share no
more with Tancred than they had already shared. He
had given her a choice and then abided by her decision. He had been honorable. More than honorable.
Rosamund pressed her lips together against the tears
that thickened in her throat. She must live with her
choice.

"My lady, did my song move you to tears?" Will
exclaimed happily. Then he seemed to remember that
his intention had been to *cheer* her. "Oh! I am such
a fool! Next time I will know not to make a song
about birds and daisies, my lady. I did not know they
would cast you down. I meant to make you happy,
truly I did. I'm such a . . . such a . . ." Upset, he
searched for a word.

"Dolt?" Piers offered helpfully.

" 'Tis a splendid song, Will," she rushed to assure
the lad, feeling guilty for having upset him. "Your
song honors me, and I thank you." She waved a hand
airily. "I have a touch of spring fever, that is all."

"You do?" he asked doubtfully.

"You made her weep," Piers accused hotly, glaring
at Will. "You and that stupid song." The boy bunched
his small hands into fists.

Quickly, Rosamund sat down on the bench between
them. "I am not weeping. These are . . . tears of joy.
Yea, tears of joy is what they are." She curved an arm
around each boy and hugged them to her sides. "Joy
that I have two such gracious young men to cheer
me." She gave them each a loud kiss on the cheek.
"Thank you. You have aided a damsel in distress."

Will's face flamed bright pink.

"Eeuw!" Piers rubbed at the spot where she had

kissed him, and earned a sharp poke in the ribs from Will. "What?" he demanded indignantly.

"A knight doesn't do that," Will scolded him in a whisper that could be heard clear across the hall.

"I'm not a knight yet!"

Before Will could respond, a man-at-arms attired in his helm and bossed gambeson strode into the hall and straight to Rosamund. She guessed him to be a sentry.

"My lady," he said, "a messenger from Lord Fitz Clare awaits without the gate."

A stone dropped in Rosamund's stomach. What did Lord Trufflenose want now? The last time he had come when there was no lord present in Wynnsef, he had brought with him mercenaries and a war machine. "Does he come alone?"

"No, my lady," the sentry replied. "He comes in the company of an escort. He says he bears a message of some import and craves your indulgence in allowing him to deliver his message directly to you, so that there can be no misunderstanding."

Rosamund considered. It was not unusual to send an escort with a messenger. Travel was always hazardous.

The sentry hesitated, then added, "The captain says it would be safe enough to let him alone in through the wicket gate."

She trusted John's appraisal of the situation. "Very well," she said. "Let in the messenger, but just him." Her lips curved in a grim smile. "It will do no harm for him to see that the castle is fully garrisoned. Bring him here to the great hall. I will return shortly."

Piers and Will ran off to watch what happened when the messenger was allowed into the bailey. Rosamund swept away to her chamber, still in the old keep. She could not bring herself to move to the master's chamber above the great hall, that room where Tancred had taken her to his bed. Where she had spent the most joyous night of her life. Perhaps someday she could move there, but not yet . . . not yet.

Aefre met her to help her dress. When Rosamund reentered the great hall, she was attired as befitted a baron's daughter.

She ascended the dais and sat in the high seat. The messenger, who had been offered refreshment while he waited, swiftly rose to his feet. He bowed with a flourish.

"You have brought me a message," she said, cutting directly to the purpose of the man's presence. "I would hear it now."

"My lady Rosamund, my lord Godfrey does esteem you greatly as a neighbor and does value your estimable strength of character, but more than that he wishes to pay homage to your womanly grace and charm. He knows that this can be a cruel, confusing world for a woman alone. It grieves him to see you struggling, though so very valiantly, on your own. He observes that you have not grown too old to bear children, and doubtless ache to hold your own babe in your arms, as women are wont to do—"

"Get to the point," she said. What sort of prelude to war was this?

"Ah," the richly dressed messenger said, "a woman of few words. That will please my lord. Very well. I am come to convey Lord Godfrey's offer of marriage to you."

"My lord bishop, Lady Rosamund of Wynnsef," the chamberlain announced to the justiciar of England, King Richard's administrator in the royal absence.

Only reluctantly had Hubert Walter, Archbishop of Canterbury, agreed to receive the heiress. He was hard-pressed to find the time. From his desk, he waved the chamberlain to admit the female.

As he had heard, Rosamund Bourton was exceptionally lovely, though she was far too thin to be considered beautiful. So, he thought as he studied her, this was the woman who had broken the heart of the mighty Moon Lord.

Hubert had always liked that lad. Tancred's sincere
modesty was refreshing in one so comely and accomplished, particularly among the vipers who called
themselves barons. Indeed, those very accomplish-
ments had helped his king gain a reputation for being
a superior warrior and good leader, but Richard did
not give credit where it was due, and Tancred did not
say otherwise. Hubert smiled, pleased with the way
things had turned out. Fortunately, kings had their
ways of learning things, and not all knights were as
quiet as Tancred. Enough powerful princes and lords
had discovered the truth.

Now, as to this chit who had cast the lad aside . . .
Hubert regarded her down his nose as she curtsied
and waited for him to speak.

He allowed her to wait a long moment before he
said, "Arise, Lady Rosamund. You may approach me.
I am not the king, but his humble administrator."

Hubert could almost hear the thoughts of his chamberlain. *Humble, my arse.* Well, but it did not do to
be humble when one ruled a kingdom, which he did
in Richard's stead. The ambitious had no respect for
humble men, and it was the ambitious against whom
Hubert must guard England.

"So, Lady Rosamund, to what purpose have you
come to me?" he asked when she came closer.

She looked surprised. "My lord bishop, I did tell
your clerks—"

"I would hear it from your lips." He liked the way
she lifted her chin and squared her shoulders. This
one had courage.

"I have come to ask for a champion, my lord
bishop," she said directly. "My neighbor seeks to
annex my lands and my person."

"You are twenty years of age, lady. You do need a
husband. Perhaps this man will answer."

Even from this distance, he could see her eyes blaze.
Such spirit!

"I find him abhorrent," she declared, her words ringing in the audience chamber.

"Have you had no other offers?"

He saw her throat work. Abruptly she looked away. "Yea, my lord bishop. I have had one."

"But you did not accept this offer?"

She shook her head.

"Why?"

Rosamund of Wynnsef drew a deep breath, then looked back at him. "Family loyalty."

"Ah." So the matter still distressed her. Perhaps she was not so unfeeling as rumor had it. Family loyalty was no small thing, though he had all too often seen it be misguided. Still, she was a woman. She had been taught to consider family first. It was, in a female, an admirable quality.

"Have you anyone in mind for your champion?" he asked, just to be polite. She had satisfied his curiosity. Politics and expediency would determine what happened to her now.

"Yea, my lord. Tancred de Vierzon. I would have him as my champion."

Hubert stroked his beard. Hmm. This was unexpected. He was familiar with the story of that fateful day at Wynnsef Castle between her brother and Tancred—who in this kingdom was not? She had entered Hembley Abbey rather than wed her brother's killer. And she had struck a heart-deep wound in a good man.

"Lord Tancred is now a baron with vast lands of his own to concern him," he informed her coolly. "Choose another."

The look that came into her eyes caused Hubert to think of wind moaning through a broken tower. How strange.

"If I cannot have Tancred de Vierzon as my champion," she said tonelessly, "then I must rely upon your wisdom."

That small, almost indiscernible catch in her voice

when she spoke Tancred's name, nipped at Hubert's heart.

"Will you willingly wed a champion of my choice?" he asked, thinking of names who might qualify. Perhaps it was foolish of him, but he would try to find her a man who would at least be kind to her.

She bowed her head. "Yea, lord. I will . . . wed him."

"Then return to, eh"—he searched his memory for the name of the castle where she dwelled—"Wynnsef. I shall send you a champion."

"May I inquire when, my lord?"

The question ruffled Hubert. As if finding her a husband was his sole duty! And while he was doing that, what of the rest of England? "Soon," he snapped.

By the time she had reached the door, he had already turned back to his clerk and the many papers demanding their attention.

Rosamund wept that night, alone in her tiny palace room. Fool! Fool! She should have known better than to allow herself to hope. Tancred was gone from her forever.

If he had not forgiven her, it appeared that he had at least forgotten her. Once again reduced to the status of landless knight, his fastest path to property would have been to wed an heiress. It seemed some fortunate woman had been wiser than she. She tried to comfort herself with the knowledge that Tancred prospered, yet the thought of another woman lying in Tancred's arms, of another laughing with him, tore Rosamund's heart to shreds.

A stranger would win the honor including Wynnsef, and would take Rosamund to his bed. A stranger would father her children and rule over her and her home.

She wept until she grew numb with emptiness. In that state, she made the journey back to Wynnsef.

Each night she haunted the walled garden, as hollow as a ghost. Each night she took out the silver disk with the single perfect moonstone. That and her memories, must be enough to last the rest of her life.

A month passed, with Fitz Clare demanding she wed him, threatening to take Wynnsef by siege. Although the Church forbade it, more than one heiress had been forced to the altar by an ambitious groom. Against that event, Rosamund kept a dagger concealed beneath her skirts, though she knew well that the champion sent her—should he arrive in time— might be worse than Fitz Clare.

When a trumpet sounded in the distance, her blood went cold. With unwilling steps, Rosamund joined John on the wall walk. A mounted force of knights and men-at-arms approached from the south. Pennons fluttered here and there among the force, and a dark, unfamiliar gonfanon flew at their head.

Rosamund swallowed hard. She pressed her hand over the place on the breast of her kirtle under which hung the crimson pouch. Whoever it was, she prayed he was better than Lord Trufflenose. Someone better than . . . Arnaud.

She murmured a short prayer. *Thy will be done.*

When the force reached the gates of the castle, a herald riding a gleaming gray palfrey loudly announced that the champion of Lady Rosamund of Wynnsef had arrived. A letter from Hubert Walter was submitted. She barely glanced at it, noticing only the official signature and seal verifying that the man waiting without was, in fact, the true champion. Reluctantly, Rosamund gave the signal to lower the drawbridge and raise the portcullis.

Into Wynnsef Castle flowed the men of her new lord. The man she had promised to wed, sight unseen.

Feeling numb, untouched by events, she surveyed the flood of men pouring into the inner bailey, dully seeking some indication of which man was the champion.

It was not hard to find him.

When she saw him, her breath stopped in her throat.

Uncommonly tall and broad-shouldered, he wore his helmet, his dark mail, and his black surcoat bearing a blazon of stars and a moon.

Her heart began to gallop. Pray God, this was not a dream, not some cruel jest.

Just then, he turned his head. Their gazes collided, sending a wave of weakness through Rosamund. Her lips moved silently.

Tancred.

He remained still upon his destrier, unsmiling. His eyes blazed like silver fire.

Did he hate her? Had he been forced into coming to her aid? What of his wife? The questions vanished from her thoughts as soon as they entered. All that mattered in the world was that Tancred was here.

"Tancred!" she cried. She plunged into the crowd, pushing her way through the mob of men in mail, between skittish destriers and chargers, unmindful of her peril. "Tancred!"

Long-fingered, capable hands swept up to pull off his helmet, revealing his rumpled cap of black hair and his fiercely beautiful face. In the time it took her heart to race five beats, he had leaped from his destrier and shouldered his way to her. He caught her up in his arms and pressed his way through to set her down on the steps of the great hall. "Jesú, Rosamund," he murmured, "you could have been hurt." His gaze moving over her face as if he would impress upon his memory every detail.

She clutched her hands together to keep them from reaching for him, but she could not school her eyes against taking their fill of his beloved face. "I did not know you would come," she said, her voice unsteady.

He regarded her solemnly for a long moment. "How

could I not?" he asked in a soft voice. His eyes crinkled. "I applied to Hubert Walter as soon as I heard you were desperate for a husband."

Her bright smile contradicted her husky hiccup. "Oh, yea, but only the right husband." Tears rolled unnoticed down her cheeks. "One who likes gardens. And baths, he must like baths. And babies. Beautiful, dark-haired babies."

He lowered his head to touch his forehead to hers. "I crave gardens, damoiselle, and I cannot have enough baths to suit me. I do promise to be diligent in the getting of all the babies you want, though I cannot promise they will have dark hair. I am partial to golden locks myself. And blue, blue eyes."

With a sob of wild joy, Rosamund flung her arms around him, and he pulled her to him. Without another word, he lowered his head and took her mouth in a claiming kiss that left no doubt as to his feelings.

A cheer started among Wynnsef's men, up along the wall walk. Quickly it grew into a roar as Tancred's knights and men-at-arms took it up. Its powerful thunder shook the castle walls, echoing, growing, moving out over the countryside.

Rosamund scarcely heard it. Her heart raised a clamor of its own.

Tancred's gaze never left hers as his smile grew into a grin. Then he threw back his head and hurled his laughter heavenward, even as he drew her closer to his heart. In answer, she embraced him fiercely. Never again would she be foolish enough to let him go. She would take this man as her husband and count herself the most fortunate among women.

Only together could their hearts ever be truly soar free.

EPILOGUE

As twilight deepened into dark, and the stars came out, Rosamund found Tancred standing alone on the wall walk, looking eastward. The strong autumn breeze ruffled his hair, lifting his long mantle as if it were a flag. Kadar, Edeva, their children and household had departed that afternoon, on their way to the land of Kadar's birth.

Quietly, Rosamund came to stand beside Tancred, slipping one arm around his waist. "I will miss them, too," she said.

With one arm, he cradled her against his side, pressing a kiss to the crown of her veiled head before returning his gaze toward the east. "Kadar needs to be with his family again. He fears his father or mother will die before he sees them again. Before they see Edeva and their sons."

With a sigh, Rosamund leaned against the reassuring strength of her husband. "I hope they will accept Edeva."

"As she pointed out, she is one of the People of the Book. According to the Qur'ān, it was lawful for Kadar to take her to wife. His family may be unhappy at first, but I believe they will discover she is a good addition to their family when they realize that she honors their faith. And they will see how devoted Kadar and Edeva are to each other. What his family may object to is that there will be no additional wives for him."

"Yea," Rosamund said. "She was quite firm on that point before they spoke their vows four years ago, and naught has changed that I can see."

"I do not believe Kadar will take exception to her restraint when they marry again according to the customs of his people." He smiled. "They are too wrapped up in each other to accommodate other wives in that marriage. But perhaps there will be no urging from his family. She has, after all, given him two sons."

Rosamund nodded. "They will make their way, *mon coeur*. Their devotion is strong and true. Kadar is so fierce in his protection of Edeva, I doubt he will tolerate anything that makes her miserable."

Tancred smiled into the distance. "She is spoiled." He looked down at her, and Rosamund's heart quickened at the loving light she saw in his eyes. "Like you."

She laughed. "Yea, you have made me the object of every woman's envy."

"I would have you be comfortable," he told her, with a touch of masculine satisfaction.

His ability to provide her with every luxury he thought she might desire had filled the great hall and chambers of Wynnsef with furs, richly hued tapestries, with pillows and curtains, carved ivory boxes, exotic brass braziers, and vessels of glass, of silver, and of gold. For their clothing, she could choose from the finest fabrics brought from Italy, from France and Damascus. Exotic plants arrived from various parts of the world regularly. Their stables were filled with sleek, well-formed horses, and their mews with superbly trained falcons and tiercels.

After Rosamund had gone to Hembley Abbey, and Tancred had returned to the status of landless knight, he had decided to place his services at the disposal of the highest bidder. As soon as word of this spread,

offers poured in, including one from Philip Augustus,
King of France. King Richard had promptly awarded
Tancred a vast honor that included a few castles and
many rich estates in order to bind the Moon Lord to
the English Crown. After all, if anyone knew the
deadly value of Tancred's skills, it was Richard.

While a couple of Tancred's castles and several of
his manors were more commodious than Wynnsef, it
was here that they spent much of their time. Even so,
when they traveled to one of their other properties,
Rosamund worked to turn it into a garden place.

Of all that Tancred had given her, most precious to
Rosamund were his love and his children. Their infant
daughter and two toddling sons were a source of great
joy to them both.

Thy will be done.

"You have made me the object of envy among all
women for more than the many comforts you have
provided," she told her hasband, lowering her lashes.
Beneath his mantle, her fingers slowly stroked his
back. Gradually, they moved down to the tight curve
of his buttocks.

With the side of a knuckle, Tancred tipped her chin
upward. His mouth brushed hers. "It has been too
long since I took you on the flowery mead of the
garden," he murmured against her lips.

Rosamund's body flushed with desire at the memory. Fragrant grass and daisies had cushioned her
naked back as Tancred had thrust into her. "Yea,"
she agreed breathlessly. "Far too long."

He slipped the tip of his tongue along the tender
inner flesh of her bottom lip. "You did say that you
thought Isabeau was conceived that night."

"Mmm. Perhaps it was the music of the nightingale.
Or the perfume of the flowers. Or the ardor of my
potent husband."

He kissed her neck. "Always the ardor of your potent husband."

Heedless of the sentries some distance away on the

wall walk, she twined her arms around Tancred's neck and kissed him back. "I am certain our daughter was conceived there on that flowery mead."

He lifted the black slashes of his eyebrows. "Are you feeling lucky tonight?"

Rosamund smiled, filled with the glow of her love for him. "With you, my heart, I am always lucky."

So he took her hand, and together they ran through the starry dark to the walled garden, where two prisoners had found their freedom.

And where they would always return, bound by love.

For only $3.99 each, they'll make your dreams come true.

LORDS OF MIDNIGHT

A special romance promotion from Signet Books—featuring three of our most popular, award-winning authors...

Lady in White by Denise Domning
"Excitingly wicked."—*Rendezvous*
❑ 0-451-40772-5

The Moon Lord by Terri Lynn Wilhelm
"An impeccable storyteller."—*Romantic Times*
❑ 0-451-19896-4

Shades of the Past by Kathleen Kirkwood
"A marvelous writer."—Julie Beard
❑ 0-451-40760-1